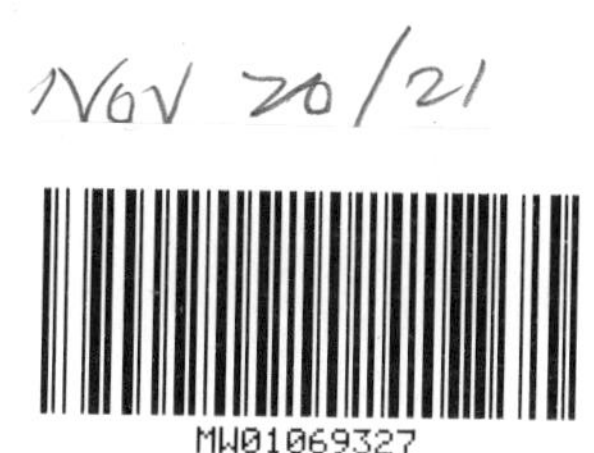

DEAD MAN LAUNCH

A TODD INGRAM NOVEL

JOHN J. GOBBELL

Severn River Publishing
www.SevernRiverPublishing.com

ISBN: 978-1-951249-82-3 (Paperback)
ISBN: 978-1-951249-91-5 (Hardback)

ALSO BY JOHN J. GOBBELL

The Todd Ingram Series

The Last Lieutenant

A Code For Tomorrow

When Duty Whispers Low

The Neptune Strategy

Edge of Valor

Dead Man Launch

Other Books

A Call to Colors

The Brutus Lie

Never miss a new release! Sign up to receive exclusive updates from author John J. Gobbell.

SevernRiverPublishing.com/John-J-Gobbell

This novel is dedicated to

Commander George A. Wallace, USN (Ret.)

A submariner's submariner.
When George was on watch,
our nation slept soundly.

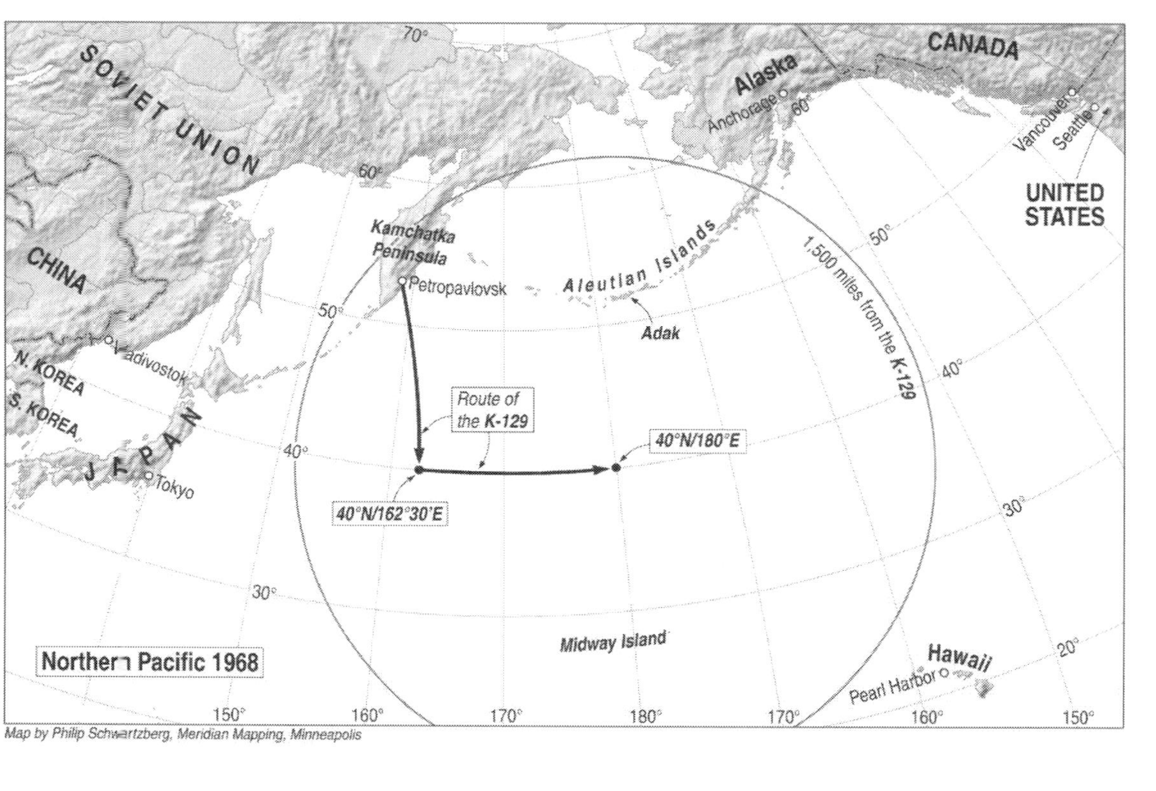

Map by Philip Schwartzberg, Meridian Mapping, Minneapolis

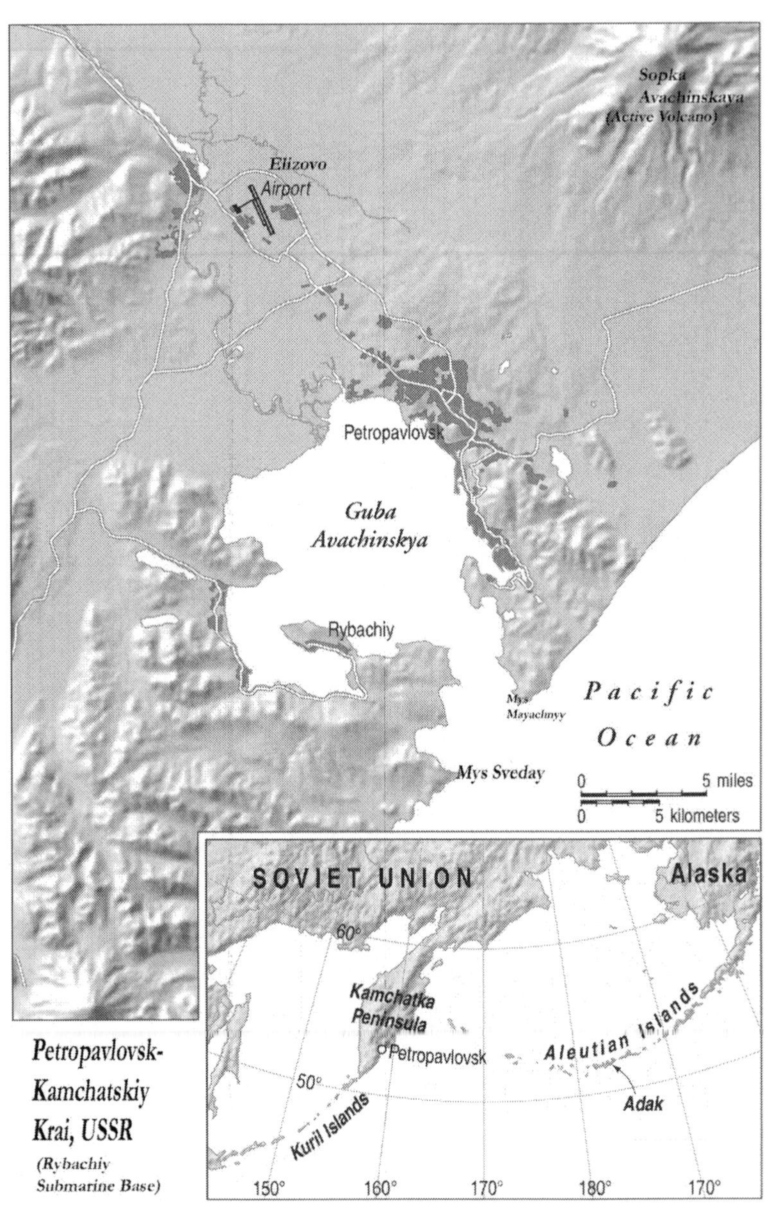

Petropavlovsk-Kamchatskiy Krai, USSR

(Rybachiy Submarine Base)

Map by Philip Schwartzberg, Meridian Mapping, Minneapolis

CAST OF CHARACTERS

American

U.S. Navy/USMC

Adm. John J. Hyland, commander U.S. Pacific Fleet, Pearl Harbor, Hawaii

Vice Adm. Alton C. "Todd" Ingram, USN, commanding officer, Kunia Regional SIGINT Operations Center (KSOCK), Oahu, Hawaii; Jerry's father

Capt. Hudson R. "Rusty" Fletcher, USN, chief of operations, Regional SIGINT Operations Center (KSOCK), Oahu, Hawaii

Capt. Gregory N. Fowler, USN, commanding officer, VP 72, Barber's Point, Hawaii

Cdr. Anthony P. Wade, USN, commanding officer, USS *Wolfish* (SS 562)

Lt. Cdr. Frank F. Hill, USN, executive officer, USS *Wolfish*, (SS 562)

Lt. Cdr. Michael Quinn, USN, JAG, legal officer, Sigonella Naval Air Station, Sigonella, Sicily

Lt. Cdr. Ronald T. Carmichael, USN, JAG, legal officer, Naval Air Station, Barber's Point, Hawaii

Lt. Phillip L. Saltzman, USN, operations officer, USS *Wolfish* (SS 562)

Lt. Harvey T. Ganz, USN, weapons officer, USS Wolfish (SS 562)

Lt. Noah A. Butler, USN, aide to Admiral Hyland, later pilot VP 72 (P-3 Orion), Barbers Point, Hawaii

Lt. (j.g.) Jeremiah O. "Jerry" Ingram, USN (USNA '65), copilot (P-3 Orion), VP 45 Sigonella, Sicily, later VP 72, Barbers Point Hawaii
First Lt. Ernesto "Ernie" Hernandez, USMC, (USNA 65), helicopter pilot, VMA 69 (Fighting Devil Dogs), Rita's brother
CWO John Anthony "Smilin' Jack" Walker, USN, watch officer, Atlantic Fleet Submarine Force headquarters, Norfolk, Virginia

CIA
Oliver P. Toliver III, commander, USN (Ret.), field agent, Los Angeles, California

Civilians
Helen Z. (née Durand) Ingram, major, RN, U.S. Army (Ret.), Todd Ingram's wife, Jerry's mother
Rita (Hernandez) Ingram, Jerry's wife, Ernie's sister
Jeremiah T. Landa, captain, USN (Ret.), harbor pilot, Los Angeles, California
Barton Seidman, chargé d'affaires, U.S. State Department, Rome, Italy

USSR
Soviet Navy
Submarine K-12
Kontr Admiral Stanislaw Kudrevich, commanding officer, submarine *K-12*
Captain First Rank Eduard Ianovich Dezhnev, political officer (*zampolit*) K-12, later instructor, Nakhimov Black Sea Higher Naval School, Sevastopol, Crimean District of Ukraine

Submarine *K-129*
Captain First Rank Vladimir Kobzar, commanding officer
Captain Second Rank Aleksandr Zhuravin, executive officer
Captain Second Rank, Vladislav Leonid Yusopov, engineering officer *K-12*, team leader DPRK SO 1 expedition (*Pueblo*), and political officer (*zampolit*) *K-129*
Captain Third Rank Nikolay Nikolayevich, chief engineer
Starshiy Leytenant Vladimir Utkin (Dezhnev), communications officer, son of Eduard Dezhnev and Roxanna Utkina

Starshiy Leytenant Vitalij Gurin, Strategic Rocket Forces, KGB
Kapitan Leytenant Aleksey Boleslav Logonov, commander special, KGB
Ivan Stepan Sudakov, rocket-fueling specialist (civilian), chief scientist (fuels), NPO Energomash, Moscow region, Russia
Kapitan Leytenant Yevgeny Maksim Mullov, assistant, DPRK SO I expedition

Army
Colonel General Maxim Yusopov, Soviet Energy Institute, (acronym for atomic energy development); father of Vladislav Yusopov
Oleg Caroni, former *Spetsnaz* (special forces), Yusopov's batman
Colonel Bogdan Arkady Jelavich, GRU, in command, DPRK SO I expedition
Major Yuri Geckos, GRU, DPRK SO I expedition, translator

Civilians
Roxanna Utkina, formerly Kirov Ballet dancer, now director Utkina School of Ballet, Sochi, Krasnodar Krai, Russia, Eduard Dezhnev's lover
Anoushka Dezhnev, Eduard Dezhnev's mother and world-famous film star
Iliana Kwolochek, Maxim Yusopov's girlfriend; actually a KGB plant

Italian
Michelangelo Rugani, Olympic skier and wealthy international playboy; handsome poster boy for Enzio Fragrances, Milan, Italy
Giorgio Michelleti, Michelangelo Rugani's stiletto-wielding bodyguard; of the Salvati Mafioso family of Sicily

Democratic People's Republic of Korea (DPRK)
Navy
Commander Dae Jung Lee, DPRK, commanding officer, *Seyung Kwon*, SO I
Lieutenant Chin Ho Jang, DPRK, executive officer, *Seyung Kwon, SO I*

Army
Colonel Sang Ki Choi, expedition commanding officer
Major In Ho Park, DPRK, boarding officer
Major Young Soo Lim, interpreter

PREFACE

It was 1968. Crisis abounded throughout the world in terrifying proportions.

In January, the Viet Cong initiated the Tet Offensive, taking the city of Hue and killing at least five thousand civilians during their month-long occupation. The U.S. Marines took it back in a series of bloody skirmishes.

In February, in a remarkable slap to the face of the United States, the Democratic People's Republic of Korea (DPRK) seized the intelligence-gathering ship USS *Pueblo* (AGER 2), which was clearly steaming in international waters off Wonsan, North Korea. With that, the United States dispatched two carrier groups, one on each coast of North Korea, ready to do their deadly business. To counter the U.S. Navy, the Soviets sent submarines from their naval base nearby in Vladivostok and from Petropavlovsk farther up the Kamchatka Peninsula. Diplomacy sputtered during this standoff, and the *Pueblo*'s crew suffered. They were tortured and held hostage for eleven months until their release in December 1968. To this day the *Pueblo* is still captive, on display as a tourist attraction in Pyongyang, North Korea, where she's moored on the Tedong River. The U.S. Navy considers her still in commission, the only Navy ship seized since the early-nineteen-century wars in Tripoli.

Fingers hovered close to red buttons when the Soviet ballistic missile submarine *K-129* went missing in early March 1968. Under orders from the

GRU, she steamed a fixed track and failed to transmit position reports at designated times. Finally, the alarm was raised, and it seemed the entire Soviet Pacific Fleet got under way to look for her. But they didn't know where to look. They didn't know *K-129* sank inexplicably about 1,825 miles northwest of Hawaii and lay on the bottom in 16,500 feet of water.

Cooler heads did not prevail. The Soviets openly blamed the United States for the loss of the *K-129*, saying she was rammed by the submarine USS *Swordfish* (SSN 579). The *Swordfish* was in the Sea of Japan then, where she hit an iceberg, but for years the Soviets refused to believe it.

Amid all this, civil unrest thrived in the USA, with riots breaking out in more than one hundred cities. Burning of the U.S. flag became commonplace, usually accompanied by an unheard-of amount of antimilitary sentiment. Servicemen in uniform were pushed, yelled at, and spat upon in public.

Political tumult erupted later in March when President Lyndon Johnson, disenchanted with the terribly uneasy times, declared he would not run for president in the fall election.

April was not any easier. Martin Luther King Jr. was assassinated.

Things got worse in May, when the USS *Scorpion* (SSN 589) sank with all hands in the Atlantic off the Azores. Her remains were soon found, with conjecture running strong that the Soviets sank her in retaliation for their *K-129* loss.

June was another black month. Presidential candidate Robert F. Kennedy was murdered by a young man in Los Angeles.

And the riots continued throughout the nation. Perhaps the most notable were those during the Democratic National Convention in Chicago in August. Police and the National Guard had to be called out to keep peace.

But quietly and very secretly, also in August, the USS *Halibut* (SSGN 587) discovered the wreck of the *K-129*. They found her with the help of the Navy and Air Force's extensive SOSUS network—a field of underwater microphones connected to shore bases around the Pacific Rim.

Through all of this, finger pointing, ugly rhetoric, and yellow dog journalism prevailed. An uneasy feeling gripped the world as Richard Nixon was elected president in November.

The Navy and then the CIA, with a large and secret budget, convinced

President Nixon that the Soviet submarine could be salvaged; that secrets of her R-21 rockets with 800-kiloton nuclear warheads and coding systems could be exhumed from 16,500 feet of ocean and examined.

Thus began Project AZORIAN, a massive undertaking faced daily with major engineering challenges. To raise the *K-129*, a gigantic purpose-built ship was constructed at a cost of $350 million. She displaced 50,000 tons and was 619 feet long, about the same general dimensions as the U.S. Navy's *Iowa*-class battleships but far different in configuration. Named the *Glomar Explorer*, she was built under the guise of mining high-value manganese nodules from the ocean floor for Howard Hughes. Kept secret were the gigantic doors in the bottom of the ship where *the K-129* could be hauled into the midships section, stored, and examined in an area called the "moon pool." The *Glomar Explorer* was launched in 1972 and arrived over the wreck site in June 1974 while the United States was still deep in political turmoil. The Watergate investigations were fast unfolding, and people were demanding the resignation of Richard Nixon.

But in the Pacific, right under the nose of a Russian spy trawler lurking nearby, the forward section of the *K-129* was indeed seized and raised to just below the recovery ship. Unfortunately, a large section of the wreck's after portion broke off and fell in pieces back to the ocean floor. This included the conning tower, control room, and R-21 missiles. But a thirty-eight-foot piece of the forward section was successfully raised and captured in the moon pool. Ironically, this engineering victory occurred on August 9, 1974, the day Richard Nixon resigned his presidency and left office, to be replaced by Gerald R. Ford.

Thousands of artifacts were discovered and categorized, including the bodies of six Soviet sailors and two nuclear-tipped torpedoes. During the sinking and with enormous sea pressures, the torpedoes' plutonium charges underwent harmless one point detonations, scattering plutonium that contaminated the wreck, requiring extensive detoxification.

Much of AZORIAN is still highly classified, and it's unclear what the CIA has done with the artifacts. Nor is it entirely clear that just the forward section was the only portion raised. Perhaps there was more.

What the CIA has stated is that the Russian bodies were cleaned, arranged, and buried at sea while the ship was en route to Pearl Harbor, the ceremony respectfully photographed. Things quieted over the years until news leaked out that a secret CIA project, for some reason called JENNIFER, had raised a Soviet submarine back in the 1970s.

Finally, after the collapse of the Communist regime in 1991, Director of the CIA Robert Gates visited the Russian Federation's first president, Boris Yeltsin, in Moscow in an official attempt to reach out and explain what happened to the *K-129*. Gates presented evidence of the recovery, including the ship's bell that had been stowed in the forward torpedo room. Gates also turned over film of the burial ceremony of the six Russian sailors and the flag used to cover their coffins.

Much of this story began or occurred in 1968, the basic period of this story. It was a period with challenges that seemed insurmountable at the time. And yet somehow we muddled through.

Система Периметр = Systema Perimetr

In the cold war, Perimetr was an automatic trigger system for Soviet ballistic missiles to be launched in the event their top political and military leaders were killed in a preemptive strike. American intelligence experts referred to this system as—

Dead Man Launch

PROLOGUE

16 June 1962
COMCRUDESPAC Headquarters
USS *Prairie* (AD 15)
San Diego, California

Santa Ana winds blowing from the northeast at twenty knots brought a fine, dusty grit, the sun laboring through a brownish sky. San Diego Bay was choppy with just a few small boats bouncing about. To the east over San Diego, a P5M amphibian clawed its way through a bucking descent, the wind tossing it around as it drew close to the bay.

When it flashed over the water, the pilot gave up trying to make the thing fly and simply chopped the throttles. The twin engine plane stalled and fell onto the fairway with a great splash. It stopped almost immediately and then began the laborious task of taxiing a half mile over to the North Island Naval Air Station where Sailors would swim out to her with beaching gear attached to buoys. With the beaching gear seated in place, a cable was hooked to a pad-eye beneath the tail and the P5M was towed ashore for maintenance and re-fueling.

Aboard the 530-foot, 16,700-ton destroyer tender *Prairie*, solidly moored in midstream, one could barely feel the gusts. Her axis was north–south, with downtown San Diego to starboard and Coronado to port. Five hundred yards to the south of the *Prairie*'s mooring, work was underway on a new bridge that would span the Bay, connecting Coronado to downtown San Diego and eliminating the crowded and frenetic ferry service at rush hour. Moored to the *Prairie*'s starboard side was a brood of five destroyers; inboard were three *Gearing* class and outboard were two older *Fletcher* class.

On the quarterdeck, the phone buzzed and Lt. (j.g.) Walter Peacock yanked it from the bracket. "Quarterdeck, Lieutenant Peacock speaking, sir."

"Walter, it's Briggs. He's on his way down. Boat ready?"

"Got it, thanks." Peacock bracketed the phone and announced to his messenger and boatswain's mate of the watch, "Get ready."

Peacock, having just relieved the watch as OOD, automatically moved beside the quarterdeck's well-varnished accommodation ladder. The watch messenger stepped to the podium with the logbook while the boatswain's mate leaned over the rail, braced two fingers to his mouth, and gave a shrill whistle to the boat crew.

Twenty seconds later, Rear Adm. Todd Ingram walked around the corner. At forty-six, Ingram had held his weight. He was still trim even though he seldom worked out anymore—except for the constant climbing and descending of ladders aboard ship. His legs were in fine shape. His cheeks sagged just a bit, and his hair had thinned and grayed at the sides. One couldn't help but notice the twin silver stars of a rear admiral at his collar points. With his stars went the office of Commander Cruisers and Destroyers, Pacific—COMCRUDESPAC.

One glance told Peacock the Old Man was off in space. Usually the admiral would deliver a smile and make small talk while waiting for his barge to disconnect from the boat boom and pull up to the accommodation ladder. They would discuss football or sailing or Peacock's three little children or the admiral's two children: a daughter at Coronado High School and a son at the Naval Academy, now on a WESPAC summer cruise. But today the admiral stood alone at the rail and gazed into the distance, lost in his thoughts.

No chit-chat today. Peacock snapped his fingers at the messenger of the watch. The Sailor, a signalman striker in undress whites, checked the Chelsea clock and logged Ingram's departure at 1604. Another snap went to the boatswain's mate of the watch, also in undress whites, who flipped switches on the 1MC. His metallic announcement echoed on speakers throughout the ship, "COMCRUDESPAC departing."

"Ten-hut!" barked Peacock. Along with the boatswain's mate and the watch messenger, he snapped to attention and saluted.

"Permission to leave the ship, sir?" asked the admiral, returning the salute.

Peacock barked, "Granted, Admiral. And have a wonderful evening."

The admiral's face softened. He looked up with, "Thank you Lieutenant. Please do likewise."

"Thank you, sir." Peacock watched Ingram salute the colors and descend the ladder with practiced steps. At the lower platform he jumped easily into the barge. The coxswain saluted him aboard, the bow hook pushed them off, and the boat lunged away with a roar. Soon it was lost in a mist of diesel smoke and spray.

The last time Peacock had seen Admiral Ingram like this was in August of last year when the Soviets started building their wall through Berlin. The times were tense, and everyone seemed to be on alert. And now, the wall was still under construction and was a news item on TV at least once a week when an East Berliner was either shot at the wall or successfully escaped to the other side.

In a way, Ingram was transparent, Peacock decided. When things were okay, he joked and smiled with you as if he were just another lieutenant (j.g.) desperately trying to qualify for something. But for the past few days his face had alternated between sadness and ferocity. Peacock couldn't tell which was more obvious. He hoped the admiral's wife could help him unwind.

Helen had made another tamale pie. At dinner, their daughter, Kate, a ninth-grader at Coronado High School, prattled on about her Spanish class while Ingram absently buttered a tortilla and sipped his frosted bottle of San Miguel beer.

Kate reached over and touched his arm.

"Huh?"

"Daddy, I said my Spanish teacher wants you to come in and speak. Is that okay?"

"Sure. No problem." He slathered more butter on his tortilla.

With a wink to her mother, Kate said, "On second thought, they want you to just clean toilets on Saturday."

"That's okay, too." Ingram bit into his tortilla and munched.

Helen barked, "Todd, wake up."

Ingram jumped. "I heard you. You want me to speak to your Spanish class and then clean toilets. That's okay." He looked over and smiled at Kate, now fourteen years old and looking every day more like her mother with her hair pulled into a slick ebony ponytail. And like her mother's, Kate's eyes grabbed you. Amazing. "Yeah. Spanish class. Toilets. I can do it all." He raised a fork and dug into his tamale pie. "Wow. This is really good."

Helen sighed. "Welcome back."

Later, he sat in his office looking out the bay window onto the street with the odd name of Encino Row. They lived just two blocks from Ocean Boulevard and the expansive beach that looked onto Point Loma to the west and the Del Coronado Hotel to the east. With the lights dim, he sipped coffee as a quarter moon rose overhead. Kate was watching *Gunsmoke* in the living room while Helen was cleaning up in the kitchen.

Damn. The kid is growing up. She's nearly a woman. Kate was almost as pretty now as Helen had been when he first met her as an Army nurse on Corregidor in 1942. Now it was 1962. He pursed his lips. "Wow."

"Wow what?" It was Helen at the door, drying her hands with a towel. "Leave off the lights?"

"Please."

She slipped into his lap and kissed him on the forehead. "What is it?"

"What is what?"

"Todd, come on." She kissed him on the ear.

He held her tight. "Is that old bed still in the garage?"

She gave a healthy giggle, then repeated. "Come on. You forgot your salad."

"What?"

"And your hot sauce. You always dump in a little Tabasco."

"Guilty as charged."

"So, tell me."

"I can't."

"Not where Jerry is concerned. So tell me."

"What do you mean?"

He could almost see her better in the darkness than in normal light. Her eyes. They dominated everything. She riveted him. And soon Kate would be able to do the same thing.

Helen read his mind as if it were a simple grocery list. "It's Jerry, isn't it?"

He forced a smile. "I can neither confirm nor deny." What he couldn't say is that COMSEVEN had designated the USS *Mallilieu* and the USS *Griffith* to chase a Russian nuke. And the only reason the *Mallilieu* was assigned was that she'd had an engineering casualty in Yokosuka and couldn't get away on time to sail south with the rest of the Seventh Fleet. So his son's ship was stuck with the duty going after that damned Commie. Normally, Ingram didn't worry, but intel from SOSUS had tracked the Soviet submarine soon after she'd left Petropavlovsk. Most likely she knew a posse was on her trail. Her captain might do something desperate like shooting one of the boat's two type 53 torpedoes. And the *Mallilieu* couldn't outrun the type 53 torpedo. It had a fifty-five-knot capability. Worse, it had a nuclear warhead with a twenty-kiloton yield. The *Mallilieu* would be dead meat anywhere within a two-mile radius.

"Todd, I'm still here and I hear the gears grinding."

"Ummm." And it just wasn't this Russian nuke. Over the past few days he'd sat through several briefings. Things were getting worse everywhere. The situation in Viet Nam was going downhill and there didn't seem to be a clear way out. Closer to home, Fidel Castro had turned up the heat on the U.S., especially after last year's disastrous Bay of Pigs invasion. Suddenly, assets intended for the Pacific fleet were being detained in the Atlantic and Caribbean. And the Soviets were cranking out submarines like tenpins: many of them on patrol were armed with type 53 nuclear-tipped torpedoes. Sometimes the daily briefings were too much. It was a dangerous world, and this mushrooming Soviet submarine threat had wrapped itself around him —especially now that his son was involved.

He looked up at his wife. "Twenty years."

"Since when?"

"We've been married nearly twenty years."

"Not bad for a couple of old retreads."

"I'll say." He kissed her on the nose.

"What about Jerry?"

He held her close. "I can't."

"He's in danger." A statement.

Twenty kilotons worth. Today, he'd been copied on messages from naval commands up and down the line and even the State Department and the CIA. The lines were buzzing and he felt he was in over his head. Everybody wanted information about this one. But nobody seemed willing to take action. And now Helen with her mother's knack at clairvoyance was dialing in. Helen felt these things as her mother, Kate, did. It was uncanny. Wherever Todd or her children were involved, she knew. He looked at Helen again in the semidarkness. *She knows.*

"Is he going to be all right?"

"He'll do just fine."

They heard Kate in the next room. Pat Boone was singing, and the enticing odor of popcorn wafted in. She'd found a movie on TV: *Friendly Persuasion* with Gary Cooper.

Ingram hadn't felt this jittery since the war. Back then, there were a few times when he was sure he was about to die and he genuinely had been scared. He felt it now; it gnawed at him. *What a crazy world. How can we stop these people?*

But then he thought of something else. "I got word today."

She faced him. "Word? You're always getting word. You're going to tell me that you've been fired."

"Not as lucky as that."

"What, then?" She faked a pout.

"I'm on the selection list for a third star."

Helen shrieked. "Vice admiral? You have to be kidding!"

"Straight scoop. Detailer called me a couple of hours ago."

She plopped his shoulders with both hands. "Congratulations, Sailor." Then she gave him a long kiss. "Where to?"

"Not sure yet. It requires confirmation by Congress; then I'll know more."

"You think maybe that job in Hawaii?" she persisted.

"Could be. And It'll be my last stop, for sure."

"That's what you said about this job."

She felt good. He held her closer and she wiggled in his lap. Her breath grazed his ear. It was warm. And he felt her lips.

"You know, there's either a mattress in the garage or the one upstairs," he said. "Your choice."

"A victory lap, huh?"

He gave a lopsided grin. "Well, sort of."

"The mattress in the garage is musty and full of bugs."

"And oil stains."

Her voice was husky. "I guess that means will have to use the one upstairs."

PART I

For whatever is hidden is meant to be disclosed, and whatever is concealed is meant to be brought out into the open...

Mark 4:22

1

17 June 1962
Project 627A, Submarine *K-12*
Voenno-Morskoi Flot SSSR
25°52'28" N, 128°09'12" E
214 kilometers southeast of Buckner Bay, Okinawa

Displacing 3,118 metric tons, the *K-12* was 357 feet long with a beam of 27 feet and a draft of 21 feet. She was powered by two water-cooled VM-A reactors of 70 megawatts each, with steam generators and two steam turbines capable of 35,000 shaft horsepower. All this could drive her at 15.5 knots on the surface and an incredible 28 knots submerged—almost twice that of the Soviet Union's newest diesel powered submarine.

Project 627A initially had a bizarre purpose: to launch T-15 torpedoes into enemy harbors. The T-15 was a gas-steam-powered torpedo seventy-seven feet long with a range of at least thirty-one miles, and carrying a thermonuclear warhead. But the project designers cast that aside early on as unworkable and changed the 627, 627A, and 645 classes to the role of attack submarine—meaning they would conduct torpedo attacks on enemy warships and transports.

Captain First Rank Eduard Dezhnev, the *K-12*'s *zampolit* (political officer), glanced at the bulkhead display over his bunk: course 197° true, speed 15 knots, depth 150 meters, time 1301. He just had time for a quick nap before his afternoon "interrogations." He was to give political instruction to three of the harder cases aboard the *K-12*, one of them Starshiy Leytenant Isidor Volkov. But Roxanna's letter beckoned. There was no one else in his stateroom but he still looked from side to side as he dug into his tiny desk drawer and pulled out her letter. It had come in the mail just before they'd cast off from Petropavlovsk seven days ago. He'd read it three times already but he couldn't get enough of it. He wanted to see it again, to think of her; to imagine her. He raised it to his nose and sniffed. She'd perfumed it. He was overwhelmed with that compelling feeling of home and comfort and love, and what goes along with a damn good woman.

He'd met Roxanna Utkina—Russian for "duck"—at a party his mother threw at her home in Sochi. Roxanna had been a soloist/dancer with the Kirov Ballet and was home for a holiday. Claiming ballet dancers were stiff, self-centered, and narcissistic, Anoushka warned her baby, Eduard, to pay no attention to the stately girl. But once they saw each other, that was it. She was tall for a ballerina, athletic and lanky at the same time, with thin arms and legs and a long, graceful neck. And she could unleash a dazzling smile while her ice-blue eyes drilled right though you. She was just as captivated by Eduard, the bemedaled captain third rank, hero of the Great Patriotic War, who walked with a limp but had a lilting timbre to his baritone voice. Dezhnev immediately dismissed Anoushka's admonitions, and for the next two weeks the two were inseparable, the dancer becoming his Utochka, his Little Duck. On the sixth night they went too far, both realizing what could happen but unable to control themselves. Still, they clung to each other for the rest of Dezhnev's time. The night before he was to return to duty, he dropped to a knee, hauled out an engagement ring, and asked her to marry him. To his astonishment, his Utochka begged off for the time being, saying she didn't want to stifle her career in the Kirov while he seemed to be always posted to assignments in eastern Russia's provinces—Kamchatka being one of the most remote locations.

They kept in touch. Roxanna, his Utochka, had her baby. They agreed to name him Vladimir Utkin, taking her last name. Even so, he doted on the child as much as he could, visiting at least twice a year. He was devastated when Roxanna married Ilya Gurov, one of the Kirov's flamboyant managers, with his long, impeccably combed shoulder-length blond hair. It was a poor arrangement from the beginning. Gurov was gone constantly currying favor with the higher-ups in the Communist Party. And worse, he completely ignored his step-son. At age five, little Vladimir Utkin was put into a private boarding school with Dezhnev paying the bills. Roxanna became distant as time went on, but Dezhnev doggedly kept up the payments for his son, making sure he had the best schooling possible and trying to maintain the romance. Dezhnev flew west to see his son and Roxanna as often as possible. In the meantime, Roxanna's career blossomed while Dezhnev felt trapped emotionally. At times he sought the comfort of other women, but that always ended in disaster. He could not forget his Utochka; could not put her out of his mind. When he sought Anoushka's advice she scoffed and told him to grow up. Secretly, Anouchka just couldn't let go of her little Eduard.

But then two things happened. Two years ago, during a rehearsal, Roxanna's dance partner lifted her, stumbled back, and dumped her into the orchestra pit. She crashed through a chair and her Achilles tendon was ruptured—a career-ending accident. With Roxana's career suddenly shattered, Gurov left her and disappeared into his job. Divorce papers came through six months later, Roxanna only too happy to sign while looking for other ways to make a living.

Dezhnev lost no time swooping in. At first she refused to see him. But later on, as her surgery and therapy took hold, she would agree to see him and even held his hand on occasion. Six months ago she started a dance school in Sochi and already had ten students.

And now, she was writing perfumed letters. Amazing how things had changed.

25 May, 1962

Eduard, my lovely,

I hope this finds you well. Just a few moments to dash this off between classes.

Some of these children are such brats! I thought you should know your mother is sort of down. Apparently, she missed out on the part of Anna Gromeko in Dr. Zhivago. One would think she was a natural with her language and culture, but MGM gave it to a younger woman, Siobhan McKenna, an Irish Catholic of all things. Admittedly, she is only 39, much younger than Anoushka. And that's what counts in Hollywood, I hear. Further, Anoushka tells me her agent does not answer phone calls—the kiss of death. When she's working, she makes lots of money, but then she squanders it on the most foolish things. The Hollywood two-step, she calls it. But it seems she must keep up with the Hollywood people so she can get jobs. That's expensive. And now, she tells me she may lose her house in Venice Beach. It makes me think I'll take the Kirov anytime...

Once again Dezhnev found himself surprised. All this information. They must have become pretty good friends. He felt a lot better realizing his chances had vastly improved.

...but the reason I tell you this is that we're seeing quite a bit of each other. She drops by my school and even helps out a bit working with the five-year-olds. There is something in her that brings out the best in them.

Speaking of best, two of my fourteen-year-olds were accepted at the Kirov and begin training next month. Very exciting.

Even better news is that Vladimir seems to be buckling down. He's given up smoking—I think your last visit did the trick—and is doing much better in mathematics. Now he says he wants to be a naval officer, like his father. Things could be worse, I suppose. But I'm glad about the smoking. Also gone with the cigarettes were those hoodlum friends. They were awful. It seems there was a fight. A bad one. He came home with a black eye and bruises on his back and legs. Whatever it was, he isn't seeing those people anymore. He needs a father, and you're the best one he's got. I'm glad you're there for him. If only it could be more often.

He misses you and ... here it is, I miss you, too. Write soon and write often.

Off to class. Hope to see you soon.

Your Lovely and Your
Utochka

. . .

Utochka! His Little Duck. Clearly, she wanted to see him. Maybe even marry him? Astounding!

Fortunately, he had figured a way to get out of submarines and into a shore-based assignment much closer to home. In two years he would be posted to the Nakhimov Black Sea Higher Naval School in Sevastopol, Crimea. The joke was that he'd be teaching politics, but the flip side was that he would be only six hundred kilometers from Sochi and Roxanna; an hour's flying time. Very nice.

He lifted the letter to read it again——and jerked back at —a knock in the passageway.

Dezhnev barked, "Come."

Starshiy Leytenant Isidor Volkov, his first appointment, stepped in and drew to attention, his hat in his hand. His face was gaunt and he had bags under his eyes. He looked straight ahead at the bulkhead.

Dezhnev waited twenty seconds then said, "Volkov. When was the last time you had eight hours' sleep?"

Volkov blinked; sweat beading on his forehead and above his lip. "I ... I don't know, sir."

"Six hours?"

Volkov shook his head.

"How much sleep did you have last night?"

Another head shake.

"Why?"

"Sir?"

"Sit down, Leytenant, please."

Carefully, Volkov took a chair opposite Dezhnev. "Yes, sir."

"Volkov, how much sleep did you get last night?"

The man shook his head, his eyes a bit bewildered. "Don't know, sir. Maybe three, four hours."

Dezhnev leaned forward on an elbow. "Do you realize what that means? You jeopardize your shipmates with so little sleep. Your judgment is impaired, you become unreliable. How can you—?"

"Mr. Dezhnev, I have no choice. Mr. Yusopov has me smoothing his logbooks every night." Captain Second Rank Vladislav Yusopov was the ship's engineering officer. "Then I must study for my engineering quals."

"I thought you took your engineering qualifications?"

"No, sir. Not yet."

Dezhnev whipped through Volkov's file. A separate document signed by Captain Second Rank Vladislav Yusopov stated he'd taken the exam a week ago and failed.

"When do you go next on watch?"

"Two hours, sir."

"Where?"

"Shaft alley, after spaces."

"What the hell for?" Standing watch in the shaft alley was like watching grass grow.

"Packing gland leak, sir. Starboard shaft. Mr. Yusopov is worried."

Dezhnev fumed silently. A packing gland leak was very serious. The ship's commanding officer, the ruddy-cheeked Kontr Admiral Stanislaw Kudrevich, was playing a dangerous game. Dezhnev could have him up on charges for such an error.

And Yusopov. Just yesterday Yusopov had been OOD on the bridge with Dezhnev and Kudrevich enjoying the night sky before diving.

Kudrevich had called out to his OOD. "Mr. Yusopov. Have you completed the checkoff for diving?"

Vladislav Yusopov, a thin, sallow-cheeked captain second rank, called over his shoulder, "I'm doing that now, Captain."

Kudrevich chuckled and said to Dezhnev *sotto voce*, "You notice? He always says, 'I'm doing that now.'"

Dezhnev smirked. Yusopov was well known among the fleet. A KGB protégé, he had gained notoriety with his first assignment in the Strategic Rocket Forces. But the notoriety was negative. He had been seconded to the duty watch officer during a midnight shift in the deep underground rocket warning bunker in Serpukhov, twenty kilometers south of Moscow. The duty watch officer, Colonel Kupetsky, was seized by an attack of food poisoning and was atop the toilet in the next room with raging intestinal upset. His relief had been summoned. In the meantime, Yusopov was temporarily in charge. It was at this point that the screens covering the United States blared a launch warning. Six missiles were detected coming toward the Soviet Union, their projected point of impact: Moscow.

Yusopov, seeing his chance to become a Hero of the Soviet Union, upgraded the Rocket Forces to full alert and ordered a counterattack on the United States. Then he ordered the launch of *Perimetr*, a series of rockets that, through special radiotelemetry, would launch the USSR's entire ICBM arsenal against the United States. Once airborne, there was no stopping the *Perimetr* system. Yusopov, with his Hero of the Soviet Union medal as good as pinned to his tunic, was poised over the launch panel, ready to push the buttons. It took five shouting officers and a screaming Colonel Gurin, his pants still down, to drag Yusopov away from the launch panel. While they grappled with Yusopov, the warnings went green. A glitch in the system. Somehow their radars were tracking sunspots. The world was at peace and remained so due to the efforts of four warrant officers and two commissioned officers, one with his pants around his ankles. Shortly after that the system was changed to include a two-key system for launch authorization.

The KGB decided that even though Yusopov's father, Colonel General Maxim Yusopov, was a member of the Soviet Energy Institute (Atomic Energy Commission), young Vladislav would be better off in submarines rather than the Strategic Rocket Forces. And now the *K-12* was saddled with him as chief engineer.

Dezhnev brought his mind back to the problem at hand. "All right, Mr. Volkov," he sighed. "Let's start at the top. Suppose you explain the differences to me between the pressurized water reactor and the light water graphite reactor.

Volkov blinked for a moment. The corners of his mouth turned up.

Dezhnev said dryly, "You don't expect a political officer to know such things? Try me. And if you make a mess of it you'll be living in the shaft alley for twenty four hours."

Volkov sat up straight and like a toy soldier began, "The pressurized water reactor is the main power source for the Soviet nuclear fleet using uranium enriched to about thirty percent. The coolant and moderator is water that is fed into the ..."

Dezhnev began reviewing Yusopov's file, then compared it with Volkov's. Amazing that no one had pointed this out before. Captain Second Rank

Yusopov had been educated at the Makarov Pacific Naval Institute in Vladivostok, a school for ordinary officers. Instead of going into the surface fleet, though, he was posted to the Strategic Rocket Forces, a plum assignment—with his father's help, no doubt. Sadly, Yusopov's experience in naval reactors was limited to surface ships. Prior to the *K-12*, he'd only served in diesel submarines.

Volkov droned on, "...whereas the RBMK light water reactor uses enriched uranium with graphite as its moderator. Efficiencies are achieved in this area by using ..." He stopped and looked at Dezhnev with raised eyebrows.

"Go on."

"...with the graphite reactor, it is possible to run it on natural uranium rather than enriched uranium, the natural uranium basically having the same elemental composition as when it was mined..."

Dezhnev nodded politely and turned back to Volkov's file. He came from a broken family, raised by his mother, who worked on the janitorial staff at Red Banner Fleet Headquarters. But that was to Volkov's advantage. He earned top grades in the lower schools and was admitted to the Frunze Higher Naval School. He did well in his academics, taking classes in higher mathematics, physics, and chemistry. His grades at the nuclear power school were top-notch. The *K-12* was his first ship.

Quickly, Dezhnev flipped to his test scores. Captain Second Rank Yusopov had checked the "no pass" boxes on two evaluations. So had Captain Third Rank Dmitri Matvonkye, the operations officer, and Captain Third Rank Lev Keslor, the weapons officer. Except Matvonkye had marked Volkov as "pass" on the first evaluation and then struck it out and marked "no pass." Same thing with Keslor. Changed from "pass" to "no pass" on the first evaluation. Both had checked "no pass" on the second evaluation.

Dezhnev understood. He'd seen it happen many times. Yusopov was a dunderhead who, as senior watch officer, had influenced the markings of two subordinate officers lest they receive poor evaluations. They'd passed it on to the executive officer, who looked the other way and sent it on to Kudrevich, another influence peddler, who endorsed the evaluations.

Volkov, a nobody, was being railroaded off the *K-12* because his superior officer was afraid. Afraid of a man who knew more about the *K-12*'s nuclear power plant than his superior officer.

Volkov prattled on about the corrosive properties of graphite.

Dezhnev raised a hand. "Okay. Listen to me. When was your last oral evaluation with your boss?"

Volkov seemed surprised. "Not yet, sir."

"What?" Regulations required that superior officers sit with subordinates at least once every six months. "Okay then, when was—"

The lights blinked twice. Men walked quickly in the passageway outside. His phone buzzed. He yanked it from the bracket. "Yes?"

It was Kudrevich. "Action stations, Eduard. Get off your dead butt and get up to the control room."

"What is it?"

"American sonar blazing away. Sounds like he's about thirty kilometers out." Ironic. Kudrevich depended more on Dezhnev than he did his senior officers, including the executive officer. Perhaps it was because of his war record.

"Yes, sir. Be right up." Dezhnev hung up and said, "Looks like we're going to action stations, Mr. Volkov. Yankee Doodle Dandy is sniffing around up there."

"Who?"

The man was smart, but he was also dense. Even at that, Dezhnev decided he had potential. Worse, he decided he liked him. "Look, let's meet again later. There are some things you have to know."

"I don't understand."

"You will, my boy. You will."

2

17 June1962
USS *Mallilieu* (DD 768)
25°52'28" N, 128°09'12" E
97 miles southeast of Buckner Bay, Okinawa

Midshipman Third Class Jeremiah Oliver Ingram yawned loudly and scratched his chest. It was 0115 and he'd been on the midwatch for an hour and a half: two and a half hours to go.

Damn! He yawned again, yearning for his nice warm bunk.

He was in the forward fireroom where the temperature soared above 100°, alone on the upper level seated in a chair tilted back against the guard rail of boiler number one. The rest of the watch was on the lower level tending the fire in boiler number two. For company he had a grease-stained paperback copy of Ian Fleming's *Thunderball.* Jerry yawned as he flipped pages, envying James Bond as he thwarted assassins and terrorists, darting from close call to close call and from bed to bed, barely lingering to enjoy the scent of the gorgeous women who found him irresistible.

The destroyer USS *Mallilieu* plowed through a belligerent state six sea, headed for the Bashi Channel and eventually Subic Bay in the Philippines. Outside, the wind gusted up to sixty knots. It was on the nose, making the *Gearing*-class destroyer buck and pitch heavily. From time to time, the 2,400-ton *Tin Can*, as her Sailors fondly called her, rolled drunkenly, sometimes sliding toward a broach. Then the stern would catch up to the bow, threatening to roll the ship. At times like this Jerry savored the relative warmth and comfort of the engineering spaces despite the heat, because he knew the bridge watch far above were wet, miserable, and scared out of their skins as the cursing helmsman worked frantically to keep the ship's head on course.

Midshipman Third Class Jeremiah Oliver Ingram looked more like his mother than his father. At five-ten, he had dark, almost ebony hair, close-cropped like that of his classmates. He had Helen's dark brown, captivating, intense eyes—eyes that challenged you with almost every glance. The rest of Jerry Ingram was complemented by a strong chin and compact, well-defined build concentrated into 175 pounds.

For now, his only job on this watch was to keep a vigilant eye on the sight glass of number two boiler as it delivered superheated steam to the starboard turbines in the engine room. It was a simple gauge, about twelve inches in length. If the water level fell below a black line near the bottom of the gauge, he was to summon Boiler Tender Second Class Arnold Schumacher, a corpulent snipe who was proudly skilled in the operation of the Navy's "M" type boiler and its associated equipment. Like an overgrown viper, Schumacher's beady eyes were just two inches apart, and he now lurked on the lower level drinking coffee with four others while hogging a spot beneath a forced-draft blower.

If the water level of boiler number 2 went above a black line at the top of the water gauge, young Ingram was also to summon Boiler Tender Schumacher. Jerry wondered: after summoning Schumacher, should he simply stand by and watch this drooling idiot twist valves and push levers? What else could he do? Maybe he should simply pray for the steam drum not to explode and obliterate the ship.

The engineering spaces absorbed nearly two-thirds of the ship. There were two firerooms and two engine rooms, which were usually intolerably hot and noisy. Even now, steam boiling in number two boiler's steam drum screeched as it raced aft to the forward engine room. The sound was loud and continuous; one always had to shout to be heard. Jerry could hardly hear himself think, let alone decipher what Schumacher or anyone else was trying to scream into his ear. Grease and noise and intolerable temperatures were a way of life for the snipes, eternally trapped below-decks in the engineering spaces.

It was Jerry's third watch in the boiler room, and by now he was sure he didn't like it, even though he was warm and protected from the elements outside. He and fifteen of his Naval Academy classmates were two weeks into their summer cruise. He was grateful to have survived his plebe year, scraping by near the bottom of his class. They'd scattered his classmates, along with a number of NROTC sophomores, among destroyers in the Pacific. The *Mallilieu* was steaming in company with a sister ship, the USS *Griffith.* They had been detained in Yokosuka, Japan, for unscheduled repairs and missed their deployment by four days. Now, having just refueled in Buckner Bay, Okinawa, they were again headed south to catch up with their task group in Subic Bay, Philippines.

After standing watches in engine rooms and fire rooms, Jerry had decided he didn't want anything to do with destroyers or the rest of the surface Navy. They'd rotated him through watches on the bridge, in the gun mounts, in sonar, in the engineering spaces. He'd seen enough of the destroyer Navy to let him know these little tin cans weren't for him. Too much bouncing around and too much spit and polish. Even officers on the *Mallilieu* spit-shined their shoes. *How stupid.* Jeremiah Ingram had vowed to put in for pilot training as soon as he graduated from the Academy, hopefully receiving orders to Naval Air Station, Pensacola.

The ship tilted up like a truck climbing a steep hill, then pitched over the top of the wave, her twin screws momentarily lifting from the water. Cursing throttlemen in the engine room couldn't twirl their valves quickly enough to stop six-hundred-pound steam from spewing on the turbines, making the screws race and setting up a terrible vibration and racket aft. Four or five miserable seconds later, the fantail crunched back in the water to begin the process all over again.

Jerry eyed the water level for a moment and then went back to James Bond. He was speeding through northern Italy in a—

Somebody bumped his shoulder. He looked up into Schumacher's lizard eyes.

"Don' read no horney-books in the bahler room."

"Huh?"

"You hear me, college kid?" Schumacher yanked the book out of Jerry's hand and dropped it through a grate opening to the lower level.

Jerry shot to his feet. "What the hell?"

Schumacher pointed. "You watch that gawdam sight glass, college kid. Nuthin' else."

Technically, Jerry outranked Schumacher, but that was a stretch and both of them knew it. Plus, Schumacher was the top watch-stander in the forward fire room responsible for five men, two "M" type boilers, and the associated equipment. He had supervisorial authority. It occurred to Jerry that he'd been hazed so much over the past nine months as a plebe that this guy was a joke. Even so, a voice inside said, *Shut up, Jerry.* "Okay, I got it. No more reading."

With a final stare, Schumacher turned and descended the ladder to the lower level. Through the grate, Jerry watched him return to his coffee and stand under his cool blower.

At 0355 Jerry returned to the compartment up forward where his fellow midshipmen were bunked. They'd cleared out the second division and sent them aft. Now, the regular crew called the compartment Boy's Town. Also, some ghoulish detailing officer decided to try a social experiment and put fifteen Naval Academy sophomores with fifteen NROTC sophomores in the same compartment. The Naval Academy middies had the starboard side of the compartment, the NROTC middies the port side. Predictably, they clashed, and once, a fight started after lights out. But they quickly put that to rest lest an outsider find out. Now there was an uneasy peace, with each side barely speaking to the other.

Bright lights were out, red lights were on, and the place was cool, the compartment very quiet as the ship bucked and plunged into waves. But the motion was less violent than before. She no longer snapped from her rolls; she only eased back to the perpendicular and rolled gently to the other side with a smooth recovery. Except for occasional snores, the midshipmen were silent in their sleep tonight—finally getting solid rest rather than clutching bunk chains for dear life while the ship gyrated wildly and threw them around.

Removing grease-stained dungarees, Jerry stripped to his skivvies and swung up into his bunk—the top in a tier of three. With the storm abating, the blue Pacific worked its wonders, rocking everybody gently like babies in a crib. Jerry pulled the thick Navy blanket over his shoulders, rolled to his side, and was soon gone with the rest of them.

Something smacked his shoulder. "Off and on, Middie."

"Go away."

The hand pushed harder. "Com'on, pissant."

"Hey!" Jerry flipped over, checking his watch: 0725. "What's the idea?" He looked into the face of Fredericks, a buck-toothed third-class boatswain's mate with tobacco-stained teeth and fuzz concentrated under his nose that was supposed to pass for a moustache. "Out of the sack, Middie."

Jerry blinked sleep from his eyes. "Huh?"

"You got the watch in sonar: 0745."

"Something's wrong. I'm not up until the noon watch. And that's supposed to be on the signal bridge."

"I don't make the rules, Middie. I'm supposed to wake you and that's what I done."

"Who changed the watch bill?"

"I dunno know. The exec, I guess. You better get dressed and get some chow." Fredericks exited through the aft hatch into the mess decks, flipping on the bright compartment lights as a final "screw you."

Jerry rubbed his eyes. Except for one other bunk, the compartment was empty—all of the other middies were either having chow or were on watch somewhere. It hit him: Cookson—an NROTC jerk. Lying groaning in his bunk, Cookson was claiming seasickness again. Cookson stood at the top of his class academically. But at sea he was about as effective as a fart in hurricane. Cookson simply disappeared when people depended on him. Jerry realized Cookson must have been the one booked in sonar for this watch. Now they'd accelerated the schedule and shoved Jerry in there to take his place. Jerry eased off his bunk, ready to go over and toss the sniveling little jerk on the deck. After a moment's reflection, he walked forward to the crew's head where he took a quick shower, shaved, and dressed, this time in khakis; they let the midshipmen wear khakis for watches on the weather decks. Sprinkling on aftershave, he stomped by Cookson's bunk. The man didn't make a sound.

Jerry reached the aft hatch, undogged it, and swung it open. The thick odor of greasy food gushed in, followed by the sounds of Sailors moving about, sitting at chow, clanking their tin cups and trays, and laughing and shouting at one another.

"Ingram." It was Cookson. *Speak of the devil.*

"Yeah?"

"Kill the lights and dog the hatch, will ya?"

"Sure." Jerry slammed the hatch against the bulkhead and clipped it open. Leaving on the compartment lights, he stepped through and headed for the chow line.

Behind him Cookson shrieked, "Ingram, Ingraaaaam..."

He checked the mess line: pancakes, bacon, and scrambled eggs fresh from Okinawa. Not bad for a surface ship. Being an oncoming watch-stander, he ducked into the head of the chow line that stretched up two decks to the main deck and began filling his tray. Someone tapped him on the shoulder.

He turned to find Fredericks, the third-class boatswain's mate. The man's Dixie cup hat was stuffed in his web belt. Also on his belt was the boatswain's mate's coming-of-age badge: his knife. All boatswain's mates swaggered, and all boatswain's mates carried a knife, usually personalized. Usually a big one. Frederick's knife suited two criteria: (1) it was inexpensive, and (2) it was very reliable for slicing anything from a piece of tag line to a four-inch manila dock line. It was a bayonet honed to razorblade sharpness and sheathed in a Navy scabbard that rode on Fredericks' hip at a jaunty angle. His only regret was that he couldn't carry it ashore where it could do some good in the bars he frequented.

"Sorry, didn't mean to pop in front of you," Jerry said quickly, "but I got the watch."

"I know, I know. Lissen. The Exec's all over me about your compartment.

Sez it looks like a shithouse. And after my earlier visit with you, I gotta say I agree with him. Smells like one, too."

"Yep." Jerry held out his tray for applesauce.

"So, who's your compartment cleaner for today?"

Jerry hadn't checked the schedule; he had no idea who was up. "Cookson. He's already in there."

"I better check on him after chow. The Exec's really pissed."

"I think that's a good idea."

A mess cook shouted, "Hey, Middie; someone screaming in there?" He nodded toward the open compartment.

"I dunno."

Jerry went to the bridge first to look around and get the overall picture. Everyone there ignored him, intent on little tasks. The lookouts peered straight ahead, binoculars pressed to their faces. The *Griffith* and the *Mallilieu* were side-by-side at about a five-hundred-yard interval, racing into a beautiful sunrise and a clear day, bones in their teeth. Through the deck, he felt the determined drive of the *Mallilieu*'s geared turbines, driving her at twenty-two knots, he guessed.

Jerry stepped into CIC, then walked back toward the sonar compartment. It was quiet in this space. In the past two weeks he'd stood watches on the bridge, CIC, and sonar. Usually, there were smiles and low conversations, a lot of teaching, and at times a bit of grousing. In CIC there was popcorn on the midwatches.

But not now. As always, CIC was dark. The faint odor of popcorn lingered from the midwatch. But now it was different. There were nearly twenty people in here, most of them wearing voice-powered phones. Things were subdued. Conversations were brief. Faces were lit by the glow of cathode ray tubes and the backlighted plotting boards mounted on the bulkhead. Men were bent over the DRT plotting table muttering to one another. A radarman striker was keeping a surface plot on a bulkhead-mounted status board. It was a backlighted PPI plot and he was running a track. The skipper, exec, CIC watch officer, and the ASW officer, Lt. (j.g.) Ralph Jacobi, were off in a corner in hushed conversation, their faces a putrid dark green from the glow of radar repeaters.

Jerry walked over to them, but Jacobi looked over and held up a hand. *Wait.*

Jerry stood rooted to the spot. To his right he noticed a large yellow triangle drawn on the PPI track. There was a word beside the triangle. He leaned closer to look. *Sonofabitch*!

DATUM!

3

17 June 1962
USS *Mallilieu* (DD 768)
25°51'36" N, 128°09'22" E
149 miles southeast of Buckner Bay, Okinawa

Jerry Ingram stood under a blower, cool air rushing down his neck. But he didn't notice as he stared at the status board.

Datum.

That meant a submarine, or a submarine's last known location. And if Jerry interpreted the plot correctly, it appeared to be about thirty miles ahead of them steaming on a southeast course. At this rate they'd be on it in about an hour and twenty minutes. He checked the pit log over the DRT: twenty knots, just a shade above. That made sense. Any faster and the sonar's listening gear would have been drowned out by their hull noise.

He cocked an ear to Cdr. Ralph Decker, the ship's heavyset captain, who said, "Tony, I'm thinking we should go to condition 1AS."

"Makes sense to me, Skipper," said Lt. Cdr. Anthony Tilton, executive officer and CIC evaluator. Jerry detected a New England accent.

Leon Jacobi, the ASW officer, a tall, thin man, had a five o'clock shadow that became noticeable shortly after lunch. Tilton called it a two-o'clock shadow and was always on him about a closer shave. He asked, "Torpedoes too, Captain?"

"What do you have?" asked Decker.

Jacobi replied, "All six tubes are loaded, but there's four practice rounds and two war loads, both on the portside mount." The *Mallilieu* carried two Mark 32 launching tubes, both amidships, one to starboard, the other to port. Each cluster consisted of three tubes that could be rotated outboard to launch a Mark 44 acoustic torpedo toward a target.

The skipper rubbed his chin. "Okay. Shift one war load to the starboard mount and stand ready to swap out the rest of the practice rounds with war loads. May as well start with the one you're swapping out of the port mount."

"Yes, sir, said Jacobi. "Hedgehogs, too?"

"Make it so."

"Jesus," exclaimed Tilton.

The skipper turned to him. "Any objections, Tony?"

Tilton stammered. "War loads, sir? Aren't we overreacting?"

The skipper looked at each of them in turn. "This message authorizes us." He waved a flimsy in the air. "And as long as we're authorized, I'm doing it on the supposition that the guys who sent this message know more about the threat than we do. And if they're taking it that seriously, then I am too." He paused. "I'm not screwing around, gentlemen, got it?"

"What's so hot about this contact?" asked Tilton.

"Don't know," said Decker. "Except that it's based on SOSUS; they must have been tracking this guy for a while and they want us to hold him down."

"Do you suppose he's a nuke?" asked Tilton.

"Message doesn't say so," said Decker. They looked at Jacobi.

"...Uh, we don't have any intel on that, Skipper. They do have nukes, but they're all with the Northern Fleet as far as we know," said Jacobi.

Decker exhaled loudly and said, "Yeah, I don't think so either. But who knows?" He shrugged.

When they didn't respond he said, "Okay, let's get moving. Sound condition 1AS."

The exec turned to the CIC watch officer and barked, "Mr. Hunter, call the bridge and tell them to set condition 1AS."

"Aye, aye, Commander." Hunter was off in a dark corner wearing headphones. Jerry could hardly see him grab a hand phone and buzz the bridge. Five seconds later, "Set Condition One AS" gonged throughout the ship.

A hand yanked at Jerry's sleeve. It belonged to Lieutenant (j.g.) Jacobi. "Sir?"

"Where's your GQ station?" His eyes were like black embers.

"Mount 51, sir."

"No, I mean 1AS, damn it."

Jerry stammered, "Th-they never assigned us one, sir."

"So I end up with that deadbeat Cookson?"

"Er, he's on the binnacle list."

"With what?"

"Seasick, I think."

"Well, from now on, you're in sonar with me. I'll square it with the exec and we'll excuse Mr. Cookson from further duty. Come on."

Without waiting for an answer, Jacobi turned and headed for the sonar shack. With Jerry right behind, they stepped into the space that was a small part of CIC behind a thin bulkhead accessed through a plastic accordion door. Instruments and control boxes were mounted on the aft bulkhead. One of them was a suitcase-sized console called the attack director that was the heart of the underwater fire-control system. Jamming on a set of headphones, Jacobi stood before the attack director and flipped switches, energizing the machine as a multitude of dials and indicator lights jumped to life. Beside Jacobi was Sonarman Third Class Ray Flannigan, a muscular blond man of average height. His sleeves were rolled up to his biceps, and a pack of Pall Mall cigarettes was tucked into the left-side fold. Occasionally, on long 1AS watches, Jacobi permitted smoking in the sonar shack as they did in CIC. But for now the cigarettes remained where they were. Flannigan stood with his legs apart before a series of brass-plated handles and switches that controlled the ASW underwater battery.

"Flannigan," said Jacobi. "Call the chief. Tell him war loads, all mounts. Torpedoes and hedgehogs."

The normally unflappable Flannigan turned to look at Jacobi, his eyes wide. The others did too.

"That's right. We're getting serious today."

Flannigan nodded, "Yes, sir." He pushed his voice-powered phone mic and began speaking.

"And have him report when all is completed."

"Yes, sir."

Beside Flannigan stood the sonar talker, a short, chubby striker by the name of Betts wearing headphones over his crew cut. In a squeaky voice, he said, "Torpedo mounts, hedgehog mounts, and mount 52 all report manned and ready."

Jacobi said, "Very well." He pushed his talk button. "Bridge sonar, all stations manned and ready. Yes, that's right, Larry. We're set in here. What? Not yet. Tell the captain I'll let him know as the loadouts are completed on the torpedo mounts." He paused, then, "Yes, I said loadouts. War shots. You bet it's scary. I'm biting my nails like everyone else. What? No ... I won't shit my pants. Not yet anyway."

On the port side a large floor-mounted CRT (cathode ray tube) console provided a PPI read-out from the sonar signals—sound pulses (pings) transmitted underwater from a transducer mounted beneath the ship. If a metallic target was nearby, hopefully a submarine, the signal bounced off the target and back to the ship, where it was received by listening gear. Using a cursor, the sonar operator could determine an accurate range and reasonable bearing to the target. Right now, the volume was turned down and the sonar was pinging without any echo return on the PPI.

Sonarman First Class Earl Weiner sat at the sonar console—called the "stack"—making adjustments and working the cursor through blotches of false returns. Weiner had a long, thin face accentuated by a Van Dyke beard, and he too was wearing headphones. He had a clipped New England accent, and the crew called him the Earl of Neptune. Weiner seemed to live in the sonar shack, either sitting before his beloved stack or sometimes with the cabinet wide open, tracing diagrams and fixing errant circuits.

Jacobi asked, "Tape recorder still busted?"

Weiner said, "Parts been on order for two weeks. Nothing yet."

"Damn." Jacobi stepped next to Jerry. "Okay. We may really need you.

Here, I want you to enter this log with everything we do. Loadouts, course changes, speed changes, contact information, even when somebody farts. No, belay that last. Now, here's the logbook. Just write everything you see and hear. Date the page, then enter time in the first column; twenty-four-hour clock, got it?"

"Twenty-four-hour clock, yes, sir."

"The event goes after that. Print everything. Upper case; be economical with your words. Do it just like the quartermaster's rough log. You've seen that?"

"Yes, sir, I have."

Jacobi plopped a large cloth-bound volume in Jerry's hand, "And use pencil. Any questions?"

"No, sir. Er, yes, sir, actually. Where can I find course and speed changes?"

Jacobi pointed to a cluster of dials on the attack director. "Here is our course and this one is for our speed. Above this you can read target course and speed and sometimes depth although it's usually a crappy guess. Now, over here," he pointed to a group of gauges before Jerry, "is a pit log and gyro repeater where you also can get our ship's course and speed. Got it?"

Jerry nodded. He felt good about this. He actually had a job to do, not just scrubbing bilges or watching water levels in the forward fireroom. "Yes, sir. I do. Just one more question, though."

"Shoot."

"Why me? Why not someone else?"

"Because you're a hotshot midshipman who should be used to taking notes by now. Also, Mr. Bramlett tells me you're doing a bang-up job smoothing the engineering logs. So it's time to stop screwing around and start earning your pay. Got it?"

"Yes, sir." Jerry snapped to attention.

"We don't do that in here. Now get to work. Things can get hot and heavy, so stand by. In the meantime, coffee's over there if you need some." He pointed to a small coffee mess on the portside bulkhead. "Just don't spill or there will be shit to pay."

"Yes, sir. And thank you, sir."

Jacobi slapped him on the shoulder then stepped before his attack director. He called over to Weiner and said, "Okay, Earl, give us a little sound."

Weiner said, "Of course, sir. Volume coming up." And

"... ping...ping... " On it went; the sound waves searching the depths.

"That okay, sir?" asked Weiner.

"Good enough for government work," said Jacobi. He turned to his right. "Betts?"

"Huh?" In the dark, the sonarman striker was faceless. Nevertheless, he jerked.

"Betts, damn it!"

"...Sir?"

"I catch you sleeping again on watch and you're going up on charges at captain's mast."

"Yes, sir. Sorry, sir. It won't happen again." Betts was an eighteen-year-old with copious pimples.

"Do you realize, Betts, that in wartime, sleeping on duty is a court-martial offense?"

"Er, no, sir."

"And is punishable by death?"

"No, sir!" blurted Betts.

Weiner snickered. Flannigan wiped a hand over his mouth.

"By firing squad!" barked Jacobi.

"No, sir. I didn't know that, sir," said Betts.

"Do you smoke, Betts?"

"No, sir."

"Well, you better learn because they tie a black handkerchief around your eyes and give you a last cigarette to enjoy. That'll give you a few minutes more to live. Understand?"

"Yes, sir!"

"Then, that's it. BLAM! Lights out!"

Betts snapped to attention. "Yes, sir!"

By this time everybody was laughing. Even Betts began to grin.

"What's more Betts, do you realize there is no relief to next of—"

"...ping...bleep...ping...bleep..."

"The shit?" Weiner stiffened at the stack. "Sonar contact: bearing one-zero-one, range eleven thousand yards; no doppler, echo quality sharp, classified possible submarine."

Jacobi jammed his microphone button, "Bridge, Sonar. We have a possible submarine, bearing one-zero-one, range eleven thousand ... what? Okay, Larry." Jacobi turned to Weiner. "Pipe that to the bridge speaker, Weiner."

"Yes, sir." Weiner threw some switches.

"What are you doing, Midshipman?" Jacobi stood directly before Jerry.

"I...what should I do, sir?"

"What do you think we're paying you for? Log the damned contact data. What do they teach you at the Academy, anyway? Am I wrong about this?"

Jerry had been mesmerized. "Yes, sir. Sorry, sir." Grabbing the logbook, he carefully entered own course and speed and then target bearing and range.

Looking over Jerry's shoulder, Jacobi said, "Don't forget what your man on the stack said, 'No doppler, echo quality sharp, classified possible submarine.'"

"Yes, sir." Jerry wrote that, vowing to listen intently and write it all down.

They were on the contact within minutes, with the *Mallilieu* settling about five hundred yards behind the contact, course one-nine-one; speed three knots. Weiner droned aloud with his contact information; the attack director jumped, buzzed, and clicked; Jerry scribbled furiously while Jacobi occasionally looked over his shoulder and nodded.

After a while, Flannigan held his hands to his earphone and then said, "Sonar, aye." He reported, "Port and starboard torpedo mounts report all tubes loaded with war shots."

Jacobi sighed, "Very well." He pressed his mic button and said, "Larry... yeah, sorry. This is Sonar calling the Bridge. Okay?...All torpedo tubes set with war loads...Pardon?...Okay, tell the skipper I recommend search pattern alpha...that's right. Okay...will do. Sonar out."

He said to Flannigan, "Set search pattern alpha."

"Yes, sir, search pattern alpha. All torpedoes?" Flannigan asked.

"Affirmative."

"Yes, sir." Flannigan relayed the message.

Jacobi clacked open a Zippo lighter and lit a cigarette. "Smoking lamp is lit in Sonar." He leaned over to Jerry and said *sotto voce*, "Don't log that."

"I didn't think so, sir."

Jacobi released a smile and took a drag.

The attack director buzzed. Jerry noted target speed had crept up to five knots. He logged it and pointed to another dial. Target depth: three hundred feet.

"Yes, log it," said Jacobi. He took another drag and looked at the clock, a black-faced twenty-four-hour Chelsea. "Damn, nearly chow time, except we can't go. I'll get something sent up after a while."

The attack director clicked. Target speed had jumped to ten knots. Jerry logged it as Weiner called, "Hearing screw noises, down doppler. Range now fifteen hundred yards."

Jacobi punched his mic. "Larry? Yeah. Go to twelve knots. Target speed now ten knots and we've fallen behind. We have screw noises. Say again? Right." He stiffened. "Stand by everybody. The skipper's on his way in."

The accordion door whipped open and Cdr. Ralph Decker filled the doorway with his linebacker's build. He faked a spasm of coughing and waved his hand over his face. "Holy crap. What are you guys smoking? Manila dock line?"

"Welcome to Dracula's chamber, Skipper," said Jacobi.

Decker whipped off his garrison cap revealing dark salt-and-pepper hair. "Have you tried him on Gertrude, yet?"

"Been thinking about it, sir."

"Okay, then, go ahead. Let's see what this guy does ... Jeez," he pointed to the attack director. "Target speed twelve knots. Range?"

"Seventeen hundred, Captain. Down doppler."

Decker said, "We're falling behind. Tell Larry to go to fifteen knots."

Jacobi called the bridge and gave the order.

Jerry logged it all.

"Okay, do it," said Decker who by this time had stepped all the way in, filling the sonar shack with what seemed his massive 210 pounds.

Jacobi yanked a hand microphone off a small console. He turned to Jerry and said softly, "We're trying to raise him on the underwater telephone and determine if he's an allied submarine or a dirty commie rat. So listen carefully. See if you hear anything different than any of us. Okay?"

Jerry gulped and nodded, his pencil poised.

Jacobi pressed the mic and said in precise, clipped tones, "Comrade Boris,

Comrade Boris, Comrade Boris. This is the United States destroyer *Mallilieu*. Please respond. Over?"

He turned up the underwater telephone's speaker only to hear static scattered among ocean noises.

Decker pointed a finger. "Again."

"Comrade Boris, Comrade Boris, Comrade Boris. This is the United States destroyer *Mallilieu*. Surface and identify yourself. Over?"

Decker nodded.

They waited.

Flannigan lit a Pall Mall.

Weiner reported, "Definite screw noises. And I hear machinery. Range eleven hundred. He's pulling away again. God, listen to him clanking and farting."

Jacobi said, "This thing's about as subtle as the San Francisco earthquake."

"One more time," ordered Decker. "And go to eighteen knots."

Jacobi called the bridge with a curt, "Eighteen knots, Larry." Then he grabbed the Gertrude mic and repeated, "Comrade Boris, Comrade Boris, Comrade Boris. Surface and identify yourself. Over?"

Jerry felt the screws dig in as he wrote in the log. The ship lunged to the greater speed.

Decker and Jacobi locked eyes. Decker asked in a soft tone, "Think we got a nuke, Ralph?"

Jacobi rubbed his chin. "If he holds this speed and we keep hearing machinery noise, then I'd say 'Yes, sir, that's a steam plant and that means nuke.'"

4

17 June 1962
Project 627A, Submarine *K-12*
Voenno-Morskoj Flot SSSR
25°52'28" N, 128°09'12" E
214 kilometers southeast of Buckner Bay, Okinawa

Dezhnev stood and grabbed his cap. "Where's your action station?"

"Engine room, lower level," replied Volkov.

"Well, get going,"

"Yes, sir. Excuse me, Captain." Volkov squeezed past Kudrevich and ran aft.

Kudrevich gave Dezhnev an eye roll and said, "If you please Father Dezhnev, we would be most honored if you could join us in the control room?"

Suppressing an urge to meet Kudrevich's sarcasm, Dezhnev said, "Yes, sir."

Kudrevich turned into the passageway and took a ladder to the next deck. Dezhnev followed him into the control room, an area about four by eight meters. Men were still piling into in a space that normally accommodated ten or so for an underway watch. Squeezing among them, Kudrevich and Dezhnev took station on an elevated platform between the two periscopes.

By now, about twenty men had stuffed themselves into the control room. On the port bulkhead to Dezhnev's left were a number of large levers and switches to control the submarine's trim and water ballasting. There was also a large panel with gauges and lighted read-outs and controls for the ship's twin reactors and auxiliaries.

Seated at the forward bulkhead were the planesman-helmsman and stern planesman, both wearing headphones and concentrating on large gauges indicating the ship's speed, depth, course, rudder position, and fore and aft trim. Five men were clustered around the machinery to starboard that constituted the ship's "attack center." There were four large consoles controlling the ship's Arktika-*M* sonar and torpedo fire control systems. For navigation, a plotting board and chart table were mounted against the aft bulkhead.

The chief starshina rumbled in a deep voice, "Captain's on deck."

Seated or standing, the men in the compartment snapped to attention.

"As you were," ordered Kudrevich. He turned to look over the chief sonar operator's back, a bald, heavyset *starshina*, petty officer first class, named Bonderchuk.

"When was the last time we went active?" he asked, peering at the sonar scope.

"Yesterday, sir, for some tests. And then only three pings," replied Bonderchuk.

"And what do we have now?"

"A sonar is blasting away out there. Most likely an American destroyer."

"Where from?"

"About two-eight-five. Looks like he's headed right for us."

Kudrevich looked over at Leytenant Zolyar, their navigator.

Zolyar said, "Okinawa is a little over a hundred kilometers in that direction."

Kudrevich turned back to Bonderchuk. "Can you tell if he's acquired us?"

"Not for sure, sir. But sonar conditions are excellent out here. Signal strength is about thirty-five decibels, which tells us he could have contact. I estimate his range at about twenty-five kilometers." A veteran of three patrols with Kudrevich, Bonderchuk had anticipated the question with the American's range.

"American for sure?"

"To me it seems right, Captain. He's working four kilocycles. That's one of their frequencies now. I'd say yes."

Kudrevich patted Bonderchuk on the shoulder. "Good. Stay on him." To the OOD he said, "Mr. Matvonkye, what's the most recent thermocline?"

"Ninety meters, Captain, taken about two hours ago."

"Very well. Rig ship for quiet routine. Speed six klicks. And let's get below this. Make your depth two hundred meters."

"Close watertight hatches, sir?"

"Yes, of course."

Hatches thumped shut throughout the boat. Dezhnev watched the speed gauge drop slowly to six klicks as Matvonkye nursed the ship from eighty down to two hundred meters.

Kudrevich turned to Dezhnev and winked. "So now, Eduard. Cat and mouse. On the one hand, we have a live one; on the other, we aren't even close to that carrier."

Fifteen minutes later, the American destroyer had taken position deep on their starboard quarter, matching their six-klick speed and still pinging away.

In spite of air conditioning, the compartment was getting warm due to all the men and the activated machinery.

It was quiet except for an occasional outburst when the boat chief snapped at one of the planesmen.

But then...Kudrevich drummed his fingers. He called, "Mr. Matvonkye, Increase your speed to fifteen klicks, please."

"Sir?"

"What did I just say? Fifteen klicks, damn it."

"Yes, sir." Matvonkye gave the order and the ship vibrated a little as the screws bit the water.

Kudrevich rubbed his chin and muttered to Dezhnev, "He still has us, damn it."

Dezhnev shrugged.

Kudrevich said, "Mr. Matvonkye, make your depth three hundred meters."

Matvonkye stammered a bit knowing the order would take them close to test depth. "Th-three hundred meters, aye, Captain." He gave the order with the boat taking a slight down angle, the depth gauge clicking off the meters.

They were passing through 250 meters when Kudrevich said, "And make sure to—"

There was a low buzz. Dezhnev turned to look at the engineering panels. Lights turned from green to yellow. A few clicked to red. Then many turned red.

"Litvin," demanded Kudrevich, "what the hell is going on?"

Everybody turned to look at Leytenant Zoltan Litvin, the action station engineering officer. Many lights on his indicator board were changing quickly from green to yellow to red. He raised a hand for quiet. "Shit! Flooding in the engine room!"

"What is it?" demanded Kudrevich.

Litvin raised a hand and pressed it to his headphones. "Auxiliary seawater cooling line to the A/C system. Two men dead. And reactor number two has scrammed!"

Dezhnev pointed to the hydraulic panel. "Close the damn valve."

Litvin looked to Kudrevich for confirmation.

"Do as he says!" said Kudrevich.

While Litvin bent to throw the valve, Kudrevich ordered, "Mr. Matvonkye, stop the dive. Full rise on the planes. Make your speed thirty-three klicks and come to fifty meters."

Matvonkye stammered, "Did you say fifty meters, Captain?"

Kudrevich's face turned red. He stepped off the platform and moved to within centimeters of Matvonkye. "Idiot, do you want to die? With all of the Rodina's marvels of hydraulic engineering failing around us, how else do you reduce the water pressure back there?"

Matvonkye barked, "Sorry, Captain. Depth fifty meters. Bow planes full rise, speed thirty-three klicks."

Kudrevich returned to his platform and said to Litvin, "And close all hull valves in the engine room."

"Yes, sir."

"Which reactor scrammed?"

Litvin leaned over to examine his board. "Uhhh, number two captain." He started throwing valves and added, "Closing hull valves in the engine room, sir, except..."

"Except what?"

"The auxiliary seawater valve to the A/C system is stuck. Argggh." He kneeled on the deck and pulled with both hands. "Argggh."

"Damn it!" Kudrevich yanked a phone from the bracket and punched a call button.

Yusopov shouted, "I'm here."

"What do you have, Vladislav?"

It was hard to hear the chief engineer. People were shouting and there was an eerie loud screeching in the background. Kudrevich knew that sound only too well. They'd practiced it many times in the simulator. When water pipe broke it was almost impossible to hear because the noise was so loud.

Yusopov said, "Secondary seawater coolant line burst at one of the flanges. You know one of those high-quality jobs done by our marvelous workers back in Severodvinsk."

Kudrevich swore. The shipyard workers had not properly cleaned the flange surfaces, and the joint had let go. The seawater coolant line was a three-centimeter line. At this depth, the water pressure would be enormous. No wonder all that noise and the water blasting around, shorting out electrical panels.

"...water filling up the lower level. Two men dead: Gerobits and Kosinov. Number two electrical panel has shorted out. That's what caused number two reactor to scram."

"What the hell?" muttered Kudrevich. He looked at the depth gauge. Speed was up to twenty five klicks and depth was nearly two hundred meters. "What else?"

Someone in the background sounded panicked. Another screamed. It was chaos. "So much mist, we can hardly see."

"How about the globe valve?"

"Jammed open. Too much shit in the hydraulic line. How about yours?"

"Ours is jammed open too. Can you get someone down to the gate valve?"

"It's under nearly two meters of water. Can't see."

"Get a diver in there, Vladislav. I don't want to surface this pig. I have an American destroyer on my ass. Maybe more."

"...trying."

"Well do it! If it means you taking off your clothes and diving down there yourself, it must be done."

"Gladly. Who takes care of the reactor scram?"

"Don't threaten me, Mr. Yusopov. You will safeguard reactor number one with your life. Make sure water doesn't short out number one's electrical panels. Do you understand me?"

"Yes, sir."

"And you will restart reactor number two as soon as possible."

"That means drying all those damned electrical panels."

Dezhnev felt the ice in Kudrevich's voice as he spoke slowly and precisely. "I'm not looking for excuses, Mr. Yusopov. You will restart reactor number two as soon as possible."

"Yes, sir."

"Do you need a doctor?"

"Not now. Gerobits and Kosinov are floating face down in the mess. I don't think he can help them. We'll pick them out later."

"Anybody else?"

"All right for now."

"Visibility any better?"

"Worse, actually. I can barely see Kosinov floating down there at two meters. And number two...wait," Yusopov muffled the phone and shouted something. "I can't..."

Kudrevich knew the man had his hands full. "Find somebody to close that damn gate valve," said Kudrevich. "And hurry up. We're getting tail-heavy. I'm calling back in three minutes." He hung up.

Kudrevich checked the inclinometer. The ship was still rising in spite of all the weight back aft: 160 meters.

He caught Dezhnev's eye. "It's a pile of shit back there. We may have to blow."

"Then the game is over."

"Those damned Americans up there," Kudrevich nodded upward,

"cooking their hot dogs in the sunshine." He checked the depth gauge. Rate of ascent was almost nil. And they were getting more tail-heavy: down seven degrees aft. "Litvin," he called, "blow stern tanks, two thousand kilos."

"Two thousand kilos, aye, Captain," replied Litvin. He threw some hydraulic levers. Instantly the sound of compressed air ranged through the ship.

"Captain." It was the weapons officer. He turned. Over the roar of the air rushing into the ballast tanks they heard a voice drift through the sonar speaker. With much static, it sounded like an obsolete radio set tuning to station thousands of miles away. "... Boris, Comrade Boris, Comrade Boris. Surface and identify yourself."

"Any answer, Captain?" asked the weapons officer.

"No. Absolutely not," barked Kudrevich. Then he muttered to Dezhnev, "'...surface and identity myself.' I hope that damned fool gives me an excuse to stick a torpedo up his bum."

5

17 June 1962
USS *Mallilieu* (DD 768)
25°51'38" N, 128°08'22" E
153 miles southeast of Buckner Bay, Okinawa

Jerry logged the time: 1017 UQC XMIT: COMRADE BORIS, COMRADE BORIS, COMRADE BORIS, COMRADE BORIS, SURFACE AND IDENTIFY YOURSELF. 1018/19 NO REPLY.

Jacobi peeked over to double-check and grunted.

Decker leaned outside the sonar shack and snapped his fingers at the CIC watch officer. "Safe, Mr. Hunter."

"Sir?"

"Pull the pub on Soviet submarines."

"Yes, sir."

Jacobi turned to Weiner on the stack. "Doppler?"

Weiner held up a hand, listened for a moment, then said, "Sheeeyat."

"What?" said Jacobi and Decker.

Weiner said, "This is not a submarine, it's an underwater trash hauler.

Just a ton of noise not usually made by a Soviet submarine, and I've tracked a few in my time."

Jacobi checked the attack director. Target speed was holding steady at twelve knots. No. It began to jump again. Jerry squeezed next to Decker to watch it flicker up to fourteen to sixteen to eighteen knots in a period of ninety seconds.

Jacobi asked, "Got it, Midshipman?"

"Yes, sir, I do." Jerry hoped his voice sounded normal. But anxiety was catching and he felt it with the others. They spoke faster, their language clipped, precise. And it seemed to be much warmer in here. His body felt clammy and perspiration broke out on his forehead and lip.

"Captain?" A hand passed a thick cloth-bound manual through the doorway."

"Thanks, Hunter." Decker flipped pages in his Soviet submarine manual. Finally, he stopped. "This could be it. November class. Three thousand tons surfaced, forty-seven-fifty submerged; two water-cooled reactors, twin screws, thirty-knot capability; test depth, a thousand to thirteen hundred feet."

Then Decker whistled. "How do you like this? Carries two nuke-tipped torpedoes."

Jerry realized Decker was talking about the submarine down there. Nuclear-tipped torpedoes: he felt as if he'd been kicked in the stomach.

Jacobi nudged him with an elbow. "You okay, Jerry?"

"Never better, sir."

Decker asked Jacobi, "Any other Commie nonnuclear submarine that can exceed eighteen knots?"

"Not that I know of sir, and," he rapped a knuckle in the glass front of his attack director, "he's now at twenty-two knots."

"Damn," said Decker. He leaned out the hatchway again, and called, "Mr. Tilton. Do we have Kadena on the net?"

"Affirmative, Captain."

"See if they can give us a P2V."

"Yes, sir."

Decker said, "As much as I'd like to be in here with you boys, I'd better go back to the bridge. But keep me in the loop, please."

Tilton's voice echoed from CIC. "We're in luck, Captain. P2V two-six Bravo is ten minutes away and inbound."

Decker asked, "Do you have him?"

"Wait...yes. Mr. Hunter just raised him."

"Well, give him a bearing and range and let's see what this goblin is made of."

"Yes, sir."

Decker said, "Okay, fellows, it's all yours." With a wink, he walked out, closing the accordion door behind him.

"How's the doppler?" asked Jacobi.

"About even now, sir. Looks like we're matching speed."

"Okay." Jacobi called Lieutenant Larry Hartford, OOD on the bridge. "Larry, hold it at twenty-two knots. That's what he's doing now."

"Okay," said Hartford. "What's the range?"

"About two thousand yards."

"Do you want to close him?"

"No, that should be good enough for now. We have good sonar conditions out here and I'd like to stay back here in case he jumps to the right or left and tries to lose us."

"Sounds good to me. I'll let the skipper know."

Tilton broke in on the line. "Two-six Bravo is one minute out. He'll be passing directly overhead on the sub's bearing, which is..." He left the question open.

"Roger, XO ..." Jacobi checked the attack director and then pushed the sound-powered phone button. "Tell him one-nine-seven magnetic."

"One-niner-seven magnetic it is, Ralph. Thanks."

Ten seconds later they heard the distinctive roar of the P2V's twin Curtis-Wright 3350 engines as it swooped over at near masthead height and headed for datum.

Ten seconds later the exec shouted, "Madman! Wait one... Okay, he's laying a pattern of sonobuoys."

Jacobi asked, "Did he give you a loiter time, XO?"

"Four hours."

"Wow." Jacobi turned to Jerry. "Are you getting all this?"

Jerry stammered at first. "As best as I can, Mr. Jacobi. First was 'Madman' from the P2V. That's positive submarine, right?"

"Check."

"Okay." Jerry scribbled and then said, "Last I had was that he's laying a sonobuoy pattern."

"That's right. And don't forget loiter time, four hours."

Jerry's pencil twirled. "Yes, sir."

Jacobi clapped him on the shoulder then said to Weiner, "You about due for a relief, Weiner?"

Lighting a cigarette, Weiner said, "Hell, I'm just getting started, sir. I got the rest of this watch to do anyway."

"Well, you better—hold on. The depth solution has changed. This says he's now up to two hundred feet and rising." Jacobi called the bridge with, "Larry, you got that?"

"Bridge, aye," snapped Hartford. "Uhhh, are you sure about the depth?"

"No, not really." For all of its good qualities, the attack director's depth solution was a guessing game.

"Air!" Weiner clamped a hand over his earphone. "Tons of it!"

"Speaker!" demanded Jacobi.

Jerry scribbled while they heard the unmistakable sound of compressed air.

"Torpedo doors?" asked Weiner.

"No. It's gotta be ballast tanks. Something's not right with this joker." He tapped his mike button. "Larry, tell the skipper that he's—"

"Holy shit!" shouted Hartford.

In the background Jacobi heard shouts of incredulity. "What?"

"Ivan has surfaced, about twelve hundred yards off our port bow."

"Son-of-a-bitch."

"Yes, I'd say that—oops—here's the skipper."

Decker came on the line. "Jacobi. As much as I appreciate your ASW crew following doctrine, I'd appreciate if you'd tell mount 52 to stop tracking the submarine lest Ivan shoot a live one at us."

"Right away, Captain." Following World War II doctrine, antisubmarine procedure was to have an active five-inch mount, with both guns loaded, aiming at an enemy submarine when it surfaced. Jacobi turned to Flannigan, "Quick, tell mount 52 to train off the target, go centerline and ready-air."

"But they just reported on target and tracking, sir."

"Do it before Ivan sticks a torpedo up our ass!"

Flannigan relayed the order. Fifteen seconds later, Hartford came up with, "Skipper says that's good, Ralph. But keep 'em ready to go, just in case."

"Permission to come on deck, Larry?" said Jacobi.

There was a pause. "Skipper says don't forget your sunglasses."

"Be right there—come on Ingram, bring that damned log book." Jacobi and Jerry walked out into the bright morning sun. They made their way to the top of the pilothouse, now crowded with officers and men.

The cloudless sky was a deep blue. With barely any wind, the sea was calm with small groundswells: a perfect day.

Glittering in sunlight, the submarine was clearly visible off their port bow.

With white topsides and blue underbelly, the P2V came up from behind and roared over the top of the submarine. A figure popped up in the submarine's sail and made a rude gesture. Then there were two, then two more.

Decker turned, and like a victorious football coach, threw an arm around Jacobi and pointed. "There's Ivan. He looks pissed. You have anything to say to him?"

"How about offering assistance, Captain?"

Decker grinned. "Damn, Ralph. I knew you were good for something." He called down to the OOD on the bridge. "Mr. Hartford?"

"Sir?"

"Approach that submarine slowly to within hailing distance—say, two hundred yards, no less—and lay to off his starboard side. Make sure we do not point our bow at him. Do you understand?"

"Approach slowly, carefully. Do not ram the son-of-a-bitch, and come within hailing distance, two hundred yards, and lay to, aye, Captain."

"That's the idea, Mr. Hartford. Now proceed please."

Jerry scribbled, and when he had time, sketched the submarine on the facing page.

More and more were crowded on the pilothouse. A photographer armed with a Hasselblad high-resolution camera crowded beside Jerry and snapped pictures.

Hartford called up to the bridge, “Message from two-six Bravo, Captain. Upon orders from the United States State Department, he has been told to break off and return to Kadena.”

“Damn, I thought I was OTC,” groaned Decker.

“I did too, Captain,” said Hartford. “Wait one, sir.” Someone handed him a radio flimsy. “Message from COMSEVEN, Captain.”

“Telling us to leave little Ivan alone and head south.”

“In so many words, Captain. It says ‘proceed on duty assigned.’”

“Why am I not surprised?” said Decker.

“One more thing, Captain.”

“What’s that?”

Hartford looked up with a grin. “COMSEVEN signs off with BRAVO ZULU.” Well done.

In a falsetto, Decker mimicked, “Well bless-a-my soul.”

The P2V did a last grand sweep over the submarine, waggled its wings, and then turned and headed straight for the *Mallilieu,* no more than twenty feet off the deck. Jerry looked down upon the fast approaching patrol plane. Quickly growing in his vision, it was lower than where he stood at thirty-seven feet above sea level. Pilot and copilot were clearly waving as the Neptune pulled up and blasted over the top, their world completely filled with sound from the thundering Curtis-Wright 3350 engines.

Men waved and cheered as the P2V vanished into the distance, again waggling its wings.

Decker clapped Jacobi on the back. “Damn, did you see that, Ralph?”

“How could I miss it, sir?”

“I mean that damned copilot was giving us the finger.”

Just after they struggled to the surface, Kudrevich ran for the ladder, undogged the hatches, and scrambled to the bridge. Two lookouts and a junior officer followed. Dezhnev struggled up the ladder to the conning station at the top of the sail, his eyes squeezed shut in pain. Somewhere during all this he'd banged his knee, and it hurt like hell. The prosthesis needed adjustment, and that made it worse. He managed to wiggle up the last rung of the ladder without groaning. He rose to the little bridge in time to see an American plane roar over.

At length, Dezhnev stood and looked over to see Kudrevich avoid his gaze. The captain was embarrassed. Litvin had overcompensated with the blow back aft. Kudrevich ordered a blow forward hoping to even things out. But they had blown too much ballast and the *K-12* popped to the surface like a cork. The jig was up, and everybody looked the other way.

As Dezhnev worked kinks out of his leg, Kudrevich yelled into the squawk box, "Yes, Mr. Yusopov, We're on the surface. The Americans are over there laughing at us. I said pump the damn bilges and get that mess straightened up down there."

"Yes, sir. Uh..."

"What, damn it."

"We need the doctor, Captain."

"What the hell is it, now?"

"It's Volkov, sir."

Looking to Dezhnev, Kudrevich gave an eye-roll. "What's he done now?"

"Er...a..."

"Speak, you stupid son-of-a-bitch!"

Yusopov sputtered. "He swam down and found the gate valve. Nearly drowned, but he got it closed. The broken line is now secure. But Volkov is unconscious; ingested too much water. He's turning blue and we can't make him come around."

Kudrevich slumped for a moment. Then he called down to the control room and ordered the doctor aft.Volkov had made it easy for Dezhnev. Yusopov was exposed without turning a finger. The klutz would be out of submarines the minute their lines hit the dock at the Rybachiy Naval Base in Tar'ya Bay.

Kudrevich gave a curious glance and asked, "What the hell are you gloating about?"

"Not gloating; banged my leg on the way up, Captain."

"Too damn bad."

6

14 May 1967
Mason residence
114 Sound View Drive
Sag Harbor, Long Island, New York

Sad Sack Mason poured. The four of them drank—Mason, Jerry Ingram, Hudson Fleming, and Ernie Hernandez. Bowing to their parents' request, the three lieutenants (j.g.) and First Lieutenant Hernandez, a fellow Naval Academy graduate who had taken the Marine option, were turned out in whites with gleaming gold pilot's wings mounted on their left breast. They had just graduated from Pensacola and were enjoying a wetting-down party, courtesy of Sad Sack's parents in their Sag Harbor, Long Island, home. It was out in the Hamptons or, as the Iowa-born Mollie Mason loved to say with a tipped-up nose, "... the Hahmptons." With that, Sad Sack's mother would feign raising a monocle to her left eye, give an eye-roll, and strut about, subtly wiggling her ample derriere.

But to Sad Sack's disappointment, the bar was not well stocked today. All that remained was a lonely fifth of Jim Beam bourbon. Gone were the

Johnnie Walker scotch, the devastating Wild Turkey bourbon, Beefeaters gin, and Ron Rico rum. Even the vast array of liqueurs, wines, and champagnes was gone. Today, it was scattered about three different bars serving the guests. Indeed, Tyler Mason, Sad Sack's father, knew how to enjoy himself. His son, Randolph, nicknamed Sad Sack in high school because of his droopy eyes, fully intended to follow in his father's footsteps this beautiful May afternoon.

In fact, all four intended this day to finally step up to the lifestyle to which they had long aspired. They had met as plebes and survived to graduate with the Naval Academy's class of 1965. Now, they'd just emerged from flight school but were going in different directions.

Sad Sack Mason and Hudson Fleming had made it into jets and were scheduled for advanced training next month. Ernesto "Ernie" Hernandez had finished Marine officers basic training at Quantico, Virginia, on an accelerated program. After he finished flight school he was assigned to helicopters and would soon be off to his flight training component.

Jerry Ingram was glad he wasn't going off to jets. Outwardly he implied he didn't like the culture. Secretly he didn't trust himself to strap a flaming torch to his ass and blast through the speed of sound. He felt he just couldn't think that fast. On the other hand, helicopters didn't attract him either. Not fast enough.

He'd decided he liked the ASW culture from the time that P2V buzzed the *Mallilieu* and the copilot flipped them the finger. That was funny and showed character. But it seemed an eternity ago—1962. So much had happened since then. He'd finished the Naval Academy and now, flight school, the golden wings on his tunic a dazzling testimony. It was five years since the *Mallilieu* had tangled with the Soviet November-class submarine on his midshipman cruise. He could still hear the thunder of the P2V's 3350s as it thundered overhead. Later that summer he met some ASW flight crew and really bought into it. He liked their skills, their silent dedication, their camaraderie and commitment to one another. So Jerry Ingram signed up for multi-engine, passed, and was assigned to the newer antisubmarine Lockheed P-3 Orion, a four-engine turboprop with long legs. Right now he was assigned to a RAG (replacement air group) squadron in Jacksonville, Florida. Starting in a P-3's right seat, he was told he'd be there for three or four months' training and then would be off to a permanent squadron assignment.

"How 'bout another shot?" Not waiting for a reply, Sad Sack slopped more Jim Beam into their gleaming Waterford tumblers.

"Wow. That's enough," said Jerry. This would be his third. Already he felt himself losing control. And soon he would have to go out and mingle with the legions of parents and friends invited by the Masons.

Sad Sack gave a wink. "Aw, come on, Ingram. You only live once—uh, well, not once, but at least twenty times."

"Well, I'm burning that up fast. I think I'm working on my fourth or fifth life just this afternoon."

Hudson Fleming, his hat tipped back on his head, threw an arm around young Mason. "Hey, Sad Sack. You see your old man and my old man out there? Suddenly, they're close buddies."

"Doing a deal, you think?" asked Sad Sack. The two fathers were meeting for the first time.

Sad Sack made a show of peeking through the pass-through window of the mahogany paneled bar room into the main living room. "I'll say. Those guys are really into it."

Fleming lowered his voice and said in a near whisper, "These guys are trying to figure out what's going to happen to the stock market if the United Arab Republic attacks Israel."

"Ummmm," the others nodded sagely.

"My money is on Nasser," Fleming went on. "He was military before he became president of Egypt."

"What, you don't think little Israel can beat the combined forces of Egypt and Syria?" Hudson said sarcastically.

Ingram peeked into the living room. About fifty people mingled there. Outside, more guests crowded around a bar on the veranda. Beyond was a Cape Cod–style boathouse, all giving way to a spectacular view of the beach and Sag Harbor Bay. The two fathers, their brows knit, stood off in a corner by themselves. Tyler Mason, the commodities broker, waved an unlit cigar at Harold Fleming, a senior business analyst for the *Wall Street Journal*.

"There'll be the devil to pay," said Fleming. "The market will go down two hundred points tomorrow."

"Maybe more," agreed Jerry.

Hernandez stepped over. "What do you think they're talking about now?"

"What else? The price of pig shit in September," said Sad Sack.

They giggled, Jerry more than the rest. The bourbon was creeping up on him, and he was having trouble talking. He looked fondly at the other three and wondered, not for the first time, how four young men from very different backgrounds had become such good friends. Sad Sack was undoubtedly the wealthiest, and yet he didn't wear it on his sleeve. He'd been a star forward on the Academy basketball team. Without knowing, one would not have guessed he was born to the purple. Fleming's father had been with the *Wall Street Journal* for twenty-five years, his opinion highly respected in domestic and international circles. Securities rose and fell upon his pronouncements.

Jerry Ingram was from a Navy family. His father, Vice Adm. Todd Ingram, was also a Naval Academy graduate but a surface officer without the benefit of gleaming Navy wings on his breast. However, the elder Ingram made up for it with three Navy Crosses and other medals of the World War II era, making his son a shoo-in to the Academy. With close to thirty years in the Navy, the elder Ingram was now in his final position before retirement: officer in charge of the Fleet Operations Control Center—Pacific located in Kunia, Oahu, Hawaii. More often people called it the regional SIGINT (signal intelligence) Operations Center, or KSOCK for short. Reporting to Adm. John J. Hyland, CINCPAC (commander in chief Pacific Fleet), Ingram's task was tracking all Soviet submarines in the Pacific.

Unlike his father, Jerry was a bit of an underachiever. His high school grades were barely good enough. And he'd scraped by at the Academy also, not so much from lack of ability as from sheer laziness. Predictably, he'd graduated in the lower third of his class. It was a miracle he'd been admitted to flight school.

Ernesto, on the other hand, was the son of Don Francisco and Doña Delores Hernandez, vintners in Vera Cruz, Mexico. At a young age, Ernesto and Rita, his younger sister, moved to Riverside, California, to live with their Uncle Julio and Aunt Olga Hernandez, owners of Raymond Vintners. They attended American schools, and each became an American citizen in their eighteenth year. Julio Hernandez turned out to be a marvelous taskmaster and inspired Ernesto to study hard. Even with that, everyone was surprised when the youngster won an appointment to the U.S. Naval Academy. As it turned out, a congressional appointment was the least of his problems.

Over the years he struggled through the racial and cultural push-back. But Uncle Julio taught him how to handle himself and the prejudice he faced, which helped him in the Navy. Rita grew from a cute little girl into a stunningly beautiful raven-haired woman and marched off to New York City at the age of nineteen to seek her fortune in the fashion industry. Her goal: the cover of *Vogue* magazine.

And now here they were, the four young men crowded around the pass-through window watching Vice Admiral Todd Ingram, resplendent in his dress whites, walk up to Tyler Mason and Harold Fleming and shake hands.

"Your dad just killed the deal. All shot to hell," said Sad Sack.

"Yeah," agreed Jerry. "Millions down the hole. He thrust out a hand to the sideboard to steady himself. "Sorry, Sad Sack, no Corvette for your birthday."

Sad Sack smiled. He was happy with the Corvette his parents had given him last year. He hadn't had time to drive it much. Only 4,500 miles while he was in flight training. He shrugged. "The one I already have is still brand new."

"Looks like they're all having a good time," said Ernie.

"Whooosat?" said Sad Sack. He pointed at Gen. Bucky Radcliff, a long-time Ingram family friend. The general was making a beeline directly for the group of young pilots. "Geez, a major general."

"Getchershit together," said Hernandez. "Here he comes."

"Holy cow," said Fleming. "Look at all those medals, from the top of his breast to the bottom of his balls."

They did a poor job of standing to attention.

Radcliff walked up. "Gentlemen. And I do use the term loosely."

Fleming snickered.

"That's more like it," said Radcliff. He turned to Ingram. "I'm proud of you guys, even though you had the poor judgment to go Navy. You still made it through flight school." He draped an arm around Jerry's shoulder. "You too, kid."

"Thanks, Uncle Buck." The others gasped, but it escaped Jerry's lips before he could think about it. "Bucky" Radcliff had been his "Uncle Buck" forever. It was natural.

"What kind of duty you all headed for?" asked Radcliff. He smacked his lips and grabbed a handful of peanuts from a crystal bowl. "Plenty of opportunity to see Ivan?"

"Yes, sir," they answered.

"Don't forget. Ivan's not too pleasant. He'll drive you to the brink."

"Why does he do that, General?" asked Fleming.

Radcliff grabbed a crystal tumbler, sloshed in what was left of the bourbon, and drank deeply. "Ahh, good stuff. Remind me to thank your folks, Mason."

"Yes, sir," said Sad Sack.

Radcliff looked squarely at Fleming. "Because Ivan doesn't have any wavoes. That's why. He lacks confidence. He has inferior equipment, training, and personnel. He pushes the envelope because he knows we won't shoot back and it makes him feel big."

They stepped close.

Radcliff said, "Seriously, your job is to stay off his back unless he really sticks it to you. When that happens, your training takes over and you'll do just fine."

"Has that happened?" asked Sad Sack.

Radcliff clapped the young j.g. on the shoulderboard. "Many times, Mr. Mason. More than I can tell you. We just don't shout it from the rooftops."

Silence fell. The sound of the cocktail party seemed an intrusion.

Radcliff turned to Ingram. "Just yesterday one of their destroyers tangled with one of ours in the Sea of Japan." He shook his head slowly.

Eyebrows went up.

Radcliff looked from side to side then dropped his voice. "TINS message, okay?"

"TINS?" asked Ingram

Radcliff smirked. "T-I-N-S: this is no shit."

"Got it," said Ingram.

Radcliff gulped more bourbon and then said, "Ivan pulled alongside your destroyer and actually bumped him a couple of times. Your destroyer pulled well clear and got on the net calling for help and asking for advice. But Ivan kept at it."

"I was eavesdropping on the circuit and heard your poor CO trying to keep his cool while his crew was giving Ivan the finger and throwing tomatoes at him."

Ingram nodded. Radcliff was right. In flight school he'd heard about these encounters many times. The Russians were really pushing it these days and were looking for trouble.

"So, guess what we did?"

Eyebrows went up further.

"We happened to have two F-102s just out of Cadena at ten thousand feet doing training maneuvers. I got on the circuit, put them on the deck, and told them to let it rip." Radcliff smiled. "Those bastards flew in at deck level and lit their burners right over the top of Ivan while pulling straight up. Then they came down again pushing them further away. It took three runs, but Ivan finally steamed off for Vladivostok looking for peace and quiet."

"Amazing," said Sad Sack.

"Best use of the taxpayer's gas you'll see all year."

"What happens to the F-102 pilots?" asked Fleming. "Do they get commendations."

Radcliff shook his head. "They don't get squat. It's an unreported incident that's sort of reported. We're not supposed to talk about it. So I called out to the Cadena O club and had them buy those guys steak dinners and put it on my tab. It's all we could do."

There was laughter in the living room. Someone must have told a whopper. Jerry marveled that his Dad could mingle so easily with all these important civilians. How did he do it?

His mother, Helen, walked up to them and gave a broad smile. Tyler Mason and Nelson Fleming were really grinning and making nice. Mason reached over, grabbed a glass of champagne from a passing waiter, and handed it to Helen. With a slight headshake, she tried to wave it off. Mason insisted. Jerry Ingram caught his father's imperceptible dark look. Switching gears, Helen gratefully accepted and took the tiniest of sips, smiling broadly. She was a teetotaler. As she walked away, Jerry knew she'd get rid of it when nobody was looking.

While the others guffawed, Helen looked about the room. At length, she looked back, caught her son's gaze, and beckoned. *Come on out. It's time for you to go on.*

Mom, I'm too drunk, he thought.

She beckoned more fiercely. Then she beckoned to the others as well.

Radcliff said, *sotto voce,* "Duty calls, gentlemen."

"Bucky, I'm toasted," protested Jerry.

"You'll do fine," said Radcliff. "Just get out there. All of you."

"Screwed," said Mason, buttoning his tunic.

If I go out there, I'll puke on that white Persian rug in the middle of the living room.

Mollie Mason leaned around the corner with a scowl. "Ssssst. You boys. Get out here. It's your damned party."

"Sorry, Ma," said Sad Sack, brushing imaginary dust off his tunic.

"Look at you," she mimed a scold. "Drinking your father's liquor like a bunch of downtown hoodlums."

"Sorry, Mrs. Mason. Won't happen again," said Fleming. His white tunic buttoned, he walked out, running a hand over a neatly trimmed butch haircut.

Ernie walked past with a grin.

Sad Sack tried to walk past, too, but Mollie stood before him and gave him an angry look. "After all, Rudy, this party is for you. Act your damned age."

"Yes, ma'am." Sad Sack weaved at near attention.

Jerry tried to sneak around the other side.

"You too, you little twit," said Mrs. Mason.

Radcliff gave a light belch behind Jerry. "Little twit."

"Yes, ma'am. Sorry, ma'am." Jerry Ingram hustled on. But he caught the twinkle in her eye.

With Sad Sack Mason trailing behind, they walked into the living room to the admiring glances of the guests. Jerry headed for his mom and dad but then stopped cold in his tracks. Ernie had joined up with the most gorgeous creature he'd ever seen. Tall and very slender, she had jet-black hair, a long, thin face, and the largest green eyes he'd ever seen.

She smiled up at Ernie, teeth glistening like popping flashbulbs. Suddenly, she dropped her gaze to Ingram and held it there for three long seconds.

Wow! Ernie, where the hell did you come up with that?

A proud Helen and Todd Ingram were five feet away, waiting to greet Jerry and show him off. He started to turn left toward the beauty queen when a palm grabbed his right elbow and steered him on. It was Mollie Mason. "Jerry, you are so lucky to have such nice parents." In a low voice she added, "One of your better features, I'm sure."

Jerry walked into his mother's arms as she gave him a big squeaky kiss on the cheek. "Good to see you. It's only been since last Christmas." As always, Helen looked beautiful. Her hair was now streaked with bits of silver rendering an aura of wisdom and grace.

Todd Ingram would have none of it. Hugging his son, he said, "Congratulations, Jerry. Great to have a zoomie in the family. Love those wings." With a grin, he knocked the wings with the back of his knuckles. "And now, you're a jay gee. Amazing."

Jerry was introduced to Tyler Mason and Nelson Fleming.

And over there all that time was that girl. She glanced at him again and then rejoined a conversation with Ernie and two older men.

Ernie, you are one lucky sonofabitch.

Molly said, "Dear me, the way you men are all ogling her we'll have to build a runway next time.

"Runway for what?" said Tyler.

Deftly, Helen pitched her champagne in a potted fern. Jerry saw her do it and tried to catch her eye. But she looked on as if nothing had happened.

Mollie planted her hands on her hips. "You mean you don't know who Rita Hernandez is?"

"Hell, no," said Tyler lighting his cigar.

"She's a model, a *Vogue* model, you drooling idiot. She makes three thousand dollars an hour."

"Now you're talking," said Tyler.

"I thought you read the paper every morning, Tyler."

"Well, if I'm in a hurry, just the business section."

"If you'd looked this morning you would have seen her on the front page of the entertainment section with Ernest Borgnine and Lee Marvin."

"No kidding? For what?"

"Promoting their new picture, "*The Dirty Dozen.*"

"Dirty what?"

"*Dozen*. It's about Army soldiers who raid a German hideout to kill their high command."

"Well, then, we have to meet this young lady. Let's go say hello."

Helen took Jerry's hand and squeezed.

Tyler started to walk over but stopped. The girl was headed toward them accompanied by Ernie Hernandez. They drew near and stopped. Ernie said, "Good afternoon, Admiral. And good afternoon Mr. and Mrs. Mason. We wanted to thank you for inviting us here. What a wonderful party. Please meet my sister, Rita."

Sister?

Helen squeezed harder.

There were handshakes all around. Rita gripped Jerry Ingram's hand coolly. But her eyes flashed for a moment, taking him in.

Helen's nails dug into his palm, but she had to let go to take Rita's hand as Ernie finished the introductions. With the thinnest of smiles, Helen said, "Pleased to meet you," her greeting the temperature of fudge bars in the freezer.

A waiter passed with a tray of bacon-wrapped duck liver all jabbed with tooth-picks. The others gave oohs and ahhs. Jerry's stomach wrenched into a knot.

Helen said, "Look, Jerry, rumaki. Have one, it'll do wonders," She grabbed the hors d'oeuvre by the tooth pick and popped it into her mouth. "Ummm, good."

"Uh ... not now, Mom, thanks."

Todd slapped him on the back. "Come on, Jer, lots of protein. Chestnut too. Make you grow another two inches." Everybody laughed. He grabbed the toothpick and handed it over.

"Thanks, Dad." Jerry took it and munched, forcing a smile. Maybe it would settle him down.

It did the opposite. His stomach rumbled, touching off a minor earth-quake inside. There was no stopping it. He said as casually as he could, "Excuse me for just one moment, I see someone I haven't seen since my plebe year." He strode out the French doors, onto the veranda, ducked around the boathouse, and ... lost it all in one croaking blast.

Weak. He sank to one knee on the boathouse porch, breathing heavily and gagging. Sweat broke out on his face; another wave swarmed inside. He bent over.

From behind, a cool hand wrapped around his forehead as he retched again. Finally, it was gone. He felt a little better. The hand was that of a woman. *Mom! She'll kill me.*

He rose with, "Look, Mom, I'm sorry. Those guys..." He turned to find Rita Hernandez wearing an amused smile.

She dabbed a napkin at his mouth. "It's okay. I saw those guys force-feeding you. Ernie told me. You don't like bourbon?"

He belched. "Sorry. Feel a little better." He did feel better. "Bourbon does this to me. But it was the only stuff available. The rest was scattered about the party."

"Well, Ernie apologizes for the rest."

"He sent you?"

"Well, er, yes."

Jerry laughed. "I'll kill him."

"Whatever for?"

"He knew what I was doing. And then he sends in his little sister." He focused on her. "I'm sorry."

"It's okay. I've seen worse."

He thought that unlikely. She looked as pure as the driven snow. "I don't believe you."

Right away, she came back with, "I'm sure you'll get your revenge. Look, you in town long?"

"Thirty days, then it's off to Florida."

"For..."

"For training. They're going to teach me how to kill Communist submarines."

"I have a shoot coming up in Florida next month."

"Maybe I'll see you there."

She flashed an amazing smile. "Maybe sooner. I have two tickets for Lincoln Center tomorrow night. Leonard Bernstein is doing a special performance of *West Side Story*. How does that sound?"

7

16 October 1967
Bamboo Snack Bar
Highway 78
Ladsen, South Carolina

John Walker stared at the ledger for a long time. He owed $4,233.76 by the end of the month; most of it for beer and food. There was no possibility that his Navy pay, even as a chief petty officer, would cover it. And the income from the Bamboo Snack Bar, which he owned outright and had invested in heavily, was dismal.

Outside, it was cold with low-hanging clouds. Rain maybe. Inside, the jukebox played a slow, mournful hillbilly tune that made the place seem colder than it really was. He raised his USS *Simon Bolivar* Zippo cigarette lighter and fired up another Viceroy. The ancient wooden chair protested loudly as he leaned back, exhaled, steepled his fingers, and looked out the door of his closet-sized office. It was noon and there were only three patrons out there: Henry Berman, the town drunk, and a young couple who had walked in five minutes ago. Froggie Prendergast, a buddy and retired Navy submariner chief, a stink-potter who worked for nothing most of the time, stood behind the bar polishing glasses.

The couple was hunched together in deep conversation. He had a draft beer, she had a coke. He looked Navy all right, maybe a zoomie. She looked Mexican and was an absolute knockout, with pulled-back ebony hair, a simple peasant blouse, and a short skirt. By the way she carried herself, her graceful gestures as she spoke, and her near-perfect makeup, she might have just stepped from a magazine ad.

Shaking his head slowly, Walker closed the ledger. He and his wife, Barbara, had tried so hard, had scrimped and saved to make this a go; to create a nest egg. Instead the Bamboo Snack Bar had sucked them dry. There was no money left. And Froggie, his old and loyal friend and fellow submariner, hadn't been paid for four weeks. *How are you going to handle that?*

Not my fault, decided Walker. *We live in a sick system. It's not the Soviets' fault this planet is so screwed up. It's the place where we live, the politicians and the military leaders and corporate demons that slop up everything in sight, leaving nothing for the little guy*. He'd concluded the Soviets were not the aggressive adversary Americans feared. *This Cold War and the billions upon billions spent on national defense is a sham. Those people are just stuffing their pockets. And here am I, another one of their millions of victims, awaiting slaughter.*

For the past few days he'd been pondering this. There was one thing he could do that, perhaps, might even the balance; might help solve the political situation and at the same time save him from bankruptcy. He took another drag off his Viceroy and laced his fingers behind his head, thinking about his plan. *Yeah, maybe; just maybe.*

John Walker's chair protested loudly as he shifted his weight upright, stubbed out his cigarette, and rose. He locked the ledger in his desk and walked out of his office and into the bar. Approaching the jukebox, he selected a key from a large, jangling key ring, inserted it into the jukebox, and punched selection H2. Immediately the Turtles started singing "Happy Together." The couple looked over, smiles darting across their faces. He strode over to them. Holding out a hand, he said, "Welcome to the Bamboo Shack Bar, America's finest repository of bubbleheads."

The patron took his hand. "Nice to be here. You the boss-man?"

Walker gave a broad smile. "Yes, sir."

"And you were a bubblehead?"

"Still am."

The woman looked up at Walker and threw him a dazzling smile. With a nod to the jukebox she said, "That's our favorite song."

Oh, my God. Her voice was low, sultry. Walker replied, "Five free replays on the house."

Her smile lit up the whole room. "Thank you."

He turned to the man, "And you sir, a zoomie?"

The man smiled. "Guilty as charged. How could you tell?"

"By that obsessed expression on your face."

They laughed.

"I'm Johnny Walker, owner, sole proprietor, chief petty officer, husband, and father of three."

"Any relation to, you know," the zoomie nodded toward the Atlantic and Scotland, *Johnnie Walker Scotch.*

It was a question he heard at least once a day. "I wish."

"Nice to meet you. I'm Jerry Ingram. My friends call me Jerry."

"I'm Smilin' Jack to my friends." They shook again.

"And this is my er, ah...wife, Rita."

Walker's jaw dropped. "Wife? Just married?"

Jerry waved a hand. "Join us, please. And yes. We just hooked up last night with a justice of the peace. The one down the road. Paradise Chapel? You know the guy? Reverend Stevens?"

Thaddeus Stevens was a regular patron who often occupied bar-stool number four beside Henry Berman, slopping up beer. Walker didn't know much about Stevens except what Berman slurred on occasion. It seemed the Paradise Chapel, which at one time served all the quickie wedding needs for the Navy base at nearby Charleston, had fallen on hard times. Newer and more progressive chapels had sprung up closer to town, cutting deeply into Reverend Thaddeus Stevens' revenue for ten-minute wedding services. Stevens' only recourse against the newer chapels was to stay open until midnight. That must be why these two looked so tired. Married at 11:30. In bed by 12. Awake the rest of the night. Suppressing a grin, Walker sat and said, "Yes, he's a fine man. So is his wife, Alice." He'd never met Alice. But Berman had let on that she was a teetotaler and was the one who really ran the Paradise Chapel. She also played the organ. "Together, they're a fine couple and do a great job."

The two looked relieved. "We thought so."

"Got an idea. 'Scuse me." Walker popped up and walked over to the jukebox, pulled out his key ring, and selected D6. It began playing "The Hawaiian Wedding Song" with Andy Williams.

He walked back and sat. "That's better. Congratulations."

"Thanks, Smilin' Jack." She flashed her ring finger: a cigar band.

What an absolute knockout. Walker pointed. "Ah, honey. You should have the best. Look, I can get you a beautiful ring, cheap. Full karat diamond, emerald cut, set in white gold. Perfect clarity for just a thousand dollars." What he didn't say is that it was his wife's ring and he'd only paid four hundred for it in Yokosuka, Japan. And it had faults.

Jerry said, "Thanks. We'll work all that out. I'm shipping out day after tomorrow." He sighed. "Yeah, we're in a hurry. From the quickie wedding to shipping out. My orders were accelerated. Instead of three weeks' leave they want me out there now."

"Where's 'there?'"

"Sigonella, Sicily."

"Ah, you'll love the Med. Better than Vietnam."

Jerry nodded, "Roger that. Over 400,000 Americans mucking around the jungle. Just as many Communists. Maybe more. Yeah, it's quiet in Sigonella. Beautiful countryside."

"Nice big volcano," grinned Walker, meaning Mount Etna.

"So I've heard. But so far, things are quiet. And that's just right." He looked at Rita and squeezed her hand.

Walker felt a hot flash. *God, she's amazing. Look at her skin; it's so smooth, her teeth are impossibly white, her arms are delicate and just ... just perfect.* He wanted to know more. "You're flying multi engine?" he fished.

"P-3s. Just finished with a RAG group in Florida."

"So you've become a right-seater."

Jerry grinned. "Finally earning my pay. How 'bout you? How long you been in submarines?"

"Seven years."

"Doin' what?"

"Oh, this and that."

Jerry sat back. That meant spook work, and on submarines that was cryptography. "Oh, er, you been on nukes?"

Walker held up two fingers. "The *Andrew Jackson* and the *Simon Bolivar*."

"Wow. Boomers. Er, ah, lemme see, you're a torpedoman."

"Nossir. Chief warrant in the radio gang."

"I see. And what's it like to be on patrol for sixty days?" Jerry looked at Rita and rubbed her neck.

She made a purring sound.

That drove Walker crazy. *What I would do for sixty days with her*. "Boring."

"You don't get a chance to send messages."

"Right. Most of the time, we just put up the mast and monitor chatter."

That was interesting. That meant the submarine was at periscope depth, which meant she was exposed. Jerry figured Russian boomers would be doing the same thing.

Walker must have been guessing because he said, "Ivan does a lot of that." He looked at his watch. *Jeez, late*. He rose. "Have to go Mr. and Mrs. ah ..."

"Ingram."

"Must get back to my day job."

"Charleston?"

"Used to be here. Now, with the Atlantic Fleet Submarine Force headquarters in Norfolk."

"Wow. Neat job. Pushing paper?

"Sort of. Watch officer." He didn't add that he was in charge of the crypto section.

"I'll bet it's important." Jerry pushed away his glass.

"Have another. It's on the house."

"We'd like to, but time for us to get going as well. Got a plane to catch..." he checked his watch, "in forty-four hours."

"But we're not going together." Rita added another sizzling smile. "Until dependent housing becomes available." She turned to her husband. "Did I say that right? Dependent housing?"

"That's right." Jerry said glumly. "Only a few days. I'll fly you over and you can bunk in a hotel until a place turns up."

Rita gave a faux pout. "How long?"

"Just a few days," said Jerry. "It's the Navy way."

She said, "I'll never get used to Navy life." She tapped a long finger nail on the counter to "Happy Together."

It drove Walker crazy.

She turned to him. "You've been in for a long time. Did your wife get used to it?"

Walker flashed a broad grin. "Sure. You do get used to it. But it's not easy at times." Desperately he'd been trying to think of a way to find out where Rita would be staying after her new husband left the United States. "It depends on how you keep yourself busy."

They looked at one another.

"I don't know much about cooking," she said. "I'm not sure what I'll do."

"There are other things," said Jerry.

With a sigh, Walker stuck out his hand. "Congratulations, you two. And best of luck in P-3s, Lieutenant."

"Thanks, Smilin' Jack." The newly married couple stood and walked out, arm in arm.

8

16 October 1967
Atlantic Fleet Submarine Force headquarters
Norfolk, Virginia

Chief Warrant Officer John Anthony Walker Jr. uncorked his red MG and zipped north on Highway 95 in clear traffic under overcast skies. For the first two hours he daydreamed about Rita Ingram. She had nudged his leg while they sat. Accidental or otherwise, the feeling was exhilarating, demanding. He'd looked quickly at her and he swore she'd given him the slightest of smiles. Her new husband was going to the Med so she'd be here alone for a few days, and if his guess was right, without friends or relatives. Come to think of it, they'd had a quickie wedding at the Paradise Chapel. A hot night in the sack—both probably drunk. Most likely, they didn't remember a thing.

Just ripe for the picking. How the hell could he find her? Maybe Ted Stevens at the Paradise Chapel might have something in his paperwork. In addition to calling upon the Reverend Stevens, he decided to look up their bill when he returned to Charleston. Maybe that would give him more information on Rita.

Eventually, his mind turned to the business at hand for the rest of the 450-mile trip. After 380 miles he made his decision.

Do it! Just do it!

Chief Warrant Officer John Anthony Walker Jr. would contact the Soviet Union via their embassy in Washington, DC. The overriding principle would be—**K**eep **I**t **S**imple, **S**tupid: the KISS principle he'd learned in a computer class. Even so, he had the eerie feeling someone was watching as he drove through the Norfolk Navy Yard main gate.

The Marine saluted him without making eye contact. Walker pulled away and shifted into second gear. He quickly scanned the bushes in the side-view mirror. No FBI agents popping out to clamp a hand on his shoulder. Nobody chasing after him waving a .45.

Even so, there was a low growling in his belly as he pulled up to the Atlantic submarine headquarters building. He switched off the ignition and set the parking brake. When he exited the MG, his stomach was nearly roaring, almost like a bad pizza or too much booze last night. *Diarrhea? Knock it off! Grab hold. If you don't do this, you'll really be shitting your pants as the sheriff throws you into the street and seizes your property to give to greedy creditors,* including his precious MG. He checked his watch: 1737, five thirty-seven. He'd made good time from Norfolk, and tonight's watch, a Monday, should be fairly quiet unless somebody decided to declare World War V.

KISS! Do it in the open? Nobody will notice.

It wasn't until 0130 that John Anthony Walker Jr. made up his mind what to steal. He decided on the current month's key list for the KW-47 cryptographic machine, a near-obsolete typewriter-like machine in use by all the services through World War II to the present. Walker figured his Russian contacts would accept that as an inducement for more lucrative data on machines such as the new KW-7. Then he figured, *what the hell, why not?* Scratching his bald spot, he decided to include the monthly SIOP summary. *The Russkies' socks will go up and down when they see this.* The Single Integrated Operational Plan (SIOP) was a monthly overview of the disposition of all U.S. nuclear weapons and their targets in case of nuclear war with the Soviet Union. If he did it right, he could supply this material to the Russians on a monthly basis for a fabulous price. Perpetual employment, perpetual motion, perpetual riches.

At three in the morning, Walker sat at his desk in the cryptographic office of SUBLANT's Norfolk Virginia's headquarters. It was quiet. He took a casual look around. Nine men worked in here manning teletypes and radios. Seven fiddled with paperwork, acting like they were busy. Two faced away, as if concentrating on something; those two goldbricks were asleep, Walker knew. He always knew which ones were awake and which ones slept. How could he not? He was an expert at faking it. Walker knew every trick. But now? It was a very quiet and sleepy watch, as he had hoped.

Faking a yawn, he stood, reached in his briefcase, and pulled out a copy of the latest *Sports Illustrated,* Joe Namath on the cover. Magazine in hand, he walked into the vault—a 10 x 15 area to which only he, the watch supervisor, had access. Safes and file cabinets lined three walls. The watch captain's desk was a small, gray steel government issue with a green utility lamp that stood against the far wall. In gay profusion, red or yellow placards attached to safes and cabinets silently screamed TOP SECRET. There was a red telephone on top of the desk. Nobody used it; perhaps because nobody knew the extension number to the desk in the main vault. Now, he plopped the magazine on the desk and walked over to the bank of safes to his right.

Walker looked out the massive door. His motions were jerky. Where were the FBI agents? He was sure someone—FBI, ONI, CIA—would reach out and grab him.

No one? Amazing.

Get to it before you really crap your pants.

Someone turned on a rock station playing "Cry Softly Lonely One." Walker liked that tune. It was by Roy Orbison, and he began humming along. A vision of his wife, Barbara, flashed before him as he stooped to spin the dial of safe 23 WX. He and Barbara were having such trouble and he was sure that with some money, happiness would return.

One more glance over his shoulder. *Okay.* Carefully, he opened the safe and found the drawer marked **KEYLIST KL-47 OCTOBER 1967**. Quickly, he pulled out four pages and casually tossed them on his desk. He closed the door to safe 23 WX without locking it and then quickly spun up the dial to safe UV 652. Opening that, he found a folder marked **SIOP OCTOBER 1967** and pulled four pages from that. Another glance out the door told him his watch-standers were either doing their jobs or were asleep. Roy Orbison's mellow voice implied the later.

Good for me. Bad for the Navy. Bad for my team's performance grade.

Walker casually gathered up the key lists and the SIOP pages and stuffed them between the thick pages of *Sports Illustrated*, then walked out.

He walked to his desk, sat and flipped pages, and shoved cumbersome manuals aside to make room for more cumbersome manuals. Surely the FBI would be swarming into the room soon, ready to hold him screaming and kicking on the floor as they snapped on handcuffs. He checked his watch. Ten minutes had passed since he exited the vault. No FBI or inspector generals or senior watch commanders arresting him.

Nothing. Time for the KISS principle.

Lighting a cigarette, he stood and sauntered to a glassed-in enclosure, *Sports Illustrated* in hand. Inside the room was a monstrous copy machine that was always breaking down. The irony was Walker was the key operator. Only he knew how to fix the machine. Fingers crossed it worked tonight. He pushed the start button. The machine clanked and groaned. A quick glance told him his crew was still busy trying to look busy. Now! Walker deftly and deliberately copied the four KW-47 key list pages and then the four SIOP pages. He was stuffing them back in the magazine—

"Hey, Skipper."

Walker spun around. It was Robinson, a third-class radioman. "Hi, Charlie." He forced a smile.

Robinson leaned against the door jamb, chewing gum, his hands in his pockets. With a grin, he said, *sotto voce*, "Don't let the boss catch you. Twenty lashes for unauthorized copies of Broadway Joe."

Walker wailed in a high pitch, "Oh, dear. He'll never forgive me."

Robinson guffawed and walked to his bank of radio transmitters.

Walker's heart pounded. His temples felt as if they'd burst, and an electric current seemed to run through his body. "Whew." He leaned over the machine and held tightly for thirty seconds. Then, deliberately, he stood and made sure the original KW-47 key list and SIOP pages were safely tucked in the *Sports Illustrated* along with the copies. Suppressing a great urge to wipe mist of his brow, he turned and walked back to his desk.

Ten minutes later, the original KW-47 key lists and SIOP pages were securely back in their safes.

Chief Warrant Officer John Anthony Walker Jr. was relieved of his watch at 0556. He stuffed his *Sports Illustrated* and the rest of his belongings into an old leather briefcase and walked from his office into the lobby. After a cursory inspection by a civilian guard, he strode past two Marine sentries, through the door, and into a new day. Except there was no sunrise. Just a heavy overcast and the hint of rain.

Except for the TV blaring next door, the apartment was quiet. The lights were out and Walker lay on his bed, interlaced hands under his head. He'd never felt so jacked up in his life. They'd bought it! Hook, line, and Vodka bottle. He was too excited to sleep. It was seven in the evening and he hadn't slept yet. He was due on watch again at midnight and wondered how he was going to stay awake. But damn it, he'd sold the goods to the Russians.

Again, using the KISS principal, he'd taken a cab into Washington, DC, jumped out two blocks away, and walked back to the 1100 block of 16th Street NW. A hulking 1900s mansion built by Mrs. George M. Pullman of sleeping car fame looked both sad and sour in the late fall. He'd walked past a guard at the main gate, through the front door, and demanded to see a security officer. A well-dressed man of about fifty-five who introduced himself as Oleg walked in five minutes later and, with the security guard—an enormous drooling goon—following them, showed Walker to a small office. There were no niceties. When Oleg asked the nature of his business in slightly accented English, Walker shoved the key list and SIOP pages across the table, saying that he wished to be in the employ of the Union of Soviet Socialist Republics and could produce key lists on a monthly basis, plus a lot more information. Oleg, ever so politely but, ever so penetratingly, asked if his motivation was political or financial. "Financial," Walker replied. "I need the money."

Oleg nodded and steepled his fingers. Back and forth it went for two and a half hours. Oleg digging and digging. At length Walker stated that he needed sleep. That he was due back on watch at midnight. Oleg nodded and asked for Walker driver's license. He disappeared with that for five minutes while the goon stood behind Walker. He could almost feel the man's breath.

The goon coughed. Walker nearly peed his pants. The clock ticked. Walker's skin felt clammy. Screaming headlines of this morning's paper popped into his mind: an unidentified source had disclosed to the *Washington Post* that Communist China had detonated an H-bomb last July at their Lop Nur Test Ground. H-bomb! *Jeez*. And here he was dicking around with a little key list. The Ruskies and the Chinese would soon be at it while he and Barbara—

Oleg returned silently. Still standing, he returned Walker's driver's license. Then he pushed an envelope across the table. Walker felt giddy when Oleg asked politely if he would count the money. The envelope contained one thousand dollars in used fifties and hundreds. Oleg produced something else and asked Walker to sign it. It was in Cyrillic—Russian, something he couldn't read. "What is it," Walker asked?

"A receipt, of course," replied Oleg. Then the Russian, Walker was sure he was KGB, gave instructions on their next meeting. Never again at the embassy. Walker would meet his handler in two weeks, and information and money would be exchanged only in dead letter drops, preferably somewhere in the Virginia countryside. Oleg then said that Walker would be paid between one thousand and four thousand dollars per month, depending on the value of the information.

John felt giddy. He said he could provide the key lists for the new satellite-driven coding system for the new KW-7. Oleg agreed that the KW-7 key lists would be most desirable. Walker was surprised that Oleg knew about the KW-7 but didn't press the point.

An appointment two weeks hence was agreed upon, and the two men stood. Without shaking hands, Oleg said goodbye and exited the room.

That's when Walker got another fright. The goon palmed Walker's elbow and with a grunt propelled him down a hall and to a side door, then handed him a large overcoat and droopy hat.

After Walker had donned these items the goon once again palmed the elbow of Chief Warrant Officer John Anthony Walker Jr. and nudged him through door. Under a portico was a 1964 black Buick roadster, its engine running. Two men were in the front, one was in the back, and another was standing by the back door. With an enormous hand in the small of Walker's back, the goon propelled Walker into the backseat. The other man entered after him so that he was sandwiched between them. All of the men were dressed much like him, their features indistinguishable. After a half hour of mindless driving they dropped him in Georgetown, took back the overcoat and hat, and drove off.

And now Walker couldn't sleep. He felt victorious. He lay there with the fat envelop on his chest. His key to the future. Barbara had called. But she was drunk as usual and complained about their son Michael and his schoolwork. John simply hung up,

She didn't call back.

He got up and padded into a living room filled with cheap Danish modern furniture. He sat and flipped on the light. He was going to turn on the TV when he spotted a *Vogue* magazine left by a recent girlfriend. The issue was only three months old, and he picked it up, idly flipping from back to front, as he'd seen women do. *Why do they*—he stopped. *Damn!* There she was. He was sure of it. Rita whatever her name was. A frigging bombshell! A little on the thin side but wow! There were several photos, many of her wearing a stylish line of clothing with an Italian name. Some of it nice and tight. In each photo Rita had that challenging come-and-get-me look he'd seen yesterday in his bar.

Walker rubbed his chin for a couple of moments. Finally, he picked up the phone and dialed a number.

A crusty voice answered, "Bamboo Snack Bar, Froggie speakin'."

Walker was happy to give him the news. Froggie , you old pile of crap. You're getting paid tomorrow."

"Huh?"

"I mean it. You and Gloria can go out next Saturday and paint the town."

"You're shitting me."

"Three hundred and fifty dollars, old buddy. Just wait."

"What's the catch?"

"None. How's business?"

"I think I believe you."

"That's right. How's business?"

"Eh, I seen better."

Walker took a deep breath. "Is Reverend Stevens there?"

"Yeah."

"Drunk or sober?"

"He's about to fall off the stool."

"What's his tab so far?"

"He paid some. I think he still owes us about fifty-five bucks, somewhere thereabouts."

"Put him on.

"Okay."

The phone rustled as it was handed over. "Smilin' Jack?" a man slurred.

Walker said, "Ted, I'm sorry to bother you."

"Any time, Jack."

"Look, something's come up. How would you like it if we rubbed your bar tab off the books."

"Well, it's only fifteen dollars or so. And— "

"Fifty-five."

"Oh, I didn't realize. Look, I can have it by next Monday. Honest. Me and Alice are expecting a big weekend."

"Well, I can make it bigger for you."

"Howzat?"

"All I need is an address or phone number of someone you just ahh —processed..."

9

17 October 1967
BOQ, Naval Air Station
Norfolk, Virginia

The phone line clicked and rattled as the coast-to-coast connection was made. Finally, a slurred, "Hello?"

"...Uncle Jerry? It's me, Jerry."

"You're kidding!"

Jerry visualized Jerry Landa and his glittering Pepsodent grin. It was very disarming, and he used it to the hilt. "Yes, sir. It's me, in the flesh."

Landa belched. "You realize what time it is here, son?"

Jerry Ingram looked at his watch: 9:05 a.m. here; 6:05 on the West Coast. Jeeez, he'd forgotten! "Oh, my God. I'm so sorry. I'll call later."

"Never mind, kid. I'm already up. I walk the dog at this hour. Nice and peaceful. We're up in the Santa Monica Mountains. Beautiful view this time of day. I can see the ocean. How about you?"

It rained outside. Jerry longed for California weather. But it should be like California when he got to Sicily. "It's nice here, Uncle Jerry. But not as nice as it is in Los Angeles."

"Bel Air."

"Bel what?"

"Never mind. What's on your mind, son." Jerry heard a cigarette lighter click.

"I ah...I have a..."

Rita sat beside him and took his hand.

"Spit it out, kid."

"Yes, sir. Well, that is..."

"Jeez. What's wrong with ring-knockers? They ever teach you to speak?"

"I need advice."

"I figured that."

Jerry Ingram exhaled. "I got married a couple of days ago."

She squeezed his hand and kissed his cheek.

Silence. Finally, "And what did your folks have to say?"

"Well, that's just it. I haven't told them ...yet."

Landa's voice amped up a bit. "And you want me to tell them?"

"Look, Uncle Jerry. Dad is so damned important; I don't want to upset him."

"Your dad has a very level head. Otherwise, they wouldn't have made him a vice admiral. And your mom—"

"That's just it. I don't think she likes her."

"Likes who? Your wife?"

"Here's what happened, Uncle Jerry." Jerry Ingram laid it out for their longtime family friend and his namesake, Jeremiah T. Landa, captain, USN, retired. He and Todd Ingram had served together in destroyers during the Pacific war. They were very close. Besides his grandmother Kate and his parents and sister, Uncle Jerry was his only real family.

In Landa's Navy days he'd been the flamboyant fighting destroyer skipper with Todd Ingram as his executive officer. Landa was a Sailor's sailor at sea, but ashore he'd been a disaster, getting sloshed in O clubs, making the brass angry, with Todd Ingram cleaning up the mess. His nickname was "Boom Boom" because of the fart jokes he loudly told at the O clubs. The junior officers laughed and cackled at them, the senior officers and their wives flashed stern and disgusted looks. This attitude crept into his fitness reports and killed what could have been a brilliant Navy career. He was retired as a captain shortly after the Korean armistice. After that, things hadn't gone well for Landa until recently, when he'd landed a job as a harbor pilot. Now he was happy again, telling his stupid jokes and piloting giant cargo vessels and tankers into Los Angeles Harbor, zipping back and forth to Bel Aire in a new Corvette. He could afford the Corvette and the home in Bel Aire since Laura, his wife, had become a highly sought-after concert pianist. Landa, with his broad, glittering smile and salty good looks, was the perfect complement to his beautiful wife as he drove her to and from her concerts. All he had to do was keep his mouth shut.

"Okay, spit it out, son," said Landa.

Jerry explained about his meeting Rita Hernandez at the posh house in the Hamptons and their whirlwind romance in Florida. She was on a thirty-day photo shoot, and they managed to get together almost every day. But the last night in Florida, she'd broken down and told Jerry she'd skipped her period and most likely was pregnant. They had to admit, they hadn't been careful. Then Jerry's assignment to Sigonella came through. He had two weeks' lead time, but they burned up most of that, unable to part. Finally, he was due there in five days. He chose the Norfolk Air Station since they had direct flights. She rode with him on the trip north to the air station, stopping, on the spur of the moment, to get married north of Charleston. Now they were holed up in Norfolk while he waited for a flight to Sicily.

Landa asked, "How about her job? Models make lots of money."

"More in a month then I do in a year. But she's put it on hold. They've given her time off."

"That's nice. So, what do you want me to do?"

"I'm afraid Dad will blow his stack."

"Damn it, son! Give him some credit! Your mom, too. They love you."

"I...look...I'm sorry. I shouldn't have called. I'd better—"

"Lemme think, damn it."

"Yes, sir."

"Okay, when do you take off for Sigonella?

"Three hours. I'm all packed."

"Shiiiiit. You don't give a person much warning, do you?"

"Sorry."

"Here, look kid. Let me speak with Laura. She and Helen are such buds; maybe she can smooth things out."

Bingo! Landa's wife Laura and Helen Ingram were close friends. Jerry felt as if an enormous weight had been lifted off his chest. "You will?"

"Don't expect any miracles. Laura may talk to Helen or she might tell me to tell you to kiss off. Who knows?"

"Well, thanks, Uncle Jerry. It's a start."

"Now, put her on."

"Huh?"

"Your wife, damn it. What's her name?"

Jerry felt as if the weight had been replaced. He took a deep breath. "Rita."

"Rita. Yes, your folks mentioned her at dinner the other night. Sounds like a neat girl. Put her on."

"Yes, sir." Ingram handed over the phone. With a whisper, he said, "My uncle Jerry, my godfather, really. A dear family friend. My namesake."

"Me?" Her eyebrows went up.

"You."

"Okay." Rita shook out her hair and put the receiver to her ear. "Hello?"

Jerry heard Uncle Jerry talking. Rita's mouth gradually spread to a wide grin. "Oh, thank you. Thank you."

Landa's voice blasted for a moment.

"I'm sorry. Thank you, *Uncle Jerry*. I can't wait to meet you, too."

They spoke for perhaps another minute, then she hung up. Slowly she said, "You are very lucky. What a wonderful man."

"What did he say?"

"That he and your parents love you and me and that's all that matters. They will be there for us if trouble comes along. In the meantime, things will take care of themselves." She smiled again. "He wants me to call him Uncle Jerry, just like you."

Jerry leaned back with a big grin. "Wow!"

"He sounds kind of cute."

"He is. You oughtta see his teeth."

Bag in hand, Lt. (j.g.) Jerry Ingram was about to call a cab for the airport when the phone rang. He picked it up. "Ingram." He listened for a moment, then took off his hat and began unbuttoning his blouse. "Okay. Thanks for the heads up." Slowly, he replaced the receiver.

"What?" Rita looked lost in her overcoat, the only one available at the Base Exchange.

He gave a thin smile. "You ready for one more?" He began to loosen his tie.

"What are you talking about?"

"That was base ops. Plane's delayed. Doesn't take off until thirteen hundred."

She sat on the bed and dropped the overcoat off her shoulders. "Boy, you sure don't lose time."

"*Carpe diem*."

"What's that?"

"Spanish for take off your clothes."

"Jerry!"

He reached for her. The phone rang again. "Damn. Now they're going to tell me the stupid thing's on time."

"Here, let me..." Rita grabbed for it. "Hello?"

"Hi ya, honey."

The voice sounded familiar. "Honey who? Who is this?"

"It's Smilin' Jack from Charleston."

"Where?"

"You know. We met at the Bamboo Snack Bar. You know. My place in South Carolina."

"Oh, yes, what do you want?" Although she recalled the man as sort of a boob, her heart rate picked up a few beats.

"I have your wedding rings."

"Wedding rings? They're already on order." Through *Vogue*, she'd made a deal at Tiffany's. "I don't need them."

Jerry sat up and put his ear close to the phone.

"Listen, I know this guy. He has good stuff. He has a combination engagement and wedding ring, two-karat emerald-cut diamond, white-gold setting, for just fifteen hundred bucks."

"I don't think so, you see—"

"Look. I'm here in Norfolk too. It's my duty station. I'd be glad to meet you for lunch and show you. We can make him an offer."

"I'm sorry, but that's out of the question. What I'm trying to tell you—"

"There's this great seafood place out on the bay. Everything is fresh caught. Good atmosphere, wine, and the music is fabulous."

Jerry grabbed the phone. "Negatory, creep."

"Oh, sorry, Lieutenant. I was just trying to—"

"Yeah, on second thought, how did you get this phone number?"

The voice said, "No harm intended, Lieutenant. I had this opportunity and wanted to help out. I guess it wasn't a good idea."

"No, it wasn't. Now go crawl back in your hole before I call ONI."

"Sorry about the intrusion, Lieutenant. Goodbye." He hung up.

Ingram banged the phone down. "Jerk." He lay back and scratched his head. "Wedding rings?"

"It did sound like an interesting deal, and that sounded like a neat restaurant."

"What a loser. I wouldn't trust that idiot as far as I could throw him. And I doubt if he is Navy." He rubbed his chin. "How in the hell did he get our number?"

"But still, fifteen hundred dolalrs." Tiffany's was charging twenty-eight hundred for something similar.

"Don't give it another thought." He reached and pulled her down. "Now, where were we?"

10

4 January 1968
Pantages Theater
Hollywood, California

Searchlights, there were two of them, blazed against the clear winter sky. Limousines were lined up on Hollywood Boulevard before the Pantages Theater, its tall marquee announcing *842 Days of Leningrad.* A red carpet was rolled out; sections were roped off on either side to allow movie-goers and fans to squeeze in and watch the kings and queens of Hollywood descend from their limousines, the near-freezing temperature prompting the gaudiest of furs and long winter coats. Some were interviewed by shivering reporters, the rest quickly moved into the welcoming warmth of the Pantages' gilded lobby.

It was the Hollywood premiere of the film, which had opened three days ago in Leningrad and had an all-star cast playing Russian and German soldiers. The highly publicized budget was close to that of *The Longest Day*, and starred many of the same actors. Politics had played a part in the casting.

Many refused the roles of Russian generals and soldiers who beat the Nazis back time after time. Current events dictated the favorites, and well-known stars scrambled for parts as tragically misled German soldiers and officers. The Russians were played, for the most part, by unknowns. Both the *Hollywood Reporter* and *Variety* ran interviews and editorials, and the buzz was more about U.S.-USSR brinksmanship and the horrors of mutually assured destruction than the merits of the movie. Most likely, the latter would be decided tonight.

Anoushka Dezhnev had a role, oddly enough, as the wife of a corrupt Swedish diplomat instead of her usual tragic poster-woman widow of the Great Patriotic War.

Oliver Toliver and Suzy, his regal-looking Asian wife, stood off to the side of the lobby watching the glitzy parade. Toliver fidgeted, but Suzy was enjoying a welcome break from running Wong Lee's Chinese restaurant just north of downtown Los Angeles.

A voice boomed, "Ollie, I didn't think you'd show up. What a great surprise." Jerry Landa walked up and thrust out his hand. His cheeks were red from the cold, and he wore a long wool coat. His magnificent teeth chattered as he said, "They have something hot to drink around here?"

Along with Jerry Landa, Oliver Toliver III and Suzy were also close friends with the Ingrams. Originally a gunnery officer with Todd Ingram, Toliver's hip and leg were seriously wounded when he was a gun boss aboard a destroyer in one of the vicious night battles with the Japanese in the Solomon Islands. Refusing a medical discharge, Toliver stayed in the Navy and transferred to the Office of Naval Intelligence. Just before the Korean War he became an agent with the Central Intelligence Agency. He'd also known Eduard Dezhnev back in 1942 when he was a naval attaché to the Soviet consulate in San Francisco, which led to getting to know Dezhnev's mother after the war.

Toliver took Landa's hand and they shook warmly. When Landa's wife, Laura, walked up, equally red-cheeked, he kissed her on the cheek. "You two spent the day in a deep-freeze?"

"Might as well," Laura hissed, peeling off her coat. "Jerry and his damned Corvettes."

Landa grinned. "Just got a new one last Tuesday. Pass anything except a gas station."

Toliver gasped, "You got a Stingray?"

"Owwwieee. A red one, too. Three-hundred-twenty-seven-cubic-inch engine. A kid blew out a clutch dragging me down Sunset Boulevard. You should have heard it. He didn't get past second gear. A giant *boom*; parts flying all over the place, I think the muffler fell off too."

"No cops?"

"Not yet."

"I'll kill him," Laura said. "Made me ride in that damn thing with the top down." She shook out her hair letting it tumble to her shoulders. "I wish the cops had caught him." She turned to her husband. "You're like a sixteen-year-old with that damn thing."

Toliver smiled inwardly. Landa sounded like the old Landa. His new job as a harbor pilot suited him. He said, "Well, glad you got here in one piece, and glad we're all sitting together rather than next to some unknown who's out to screw me."

"Who would want to screw you?" Landa laughed as the Toliver and Landa wives traded hugs. He reached up and tugged at Toliver's roadster cap with its ornate checkered band. "Coat of arms; House of Toliver?"

"I wish it were that simple."

"Well, it makes you look like an agent about to screw someone."

"No screwing around here; just going bald." Toliver reached over and threw an arm around Laura. "You look gorgeous, sweetheart."

Laura replied, "Hollywood talk, Ollie. Where on earth did you learn that?"

Toliver faked an accent, "Brooklyn, schweetheart, the only place there is."

Anoushka Dezhnev walked up wearing a long, black-sequined evening gown. "Wonderful. I see you all received your tickets."

Toliver drew her in and gave her a big hug while flashbulbs popped around them. "Thanks for the tickets. Wouldn't miss it for anything."

She held onto Toliver after the photographers moved on. Suddenly, he felt her hand quickly go into his coat pocket. Then she patted him twice.

What the hell?

She looked up at him, her face drawn by time and yet still incredibly dynamic, compelling, and beautiful at her unannounced age of seventy-two. To the outside world, she had just entered her fifties. "It's from Eduard," she said.

Toliver knitted his brow.

Laura said, "Oops, there's Millard. I'd better say hello." She stepped away, dragging her husband with her. Flashing his Pepsodent grin, Landa managed, "See you inside." He waved over his head.

Anoushka continued. "That's from him. He gave it to me today at the airport."

"Here? Los Angeles?"

"Yes. He called last night from Vancouver. He's on his way to Mexico City."

Toliver whipped off his cap and scratched his head. "I had no idea he was in town."

"Only for a few moments while they refueled his plane."

"Why's he going to Mexico City?"

"It's that damned Utochka. She barks; he rolls over asking for his belly to be scratched." She snapped her fingers under Toliver's nose as she said the last with a near snarl. Toliver knew Anoushka and Roxanna Utkina didn't get along. But here, Anoushka was outwardly displaying animosity toward her son's betrothed. Toliver had tried to stay out of the middle, but now Anoushka was unloading on him.

She continued, "She's decorating her damn dance studio in Latin American style. He's there to pick up fabrics and a few pieces of furniture."

"Her school must be doing pretty good to pay for all that."

"It's hush money from the Kirov. That fool Gurov is on the loose and shooting off his mouth. It's beginning to look messy."

"They're shutting her up."

"In a manner of speaking. And if Gurov doesn't shut up it's—*ggkkkt!*" She drew a finger across her throat.

Toliver blinked.

"So I think you should read Eduard's note."

"I'll get to it soon as possible."

"He said it was urgent. Go to the bathroom now while there's time."

"I don't know..." Toliver looked around. "Yeah, okay, I'll just—" Her sudden gasp startled him. "What?"

"That man." With a slight tilt to her head, Anoushka indicated a smallish man across the lobby.

Toliver spotted him right away. The man stood by himself, dressed as a chauffeur with cap in hand and black leather gloves. He wore rimless glasses and had a pencil-thin moustache. There was a slight bulge under his left armpit. *Not good*. "What about him?"

"He's tailing me."

"You sure?"

Anoushka's voice was low and husky. She leaned close, her perfume engulfing Toliver. "Let me tell you. For the past twenty-three years, these people have been after me. That one in particular is a klutz. I've seen him many times in many different guises. He actually asked for my autograph once."

Toliver knew they followed her constantly. They must be KGB. But what she didn't know was that the KGB often had people followed with an obvious tail while another, the real tail, moved unobtrusively and kept in the shadows. At one time they'd even tapped her phone. But he'd called in a special team and had that neutralized. "Did you give it to him?"

"No. He smelled of garlic. I shooed him away."

A chill swept over Toliver, telling him this might not turn out to be such a good night after all. He wondered if he should call backup. "Are you sure?"

"I know these people. All my life they've been around me. They just don't go away."

Toliver nodded. He'd seen it firsthand.

Softly, she said, "I think he has a camera." Suzy stepped over just then. They laughed and traded air-kisses.

Anoushka said, "We haven't been to your place for a while."

"We've missed you," Suzy said.

Anoushka laid on a thick accent. "Vell, I vas in Roosha making movie."

Suzy took her hand. "Thanks for asking us. I can't wait to see it."

"I hope you enjoy it. And we'll get to Wong Lee's soon, and I will bring lots of people off the D-list."

Suzy laughed, "I hope you mean A-list."

"Yes, yes, A-list. I still have trouble with my English." Anoushka had a razor-sharp mind. But she purposely smashed her English, knowing people loved it.

Toliver glanced at the chauffeur while the women talked. There. He was sure he saw the man slip a Minox camera into his top pocket. Why the hell was he doing that? He figured the chauffeur, or whatever he was, could have seen Anoushka pass the note compromising not only him but also Eduard Dezhnev, a deep-cover spy for the United States. *Damn it Ollie, think of something.*

A woman in a spangled fur coat, holding an impossibly long cigarette holder, waved to Anouchka.

She waved back and said, "I must go."

As she moved off, Toliver leaned down to kiss her. "Is he all right?" he whispered.

She offered her cheek and with a glittering smile, said, "I think so."

"Okay."

"We speak later," she muttered. Walking away she said from the corner of her mouth, "That man is dangerous."

A valet strolled the lobby with a three-chime gong announcing show time.

The chauffeur turned and walked into the theater.

Toliver made his decision. "Suzy, go on in and find Jerry and Laura. I must do something."

"Ollie?" she protested.

"Time to go potty. Be right back." He pressed a ticket into her hand and walked away. Staying on the edge of the crowd, he moved toward a broad staircase. The lobby was quickly emptying as he hobbled up the stairs, favoring his leg. On the mezzanine he found the men's room, pushed open the door, and walked in. Empty; good. To make sure, he leaned down checking the stalls. Nobody inside. He walked to a far corner, hidden from the front door, and fished out Anoushka's note. It was on lined paper written in a checkerboard code with heavy pencil. Simple, but he needed today's key word, and that was in his safe at home.

Something scraped behind him. Quickly he shoved the note back in his pocket and turned to see a dark shadow raising a sap. He tried to step away but someone else grabbed him from behind.

The blow to his head sent an electric shock through him: ten thousand volts at least. He stiffened and then sank to the cold black-and-white-tiled floor.

11

4 January 1968
Pantages Theatre
Hollywood, California

The music was stark and dissonant. After five minutes, Landa found himself squirming in his seat. They'd done a masterful job blending stock war footage with new film. He swore he couldn't tell the difference as Russians and Germans killed each other in the cruelest of ways while the credits rolled. One scene showed a Russian T-34 tank grinding up a trench full of Germans soldiers, their ear-piercing screams echoing throughout the theater. He'd seen too much of this in the Pacific. His breath became shallow; perspiration broke on his forehead, and he found himself reaching for Laura's hand.

Suzy sat to Laura's left, her husband's chair empty beside her. After an equally grisly flame-thrower scene she leaned over with, "Maybe he slipped and fell or something. I think I'd better…" She rose.

Landa raised a hand and rasped, "You stay. I'll go." Glad for a chance to get out, he gave Laura a peck on the cheek, got up from his seat, and began walking up the side aisle.

Three men moved down toward him. Unable to see their features in the darkness, he stood sideways and let them pass,

He'd nearly gained the exit when it hit him. Those three guys! Two of them flanked a man unsteady on his feet. *Damn!* The one in the middle wore a roadster cap—with a *checkered band*!

Quickly, Landa turned and walked down the aisle. The curtains rustled beneath the stage **EXIT** sign. His mind whirled and he picked up his pace to a near-run. Ten feet ahead, someone casually dropped an empty popcorn box in the aisle. He bent over, scooped it up and dashed through the curtains. The door was securely closed. He nudged the door open with his hip while folding the popcorn box. He leaned down and jammed the popcorn box in the doorway, thankful that something from his raucous youth had finally paid off.

Leaving the door ajar by two inches, he stepped out and scanned the parking lot. Where were they? Landa ran a few steps among cars looking side to side. Off to his right near the side street, he spotted a section reserved for limousines. A dozen or so chauffeurs were gathered around two flaming trash cans warming their hands, smoking, and talking. He walked toward them. One looked up, curious.

Landa opened his mouth to speak when he saw three figures crossing the side street, Argyle Avenue, fifty feet away. Walking north, they dragged someone between them. One looked like the chauffeur he'd seen in the lobby.

Landa dashed to the sidewalk. "Hey!" he shouted.

One looked around. But they kept moving away from Hollywood Boulevard, into a darker section of the block.

"Come on!" Landa quick-paced across the street, jumped onto the sidewalk, and broke into a run. "Hold up, damn it!"

He drew to within ten feet. They turned to face him. Yes, it was Toliver. He was held up between the two. "What are you doing?"

The chauffeur ducked from under Toliver's arm, spun, and fumbled at buttons on his tunic.

Landa spotted the bulge under the man's tunic. *Jeez.*

Desperately, he looked around. They were in shadows halfway up the block beside a store labeled Green & Sons Jewelry Exchange.

"Boom...Boom," Toliver slurred. He looked up; one eye was black. Blood ran from the corner of his mouth,

"Agggh!" The chauffeur was trying to undo his buttons. His companion shouted something unintelligible.

Three trash cans stood at the curb. Landa bent to pick one up. It was full, and with a growl he raised it over his head, turned, and hurled it into the plate glass window of Green & Sons Jewelry Exchange.

Glass shattered. The burglar alarm sounded shrilly. The two men stood frozen. They let Toliver go, and he crumpled to the sidewalk.

"Help!" Landa shouted. He picked up another trash can, an empty, raised it over his head, and hurled it onto the two men.

The other man, darker, taller, wearing a topcoat, raised a hand and easily parried the garbage can away. But it landed in the street with a rattle and rolled to a stop in the middle of Argyle Avenue.

"Help," Landa shouted again, reaching for the other garbage can.

There was a shot. A bullet whizzed past Landa's ear as he raised the can, "Please!" he yelled. "Someone help!"

Behind him he heard men yelling, footsteps, running as the burglar alarm clanged away.

The two men before him turned and ran. Quickly, they rounded a corner and were gone,

Landa leaned over Toliver, wheezing, water vapor shooting from his mouth. "Ollie, what the hell?"

Toliver blinked and sat up with a groan, rubbing his head. "Bastards, I should have seen it coming." Suddenly, he patted his coat pocket and pulled out a slip of paper. "Thank God, they didn't get it."

"Didn't get what, Ollie?"

The chauffeurs were almost on them. Sirens squealed in the distance.

"No cops, Jerry. I'll tell you later. Just get me out."

"Jeez, you're all busted up." He took out a handkerchief and dabbed blood from Toliver's mouth."

The chauffeurs rushed up. "What the hell buddy, you okay?" They crowded around.

"Jerry...damn it. Get...me...up," muttered Toliver.

Landa laced an arm beneath Toliver and, with both grunting, rose.

Two police cars screeched to a stop across the street,

Landa, still breathing hard, said to the chauffeurs, "My friend here had too much to drink at the pre-party and he was trying to walk it off. Then these goons attacked him and threw garbage cans at him then through the window. They looked like they were trying to jimmy the lock. He surprised them."

"Wow, right under our noses."

Somehow finding strength, Toliver grabbed Landa's arm and they worked their way through the crowd, ducking past the police.

The alarm still shrieked as they crossed the street. Toliver tried to head down the street toward the Pantages main entrance.

"Come on," Landa growled. He pulled Toliver into the parking lot and toward the fire exit.

"Hey!" A shout behind them.

Toliver looked around. "Cops. I don't need cops right now,"

"I got it fixed," said Landa, picking up the pace. He was surprised Toliver was doing so well. "You're walking pretty good."

"Knockout drops wearing off. Wait." Toliver bent over and loudly vomited between the cars. After a moment, "Better." He wiped his mouth with his sleeve. "Shake a leg."

"You bet." They were at the door. The two policemen were just ten feet behind. The door was still ajar. Landa reached down, yanked out the popcorn box, and threw it into the parking lot. Quickly, they stepped through, letting the heavy fire door click shut behind them. They heard a thud on the outside; otherwise it was quiet except the sound of machine guns from inside the theater,

They eased through the curtains, hearing Anoushka's heavily accented voice speaking to an SS officer, "But ve haf permission to leaf."

Landa rasped, "You okay?"

"Feel like passing out," They made it to their seats, the two wives looking anxious.

Toliver collapsed into his seat, his eyes closing.

He awakened ten minutes later. Suzy sat beside him wiping his face with damp towels. Landa was on the other side munching popcorn.

"Welcome back," said Landa. "How the hell are you?"

"Much better."

"Here." Suzy raised a paper cup to his mouth.

"Huh?"

"Seven-Up."

He took a few shallow swallows. Right away the sugar hit his system, making him feel like he was going to live.

The Leningrad movie lumbered on, with more and more seats becoming empty seats in the world-famous Pantages. Toliver leaned forward. "Jerry, I have to make a phone call."

"Shut up and be quiet. Cops are all over the place."

It was true. Toliver glanced to the back and saw a uniformed officer standing beside the usher at the middle entrance. "Come on. I may need help." Toliver rose.

"Jesus, Ollie, can't you take a hint?"

But Toliver was already trudging up the aisle.

"Damn it!" Landa rose and followed behind, grabbing Toliver's elbow as he bumped into the wall. They got through the side entrance into the main lobby where Toliver found a bank of three phone booths.

"This won't take long." Toliver slipped into a booth. He pulled the accordion door closed, sat, and dropped in a pair of quarters.

Two uniformed policemen flanked Landa. One said, "Evening, sir. Are you two together?"

There was a thud on the phone booth door. Toliver had slapped something on the glass.

One policeman stooped to look closely. "Jeeeez, Ernie, take a look at this."

"What?" said the other.

Landa leaned over with the others to see what Toliver, phone in hand and talking to someone, held up against the window. It was an ornate gold-filigreed badge bearing the seal of the U.S. government. A legend on the bottom read: Central Intelligence Agency.

"What the hell is the Central Intelligence Agency?" asked Ernie.

"Not sure, but I think it's that spy outfit in Washington, DC. I'll stay with these guys. You better call it in to the sergeant."

The Tolivers got home at 11:37. Ollie had to explain more to Suzy than he did to the police. Two CIA operatives from the Los Angeles field office had finally shown up and spoke quietly to the police. Five minutes later they were gone, mounting a search for a short man in a chauffeur's uniform and an accomplice dressed in dark clothes. Gone also were nearly half of the theater's patrons, reporters rushing to telephones announcing that *842 Days of Leningrad,* while having lots of action with bullets and bombs, was itself, the bomb of all bombs.

His left eye was nearly swollen shut, and Suzy doted on him for a half an hour. Finally, she yawned. "I'm sorry, nighty-night time."

"I'll be along."

"You okay?"

He kissed her. She smelled wonderful. "Top of the world."

"Ummm."

"With you in five minutes."

"Ummm." Suzy shuffled off, dragging her sweater.

Toliver stooped to his floor safe, spun the combination, and opened the door, He found his codebook among several stacks of $20 bills, a .45-caliber pistol, and three CIA operating manuals. He flipped the codebook pages to January, ran his finger down the page, and found today's keyword: SUBWAY. Quickly, he set up his page and plugged in the letters. Decoded, the message read:

SOVIETS INTEND TO STEAL A US KW-37 CODE MACHINE. I HOPE THIS IS IMPORTANT—VERY HIGH PRIORITY HERE. RETURN SEVASTOPOL NEXT WEEK.

12

17 January 1968
Café Sebastiano
Catania, Sicily

The moon was full; the band played softly; and the bottle of Nero d'Avola, a fine red, was nearly flawless. One of Café Sebastiano's large-paned bay windows looked out upon the square below and the Ingrams' two-bedroom apartment across the way. Another bay window opposite looked onto the Ionian Sea as a low fire crackled on the near wall. With just three incandescent lights and plenty of soft candles, Sebastiano's had seemed idyllic when Jerry and Rita first started coming. And now, with the place full, it felt even more so: close, friendly, intimate. Everyone knew everyone.

It hadn't started out that easy. Catania didn't like foreigners. The Luftwaffe had occupied Sigonella Air Station just eleven miles to the west during World War II, basically plundering the town during their stay. General Patton and his Third Army came in and threw them out, and times improved.

But Sicily survived Mussolini, and it survived the Germans. And now

Catania was determined to survive the Americans—with perhaps a bit more grace since the Americans didn't seem bent on looting the place.

Like many Americans, Jerry and Rita were initially ignored at Sebastiano's. But Jerry hated walking two blocks to the next restaurant for the same treatment. So they worked on Tomaso Modesto, Sebastiano's proprietor, tipping heavily and being gracious. It seemed to work because their evenings became more enjoyable. Rita and Jerry noticed that when other Americans called Tomaso "Tommy" or "Tom," the temperature in the room would plunge at least twenty degrees. Actually, it was hard not to like Tomaso. He was a giant of a man, at least 6 feet 4 inches and weighing 325 pounds with thick, powerful arms and legs. He had copious, curly hair with a bald spot in back that his wife, Rosa, who worked in the kitchen, carefully manicured. And to Jerry's amazement Tomaso, with short, stubby fingers the diameter of toilet plunger handles, played a decent guitar, but only when the moment was right. Now was not the moment. Sebastiano's was just too busy.

The salads finished, Tomaso carried out a large platter with their main dish. He nodded to a three-piece band beside the fireplace and they played a downbeat and a fanfare. In a deep, loud baritone, Tomaso announced to the whole room as if he were calling a bullfight: "*Zuppa di cozze o vongole al pomodoro.*" Clam soup with tomato sauce.

As was the custom, the crowd cheered loudly as if the bull had once again ducked the red cape.

Tomaso's son, Ugo, an aspiring look-alike of seventeen, handed his father another tray. Once again the band struck up and he announced, "*Voilá, farsumagru.*"

Again the crowd cheered.

Jerry picked up fork and knife. "What's in it this time?"

Tomaso reverted to an American accent, "Eh, half a can of tuna, some Lysol bathroom cleaner mixed in with ground-up buzzard claws."

Jerry took a bite. It was excellent. *Farsumagru* was a popular meat dish of Sicily. Both he and Rita loved it. "Any gunpowder this time?"

With a smile, Tomaso said, "The Germans didn't leave much, so we save it for special customers."

"Pity."

Rita thought it had gone too far. With a killer smile she said, "This is the best ever, Tomaso. I think Rosa added some extra...umm ... *caciocavallo*?"

Tomaso brightened. While Ugo cleared used dishes, he said, "You amaze me, *bella*. That's exactly right." After filling their glasses with the rest of the Nero d'Avola, he snapped his fingers and Ugo produced another bottle. Tomaso watched closely as Ugo uncorked it for them. With that, both men took a pace back.

"*Grazie mille*," said Jerry.

"*Prego*." With nods, Tomaso and Ugo walked away.

Tomaso was right, Jerry thought. Rita was radiant tonight. And quick glances around the dining room told him others thought so, too. That was nice because she'd told him recently that her life was boring. Not that she missed the intensity of a photo shoot, but without all that, she really had nothing to do. Jerry had tried to get her involved with other Navy wives, but she didn't fit in. She didn't dress or look or act "wifely." When she walked in a room, it was as if Rita was marching down the runway with flashbulbs popping around her.

Rita was glad to get out tonight, to be among people, for another reason. It had been a spooky two days. Two days before, there had been a terrible *terremoto*, an earthquake, on the other end of Sicily in an area called the Belici Valley, registering 6.4 on the Richter scale. Whole villages had been wiped out, hundreds were dead, thousands homeless. Many in Belici had relatives in Catania who rushed out to help. Jerry had been away on a flight and returned to a quiet and stunned Catania. The mood in town tonight was a faux gaiety.

Jerry took her hands. "You better now?" She'd been scared and hugged him fiercely when he'd returned late this afternoon. Catania had shaken somewhat, but the horror stories from Belici were beginning to pour in.

She frowned. "I knew there was a reason for not moving to California."

Jerry pulled her hands over and kissed them. She knew he'd grown up in California, too. "Piece of cake. Just like riding a boat."

"I hate boats," she pouted.

He tried another tack. Rita preferred restaurants, not home cooking, so he wondered how she knew about..."*caciocavallo?*"

She raised a corner of her mouth and lowered her voice. "Last time, remember?"

"No."

"Rosa told me. It's a cheese made locally from sheep's milk. She uses it a lot."

"Your secret is safe with me," he whispered back.

"Do your best."

Better. Jerry tried the clam soup. "Wow. This sure beats peanut butter sandwiches at ten thousand feet." Jerry had been flying constantly since last November.

She tried hers and nodded in agreement. "Amazing." She looked down.

"What is it?" He was getting used to her moods.

"I have news."

"Me, too."

"Oh?" A smile.

"You first."

"Maybe you, since..."

"Ladies first." With a wink, Jerry lifted his glass, drank, and thumped it down.

"All right. I was with Doctor Hathaway today and—"

A shadow flicked over the table. "*Mi scusi*. Rita, is that you?"

They looked up into the face of a man with Tomaso proportions. But he was all muscle and bulk with none of Tomaso's fat. He was about two inches taller than Jerry, must have weighed 225 or so, and was in his late twenties or early thirties. His face was dominated by an enormous white grin that stretched from Catania to North Africa. Over that were azure-blue eyes, thick eyebrows, and well-tended, nearly shoulder-length hair.

Rita squealed and jumped into his massive arms. "Michelangelo!"

Jerry sat back while his wife and whoever it was exchanged cheek-pecks and exaggerated hugs.

At length, Rita said, "Michael, please say hello to my husband, Jerry Ingram. Jerry, this is Michelangelo Rugani."

"Husband," Rugani boomed. "Congratulations. You've made quite a catch."

"Thanks." They shook hands.

Rita said, "I haven't seen you since...Innsbruck?"

It hit Jerry. He'd seen this man on TV blasting down the slopes of Innsbruck in the 1964 men's slalom championship, during Jerry's junior year at the Naval Academy. Michelangelo Rugani was the darling of the Italian press. But although powerful and athletic and daring, he was known as a party boy who often got drunk on nights before his races. Nevertheless, he would take off and thunder down the hill with everyone cheering and cameras grinding. Twice, he was near a world's record when he lost control and blasted into the fence in a white miasma of snow, pine needles, and often, onlookers' arms and legs. Each time he emerged waving and smiling as they carried him down the hill on a stretcher.

"Yes...Innsbruck, my sweet."

The Winter Olympics were due to start next month in Grenoble. Jerry asked. "And you are going to try it again?"

Rita waved at hand at Tomaso. "Please, a chair for our friend."

Ugo was there instantly sliding a chair behind Rugani. "Oh, I'm not so sure, Rita. I don't want to interrupt your meal."

"Please," she said. "Besides, the place is full."

Jerry looked around. She was right. He was stuck with Rugani.

"Well, thank you." Rugani sat and looked to Tommaso hovering close. "You still have the *farsumagru,* my friend?"

"*Si. Il meglio.*" The very best. Tomaso looked to Jerry and Rita. They both nodded with vigor.

Rugani snapped his fingers and grinned. "Then please bring it."

"*Subito.*" Tomaso bowed, then hustled off leaving Jerry wondering why he hadn't seen Tomaso bow to anybody else in the few months he'd been here.

Rugani looked over at Jerry. "Yes, I am most fortunate at my age. I couldn't have told you this a week ago but I just qualified for the men's ski team. Once again," he kissed the tips of his fingers, "...the world must suffer the trials and tribulations of Michelangelo Rugani."

"I can't wait," said Rita.

"You two should come. I can get you tickets."

She glanced at Jerry.

Jerry shrugged, "Maybe, when I'm not flying.'"

"You fly? You're at Sigonella?"

"Yep."

"What do you do?"

"Chase Communist submarines."

"Keeping us safe from Ivan?"

"I hope so."

A squall had drifted in, and light rain dotted the streets when they walked outside. For some reason the January air seemed warm as they snuggled under her umbrella. Just outside Café Sebastiano stood a proud Mercedes-Benz 300 SL with the signature gull-winged doors. Raindrops beaded the Benz' silver finish: the German national racing color. A wide, black stripe ran down the middle from end to end, the number 26 prominent on the hood. A stocky, dark-haired man wearing a leather jacket and roadster cap stood under an awning nearby. His arms were crossed and his feet were planted wide apart. One look told Jerry the man knew how to take care of himself. And others too. He was obviously a guard hired by Rugani.

Feeling expansive toward the end of their meal, Jerry had bought two bottles of Nero d'Avola, "for special occasions," he said with a wink.

Now, he sniffed at the rain as they headed across the square. "He does like to travel fast, doesn't he?"

"Jealous?"

"Quite the opposite."

"Meaning?" she taunted.

"I'm in something much faster."

She laughed. Then she asked, "So, how was she?" Rugani's girlfriend, Margarita, had shown up thirty minutes after he did. Waiting for her dinner order to be put through meant an extended meal, which meant a lot of wine-fueled talk. If it looked as if Jerry understood too much, then their exchange became liberally sprinkled with a dialect with the complexity of quantum physics. It also meant dancing, with Rugani swooping off with Rita while Jerry was stuck with Margarita, a short, boxy, brunette with gaudy eye makeup and gloppy lipstick. Jerry quickly judged Margarita's dancing suitable for the initiation rites to the International Jackhammer Association as she repeatedly trod across his shoes. Jerry suffered through two dances but learned toward the end of the second that Rugani was the son of Rudolpho Rugani, who owned Enzio Parfumes headquartered in Milan. Michelangelo, Margarita explained, with his skiing fame, had become the poster boy for his father's company. His gleaming white teeth appeared in tight head shots in glossy splendor for Enzio ads in magazines such as *Vogue*, *Lady's Home Journal*, and *Esquire*. In other words, the family was fabulously wealthy, and Michelangelo, whose tastes drifted from fast skiing to fast cars to fast women, didn't have to worry about crashing into fences on the downhill as long as he preserved those marvelous teeth for that perfect smile.

They were about to begin a third dance, a slow dance, when Jerry broke it off saying he had to rise early tomorrow for a full day of flying. Without too much trouble he was able to extricate himself and Rita.

"How was she?" Rita asked again as they walked in the rain.

"She" meant Margarita, and that meant trouble. He pulled her away from a large puddle and said, "Like plowing into Mount Etna." That was intended to amuse Rita.

Instead she asked, "She's a bit overweight, no?"

"Like a sumo wrestler."

"Oh. But—"

"I have a question."

"Umm."

"Are you happy?"

"What?"

"Happy with all this? The rain? Sicily? Me gone a lot? The Navy? Does all this bother you? Are you happy?"

She squeezed his arm. "Of course I'm happy, you fool. As long as you're here. It's the Navy way, remember? Whatever gave you that idea?"

"Just wanted to make sure." He bent down and kissed her cheek. Then he slapped her on the rump.

Rita squealed as they tromped through the entrance to their apartment. It had originally been a four-bedroom house; two upstairs, two down. But ten years ago it been converted to an apartment building. Mrs. Gastoldi, their landlord and the owner, sat in her accustomed spot in a small loveseat at the bottom of the stairs. A sole floor reading lamp illuminated her evening newspaper, its soft glow leaving the rest of the small lobby in gilded shadows. Overweight and with pulled-back graying hair, she arranged herself in regal prominence this time of night while Paulo, her husband, watched TV in the parlor.

Jerry straightened and cleared his throat. “Evening, Mrs. Gastoldi.”

She nodded, carefully eyeing the two bottles cradled in Jerry’s arms.

“*Ciao, Maria*,” said Rita.

With a slight smile, Mrs. Gastoldi said, “*Boone sera IL mBio piccolo tesoro*.”

Quietly, they mounted the stairs. At the top, Jerry whispered, “What the hell did she say?”

“I think it was ‘good evening, my little darling.’”

“Wow. How do you rate?”

“She enjoys good company during the day.”

Jerry muttered, “While I’m out there defending hearth and home.” He bent to insert the key. She leaned over beside him, her scent enveloping him.

“Yes?”

“I saw Dr. Hathaway today.”

“Oh, yeah. How’s it all going?” He stepped aside to let her pass. The room seemed cold; the fire had long ago gone out. He walked over and stooped to stoke it.

“I’m not pregnant.” She pulled off her scarf.

“Huh?” He rose.

She threw her arms around him. “He did some tests. I’m not pregnant after all. That’s what I’ve been trying to tell you all evening.”

“Oh.”

She gave a broad, gleaming smile—one he associated with the runway. “I’m sorry.”

“What happened?”

“He said it must have been a miscarriage of some kind. But he’s not sure. Apparently this happened before I started seeing him. You know, those dark weeks and months.”

Yes, those were terribly uncertain times as Jerry settled into the right seat of a P-3 while she looked high and low for a place to live and then to furnish. At first, they tried Navy housing at Sigonella, but that apparently wasn’t good enough. So, dipping into her savings, which were considerable, they came to Catania.

"You had some pain a few weeks ago."

"I think that was it."

"My God." He peeled off rain gear.

"You're not happy?"

"Me? What do they say here? *Che sarà, sarà*."

"You wanted this child?"

"I was good with it. But now he's gone and we're starting all over."

"Yes, we are. But in the meantime it means I can go back to work."

"New York?"

"If you don't mind."

Jerry ran a hand over his face. "Tired. Have to think about this. Too much after a long day." He shuffled off to their bedroom. Finding their tape recorder, he flipped the play switch. The soft tones of "Happy Together" drifted through the room.

"I love that song," she said, her voice subdued. She began humming with the Turtles.

"I know you do. Why do you think I turned it on?"

She chased after him and leapt on him piggy-back style. "I'm sorry, honey. We'll talk about it tomorrow." She locked her legs around him squeezing hard. Kissing him in the ear she said, "Okay?"

Jerry turned and eased her gently to the bed. "Well that's just it."

"Just what, honey?"

"It's what I wanted to tell you. They're shipping me off to school next week. Florida. I leave tomorrow."

"What?"

"It's just for a week or ten days."

"What on earth for? You've had plenty of school in the past six years."

"Now it's Classified Materials Control Center School."

"What on earth is that?"

"We learn to read disappearing ink." He flopped on the bed.

She rolled beside him. "You mean James Bond stuff? Spies and trenchcoats?"

He chuckled and pulled her close. “I wish. No, it’s classified publications. If somebody in my squadron loses a top-secret manual, then I go to jail.”

“You’re kidding.”

“That’s right. Especially when I become the classified materials control officer. And that’s in two weeks. So this is why I have to go to school.”

“I don’t understand.”

“Well, they send you to this school to learn how to put the blame on the guy that lost the manual and then *he* goes to jail.”

“Oh. Does this mean you won’t be flying?”

“It’s what they call collateral duty. I’ll still fly, but I have to do this also.”

“What if some spy steals all your books while you’re off flying?”

He brushed her chin with his thumb then kissed the tip of her nose. “Not a chance. It’s all locked up. And at CMCC School is where you learn to control it. Most junior officers get stuck with this job. Now it’s my turn to learn how to be mean to people. And then when some boot ensign or jay gee stumbles through the door, he’ll get stuck with the job.”

“Wonderful. When do you get back?”

“A week from Tuesday or Wednesday, depending on space availability.”

“This really is unfair.”

“I’m sorry. It’s the Navy way. Lots of surprises.”

13

DPRK *Seung Kwon,* SO-1 Class sub chaser
23 January 1968
39°12' N; 127°45' E
10 kilometers east of Wonsan Harbor, North Korea

Free of Wonsan Harbor, the sleek submarine chaser of the Democratic People's Republic of Korea revved to full power. Her three type 40D diesels pushed her close to her designed top speed of twenty-eight knots, leaving behind a foamy white wake over which hung a blue-gray plume of exhaust. Heading nearly due east out of Wonsan Naval Base, the slate-gray ocean heaved easily beneath the *Seung Kwon* with long, slow groundswells.

Jagged snow-capped peaks dominated the western horizon behind Wonsan Harbor under a misty sky, but thankfully there was no wind this morning. Even so, the temperature was down to a bitter -6° Celsius as the sun tried its utmost to burn through the thin, high overcast.

The Russian-built SO-1-class sub chasers were forty-two meters long but had a narrow beam of just six meters, making them prone to rolling in the slightest of seaways. They were downright hazardous when the weather kicked up. Luckily the sea was calm and the skies didn't look threatening. Yesterday, a strong wind had made the top-heavy vodka burner roll heavily. Sailors puked all over the place.

Her armament consisted of a .57-mm dual-purpose bow-mounted canon, two 37-mm antiaircraft guns amidships, and four 14.5-caliber machine guns in the waist and on the fantail. Today's crew consisted of nine officers and thirty-five ratings, not counting the squad of fifteen special assault troops huddled on the fantail.

Another SO-1-class sub chaser, the *Myung Jeong*, was late getting underway from Wonsan because of a blown head gasket. She had just pushed off from her berth and was on her way out to join the *Seung Kwon*. Both were "gifts" from the Russians, who were glad to get rid of them. Not only obsolete, the sub chasers were maintenance nightmares; "blown head gaskets...continual," was just one of many problems..

Captain Second Rank Vladislav Yusopov lit up another one of his American Marlboros and rechecked the plot. Their target was fifteen kilometers before them, well into international waters, laying to, apparently drifting.

International waters or not, they had decided to do this anyway and had worked out a plan. Besides the two sub chasers assigned to the mission they had added more muscle in the form of six P6-class torpedo boats now paralleling the *Seung Kwon*'s course; three of them six kilometers to the north, another three to the south. The slender, twenty-five-meter-long PT boats could do forty-two knots. Today, each vessel carried a squad of soldiers who were well prepped for the assault. Altogether, the flotilla's combined assault troops consisted of eighty-four men armed with AK-47 rifles with extra rounds, hand grenades, plastique explosives, bayonets, and pistols. Each man was well trained and knew how to use his weapons.

Huddled in his parka, Yusopov trained his binoculars on the American ship and ran his eyes over her once again. Although he could barely see her fantail, he visualized her well deck, which contained what Dzerzhinsky Square, KGB headquarters in Moscow, wanted. It was in a large space built over the cargo hold, perhaps twenty meters square, that housed all the top-secret radio and cryptographic equipment a Soviet intelligence officer could ever dream of. And all for the asking at twenty-two tempting kilometers off the coast of North Korea. But they had to catch her within 19.3 kilometers of the North Korean coast, the equivalent of the twelve-mile limit. And right now, as Yusopov looked into the hooded radar repeater, the American was still headed in that direction. *Getting closer...*

Seated in the chair reserved for the ship's commanding officer was Colonel Bogdan A. Jelavich. By tradition, the captain's chair belonged to *Seung Kwon*'s CO, not the GRU colonel who sulked there now. But the captain said nothing because so much was going on as they charged toward their target, now in plain sight. Wearing a parka with its hood drawn over his garrison cap, Jelavich smoked a particularly foul brand of Egyptian cigarettes.

"How far?" demanded Jelavich.

"Twenty-two kilometers."

Jelavich sat up. "Really? Why didn't you let me know?"

"Sorry, Colonel. This plot has a lot of sea return. I couldn't tell until just now."

"Sea return?" He waved a hand at the flat ocean. "On a day like this?"

Yusopov stepped close and dropped his voice, "That's what happened... shitty radar."

"Oh." Jelavich put aside his cup of tea. He rose to his feet and said, "So you think this could be it?"

"Maybe," said Yusopov. So far the American ship had come no closer than twenty-five kilometers. Now, it looked like she was about to stumble into their laps. He ran over the plot. The target was still drifting and slowly closing the coast with the current.

At this speed they would soon fall on their prey. In the meantime, Yusopov enjoyed his American cigarette while others nearby in the crowded pilothouse squirmed and fidgeted. The top-quality Marlboros were not strong and brackish like Russian cigarettes. He had acquired them through "extemporaneous means," otherwise known as the black market. The trouble with smoking Marlboros was that others would sniff at his smoke with obvious pleasure. Then the bumming would begin. But he'd figured a way to stop that. On various occasions he would load his Marlboro box with five or so coarse Egyptian cigarettes that looked exactly like Marlboros.

But they tasted horrible. Immediately after lighting up, the unfortunate borrower would be overcome by a fit of spasmodic coughing and start gasping for breath, his face turning red. Yusopov was merciless. Senior officers received the same treatment as those of inferior rank. No exceptions. No more bummed cigarettes.

Yusopov considered himself lucky he'd never had to pull the cigarette trick on Jelavich. The colonel seemed content with his own Egyptian brand and, thankfully, kept to himself.

Language wasn't the only thing that separated Yusopov and his comrades from their North Korean hosts. A natural disdain for race and culture was present on both sides. Colonel Jelavich barely acknowledged the presence of the North Korean bridge watch, let alone Commander Dae Jung Lee, the CO, whom Jelavich outranked and whose chair he now occupied. It was an unwritten law of the sea that the captain's chair belonged to the captain, no matter his rank. He alone had the power of life and death over all who boarded his ship. Jelavich disregarded that and kept his lanky frame huddled in the captain's chair and grunted acknowledgments to Dae Jung Lee when required. Otherwise, he remained silent and smoked his damned Egyptian cigarettes.

Jelavich had a reputation, and Yusopov didn't want to fool with him, even though they ranked the same. In his late teens, Jelavich had run the mile relay for the Soviet Union in the 1952 Olympics, winning the silver medal. Cigarettes, Yusopov mused, were a strange habit for one so athletic to take up. Maybe it happened when Jelavich joined the exclusive Spetsnaz forces, going undercover, blowing up installations, killing political leaders, and even serving undercover in the United States for two years.

Where Jelavich had a solid reputation as a strong, no-nonsense, dedicated disciple of Lenin, Yusopov's reputation had gone sideways. First, he'd been kicked out of the Strategic Rocket Forces because of the debacle when he'd almost started World War III. Then it caught up with him again as a submarine engineering officer aboard the *K-12*, which had nearly sunk right in the middle of an American ASW hunter-killer group off Okinawa. An investigation subsequent to the accident revealed not only that the auxiliary seawater valve to the air conditioning system was frozen open, but a number of other valves were also frozen in the open position. Many of them were impossible to shut by hand due to electrolysis and decay. In essence, the *K-12* was a death trap. Any number of valves had failed or were ready to fail.

Yusopov and his shipmates were fortunate that Volkov had given his life when he swam down and closed a functioning gate valve. It was a miracle the valve turned at all. One fact that the investigators didn't report was that the maintenance logs were all falsified, with Yusopov signing off on procedures never performed.

But once again Yusopov's father, nearing the twilight of his career, was able to move political mountains. Drawing heavily on his friendship with Admiral Nicolay Nikolayevich Amelko, commander of the Pacific Fleet, the father had young Yusopov reassigned to the admiral's staff. But Amelko was no fool and kept the failed protégé on a short leash by handing him over to a special surface force command, where a number of senior officers watched over Yusopov and kept him out of everyone's way.

But now the GRU had received an emergency request from the KGB. The operation was slapped together in Vladivostok, and Yusopov was swept into it simply because no one else was available. With blurring speed, Yusopov found himself climbing into a Be-12 amphibian and flying to Wonsan Harbor, North Korea, where he immediately boarded the *Seung Kwon*.

Beside Jelavich was his assistant and interpreter for the day, GRU major Yuri Grechko, a thin, balding man with a large handlebar moustache and round, rimless glasses, who likewise smoked Jelavich's brand of cigarettes. Unlike Jelavich, he coughed and wheezed continually. Jelavich loved to yell at him, which made Grechko all the more nervous; his face would turn red and he would wheeze so horribly that at times he would gasp for breath. Nevertheless, Jelavich knew when to lay off. Grechko was key to the operation. Of the four Russians aboard, only Grechko knew how to speak Korean, and apparently he did it well because the Korean officers kept their distance and treated him with respect. The other Russian was Kapitan Leytenant Yevgenij Mullov, a tall, athletic intelligence expert who knew more about the goal of this mission than anyone else.

Standing on the other side of Jelavich, but keeping his silence, was DPRK Colonel San Ki Choi, a man of immense proportions and an equally immense complement of medals pinned to his tunic. There were so many, it seemed to Yusopov, that they clanked from the top of Colonel Ki Choi's throat to the bottom of his crotch. On occasion, sunlight caught the medals and bounced around the pilothouse, blinding whoever was in the way. The silence between Ki Choi and Jelavich was a clear indication that neither understood the other's language, nor did they care to. Major Yung Soo Lim, a timid DPRK interpreter, stood behind Ki Choi, and his reluctance to offer interpretations reinforced the silence. He also did double duty as tactical communicator with the *Myung Jeong* and the PT boats. Another DPRK officer was In Ho Park, a slim, athletic major wearing dark aviator's glasses. He shuffled in place and cracked his knuckles. *Wonderful*, thought Yusopov. Nobody could be more appropriate as the leader of today's boarding parties.

One of Yusopov's jobs was to make sure the Russians stayed out of sight and the Koreans followed their cues and did their jobs right.

And it would be soon. They were closing on their quarry. She was a stubby-looking converted cargo ship of the AK (light cargo) class operated by the U.S. Army toward the end of World War II and then turned over to the U.S. Navy in 1966. She was 54 meters in length and displaced 895 tons. With twin diesels and twin screws, she was rated at twelve knots top speed. *Jane's Fighting Ships* reported she was crewed by six officers and seventy enlisted. Her topsides were dark gray and the vertical surfaces were a light haze gray that looked as if they'd been painted out recently. A designator on her bow read GER 2. A few international code flags drooping from her halyards claimed she was engaged in oceanographic research. Oddly, she didn't fly her national ensign, the American flag. But certainly she looked in better shape than the group of old warriors about to pounce on her.

On patrol two nights ago, Yusopov had purposely passed close to look her over and make sure she was not heavily armed. She wasn't. Her armament was a paltry two .50-caliber machine guns; one forward, the other aft, both covered in heavy canvas stiff with the cold.

Once again Yusopov pressed his head against the hooded radar repeater. The American still drifted 24.6 kilometers off the Korean coast, well outside the 19.3-km limit. The target was still DIW: dead in the water, not under way, about three thousand meters closer to the coast. Definitely still in international waters, but who cared at this stage of the game? He had his orders and he intended to carry them out.

Just then, Commander Jung Lee edged alongside, and with raised eyebrows asked Yusopov for a look at the radar. He was two inches shorter than Yusopov but was built like an ice chest. His one brown eye and one green eye gave his face an odd and off-putting asymmetry.

With a grunt, Yusopov stepped away. Jung Lee hissed his appreciation and bent over to study the plot. Then he cranked the wandering cursor and said, "He still looks to be about twenty-five kilometers off the coast."

The man spoke passible Russian. Yusopov said, "Yes, but we're committed. Continue on, please."

Following closely for a look was Major Soo Lim, who stumbled about the pilothouse with two large volumes. One was a Korean-English dictionary, its pages constantly open and rattling back and forth. The other was a cumbersome copy of *Jane's Fighting Ships* which he deftly kept open with his left thumb.

They were almost upon the American. Yusopov checked his watch: 1143. "Time to go, Captain."

"Yes, I believe so." Jung Lee stepped to the pilothouse door and shouted aft to men on the signal platform, "Hoist 'inquire nationality.'"

Jung Lee called for five knots, and the *Seung Kwon* throttled back and settled in the American's wake. At the same time, her signalmen snapped the flaghoist to the yardarm and two-blocked it.

The American ship promptly responded with her national ensign.

The signalman called out, "She answers with the flag of the United States, Captain."

"Very well," said Jung Lee. It was difficult to see through the throng of men, mostly army officers up from the main deck to watch the happenings. On tiptoes he called across to Lieutenant Commander Chin Ho Jang, the ship's executive officer, standing on the starboard bridge wing, "Are action stations manned and ready?"

The reply drifted across the crowded bridge, "Yes, sir."

"Very well." Again, Jung Lee called aft to the signal bridge, "Hoist 'heave to or I will open fire.'"

Yusopov said, "Captain, he's already dead in the water."

"I want to make sure he doesn't do something irresponsible."

Yusopov's eye-roll earned a smirk from Jung Lee.

A group of signal flags snapped up the American's yardarm.

Jung Lee trained his glasses on it. "What is it?" he demanded.

The signalman laid on his binoculars and flipped pages in a thick book. At length he read: "I AM IN INTERNATIONAL WATERS. INTEND TO REMAIN IN THE AREA."

With binoculars Yusopov scanned the decks of the American ship. A signalman aft of the bridge puffed steam as he worked his flag bag. He wore a parka and white hat. Forward on the bridge wing was just one man. He stood alone beside the pilothouse hatch. Yusopov chuckled as he realized this must be the ship's captain. He wore a leather flight jacket against the cold, and on his head was a white beanie with a red ball. The American captain was studying him with binoculars as well. Yusopov was tempted to wave.

People were crowded in the American's pilothouse; perhaps a half dozen, but there was no one else topside. *Strange. They're hidden. Why?*

Jelavich called from inside the pilothouse. "Commander Yusopov, are we ready for Lutrov yet?" Soviet Air Force Captain Gennady Lutrov and his wingman had been orbiting fifteen hundred meters overhead in brand-new MiG 21 fighters painted in DPRK livery.

"Yes, of course."

"Then do it."

It dawned on Yusopov that he had become the on-scene commander by default.

"Right away, sir." Yusopov nodded to Ho Jang. "Call in Captain Lutrov. Tell him to fire over the American's bow.

"Yes, sir." Ho Jang grabbed a radio handset, keyed it, and relayed instructions.

A look aft told Yusopov the *Myong Jeong* had almost caught up. Things were happening fast. Again to Ho Jang, "Tell the *Myung Jeong* to take station on the American's port quarter." He checked with Jung Lee, who nodded his concurrence.

As Ho Jang began sending the order, the low whistle of jet aircraft ranged from directly behind. He whipped his head back to see the MiG 21s flying side-by side and low, about fifty feet off the deck.

And coming fast.

Bright flashes bloomed from under their wings. Rockets streaked overhead to explode harmlessly near the horizon. The MiGs blasted over the top on afterburner, leaving a world of thunderous noise as they pulled up and rose quickly back to fifteen hundred meters.

Jung Lee shook his head in disgust. Laughter ranged from Jelavich and Sang Ki Choi inside the pilot house.

"Send them away," ordered Yusopov.

Ho Jang keyed his mic and the MiG 21s began orbiting, their engines barely a whisper.

Four of the PTs swooped in and took station circling the American ship. About the same time Yusopov spotted a belch of black exhaust from the American's stack. "She's getting under way."

Everyone in the pilothouse stood open-mouthed watching the American ship work herself up to a pitiful ten knots. Even Colonel Ki Choi and Colonel Jelavich seemed transfixed, awaiting the next development.

Yusopov called over to Ho Jang. "Lieutenant?"

Ho Jang gaped with the rest.

Jung Lee barked from the port bridge wing, "Lieutenant!"

"Sir?"

Jung Lee growled, "Lieutenant, damn it, pay attention."

"Yes, sir."

Yusopov said patiently, "Lieutenant, please call in the *P 14* to make our starboard side in order to offload our men."

"Yes, sir."

Yusopov added, "And tell all PTs to move close and hinder the American's movement toward the open ocean. Remind them we want him to reverse course.

Ho Jang spoke so fast Yusopov could hardly distinguish syllables.

Mullov looked up to Yusopov. "Twenty-one point five kilometers now, sir."

Two kilometers to go. *Maybe.*

"Her name is *Pueblo*," added Mullov, stepping away from the radar repeater.

"What?" demanded Yusopov.

Jelavich threw a fierce glance.

Mullov looked Jelavich in the eye. "Operation order 41-B, annex 22.3.5, sir."

Yusopov tried the words carefully. "*Pueblo*. That's in New Mexico isn't it?"

"Colorado, sir," said Mullov.

That earned a *you are insubordinate* glance from Jelavich.

Mullov repeated firmly, "Colorado, sir."

Jung Lee said, "He's speeding up. Could lose him."

"What?" Jelavich made to push him aside.

Jung Lee said, "New course, one-zero-zero, heading directly away from the coast."

"Shit!" said Jelavich. He sat heavily in the captain's chair. "We're losing him." He looked up to Yusopov. "Signal all units to form on us. We'll escort them out to sea." He gave a wry smile. "Maybe bump him once or twice."

Jung Lee looked at Yusopov and rolled his oddly colored eyes.

Mullov also looked at Yusopov, almost pleading.

Yusopov understood. It bothered him, too. "We have a job to do, Colonel."

"What?" demanded Jelavich.

Yusopov pointed at the *Pueblo*. He raised his voice, "We have a job to do. Kapitan Leytenant Mullov said it himself. We're here in accordance with operation order 41-B. Now we have a perfect chance."

"But he's in international waters," protested Jelavich.

"Who gives a damn about that? We need the equipment aboard that ship. Now is our best chance. We won't have another opportunity as good as this. Otherwise, he'll run and call in help from his friends."

Quiet descended. Yusopov looked out the port to see the American spy ship gaining headway. Within minutes she would be too far out to sea.

Jung Lee jammed his hands on his hips. "Colonel, I agree. If you want this ship, you won't have a better chance than now."

Jelavich licked his lips and then gulped tea. He fumbled for one of his cigarettes but couldn't get it going.

Yusopov whipped out a lighter and flicked it on. "Colonel?"

Jelavich got the cigarette lighted and took a deep drag. He blew thick, dark smoke and then nodded. Quietly, he said, "Very well. Do it." He pointed a finger at Yusopov. "But you'll be the one to answer to Moscow."

Yusopov muttered, "I've been answering to Moscow all my life." He barked to Jung Lee. "All right, Commander, pull alongside that ship and," he pointed to Mullov, "get into your gear and order them to lie to." Again to Jung

Lee, he said, "Captain, please call your other units in to swarm around and box her in."

"Right away."

"So, first we must get them to reverse course. Take us alongside, please."

"Exactly." Commander Jung Lee stepped over to his communicator and gave a rapid string of orders. Then he called orders to the helmsman and lee helmsman who swung the rudder and rang the engine-room annunciators. Then he called aft to his signalmen, who started running up signal flags. Smoke pouring from her funnel, the *Seung Kwon* lunged ahead and within minutes had passed the *Pueblo.* She leaned into a broad turn to port and soon had circled around the *Pueblo*'s stern. Then Jung Lee slowed her to take position on the American's starboard side. Distance: thirty meters. Both ships were doing ten knots, the water between them churning white and foamy.

Jung Lee walked out on the port bridge wing. Several of his officers and crew grouped around as he steered in a little–closing the gap to about twenty meters.

Mullov donned a North Korean Army officer's topcoat and hat. With his sunglasses it was impossible to tell that he was not Asian. He had a large megaphone under his arm.

Yusopov urged, "Time for your spot in the sun. Go!"

"Yessir." Mullov stepped onto the bridge and worked his way through the crowd.

Still in the pilothouse, Yusopov stood on tiptoes to peek at the man on *Pueblo*'s starboard bridge-wing. Alone, he stood, as nonchalant as if he were on a Sunday cruise; He wore no beanie now, and his flight jacket was zipped halfway down, his arm resting casually on the bulwark. With his hair blowing in the breeze, he sipped from a mug—rich American coffee, Yusopov supposed. Clearly some sort of rank gleamed from his collar tabs. There were still several men huddled in the pilothouse, peering out.

PT 11 and *PT 14* roared in to take station on the port side; *PT 15* took station on *Seung Kwon*'s starboard side with *PT 21* ahead off their starboard bow. He barked at Commander Jung Lee. "Where is *PT 17*?"

Jung Lee pointed. "Engine trouble. She's down to one engine. I sent her back."

Indeed, Yusopov saw the hulking silhouette of *PT 17* under a plume of diesel exhaust about three kilometers off their port quarter, limping back to Wonsan.

No matter. Off to the north, he saw the bow wave of the *Myung Jeong* slicing toward them. With or without the *PT 17*, they still had plenty of firepower.

"Mullov!" Yusopov yelled. "Do it!"

"Yes, sir." With a quick glance toward a scowling Jelavich, Mullov edged all the way outboard. He raised the megaphone at the American ship and bellowed in English, "Heave to. I intend to board you."

The man on the *Pueblo* shrugged and pointed to a new set of flags that had been run up a yardarm. The man grinned.

The signal man called forward, "He says, 'WE'RE CLEARING THE AREA.'"

Mullov repeated it.

"I can see that, you dolt," said Yusopov. He turned to Jung Lee. "Please tell units 11 and 14 to clear the port side. I intend to open fire."

"What?" from Jelavich in the pilothouse.

Jung Lee gave a thin smile and relayed the order to his communicator. Soon the two PT boats on the *Pueblo*'s port side roared away, leaving behind a great plume of exhaust.

Yusopov said, "Tell them our intentions."

Mullov gulped, raised his megaphone, and called over, "Heave to or I will open fire."

For emphasis Jung Lee had the 57 millimeter swung to port and aimed at the *Pueblo*.

The man on the bridge shrugged, pointed up to the flag, and yelled, "International waters."

"What?" said Yusopov.

Mullov shoved aside the group of DPRK sailors crowding around him and said, "International waters. He says he's in International waters."

"Nonsense," said Yusopov. He turned to Jung Lee. "Open fire, please, Captain. Five rounds from your forward mount."

14

Seung Kwon, SO-1-Class Sub chaser
23 January 1968
39°17'51" N; 127°52'41" E
21.5 kilometers (13.3 miles) east of Wonsan Harbor, North Korea

Commander Jung Lee stood on tiptoes looking for Jelavich. This was getting intense, and he wanted concurrence. There! He spotted the GRU colonel still inside the pilothouse, still in the captain's chair. He looked straight ahead, smoking yet another Egyptian cigarette, aloof and seemingly unconcerned.

"Colonel?" Jung Lee shouted.

From the bridge wing, Yusopov watched Jung Lee with disgust. Previously energized, he was now covering his ass.

But Jelavich must have gestured in the affirmative because Jung Lee yelled, "Mount one open fire. Five rounds."

The forward 57-millimeter gun mount barked. The first round hit the *Pueblo*'s foredeck, shredding the starboard anchor windlass. Two rounds went into the communications hut; another hit just aft of the bridge in the quartermaster's chartroom. The last round passed harmlessly through the aft deck and out the other side.

The *Pueblo* swerved right. She headed toward them. Everybody yelled as the gap closed.

Yusopov shouted, "He's trying to ram!"

Desperately, Jung Lee shoved people aside to get to his wide-eyed helmsman. Through all the noise, he got his point across. The helmsman swung the rudder. The *Seung Kwon*'s fantail swung away from the *Pueblo*'s blunt bow and she charged ahead out of danger.

But men kept yelling on the bridge and jostling one another. It was hard to hear.

Yusopov shouted, "Quiet!" It was in Russian, but the Koreans must have understood, for they backed away, allowing Jung Lee back onto the port bridge wing.

Yusopov stepped alongside, finding the *Pueblo* now off his port quarter. He yelled, "Get back on him, Captain!"

Jung Lee nodded dumbly as those about him pushed and shoved.

"And get rid of all these idiots up here," said Yusopov.

Jung Lee hesitated and gave Yusopov a dark look then called to Lieutenant Chin, his executive officer, and told him to get nonessential people off the bridge.

Soon people, mostly army officers, began shuffling down the ladders.

By now the *Pueblo* had shifted her rudder and was steaming directly away. Also, she had gained a bit of speed. "Shoot the son-of-a-bitch," Yusopov shouted.

They pulled alongside the *Pueblo.* It was apparent the captain felt he was no longer on a lark. He looked deadly serious as his ship pulled away and turned sharply north, perpendicular to their course. At the same time smoke began pouring from the communications hut and from an incinerator on the deck behind the bridge. A sailor was shoving in papers while stoking the fire with a shovel.

"Why the hell aren't they shooting back?" yelled Jelavich.

"All they have are two .50-caliber popguns and they're covered by frozen tarps." Yusopov had seen the weapons when they first closed the *Pueblo.* No one aboard her had made a move to unlimber the machine guns. He called to Jung Lee. "Please pull back alongside, Captain. We should fire more rounds into her."

Jung Lee nodded. He pointed to the stack billowing smoke." Must be wound up to full speed."

The smoke pouring from the communications room porthole grew darker and thicker. Valuable material was being burned. With a sense of urgency Yusopov called, "Hurry," to Jung Lee. "Keep shooting."

"All right."

The forward mount cracked out two more rounds as Jung Lee brought the *Seung Kwon* onto the *Pueblo*'s starboard quarter. At the same time *PT 11* and *PT 14* took station on the Pueblo's port side while *PT 21* slid into place just off her starboard bow. *PT 15* bobbed up and down in her wake.

Yusopov stepped over to Jung Lee and said quietly, "We have to make him turn around before he gets too far off the coast. I suggest we have *PT 11* and *PT 21* open fire now. Immediately." He moved around and stared Jung Lee in the eye.

Jung Lee blinked, then relayed the order to Ho Jang, who put it on the radio-telephone.

Almost immediately, the two torpedo boats began firing their .25-millimeter cannons. A gray-blue plume of cordite drifted above the ships as they blasted away, their bullets punching and ricocheting throughout the Navy ship. After thirty seconds Jung Lee chopped his hand. Ho Jang called the order, and the machine-gunning stopped, leaving an eerie silence.

Yusopov nudged Jung Lee. "Now, let the 14 boat and the *Myung Jeong* have a crack.

"Good idea." Jung Lee gave the orders. *PT 11* and *PT 21* stood off as the *Myung Jeong* and *PT 14* slithered in and began firing. Yusopov shouted over the din, "Make sure they hose down her bridge."

This time the two ships blasted away for a full sixty seconds. Metal chunks whizzed away from the ship. *PT 14* began shooting at the waterline.

"Tell those fools to stop!" yelled Yusopov. "We need to bring her to port, not sink her."

The order was given and the ship's fire was directed toward the bridge and pilothouse. Through the pilothouse hatch Yusopov saw men lying on the deck as the shells blasted through. Occasionally, one or two of them would spasm off the deck and then go fetal. Yusopov thought he heard a scream or two.

A man ran from the communications hut, his arms loaded with journals and loose papers. Yusopov pointed as the man ran for the side.

Jung Lee growled and Ho Jang started talking. But the gun crews on *PT 14* anticipated them and opened fire on the man. Bullets bounced and ricocheted all round him as he emptied his load over the side. With machinegun fire stitching the bulkheads around him, the man slipped and fell. Miraculously, he got up, and ran through an open hatch. Instantly, it was slammed shut behind him.

Jelavich yelled from the pilothouse, "What the hell, Vladislav? He's still under way."

Yusopov gripped the bulwark and cursed under his breath.

Dark smoke poured from the American's stack and a little wave peeled off her bow. *Yes, any fool can see he's underway. What do I do?*

More smoke gushed from the incinerator behind the stack. The *Pueblo* had worked up to her top speed of twelve knots or so. "I know. I know," Yusopov shouted back. He turned to Jung Lee. "We have to make them stop. Have the 14 boat unmask a torpedo tube and point right at them."

Jung Lee nodded and gave the order. The *PT 21* lunged forward and pulled away about three hundred meters. Then she slowed and turned toward the *Pueblo*, her forward port torpedo tube unmasked and ready to fire.

Still the *Pueblo* plodded on, now about thirty-six kilometers off the coast. Yusopov drummed his fingers. One thing left to do. "What do you think? How about hitting the *Pueblo* with a giant fusillade from all ships lined up on the starboard side?"

Jung Lee's eyebrows were up, anticipating the order.

"Whoa!" shouted Ho Jang.

"What the hell?" Jelavich stomped from the pilothouse, his massive hands grasping the bridge bulwarks.

Black smoke no longer poured from the American's stack. She was slowing; slowing. Soon she was dead in the water. From time to time they saw men flit back and forth throwing things over the side—journals, books, manuals, an occasional piece of equipment. One man stood at the incinerator stoking the fire, shoving in papers. Smoke billowed from the communications hut and up from below. But *the Pueblo* still looked intact and serviceable in spite of the beating she'd taken.

Jung Lee said, "Should we hoist FOLLOW ME?"

Yusopov's heart skipped a beat. "Yes, yes, by all means. But instead, let's have the *Myung Jeong* take station in front of her and send up the FOLLOW ME hoist. Let's see what the *Pueblo* does."

The *Myung Jeong* pulled one hundred meters in front of the *Pueblo* and raised her FOLLOW ME flaghoist. Long minutes dragged as the U.S. Navy ship worked up to five knots. The *Myung Jeong* tried to curve away and head back to land, but the *Pueblo* still headed out to sea.

Yusopov didn't hesitate. "He's stalling. Hit him with machine-gun fire."

Having not yet fired a round, the machine-gunners on *Seung Kwon* were happy to oblige. They poured a ten-second burst into the *Pueblo*'s bridge then, upon orders, ceased firing.

"Come on," urged Yusopov.

"Vladislav," Jelavich said dryly. "We can't sit out here twiddling all day. Do something."

Jung Lee shrugged.

Open fire, Yusopov decided. *Really pour it to them in sustained bursts.*

Just then the *Pueblo*'s bow began swinging, slowly, ponderously. Two minutes later she sat squarely in the *Myung Jeong*'s wake, plodding along at five knots heading directly for Wonsan.

Jelavich stepped alongside Yusopov. He lit one of his nasty Russian cigarettes, exhaled, and said, "Amazing. I'm beginning to believe Christmas is real."

"Let's hope."

"If you pull this off, Vladislav, you'll be Father Christmas."

"Almost there," said Yusopov.

"When do we board?"

"At 19.3 kilometers."

"No sooner, no later?"

Yusopov gave his first smile of the day. “We are obliged to adhere to the twelve-mile limit.”

“How soon?”

“Ummm. Half an hour maybe.”

But all the while, thick gray smoke continued to belch from the *Pueblo’s* incinerator, the operations hut, and from below decks.

Jelavich said, “I think that’s not practical, Comrade. Important material is being destroyed.”

Yusopov nodded in agreement. “I think that’s right.”

“Well?”

This from a man who just minutes ago was ready to pin all the blame on him. “Yes, all right.” Yusopov said to Jung Lee, “Order *PT 14* alongside to pick up Kapitan Leytenant Mullov and then proceed to board the *Pueblo*.”

Jung Lee, normally quiet and reserved, hesitated for just a moment. Others overhearing Yusopov did as well, realizing the moment was upon them. They were going to actually board a U.S. Navy ship and take her as a prize. “I…all right,” he said.

Yusopov turned to Mullov, now fully clad in a DPRK Army major’s uniform. He clapped both hands on his shoulders. “Yevgeniy, you know what to look for?”

“Yes, sir.”

“You know where it is?”

“Yes, sir.”

“Don’t get killed over there, and kill anyone who gets in your way.”

“Yes, sir.”

“Got your unit?”

Mullov pulled a field radio from the inside of his coat.

“Batteries charged?”

“Yes, sir.”

“Good. Any questions?”

“No, sir…uh, just one question, sir.”

Jelavich stepped alongside to listen as the *PT 14* bumped alongside, her engines rumbling. Men shouted up, urging them to hurry.

Yusopov thought he’d done a thorough job briefing Mullov. “What is it, damn it?”

"Can I keep all the Marlboros I find?"

Jelavich groaned. Yusopov spun Mullov and slapped him on the rump. "Go, before we turn you over to the Koreans."

As Mullov headed down the ladder Yusopov said to Jung Lee, "Might as well send them all in."

"I agree," said Jung Lee. Soon Ho Jang was on his radio-telephone ordering the boarding.

Mullov jumped safely to the *PT 14* and the patrol boat roared from the *Seung Kwon*'s starboard side and swung back under her stern. Fifteen seconds later she was alongside the U.S. Navy ship where her DPRK troops quickly jumped aboard. Immediately, they began ripping open hatches and pulling men on deck. Through binoculars Yusopov saw Mullov board last and head for the communications shack.

One after another, *PT 21*, *PT 11*, and *PT 15* rumbled alongside and deposited their assault troops.

Jung Lee closed to within thirty meters, where they heard shouts and saw DPRK troops pull American Sailors on deck and shove them to their knees. Those who resisted were beaten and clubbed with rifle butts. Soon their hands were tied and they were shoved out of the way against the starboard bulwark.

Men pushed and shoved on the main deck. The American captain was among them, trying to push back. A DPRK sergeant stood before him and whacked him on the side of his head with a pistol. Another soldier smashed a fist into the man's back. But he didn't go down. In obvious pain, he looked up at the DPRK sergeant and shouted at him.

A brave but stupid soul, thought Yusopov.

"Pay attention, damn it."

"What?"

"Your field radio," yelled Jelavich. "It's Mullov."

Yusopov yanked out his own field radio. Looking forward, he saw Mullov standing outside the communications hut, leaning against the starboard bulwark and waving his arms. He keyed the field radio. "Yes, go ahead."

"It's here!" shouted Mullov. His voice was shrill.

"The KW-37?"

"... great shape. They'd destroyed some equipment but hadn't gotten to this one yet."

Jelavich clapped Yusopov on the back.

"Wonderful, Yevgeniy, wonderful."

"Just one thing, though."

Yusopov's heart sank. Bad news always followed good. "What?"

"No Marlboros. I only found half a pack of Lucky Strikes."

15

23 January 1968
Bachelor Officer's Quarters
Naval Air Station
Jacksonville, Florida

Shouts. Engines roared. Gears clanked. Boots thumped.

Jerry woke to the commotion. A dull red glow crept through the blinds to his first-floor room. He leaned over and checked his watch: nearly 0530. He sat up and parted the blinds. Three trucks and a car were parked outside, a red warning light spinning on the car's roof. SPs were setting up traffic cones from the entrance all the way down to the main gate about four hundred yards away.

Something rustled at his door.

"What the hell?"

He looked over to see an envelope had been slipped beneath.

He yawned, not feeling tired. He'd gone to bed early last night so he could get up and read two more chapters before class started at 0830. And then there was a test at 1000, and he didn't want to foul that up. He wanted to do well in this boring Classified Materials Control course. He wasn't sure why, but over the past few weeks a little voice had started whispering to him, *Come on Jerry, it's time to stop screwing around and do things right.*

He looked down at the envelope. Most likely a mess bill or some stupid assessment.

A troop carrier pulled up outside. Three Marines jumped out. One was an officer. They carried rifles. They looked serious.

Jeez. Time to read. He snapped on the light and picked up his book on destruction of classified publications. Very dry and boring. But he was determined to learn all this nonsense in spite of his instructor, Lieutenant Rutka, a bald man with a colorless personality and an endless case of the sniffles. Rutka knew his stuff, though, and had a passion for it. He would look from side to side, talking *sotto voce* as if he'd just spotted a Communist hiding in the supply cabinet, "nine copies of the destruction record must be countersigned at the burn location and immediately forwarded to..." How could anybody remember all that?

His eye flicked to the envelope at the door. He sighed, threw aside the covers, and walked over. *Damn!* It was a telegram from Vice Adm. Alton C. Ingram in Honolulu. He tore open the envelope:

DEAR SON

WE LOVE YOU VERY MUCH. BUT NOW IS THE TIME FOR US TO GO BACK TO WORK AND EARN OUR PAY. YOU'LL FIND OUT SOON ENOUGH. GODSPEED. MOM SENDS HER LOVE AND WARMEST AFFECTION.

DAD

What? Somehow, Jerry knew this telegram and those Marines running around outside were connected. He walked over to the TV and flipped it on. While it warmed up, the telephone rang.

Shave. Quick breakfast. Run for the classroom and turn in his books and papers to a morose Rutka, who methodically checked everything off. Then back to his room to pack. After that, orders were delivered and he was off to catch an SNB, crowded with six other fliers, for the Atlanta Municipal Airport where they boarded separate planes. Jerry checked his watch: 1115. Unbelievable. Just six hours after he'd awakened he was aboard a Pan Am 707, Flight 416, to Rome. From there he was to board any military aircraft for Sigonella Naval Station and return to his squadron. There was no time to call anyone. No time to send telegrams. Just go.

On the way through the Atlanta Airport he got a better idea of what was happening. Televisions blared with the news that the North Koreans had brazenly captured a lightly armed Navy intelligence ship, the USS *Pueblo*, off the coast of North Korea. She was steaming peacefully in international waters, but the North Koreans had taken the *Pueblo* and her American crew into Wonsan and were holding them captive for "crimes against the Democratic People's Republic of Korea."

President Johnson was meeting with the National Security Council and then his military chiefs. An announcement would be forthcoming shortly. In the meantime, the nation was going to high alert, which included returning all active-duty military personnel to their stations.

Dad must have been really worried to send that telegram. Vice Adm. Alton C. Ingram sat at the right hand of CINCPAC. Therefore, he must know the whole skinny, and it must have looked gloomy when he composed that telegram. It was the sort of thing he just didn't do. As if he never expected to see his son again. *My God.*

It felt unusual to be in uniform. Many around him at the airport were also in uniform. He heard more than a few passengers arguing with ticket agents about being bumped off a flight to make room for a gunner's mate third class, a seaman deuce, or a Marine corporal. And there were plenty of men in uniform on the plane this morning. All heading for duty stations.

North Korea? What the hell is going on? We can squash those people in the blink of an eye. How can they be so stupid?

Jerry undid his tie and settled back in an aisle seat. The flight was smooth and sandwiches were soon served to catch up with the time zones. Then they put on a first-run movie, *Cool Hand Luke.* Jerry liked Paul Newman, but his mind kept drifting back to his father's telegram. Midway through the movie he fell asleep.

They landed in a rainstorm and taxied to one of the innumerable terminals at Fiumicino Airport. He was one of the last to jostle down the aisle and out the front hatchway. Rain pounded on the top of the 707 as he stepped into the jetway. Then two things kicked in. At the door, the stewardess took his hand and said, "Goodbye, flyboy. Thank you for flying Pan American. And Godspeed."

He looked down at her and held her hand. She wasn't smiling. Just concerned. He went to say "thanks" but was interrupted before he got it out. "Thanks for the nice flight, honey." A gravel-voiced Marine major stood just behind him. He had two rows of campaign ribbons and also wore pilot's wings. He looked Jerry in the eye. *A man in a hurry.*

She flashed a quick smile to Jerry and said, "And best of luck to you, too, Major. We're glad you were with us."

People behind pressed. Jerry was off the 707 and into a crowded terminal. He had no idea how to find a military flight to Sigonella. He scanned status boards then looked up to the gate signs. Everything was in Italian and he had no idea what he was supposed to—

A tap on his shoulder. A Navy ensign built like an NFL linebacker stood next to him. He was wearing an SP armband. "Where you headed, Lieutenant?"

"Sigonella."

"You have orders?"

Jerry tapped his breast pocket and nodded. "The ink is still wet."

The linebacker didn't smile. He pointed to a barely visible overhead gateway sign lost in a jumble of other gateway signs about fifty feet away. "Turn left there and head down to terminal 15. Go out to gate 6B. A plane leaves in twenty minutes. You'll just make it."

"Have to pick up my luggage."

The ensign waved a hand in the air. A third-class yeoman dashed up, out of breath. "How you doing, Johnson?"

Johnson whipped off his Dixie-cup hat and braced his hands on his knees, taking deep breaths.

"Atta boy, Johnson. You up for one last trip to gate 6B?"

Johnson stood and rearranged his white hat over a red crewcut. "Use to run track in high school, Mr. Browning."

Ensign Browning turned to Jerry. "You have a luggage tag, sir?"

Jerry handed it to Johnson. "Thanks."

"Go!" said Browning.

The kid disappeared into the crowd at a dead run.

It was twilight when they landed in a bucking thunderstorm. Jerry phoned the squadron OOD at Sigonella and was told to go home, get some solid shut-eye, and return tomorrow at 0800 for extended operations.

Good enough. He was exhausted. But he still looked forward to the prospect of surprising Rita. Maybe some wine, a little dinner, a hop in the sack. Or would the dinner come last? He mulled over the possibilities as the Navy bus rolled into town, jouncing over potholes. Thunder and lightning crackled about. He was the third to get off and had to walk across the square, B-4 bag in hand.

What?

Before his apartment building stood a silver Mercedes-Benz 300 SL, the number 26 on the hood. Wearing a leather raincoat and leather roadster cap, the stocky guard sat tilted in a chair under the awning, his feet propped on a box. His arms were folded across his chest, his chin down. *Asleep.*

I don't like this. To be safe, Jerry slinked a distance from the guard and walked to the front door from the opposite direction. The man didn't stir. Lightning flashed as he crept through the door. Mrs. Gastoldi sat in her loveseat, asleep, her newspaper in her lap.

The first stair creaked when he stepped on it.

Mrs. Gastoldi jerked awake. Her head snapped over to Jerry. Her jaw dropped.

Jerry tapped a forefinger to his lips. "Shhhhh."

"No, no," she muttered.

"Shhhhh." He stepped silently up the stairs. They didn't creak like the first step, but by now he didn't care. Key in hand, he opened his apartment door and walked in. It was dark. A fire crackled in the fireplace. Dinner plates and food remnants were on their dining table. A wine bottle stood half full beside one of the plates. The label read Nero d'Avola. It was to be for a special occasion. The other bottle of Nero d'Avola stood empty on the countertop.

Jerry seethed. He looked at the half-closed bedroom door, walked over, and pushed it open. It creaked.

They were in bed. A hurricane lamp cast a soft glow across their movements. Rita saw him and shrieked, "Who is it?"

"*Che cosa*?" A massive figure rose up in the bed, the covers tumbling from his naked white body.

"You dirty son-of-a-bitch!" Jerry hoisted his B-4 bag over his head and hurled it at Rugani. The skier easily parried the bag. He rose from the bed and ran to the window. He ripped it open and bellowed into the night. "*Giorgio, aiuta, aiuta*!"

Jerry was on the man's back, pulling his hair and hauling him down in a chokehold. But Rugani was big and powerful and deftly rolled out from beneath him. He rose to his knees, then his feet. He was framed in the window as lightning flashed, illuminating his face. His eyes were bloodshot and he swayed, looking frantically about. His hand whipped into the hurricane lamp, shattering the ornate glass shade.

"*Giorgio*!" he screamed.

"Jerry, stop! You don't know what you're doing." Rita yelled. She'd pulled a sheet around her and was up on her knees. "They'll kill you."

Jerry grabbed an empty bottle on a side table and ran at Rugani. Rugani thrust out his arms to parry a blow to the head, but Jerry swung it at his hip. Rugani screamed and began to topple over. The bottle slipped from Jerry's hand. But he stood and swung with his right as hard as he could. The haymaker landed squarely in Rugani's mouth. Blood spurted. Teeth crunched. The skier tumbled back toward the window, his hands grappling at space. Jerry helped him with a push. Rugani tumbled out giving a long, ranging scream.

Even above the rain and thunder Jerry heard a terrible crash.

"My God!" yelled Rita.

Jerry looked out and saw a large hole in the awning below. Apparently, he'd broken through and landed among the patio furniture.

Rita rushed to the window and looked out. "You've killed him."

Jerry grabbed her arm. "You're lucky you're not next."

Her eyes focused on something over his shoulder. He ducked. Something whooshed past the back of his head and down his back. He spun.

It was Giorgio. And he looked not only like a professional guard but like a professional fighter. "*Bastardo*," the man growled. His roadster hat was off. His dark hair shimmered from the rain that was running down his smooth-shaven face, tracing out the jagged scar that ran from his right eye to his ear.

Sirens wailed in the distance.

Jerry crouched, ready to spring.

Click! Giorgio held a stiletto, palm up. A nine-inch blade at least. Slowly transferring it from hand to hand, he said with a grin, "*Vieni, stronzo del mare.*" Come on, navy turd.

Rita smashed a small wooden chair across Giorgio's head. He sank to his knees, his arms flailing in space, blood running down his forehead. It ran into both eyes. He tried to blink it away as he struggled to his feet. Jerry hit him with another haymaker, his knuckles cracking. Pain shot up his wrist and arm. Giorgio stumbled backward and smashed against the wall. A gilded four-by-four mirror plunged to the floor and shattered.

Still Giorgio did not fall. He blinked several times, wiped blood away with a forearm, and began to stumble toward Jerry.

Rita screamed.

Cars with flashing lights swooped into the square below. Feet thumped into the lobby. Mrs. Gastoldi was screaming.

Giorgio's mouth drew into a grimace of death as he blocked Jerry's exit. Miraculously regaining strength, he now stood straight and began to feint from side to side. Jousting with the stiletto, Giorgio dared Jerry to run past. He burbled through blood-covered teeth, "*Sei morto.*"

A weapon. Anything. There on the floor lay the bottle Jerry had used on Rugani. He grabbed it and smashed it against the window sill. It bounced off, not breaking. But the sill was broken.

"Hah!" grinned Giorgio. Wiping blood from his mouth, he lunged forward.

Jerry swung again. The bottle shattered, deadly jagged edges gleamed at the neck. "Hah!" growled Jerry.

Figures crowded the doorway. "*Ferma! Polizia!*"

It took four men to jump atop the mightily writhing, struggling Giorgio and hold him down. Finally, they flipped Giorgio onto his stomach, cuffed him, and dragged him screaming downstairs.

The detective's English was horrible. Jerry didn't know much Italian, nor did Rita. But he heard the detective say to his fellow policeman, "Michelangelo Rugani" softly and with reverence. Handcuffs were snapped on Jerry. Rita dressed, and husband and wife were manhandled downstairs.

Paulo and Maria Gastoldi stood outside with neighbors, their hands jammed on their hips.

Shaking her fist, Maria Gastoldi tried to reach them but was restrained by policemen. The patio furniture under the awning was tipped over. Except for intact rear wheels, a chaise lounge was broken to the ground.

An ambulance drove off as Lieutenant (j.g.) and Mrs. Ingram were shoved into separate cars and driven away.

People shuffled back to their homes. The Ingrams' bedroom windows hung open. One window flapped back and forth with the wind, its panes shattered. The other drooped uselessly by the lower hinge, its panes also shattered. The storm passed, the thunder and lightning having done their will. Now, it just quietly rained and the Catania residents drifted back to an uneasy sleep.

16

24 January 1968
Police Headquarters
Catania, Italy

Little shafts of sunlight stabbed through a broken, grime-smeared window. Jerry blinked, swung an arm over his face, and rolled on his side. He yelped as a bolt of pain shot up his spine. His right hand throbbed. He looked down and saw it was purple and swollen. Something must be broken. He looked up to his watch: 0836. He'd slept six or seven hours but felt horrible. They'd let him keep his watch but took nearly everything else, including his Navy web belt.

Becoming fully awake, Lt. (j.g.) Jerome Oliver Ingram let the reality sink in. He was in jail. In uniform. A fine accomplishment compared to what he was trying to achieve last week: pass the course with better than a 3.0; simple. Instead, he'd returned home to find his wife in bed with a national hero of Italy, fought him, and then was attacked by a professional bodyguard who could have easily killed him. Would have killed him except for Mrs. Gastoldi, who must have called the police...who weren't gentle with him. With his duffle bag, he'd sat wedged between two enormous Italian cops who either couldn't or wouldn't speak English. The car sped into Catania, bounced down an alley, and drew up to the rear of the police station. He was yanked out and pushed through a foul-smelling room, down a flight of stairs, and shoved into this cell, with a broken window that gave onto a wet parking lot outside. A cold, nearly freezing, draft seeped in through the bars, causing him to once again wrap his arms around himself to stop shivering.

He needed a shave and shower. And his uniform, dress blues, must be torn in several places. He wondered if—something clicked loudly, then rumbled. The cell door. He rolled over and looked up with a groan. A man, a civilian, walked through and stood before him. There was a guard at the cell door, which remained open. The man waved the guard away and then looked down, regarding Jerry. He clasped a large leather briefcase, both hands around the handles. He wore a charcoal gray three-button Armani suit, with a vest. His trouser cuffs were cut precisely to cover immaculately shined wingtip shoes. Nearly bald, the man had thin lips, a thin moustache, and beady eyes. He took a step back and leaned against the wall. "Good morning, Lieutenant," he said in clear English. "Would you care to get up?"

Jerry rose and gasped when pain shot up his back.

"Feeling better?" The man smiled.

What is this crap? "Who are you?"

"I am Barton Seidman."

"American?"

"Yes."

"Well, that's something. Nice to meet you Bart, but—"

"Mr. Seidman."

"Mr. Seidman. As I was saying, you can see I'm rather short on living-room furniture. Can I offer you the other end of my bunk?"

"I'd like you to sign something, Lieutenant."

"Oh?"

Still standing, Seidman opened his briefcase and fished out a document. Made from heavy paper, it rattled in his hand. "Here it is. A waiver of your right for treatment under the Status of Forces Agreement with the Republic of Italy."

Jerry saw the document bore the seal of the United States State Department. "Whose side are you on, Bart?"

"I beg your pardon?"

"I was just wondering." Jerry pushed himself to his feet and groaned. "Coffee would be nice." He rubbed stubble on his face. "And a shave."

"I'm afraid I don't have coffee. The Polizia can take care of the other."

"Well, if you're not serving coffee, what are you serving?"

"I thought you knew. Didn't they tell you?"

"They didn't tell me anything. I just woke up, for crying out loud. And where the hell is my wife?"

"Very well." Seidman cleared his throat. "You see; I am the—"

"No, I don't see."

"—the official representative of the U.S. State Department in Palermo. You're lucky. You see, I happened to be in Palermo and they sent me over right away."

"What for? This is a military matter. Quite simply, some guy, a local native, was shacking up with my wife. I caught the son-of-a-bitch while they were going at it and threw his ass out. Then his goon tried to kill me. That's all. Aren't they in jail?"

"Do you know who you threw out?"

"A ski bum. Rugani."

"Yes, Michelangelo Rugani. He is the son of Rudolpho Rugani, who owns Enzio Parfumesline of fragrances headquartered in Milan."

"Yes, I know all this."

"Rudolpho is very upset and is seeking the full extent of justice."

"Then he should have the cops throw that bastard son of his in jail."

"No, no. You don't understand. Signor Rugani loves his son very much. Michelangelo is his pride and joy. His son's photos appear almost monthly in fashion magazines. He has become the essence of Enzio Parfumes. Sales jump every time he appears on the pages. An icon of Italy in many ways."

Jerry gave a long exhale. "Taller than the tallest mountain."

"And now, Michelangelo is in a hospital with serious injuries."

"I'm so sorry."

"Several bones are broken, and he will need extensive dental work."

"Gee."

"Your sympathy is most comforting. I'm sure the Rugani family will—"

A tall, well-dressed man with straight slicked-back hair walked in carrying a folder under his arm. He shook hands with Seidman and then spoke with him in low tones, sometimes whispering. Then he stood back against the wall beside Seidman and regarded Jerry.

Seidman cleared his throat and said, "This is Captain Leonardo Botazzi of the Carabinieri."

"The what?"

"The Carabinieri. You know, police."

Jerry's pulse quickened. This didn't feel right. "Carabinieri? I haven't been here long, but isn't that the police force of the Italian Army? Last night, I was tossed by a bunch of local Italian police."

"*La pula*," said Botazzi in a gravelly voice.

He understands English. Jerry said, "Why exactly is he here? And why exactly are you here? And where is my commanding officer? I should be speaking with him, not you."

"Actually, we're trying to do you a favor."

"By signing away my rights?"

"*Pensa, per favore*." said Botazzi.

Jerry's head swirled for a moment. "What did he say?"

"He wishes you to think about it," said Seidman. "Or else..."

"Or else what?" demanded Jerry.

"You see, it's a—"

"No, I don't see. Damn it. Make sense, will you? And where is my wife?"

Seidman said, "He wishes to have jurisdiction over you. To take you to Rome."

"Hell, no. I belong here. And we are in a state of national emergency. I am supposed to be serving my country. And I suspect they might be getting a little bit pissed because I'm not at my duty station."

Botazzi laid a hand on Jerry's shoulder and said in broken English, "I understand, *mi amico*." He sat at the bunk's other end and gave a thin smile. "*Siediti*...uh, sit!"

Jerry sat.

Botazzi said, "I will explain. The man who tried to stab you is Giorgio Michelleti. Of the Salvati family."

"What does that mean?"

Botazzi tried to form the words but then looked up to Seidman.

"What he's trying to tell you, Lieutenant, is that Giorgio Michelleti is of the Salvati family of the mafia. He operates barely above the law. Several deaths have been linked to him, but they haven't been able to make charges stick."

"Oh."

"Yes. Captain Botazzi is afraid for your life. If you are guilty to assaulting those two men, he can put you under protection in Rome. If you stay here and return to duty, you will be killed one way or the other. On or off the station. Hundreds of Italians work at Sigonella. There is no way to stop them."

"But the guy's in jail, right?"

Seidman and Botazzi looked at one another and shrugged. Siedman finally said, "Giorgio Micheletti was released last night at eleven thirty-two."

"What the hell? How could— "

"They have lawyers," offered Seidman. "It's not safe for you to return to Catania. It's a matter of pride, now. Their people will find you and ..." He tilted a hand from side to side. "You must understand the practicalities of the situation."

Jerry dropped his head into his hands. "How was I to know that?"

Seidman held out the single-page waiver and a pen. The paper rattled in his hand. "This allows you Carabinieri protection, Lieutenant, the very best. It will all blow over after a few months, possibly a year or two. Then you can return to a normal life."

Jerry said, "Whatever that means. Let me see that."

Seidman passed it over.

Footsteps shuffled outside. The guard peeked in, then ushered in a Navy lieutenant commander with a stocky build and a blond crew cut with a full moustache. A nametag on his right breast said QUINN. Jerry recognized the JAG flashes above the two and a half stripes on his sleeve. He also saw the man had two rows of campaign ribbons topped by submariner's dolphins: silver. The hardware told him that the commander had qualified in submarines as an enlisted man. After a series of duty assignments, he had gone on to college, then to law school, and then joined the Navy legal staff.

Jerry shot to his feet and almost bumped his head on the upper bunk trying to stand at attention.

"At ease, Sailor," said the lieutenant commander. "My name is Quinn and," he turned to Seidman and Botazzi, "I'm here to find out what the hell is going on. For example, he stepped close to Seidman, "What is that?" He pointed to the waiver in Jerry's hand.

Seidman said smoothly, "We're trying to save the man's life, Commodore. All that does is—"

"Commander."

"Commander."

"Commander Quinn."

"Sorry, sir. In short, the Carabinieri are trying to save Lieutenant Ingram's life."

"From what?"

"The local mafia. They've put out a hit order on Lieutenant Ingram. The Carabinieri is offering to take him in and protect him."

Jerry blurted. "That's right. These two are afraid the mafia will—"

Quinn turned on Jerry and waved a finger under his nose. "Lieutenant, henceforth you will speak only when spoken to. And only to me. Not them. Do you understand me?"

"Yes, sir." Jerry shouted it like a plebe. And he felt like one, too.

Quinn snatched the waiver from Jerry and scanned it. "Beautiful." He rubbed his chin and turned back to the others. "Let me get this straight. You are asking this man, a U.S. citizen and an officer in the United States Navy, called to his duty station in a potential state of national emergency, to waive his rights and hurry off to some safe house in Rome?"

"Yes, that's right," said Seidman.

"*Si*," nodded Botazzi.

Quinn said, "Mr. Seidman. Are you crazy?"

"I beg your pardon."

"You want to be a party to kidnapping a United States naval officer and turning him over to a foreign nation?" He snapped his fingers. "Just like that?"

Seidman didn't reply.

Quinn stepped over to Botazzi. "How long do you plan holding him prisoner?"

Botazzi remained silent.

Quinn continued, "Long enough for one of your jailers to make a mistake so you can loan him out to the Rugani family for an evening of canasta, right?"

Botazzi unleashed a burst of Italian to Seidman.

"Well?" Quinn demanded.

Seidman said softly, "What does the United States Navy plan to do with this man?"

Quinn said, "Please inform Captain Botazzi that under the Status of Forces Agreement with the Republic of Italy, Lieutenant Ingram will be called to an admiral's mast and charged as follows under the Uniform Code of Military Justice." He thrust a finger in the air. "First, he will be charged with violation of Article 109: waste, spoilage, or destruction, of property other than military property of United States. Next is violation of Article 116: riot or breach of peace. After that, Lieutenant Ingram will stand charges for violation of Article 133: conduct unbecoming an officer and a gentleman. Last, he is to be charged under Article 134, the general article for the prosecution of offenses not specifically detailed by any other article."

Seidman exchanged glances with Botazzi. The Carabinieri shrugged.

"This is progress," Seidman said.

17

24 January 1968
Police Headquarters
Catania, Italy

Weak. Jerry's knees felt as if they were giving way. And betrayed. His own government was throwing the book at him only because he'd caught a rich Italian ski bum in bed with his wife. Correction:.

"Prison time?" asked Seidman.

"Ten years' hard labor, at least," said Quinn.

This is shit. Jerry groaned, "Commander, I—"

"Something wrong, Lieutenant?" asked Quinn.

"Ten years' hard labor for kicking that son-of-a-bitch out of my own bedroom? I don't—"

"Lieutenant, I repeat, you'll speak only when spoken to. For the last time, do you understand me?"

"Yes, sir!"

Botazzi watched with steepled fingers. Then he and Seidman spoke rapidly for a minute or two.

Seidman asked, "What about dental charges? Mr. Rugani lost four front teeth."

Jerry brightened. He rubbed his hand over his fist as if patting his dog.

Quinn said, "I'm authorized to say that we can split the charges, with the stipulation that Mr. Rugani use a U.S. Navy dentist. We have three excellent ones on base in Sigonella."

Botazzi shook his head slowly." No, no. È Dottore Bergani in Roma. Nessuno altro."

"Holy smokes," said Quinn. "He's Italy's dentist to the stars."

Seidman nodded and lowered his voice. "Take what you can get, Commander. Rudolfo Rugani insists."

"Tell you what. Can Rudolfo cancel his contract with these mafia creeps?"

Botazzi inhaled deeply and took a step back.

Seidman said, "You've insulted him, Commander. The Ruganis are not mafia."

Quinn said, "Come on Bart. I know how the system works. Rudolfo issued a contract to the local mafia on Lieutenant Ingram, right?"

Quinn was greeted by silence. He continued, "I've seen this too many times. The deal is, Rudolfo cancels his contract with the mafia before we go any further. That's nonnegotiable."

Seidman and Botazzi exchanged glances, the nod of Botazzi's head barely perceptible.

Seidman arched an eyebrow. "I suppose so."

"Fair enough," said Quinn. "Let me speak with Admiral Eisenberg. We may have some wiggle room." Then he added, "One last thing."

"Yes?" asked Seidman, closing his briefcase.

"Damages to the Gastoldi residence."

"That's on you."

"Not so fast, pal. It was your client who trespassed."

Seidman shot back, "He was there by invitation."

"Nonsense."

"He was."

"Prove it."

"We—they have Mrs. Ingram to testify."

Quinn pawed the concrete with the toe of his shoe and asked, "Yes? You

—you're saying they have a signed statement?"

Botazzi exhaled loudly and shook his head.

Seidman looked from one to the other. "You two know something?"

Quinn said, "Apparently so, Bart. She's flown the coop. Found a high-priced lawyer and was released from here at 9:17 last night. I'm surprised you didn't know that."

"Well, I—"

"Flew out of here at 10:22 for Rome. And she then boarded TWA flight 1540 for Mexico City at 2:36 this morning." He checked his watch. "She should be there in about another three to four hours."

"We can extradite her."

"Take you forever. Besides, she's to Mexico what Michelangelo Rugani is to Italy. They'd never let her go."

Seidman looked at Quinn then back to Botazzi. They turned to one another and spoke in subdued tones.

Jerry was overwhelmed. *Rita's gone? What the hell? Mexico City? Probably on her way to hide out in Vera Cruz.* He blinked and caught Quinn's eye.

Quinn shook his head slightly. *I said shut up.*

Seidman grunted and said, "They will split the cost with you on that, also. Yes?"

"All right. Then it's settled?" asked Quinn.

"Sounds like it," said Seidman looking toward Botazzi.

Botazzi said, "*Hokay, ciao.*" He tossed a casual salute to Quinn and walked out.

"All done?" asked Quinn handing the waiver back to Seidman.

Seidman looked Quinn up and down. With a smile, he said, "When do you retire, Commander?"

"Not in a hog's age, Bart."

"Well, if you do, please give us a call." Seidman stuffed the waiver back in his briefcase and started to walk out. "The Diplomatic Corps can use someone of your talents."

"Mr. Seidman. Wait a minute," barked Quinn.

"Yes?"

"Next time you talk to that dirtbag—"

"I beg your pardon?"

"You know who I mean. Tell Rudolpho we have photographs of his dear Michelangelo Rugani in the Catania ER with four teeth missing."

"Yes?"

"Tell the captain we'll make sure it doesn't get to the press as long as they don't start their own media blitz. Or mafia blitz.

"They wouldn't do that. Captain Botazzi promised. And when—"

"Because if they do, there are more than a few Navy SEALs around here who could easily even the score of a mafia blitz. But then you didn't hear that from me, and Captain Botazzi is gone."

Jerry blinked. *He could do that*?

"That's outrageous!"

"In the meantime, it wouldn't look good to have those photographs floating around showing Italy's national icon looking like Alfred E. Newman."

"You wouldn't dare."

"No, Bart. Of course not. That would be unethical. But then someone, somewhere, might take a page from your State Department and leak it. Who'd know who let it out? And then Rugani sales would plummet."

"They would be most offended."

"Tsk, tsk. Really?"

Seidman spun on his heel and walked out.

Quinn turned to Jerry and jammed his fists on his hips, "Well, junior?"

"Sir?"

"Let's go."

"Now?"

"All set. Everything is all signed. Your duffle's in my car. "He tossed over a large manila envelope. "Here's your personal stuff."

Jerry rummaged through it. "They didn't return my belt."

"Hold up your pants with your hand, Lieutenant. Let's get the hell out while the getting is good."

A four-door gray Plymouth with black lettering, U.S. NAVY, stood before the police station. A Sailor with dark red hair standing at the rear door yanked it open. "Morning, Lieutenant," he said and waved Jerry inside. A torpedo man second class, also with submariner's dolphins. A Bakelite nametag read SCHOTZ. He was tall and thin with a slight overbite. But his uniform was immaculate, and he wore his white hat straight and perched correctly just two inches above his nose. His two rows of campaign ribbons were very similar to Quinn's.

Jerry stepped into the backseat. Schotz leaned in and handed Jerry a white Dixie cup of hot coffee. "You remember this?"

"I sure do. Thanks." The aroma wafted up and Jerry sipped. *Wonderful.*

"You bet." Schotz closed the door while Quinn slid into the front. When Schotz got in his side, Quinn asked, "All work out, Schotzie?"

Schotz started up and said, "Everything except the orders. Pretty sure we can pick them up from the base OOD at the gate. Otherwise, we wait."

"Damn."

Schotz drove fast and recklessly, the Plymouth creaking and leaning around the curves. Finally, they gained the road for Sigonella and Schotz floored it, the speedometer reaching 75.

Jerry asked, "Commander. Can I ask where we're going?"

Quinn snapped, "What did I say, Lieutenant?"

Jerry fumed and looked out the window, drumming his fingers. It was a beautiful day with white puffy clouds. Great visibility. Great day to fly. In the distance he saw a P-3 curving around on final and dropping its landing gear.

The Plymouth struggled up a hill and Schotz threw it into second gear. He said over his shoulder, "Pay no attention, Lieutenant. He's screwing with you."

The two laughed in the front seat.

What?

Quinn said, "Charade is over, Lieutenant. I had to play it that way. Those guys were out to screw you—. That and the U.S. government."

"You mean—"

"Seidman's on the take? You bet he is. It's so transparent, I couldn't believe it. We'll have him up on charges soon. He's done this to us a few times. I just wanted to see it firsthand. Damn fool doesn't realize how exposed he is. Let alone the damage he's doing to his country and government."

"So what happens now?"

"We're getting rid of you. *Persona non grata*. You're going to another P-3 squadron."

"What? I just got here. Where?"

Quinn looked to Schotz. "What did you come up with?"

Schotz called out, "How about VP 72 in Barbers Point, Hawaii?"

"Jeez, I don't know."

"See that package on the seat, Lieutenant?"

"Yes." Jerry tapped it. "Clothing?"

"Yes, sir. New uniforms. Blues, whites, and khakis, which is what you'll need where you're going. Even a web belt."

Jerry sat forward. "Hawaii just like that?"

Quinn said, "We have a Cairo-bound C-130 waiting for you. After that, it's commercial the long way around to Honolulu. You can shave and shower at the hanger. Then they'll feed you on the plane."

"But I—"

Quinn turned in his seat. "Of course this is all horseshit, Lieutenant. But wrecking the place didn't help. And wrecking a national hero didn't help either. You won't be prosecuted under any of those charges except maybe conduct unbecoming an officer and a gentleman. The court could find you didn't exert proper restraint."

"Yes, but—"

"Look. Forget about your wife for now. Sit up and take stock. Straighten out your life. Besides, we may be at war. You have no idea what's going to happen. You'll be a black sheep for a while."

"I don't understand any of this."

"You don't have to. Just accept the fact that you're screwed. The Navy will dump on you to make the Italians happy. Just ride with it and keep your nose clean. You're lucky we may be going to war. You'll have something to do."

Jerry said, "I can't believe this." He looked down realizing he'd gulped most of the coffee.

Quinn said, "Hey, Jerry. Look at the bright side."

"Sir?"

"We have plenty of coffee." He waved a thermos. "And guess what else?"

Jerry leaned forward and held out his cup. "I'm dying to find out."

Quinn poured and said, "No hard labor."

18

26 January 1968
Senior Officers Quarters
Kunia Station
Oahu, Hawaii

Bsssssst! What the hell?

Ingram rolled over. *That damned phone. Bssssst!* It was loud and strident.

Helen groaned. "Honey, it's on your side for a reason."

That's right. Maybe a recall. Maybe some more Pueblo *stuff.* God he was tired of that. He and Helen had picnicked on the beach last night. She'd made meatloaf sandwiches and potato salad. Pickles, olives and cookies took care of the rest, including a marvelous bottle of Chianti. After quietly watching the breakers and the stars, and letting gentle zephyrs tingle their skin, they'd trudged home, taken showers, and tumbled into bed, Ingram falling immediately into an exhausted sleep.

Bassists!

He cracked open an eye and looked at the clock: 2:27 a.m. Good God!

"*Todd*! Duty calls," she fairly growled.

"Yeah, yeah." He reached for the phone. Made sure he missed and got the satisfaction of hearing it fall off the cradle, clank on the tabletop, and then clatter to the floor. With the cord, he pulled the phone back to his face and croaked, "Ingram."

"Todd, you crusty old son-of-a-bitch. It's Tony."

"Uh, Tony?"

"Tony Lazarus, fer cryin' out loud. Wake up. Off and on. You sound like you've been asleep."

Ingram sat up. "Tony?"

"One and the same. I repeat. Are you asleep? I thought you guys worked twenty-four hours out there.

"Not on your life. What's up, Tony?" Lazarus wouldn't be calling if it weren't important. He was a classmate and old friend. While Todd was bumping around on destroyers during World War II, Tony was flying PBYs and P5M amphibians. Then they served together late in the Korean War on the COMSEVEN staff. Later, they'd been thrown together during the Bay of Pigs invasion—Ingram responsible for destroyer picket lines and blockading while Lazarus, the flier, was in charge of photo recon on Cuba and readying target payloads for Navy jets. Now, both were three-star admirals with Lazarus as commander air operations Atlantic, COMNAVAIRLANT. By now, Ingram knew something important was on Lazarus' mind, ergo the call at... at..."What time is it there?"

"Almost one-thirty in the afternoon, goldbrick. Already got in a half a day of hard work for our taxpayers while you sack out on the sands of Waikiki."

"Yeah, yeah."

"Helen there?"

"Right beside me."

"Come to think of it, put her on, old son. I didn't want to talk to you, anyway."

"Tony, damn it!"

"Okay, you're pissed and that means you're awake. I'm calling you at home because I don't want the Navy listening in. And it's not classified and is just between us two. And after I hang up, I'm gonna leave it with you. Okay?"

"Got it, Tony."

"All right, here it is." Lazarus spoke for four minutes and then finished with, "So that's it. I'm the convening authority. And that's all right. We put a dynamite JAG lawyer on the case and he took good care of Jerry. I'm going to make sure the State Department recalls Barton Seidman and hands his ass to him. The only job he'll get is scrubbing toilets. And then we have to settle damages and the dental problems, which won't be easy. But we can take care of all that. But here's the hard part." He paused.

"Go ahead, Tony, I'm a grown boy."

"I've decided to leave the Article 133 on Jerry. At least for a while, but don't tell him that. After reading all this stuff, I've decided he has a thing or two to learn. But I've also learned he's a hell of a pilot and is doing a good job, so I don't want to lose him. Thing is, we've got to stick him somewhere until this all blows over.

"He's on his way here?"

"Think so. Quinn stuck him on the C-130 to Cairo. After that, he's flying commercial to Hawaii. Actually, he should be landing pretty soon. You guys should scare up another good JAG lawyer for him. The biggest battle will be fighting off civilian authorities. That and unctuous Navy Department and State Department weenies in Washington, DC."

"Okay."

"You got it, Todd? You can't be seen to be part of whatever happens."

"That's right. The Navy always takes care of its own."

"Todd, fer chrissake."

"Tony, I'm not that stupid. Yes, I'll become the shadow and get something going. And thanks for the heads up. I appreciate it."

"Well, do it quietly, Todd. Keep your name out of it."

"I will. Don't worry. And seriously, thanks very much." He nudged Helen.

"Huh?"

He gave her the phone. "Say hello to Tony Lazarus."

"Oh yeah?" She sat up. In a vampish voice she said, "Tony, my sweet, how are you?"

Ingram let them prattle on for thirty seconds then snatched the phone back. "Okay, Tony. Time to go chase Communists. Thanks again for the heads up." He cradled the phone.

"What was that all about?"

He gathered her in his arms and explained as best as he could.

When not standing watch in the massive situation room, Ingram's daytime office was one deck below that of Adm. John J. Hyland, commander in chief, U.S. Pacific Fleet. They'd just finished the second meeting that morning over the *Pueblo* situation.

Off the Korean coasts, ships, including the nuclear-powered aircraft carrier *Enterprise* (CVN 65), Marines, land-based aircraft of the Navy and of the Fifth Air Force, stood ready to go in and exact revenge; to recover the *Pueblo* and her crew. And still the White House vacillated, looking for a path to negotiation. At the same time the White House seemed to expect a miracle from the Pacific Fleet. Except the Pacific Fleet couldn't do anything without White House permission.

For the first time since the Barbary Wars of 1801–1805, a foreign nation had attacked and captured a ship of the U.S. Navy without provocation while she was in international waters. At least one man was dead, her captain and crew imprisoned. But the White House and the cabinet were in an uproar; the United Nations, useless. Diplomacy worked slowly and grudgingly. But the cigar-chomping hawks in Congress wanted results—now. So did Ingram. So did CINCPAC and his staff.

The press was pushed off to the side. For once, they didn't object. They knew there was nothing to say. It was up to the White House, more specifically, President Johnson, who had just delivered his State of the Union address and was now being sucked into the resurgence of a very unpopular enemy offensive in Viet Nam called Tet.

Finger pointing. Cover-up. Name calling. Who did what to whom?

But Ingram had a job to do, and that was to find and track Soviet submarines slithering into the area; see that they were not a threat to U.S. naval units operating near Korea. It was a task close to impossible. The nearest Soviet submarine bases were Rybachiy on the Kamchatka Peninsula and Vladivostok on the Asian mainland. Rybachiy, inside Petropavlovsk Bay, was the Soviet Union's largest submarine base. And right now, Soviet submarines seemed to be storming out of the two harbors every day. Except they didn't head for Korea; for the time being, they veered off for the South

China Sea, another sensitive area with U.S. carrier operations off the Vietnamese coast.

Admiral Hyland was pressuring Ingram, and Ingram was pressuring his staff. They were frustrated at the inaction, and nerves were stretched piano-wire taut. There were at least three Soviet attack submarines unaccounted for. Ingram needed more assets at sea. Almost all of his destroyers were committed. It was up to U.S. submarines to find and track, or the SOSUS system of sea-floor microphones, or the land-based P-3 Orions.

The phone rang in the outer office. Ingram's door was propped open, and he heard his flag lieutenant stop his chomp-chomping at the typewriter and pick it up. His voice boomed with, "Vice Admiral Ingram's office. Lieutenant Retson speaking, sir."

After a moment, Retson's chair squeaked; he leaned back and peeked at Ingram through the doorway, his hand covering the mouthpiece. He whispered, "Lieutenant Jerry Ingram for you, sir. Do you want to...?" His eyebrows went up.

"Absolutely, patch him through, please." Ingram gave thanks for Tony Lazarus' call. He'd had time to mull it over. The line buzzed, he picked it up. "Jerry. How the hell are you?"

"Good morning, Admiral. Not so hot."

"What's wrong?"

Jerry gave him a quick run-down on the situation in Catania. Ingram oohed and whistled while Jerry finished with, "That's right. So, I got in last late yesterday and reported to my CO."

"And..."

"And they're putting me in a nonflying status until all this sh–stuff blows over."

"So the way you tell it, It sounds like it's down to one charge: *conduct unbecoming*."

"That's what they tell me. Can you believe it?"

"Well, that's what happens when you nearly kill someone and wreck a civilian's house."

"Dad, all this doesn't make sense. I was just—"

"What about your job?"

"Well that's just it; they're acting like I have leprosy or something. My CO gave me a fish grip, then told me flat out he can't let me fly until this Article 133 hearing sorts itself out."

"That could take awhile. Do you suppose they can prosecute when you're halfway around the world from where it took place?"

"Good question. In the meantime, I get to twiddle my thumbs and sit on my ass. Do you suppose you could speak to my CO?"

"Sorry, I can't do that. I think you know why."

"This is shit."

"Lieutenant!"

"Sorry."

"Get a hold of yourself."

"I...I'm sorry, Dad. I thought I would ask. I just want to get back in the air."

Ingram fumed. His son was getting twisted by an overcompensating legal system. Worse, politics were involved and it was hard to get to the crux of things. And he couldn't use his rank to make things easier for Jerry. "It'll sort itself out. Do you have an attorney?"

"Working on it. I have some promising suggestions."

"Well, take your time. This is important. In the meantime, go surfing or something."

"Dad, with all respect, I'm getting screwed."

"Come on, Jerry."

"Here's the deal. I caught this guy in my bed porking my wife. Now look what Uncle Sam is doing just because I clocked the guy. Does this make sense to anyone? Or is this part of the people-to-people program?"

"To be frank, it doesn't make sense when you put it that way. By the way, how is Rita?"

"I don't know. She left before I could talk to her. Ran home to Mexico, I think."

Ingram was not surprised. Rita Hernandez Ingram was used to striding down the fashion runways of New York City, not finding herself in an Italian jail. They'd met her only once at that party out on Long Island. But they'd since learned something about Rita that he'd bet Jerry didn't know. Rita was a major contributor to *Escuelas Para Todo El Mundo*, Schools for Everybody, a New York–based organization heavily connected to the fashion industry. *Escuelas Para Todo El Mundo* built and staffed modern schools in Third World countries, primarily in Mexico, Honduras, and Guatemala. With a little more digging, Helen had learned Rita had donated tens of thousands of dollars over the past four years and had spent five months actually living on site and building one project near Monterey, Mexico. After the season of the following year, she'd returned and taught a class for half a year.

The girl had heart but chose not to boast about it. For that reason, Todd and Helen withheld their opinions lest they break her bubble. Also, Ingram sensed she was a survivor. And to prove it, Rita had gone to ground in Mexico; probably with her parents, who they'd learned had a vineyard in the foothills above Vera Cruz. With all of her success, Rita most likely had the money to lay low comfortably and let it blow over—six, maybe twelve months and then back to the fast life in the Big Apple.

Ingram spoke up. "Sorry to hear that."

"I can't get used to it. Seven days ago, I was married with a neat job. And now…it's all in the garbage dump."

"What about the guy—what's his name?"

"Michelangelo Rugani."

"The Olympic skier?"

"That's him."

"Jeeeez, Jerry, what have you gotten into?"

"The son-of-a-bitch thinks he's Jean-Claude Killy. But unlike Killy, he didn't make the Italian Olympic ski team in Grenoble. Nobody knew except his close family. He's a has-been. And they need a cover-up. Instead of a lame fabricated announcement that he couldn't ski this time, he's stumbled into a marvelous excuse. Me. He's blaming it all on me and threatening to sue."

"That's nonsense."

"No doubt about that. But they'll shake us down hoping to extract some money before formal charges are filed. The Italian press is already sniffing it out."

Ingram drummed his fingers. "What's your unit?"

"VP 72, Barbers Point."

"Not bad. Your skipper's Gregg Fowler?"

"Yes, you know him?"

"He's a good man. We work together all the time. And right now, I need every one of those P3s to locate and track Communist submarines."

"I would imagine so. And I'm here to help."

In spite of it all, Ingram chuckled. "Listen, I'm up to my ass in alligators here. Let me call you back. Are you at the Barbers Point BOQ?"

"That's right. Not under house arrest yet."

"Sit tight. I have a couple of ideas. And don't worry about Fowler. He won't screw you. He'll give you a fair shake."

"I hope so."

"Dinner tonight?"

"I thought you'd never ask."

"I'll get Mom to whip up some of her spaghetti."

"Wow! Now you're talking. I'll bring a bottle of Chianti."

"That's a deal. What's your number?"

Jerry gave it and they rang off.

Ingram tipped back in his chair and steepled his fingers. He rocked back and forth for two minutes then said, "Okay." Leaning forward, his feet plopped on the floor. He rose and whipped out the door.

Retson's eyebrows went up.

"Captain Fletcher's office. Back in five minutes."

"Yes, sir. You need me along?"

"It's okay, Alex. Just keep up with that." Ingram nodded toward the typewriter and walked out.

"Yessir." Retson resumed crunching on his machine.

Ingram walked down the hall to the SUBPAC (Submarines Pacific) liaison office and Capt. Rusty Fletcher, his chief of operations and alternate member on the NIRTPAC Committee. It was convenient to have a "bubblehead" on hand to help with coordinated tactics, especially when dealing with Soviet submarines.

Fletcher's secretary was not there, so Ingram walked through the outer office and rapped twice on the door. Without waiting, he grabbed the handle and walked in. Fletcher was on the phone, leaning far back in his chair, the front wheels two inches off the deck. He was tall, thin, and balding with reddish peach fuzz on top of his head and well-combed hair at the sides. Rusty Fletcher had an infectious grin that had become his signature. It had neutralized arguments from coast to coast, and he had progressed well in the Navy. He'd been a second-string quarterback at Notre Dame who couldn't make first string. But he was deadly accurate, especially when the offensive line did its job. And his long ball was always on target, astounding for someone so short.

Ingram sat while Fletcher fussed over documents and wrote on a pad in his lap. He shot off three rapid-fire "yes, sirs" followed by one "no sir," all the while scribbling. Ingram guessed he was speaking with his boss, Rear Adm. John Maier, visiting the Ballast Point submarine base in San Diego. Finally, Fletcher said "goodbye," cradled the phone, and stood. "Sorry, Admiral. What can we do for you?"

"Sit down, Rusty, this is off the record."

Fletcher took his chair, sitting erect this time, his hands folded on the desk.

"Rusty, I need your assurance this conversation never happened."

"Todd, you know me better than that..."

Ingram relaxed. "Okay, remember at a staff meeting a couple of weeks ago? You guys proposed that it would be really advantageous if some P-3 jockeys could ride your submarines. It was supposed to be a series of familiarization rides so that one side could get to know bubblehead speak and vice versa?"

"Yeah, Operation SWAPOUT, except the zoomies didn't go for it. As I recall they laughed in our faces."

"Well, let me ask you, is SWAPOUT important?"

"You bet it is. Why do you ask?"

Ingram spent five minutes telling him.

Fletcher leaned back and scratched his chin. "You know; we might be able to do something. The *Wolfish* is getting ready to put to sea."

Ingram rose to his feet. "Sounds interesting. When can you do it?"

"You mean you want him out of town, soonest?"

"If not sooner."

"Well, I hope this is for you. *Wolfish* is under way in the next two to three weeks. Meantime, she's doing some refresher training. But she shoves off on patrol no later than February twenty-fourth."

"That's the earliest you have on deployment?"

"Best I can do, Admiral."

"So if we stick him aboard now, he could be out of sight."

"He may not be at sea, but I can have him down there cleaning bilges if you want. He won't come up for air for sixty days."

"Jeeez, Rusty."

"Up to you, Admiral."

"Yes, let's do it."

"Yessir. I'll get the orders cut."

"But make sure nothing originates from my office."

"For sure. This will come directly from CINCPAC. How can you lose?"

Ingram looked at Fletcher in a new light. He knew how to get things done. "That sounds good. Thanks, Rusty. I'll call after I dig out of this."

19

27 February 1968
Fleet Operations Control Center
Kunia Regional SIGINT Operations Center (KSOCK)
Level B, Room 2506
U.S. Pacific Command
Kunia, Hawaii

The 7 December 1941 Japanese air attack on Pearl Harbor threw a terrible fright into U.S. leaders on many different fronts. The immediate problem was to fix the U.S. Pacific Fleet, and fix it fast, in order to withstand the Japanese onslaught that began right away, not only at Pearl Harbor but in the western Pacific as well. This meant defending against serious challenges to American Pacific interests from the far-flung Philippines to Alaska, the Panama Canal, and the West Coast.

And, of course, the Hawaiian Islands at Pearl Harbor, where much of the U.S. Pacific Fleet now lay in ruins. Two battleships were total losses. Another six battleships were out of commission, one or two for a relatively short time, the rest repaired under gargantuan efforts that would take one to two years. The eight cruisers in the harbor at the time were mostly undamaged.

Three destroyers, out of approximately thirty moored in Pearl Harbor, were seriously damaged and required one to two years to repair. The rest of the ships present—submarines, mine layers, and sweepers and auxiliaries—were undamaged. Undamaged also were the irreplaceable fuel oil tank farm, dry docks, and ship chandleries. And the three aircraft carriers of the Pacific fleet. They were all at sea—on a Sunday. Nobody knows why.

In a matter of days the United States shifted to a frenetic war economy unheard of in previous generations. A labor force and stocks of strategic materials were assembled into a massive unit to produce the war weapons required to catch up to the Japanese–and then defeat them. Ship and aircraft production topped the list with new manufacturing plants rising from the ground right and left.

Early war production plans included an aircraft assembly factory on Oahu, Hawaii. The challenges for this were not only developing qualified labor to build the airplanes, but to bring in parts, components, and raw materials from West Coast suppliers. An abiding problem at the time was security, especially in the tense days following the Pearl Harbor attack. False reports were radioed in almost by the hour about Japanese landings and mayhem on Hawaii or some of the other islands. A curfew was laid down and people venturing out at night were indeed shot at.

With anxious thoughts of a second and more devastating attack, the government had an enormous hole dug on Oahu in an area known as Kunia some fifteen miles west of Honolulu and ten miles south of Oahu's famous North Shore. Initial planning called for aircraft assembly there. When this was done, the aircraft were to be towed to nearby Wheeler Army airfield for takeoff and deployment. But by the time the "hole" was completed in 1944, aircraft production on the mainland had caught up to the requirements of the armed forces, so the facility was converted to a code-breaking and map center. It became known as the Kunia Regional Signals Intelligence Center. The enormous facility comprised 250,000 square feet under roof, with 30,000 square feet of that given over to air conditioning and power generation. After the war, it was covered with earth for bombproofing. The code-breaking spaces were not space hungry, but the mapmaking spaces were.

During later stages of the war, an astounding 2,700,000 maps per month were printed and distributed.

Later, during the 1960s, as the Cold War escalated, CINCPAC began using Kunia as a command center. By 1966 the facility had been hardened against chemical, biological, and nuclear attacks. Ingram had reported in 1962 to a relatively open facility. But as he started his second tour there, Kunia had mushroomed into a sophisticated command center.

"Damn it!" Vice Admiral Ingram was cramped under a desk, lying on his back. But he was in short sleeves and working khakis, and the cool green linoleum floor was clean enough that he didn't get soiled. All this to fix the power supply to an ancient collator that predated World War II.

"You okay, Admiral?" asked Hawkins, a nervous yeoman, crouching down on his haunches.

Ingram wiggled further beneath the collator trying to turn the screwdriver. No luck. "Damn it all. What am I doing here?" he muttered. Utterly stupid to do this when there were people around him far more qualified. And with so much going on with the tactical situation. Plus, it was hard to crawl around in the cramped space. He'd had too much of Helen's spaghetti and Jerry's Chianti last night. And they were planning another quiet picnic on the beach tonight. With everything falling apart around him, he wasn't sure if he could make it.

"Damn it!" A screw dropped from the power supply assembly, bounced off his cheek, and fell on the floor. He reached back, fumbled the screw between thumb and forefinger, and worked it back into the power supply cover.

He was at this because he was desperate for a printout to compare contact values generated by SOSUS data collected from the Sea of Japan with the report from the USS *Dragonfish* now patrolling thirty miles outside Vladivostok Harbor. He'd been at it since being awakened at 0100 at home last night.

A voice echoed across the room. "Admiral, you gotta see this one!" Rusty

Fletcher, his chief of operations, was pointing to an enormous backlighted status board.

Ingram rolled to his side and peeked out. The tote board Sailor was tracing a yellow track emerging from Vladivostok. It meant another Russian submarine was exiting and coming south toward the waters around Wonsan, North Korea. A bright box beside the track designated it as contact AB 2276. Wonsan was only three hundred miles southwest.

Ingram's heart skipped a beat with the realization that they would have to convene the committee. It would be the first time, and he didn't feel like being part of a precedent that would most likely come under heavy criticism later. Their boss, CINCPAC, was unreachable in Vietnam while he toured Marine installations. Now Ingram had that old loose-in-the-knees sensation remembered from years before.

Fletcher tugged at an earlobe. His eyes were on fire with *get your ass out from under there, Admiral. We have Communists to deal with.*

Ingram barked, "I see it, Rusty. Damn it. Get somebody in here to fix this thing."

Just then, a wheezing Julius Hays, a cryptologist second class, ran up with a box of electrical parts under his arm. "Got it, Admiral." Hays plopped the box down, flipped to his back, and scooted under the collator beside Ingram.

Ingram gladly withdrew his hand supporting the power supply as Hays took his place.

"Got it, Admiral. Sorry it took so long."

Ingram handed the man a screw. "This fell out."

"Yes, sir." He took it.

Ingram pointed to three empty slots supporting the power supply mount. "How about these?"

"Jeeeez."

"Get going. We need this damned thing."

"Yes, sir."

Ingram rolled out and stood, his knees feeling stiff. He walked over to where Fletcher sat before a monitor, chomping an unlit cigar. "Any classification yet?"

Fletcher adjusted the screen resolution and said, "Not yet, Admiral, but if I miss my guess, it's another Echo II." He looked up at Ingram, his eyebrows raised at the thought of another Soviet nuclear-powered sub heading out to sea.

Ingram asked, "How long to classify?"

Fletcher said, "Shouldn't take too long. Echo IIs are noisy as hell. You can hear them for miles. The guys on the *Dragonfish* are probably erring on the side of accuracy before they submit their evaluation."

"We should have had it by now," Ingram growled.

"I agree, Admiral. Maybe they're having equipment problems. Maybe the Commies aren't cooperating. Maybe—"

A low buzzer sounded. Federson, a red-headed sonarman third class, called over to Fletcher. "*Dragonfish* just checked in with CTF 74, sir. Goblin Alpha Bravo 2276 is classified as an Echo II." Submarines in the Western Pacific were under the operational control of the Commander, Seventh Fleet, stationed in Yokosuka, Japan.

Fletcher stretched out his hand. *There you go.*

"So nice he could join his buddies." Ingram sat heavily at his console. Three monitors surrounded him and he nearly yielded to the temptation to sink down in his chair and hide. There were sixty-five men and women of various ranks and rates in the room, and he could feel their quick, furtive glances. Damn it. Three Echo II Commies headed out of Vladivostok straight south for the U.S. fleet now assembling in frantic response to the seizure of the USS *Pueblo*. The fleet consisted of two carrier groups, one group on the west side of the peninsula and the other on the east side close to Wonsan. The Soviet submarines were no doubt headed out there to do their best to embarrass the U.S. Navy. Maybe even start sinking ships.

Fletcher called over, "CTF 74 tells us *Dragonfish* has lost contact with goblin Alpha Bravo 2276. Awaiting instructions."

Ingram leaned forward rubbing the bridge of his nose with thumb and forefinger. He wanted desperately to be out of this dark cave and back in Oahu's glorious sunshine. So much going on here. This place was a—

"Admiral?" snapped Fletcher.

Fletcher. A good officer. But right now his impertinence is driving me nuts.

Ingram stood. "Listen up everybody," he shouted, his voice echoing in the chamber. "As you can see, we have a situation developing here. A damned-if-you-do and damned-if-you-don't cock-up. So let's not sweat the small stuff and just play it straight. By that I mean do what we're trained for. Follow protocol. And when in doubt, follow the damn book. No exceptions. Keep our cool and just do our jobs. Okay? It'll work just fine. Back to work. And the coffee is still warm."

Silence followed except for a few bleeps from the computing machines. From the corner of his eye Ingram saw Fletcher engrossed in a thick operating manual. The writers at the tote boards scribbled furiously as the tracks of the Russian submarines shaped courses for the Korean Peninsula.

Ingram steepled his fingers against his nose and tapped three times. Then he turned to Fletcher. "Rusty. Change of orders. Tell CTF 74 to have the *Dragonfish* follow goblin Alpha Bravo 2276, and not to be too stealthy about it."

Fletcher's brow knit. "You want us to light her up?"

"Yes. That's correct."

"Yes, sir. Will do." Fletcher picked up his phone and began speaking.

Hays slid out from under the collator. "All set, Admiral." He stood wiping his hands on a rag.

"Good, can we run that evaluation now?"

"Sir!" Hays punched a button and the collator blazed away, spewing out punch cards.

A phone rang with a low note. There were four telephones on Ingram's desk. Two were black. One was white. The last one was red. It was the red one that rang. He snatched it up. "Ingram."

"Todd. It's Gus." Gus was Maj. Gen. Gustavo Lorentz, USMC. He was the intelligence designee TAD from the First Marine Division Intelligence staff at Camp Pendleton, California. "I think Alex will be joining us."

Sure enough. There was scratching on the line and a third voice came up, that of Adm. Alexander Corrigan, naval aviator and Medal of Honor awardee for his actions in the Solomon Islands, now serving as Commander, Naval Air Forces, Pacific Region (COMNAVAIRPAC) at North Island Naval Air Station, Coronado, California. Ingram, Lorentz, and Corrigan, as the senior watch officers in their respective commands, were attached to the Naval Intelligence Response Team–Pacific (NIRTPAC). Reporting initially to CINCPAC, NIRTPAC was set up as a fast reaction team to report and make recommendations to the Chief of Naval Operations and/or the Secretary of Defense when tactical matters developed quickly. If needed, the team was to provide recommendations that could be forwarded to the most senior levels, even the president of the United States. Corrigan as a four-star flag officer was the team's senior member. "Gentlemen. Good morning to you," Corrigan said. It was ten in the morning on the West Coast.

Ingram and Lorentz blurted, "Hello, Admiral."

Corrigan said, "Before we get started, congratulations to you and your Marines, Gus."

"Thank you, Admiral. It wasn't easy," said Lorentz. First Marine Division Headquarters that day had reported that the Marines had retaken the city of Hue in South Vietnam, which had been under siege as part of the North Vietnamese Tet Offensive.

Corrigan said, "Surprised to hear the Marines had difficulties, Gus."

"Semper Fi, Admiral," said Lorentz. They all chuckled, realizing Lorentz and Corrigan were tossing canards.

"Enough of that," Corrigan said. "Who are these guys, Todd?"

The tote boards flipped images up on the main display bulkhead. At times they went quickly and Ingram had trouble keeping up. And his damned knees hurt from crawling under the collator. "Todd?" prompted Corrigan.

Right. He said, "The *Dragonfish* has confirmed all four as being Echo II class, Admiral."

"Bad news?"

"Not the best, I'm afraid, sir. These boats are nuclear powered, twenty-two-knot capable, and are fitted with antiship cruise missiles. They're specifically designed to take out large surface combatants."

"Namely..."

"Yes, sir. Aircraft carriers."

"Whoopee."

"Ruin your whole day."

"How do they do this?"

"Each submarine carries eight P-6 Shaddock antiship missiles. The missile's speed is Mach point nine and they carry a 2,200-pound warhead. Or, if they're really pissed, they can attach a 250-megaton nuclear warhead."

"Shiiiiit," said Lorentz.

Corrigan said, "Yes, I agree, Gus. And Todd, does this track put them to where I think they want to go?"

"They're on a direct track for Wonsan, Admiral. And at twenty-two knots, they could be in the area in about fifteen hours."

There was a pause, then Corrigan asked, "Can the *Dragonfish* take them out?"

"One or two, maybe. I just gave orders for her to pursue the most recent contact, designation goblin Alpha Bravo 2276, and to ping with active sonar. So the Commies know we're out here. Ready to stuff at least one torpedo up a kiester."

"Okay," said Corrigan. "I think," he added.

I don't blame you, Alex. Next Ingram said, "My recommendation is to stay close to that Commie and scare the crap out of her. She can only launch a missile if she's on the surface, and that takes five minutes or so for prep. She can't do that with one of us hanging around. Plus, she has to be within radar range of her target. So at least that one is screwed."

"Got it."

"And next, I recommend we put some P-3s up there and try to light up the other three. With luck we might regain contact."

There was a long pause. Corrigan posed the question they had been dodging. "You're saying we should contact SECDEF?"

That was in the operations manual, Ingram knew. He said, "No, sir. We're out of time, Alex. We should contact the White House directly." Contacting the White House was not in the operations manual.

"Jeez, what balls," said Lorentz.

Ingram added, "Seriously, gentlemen. We're out of time. The Commies have not given us the luxury of time to negotiate or even consider a decision. And we have two carriers at risk. And maybe other ships as well."

"But we don't have contact with the other three submarines," said Lorentz.

"What do we say about that, Todd?" asked Corrigan.

Ingram replied, "They don't know we've lost contact."

"Okay..." said an unconvinced Corrigan.

Ingram added, "The other three do know that we have contact with Alpha Bravo 2276 and that they could suffer the same fate."

"Maybe," said Lorentz.

Ingram said, "And it takes time, valuable time, for them to surface and prepare their missiles to launch. If we were up there waiting for them to surface they would be wiped out immediately. It's not a chance I'd take as a ship captain, Alex."

"What do you think we should say?" asked Corrigan.

Ingram said, "No time for niceties. Keep it simple. Something like, 'Hands off or we will sink you.'"

Lorentz whistled. "Balls is an understatement."

Ingram said, "Like I said. We're out of time. Take the direct approach."

Corrigan said, "What if we—"

Something clattered. Hays shouted and ran to the collator. He hit it twice with his fist, then ran to the power outlet and yanked the plug.

"Tell me it's not true," rasped Ingram, forgetting to cover the phone.

"I beg your pardon," said Corrigan.

Hays looked at Ingram and shook his head slowly, his palms up.

"Damn it!"

"Todd? Todd Ingram?" demanded Corrigan.

"Sorry, Admiral. We just lost a piece of equipment. Damn thing just quit."

"A computer?"

"No sir, a collator."

Rusty Fletcher ran to the machine. He stooped and examined the top end. Right away he snapped his fingers and extended a hand.

Hays plopped a Philips-head screwdriver into Fletcher's hand. Fletcher furiously twirled four screws securing the upper portion of the power supply. It didn't seem to bother him that it was marked in red and yellow with WARNING! HIGH VOLTAGE. He fumbled with wires as Hays stood nearby with a tool bag.

"Can you function?" asked Corrigan.

"Not to worry, Admiral. At this very moment we have an expert damage control team on it. Should be back up momentarily."

Fletcher cursed. With wire cutters, he clipped a thick wire in the power supply, detached the other end, and then threw the whole mess over his shoulder.

"Impressive," Corrigan said dryly.

There was silence. Their purpose for meeting was to protect the two aircraft carriers, four cruisers, and seventeen destroyers now deployed off both coasts of North Korea. They needed a decision—quickly. But it was Saturday. And the chief decision maker, the Chief of Naval Operations, was attending a conference in London.

Ingram said, "Admiral—"

"I have it, Todd. I agree with you. How about you, Gus?"

"Yes, sir. I say we go with the direct approach," said Lorentz.

"Spoken like a true Marine," Corrigan said. "Very well. We're unanimous. I'll send a priority to the White House recommending a démarche to the Soviets with a copy to State, SECDEF, CNO, CINCPAC, and CINCLANT." A démarche was a formal diplomatic presentation from one government to another to protest, among other things, intimidating activities.

"Well done, Todd," said Lorentz.

"Thank you, Admiral," said Ingram.

"Well, we've earned our pay today. Let's hope the Commies take heed."

"Fingers crossed," said Lorentz.

"And Todd," said Corrigan, "could you please send me a summary to include in the communiqué?"

"On the wire in the next two minutes, Admiral."

Ingram tromped through the door six hours later. "Hello?"

Helen whipped around the corner wearing a muumuu. Deep orange and white, one of Ingram's favorites. "Okay, slave driver. I packed the basket."

"You look wonderful." He hugged her, glad he'd gotten off watch on time. The scent of her Chanel No. 5 enveloped him and welcomed him home. She normally didn't wear it. She had figured something was up.

They had waited hours and hours at KSOCK without any idea of what would happen. It seemed hot in the heavily air-conditioned KSOCK. Even so, Ingram sweated and drank coffee and sweated some more, the silence petrifying.

Then suddenly, the *Dragonfish* reported goblin Alpha Bravo 2276 had reversed course and was headed back to Vladivostok. Within another half hour, the *Dragonfish* regained contact with the other three Echo IIs; all were on course for Vladivostok, USSR. An hour later the three flag officers decided the task of the committee was done. That it was time to accept their respective reliefs and go home. Just before leaving, Ingram had quickly called Helen and told her to pack the lunch for the beach.

"What's this occasion you were babbling about?" she asked, hooking a leg around his.

"Things went well today for a change," he said, kissing her on the neck. He didn't tell her that he'd decided to put in for retirement, something he should have done long ago. *It's a young man's game; things have passed me by.* Like that fire-eating Rusty Fletcher. With two submarine commands under his belt and succeeding staff assignments, he was ready for something like this. And Fletcher had just been selected for admiral. Time to turn things over to the Rusty Fletchers of this world.

"Congratulations."

"Huh?"

"Hey. You all right?" She brushed a fist against his chin.

"Never better."

"I don't believe you." She checked her watch. "But in case you didn't know, it's nearly seven o'clock. You sure you still want to go out?"

"Ummm. There's something I want to tell you."

She pulled back. "Really? Something that's not top secret?"

"Not really. Been a long time coming."

"I know what it is."

She probably did. Ever since he'd met her in the Philippines, Helen had been able to read his mind, just like her mother, Kate. "Okay, I'll tell you on the way. Then we watch the sunset and after that maybe go swimming in the nude."

"You are so gross."

20

28 February 1968
BOQ, Naval Air Station Barbers Point
Oahu, Hawaii

After Helen's fantastic spaghetti dinner the night before, Jerry spent most of the day shopping with his mother while Todd trudged off to work. In the late afternoon she dropped him at the BOQ, where he would check in with his CO the following morning.

Jerry had a burger at the base exchange, then headed toward the BOQ, wanting a good night's sleep before whatever might happen tomorrow. He walked into his room to find a roommate had been assigned—Lt. (j.g.) Frederick Cedros, a University of Kansas NROTC graduate. He was a skinny blond navigator who wore Coke-bottle lenses and nearly chain-smoked cigarettes. A new member of VP 72, Cedros was in from another RAG group in Florida and was part of the effort to beef up defenses against Soviet submarines in the Pacific.

As was the case in so many BOQs, they were pitched together in the two-man room with hardly any chance to get acquainted except for an exchange of initial pleasantries before snapping off their lights.

After that, Cedros lighted up a cigarette in the dark. "Any objection?"

"Go ahead."

The smoking kept Jerry awake until Cedros yawned, stubbed out his cigarette, and fell asleep. But just as Jerry began to doze off, Cedros began snoring. Jerry waited for ten minutes. Then he snapped on his light and walked over. Cedros lay flat on his back, his mouth wide open. Jerry visualized a fly buzzing in and out of Cedros' mouth. He shook the man's shoulder. "Fred?"

"Wha? Huh?" Cedros sat straight up, his eyes as big as saucers.

"You're snoring. Turn on your side, please."

"What'd you do that for?"

"I said you're snoring. You're keeping me awake."

"Don't do that again."

Jerry felt the bile rising. "You don't like it? Get your ass down to the front desk and change rooms."

Cedros lay back and turned on his side. "Sorry. I'm not good when I'm awakened suddenly."

"You ever get awakened for a midwatch?"

"Quite a few times. I used to fight with the enlisted. They had to send officers down to wake me."

"Well, this officer is tired and he's going to roll your ass out of bed next time you start snoring. Okay?"

"Got it. I said I'm sorry. Now adios." Cedros turned on his side away from Jerry.

"Happy landings, Fred." Jerry padded over to his bunk and climbed in. His mind raced with all that was going on in his life, including what his father had told him. Then he drifted off.

Cedros snored happily while Jerry shaved early the next morning. He made as much noise as possible and even sprayed liberal amounts of antiperspirant around the room. Cedros kept snoring.

At 0740, in dress khakis, Jerry was ready to leave. Holding the door open, he tossed a pillow across the room. It landed squarely on Cedros' head.

While the man sputtered and cursed, Jerry slipped through, slamming the door behind him.

He had a quick breakfast and then at exactly 0800 walked into Captain Fowler's waiting room to the secretary's desk. She was in her late thirties with gloppy red lipstick and upswept brunette hair. A nameplate announced MARTHA REDFIELD. A lieutenant commander stood off to one side. Martha nodded. "That's him."

The man walked over extending a hand. "Hi, Ron Carmichael, JAG Corps."

Jerry took it. "Jerry Ingram, with this squadron." Then it hit him: *JAG.* "You mean—"

The door opened. Captain Fowler stood there wearing a flight suit. His index finger hooked a flight jacket over his shoulder. In his right hand was a brief case. Fowler was tall, at least six-three, and bald with a bushy salt-and-pepper moustache. A cheroot was clamped between his teeth. "Glad to see you two have met." He pulled out a garrison cap and put it on.

"Just met," said Carmichael.

"Are meeting," said Jerry.

Fowler waved inside his office. "Use my office Ron. Give him the news. Sorry, but I have to go chase Communist submarines, gentlemen. They're popping up everywhere." He looked over to Jerry and took his hand. "Believe it or not, this will soon be all behind you. Commander Carmichael has all the dope. Just do what he says and you'll soon be back on top and flying. Lord knows I need you. Now pardon me, gents, but my plane launches in," he checked his watch, "fifteen minutes. Go on in, use my office." He tipped two fingers to his forehead. "Adios," then, "So long, Martha." Fowler walked out.

"Coffee, gentlemen?" asked Martha.

"Please," said Carmichael. "Black?" He raised his eyebrows to Jerry.

"Sounds good to me." Jerry studied Carmichael. At six-one, he had a round face, clear blue eyes, blond crew cut, a solid stance, and well-defined athletic frame. He looked familiar, but Jerry couldn't tease it out.

"Both of them black, Martha. Thank you." Carmichael closed the door.

They found a round table in the corner and sat. Carmichael took out a large file and began leafing through it. He muttered, "Mike Quinn speaks highly of you."

"Thank you, sir."

Carmichael continued leafing, "We'll find out,"

Jerry sat up. "Find out what, sir?"

"What I mean, Lieutenant, is whether or not you can weather all the crap the Navy and the Italians are going to throw at you."

Jerry felt a bit angered. *Take it easy*. Still, he sputtered, "It wasn't my fault, damn it. If that's the way you and the Navy feel, then you can have my resignation right now."

Carmichael leaned back and smiled, "Go ahead, smart-ass. The Navy will have wasted hundreds of thousands on your education, but at least they'll have your dead little ass to serve for another four and a half years beginning as a seaman deuce. What rating do you prefer? Boatswain's mate? Gunner? Radarman? We can plug you into a career-enhancing job that will carry over into civilian life. How about steward's mate? Shipfitter?" He closed the file.

There was a soft knock. Martha entered with two steaming mugs of coffee, set them down, and retired.

"Thanks, Martha," Carmichael said to the closing door. He picked up a mug, took a sip, and looked directly at Jerry.

He's got me. Then Jerry remembered one of Quinn's maxims. *Keep your mouth shut.* "All right, Commander. My apologies. What do you need from me?"

Carmichael put his feet up on a chair. Relaxed and in control. Very attorney-like. Except, Jerry remembered—

"You know, flyboy, you should have killed that guy. Then none of this would be happening. It would be far easier defending you against a murder charge then having to be dragged through all this stuff."

"I'll try to remember that next time."

Carmichael gave a slight smile. "That's the spirit. You would do well—"

"I remember now. Roland Carmichael. Didn't you go to Long Beach State?"

Carmichael slumped. "Guilty as charged."

"Wide receiver."

"Tight end."

"Yeah, that's it. Tight end. You had over a thousand yards one season. With four seconds to go you caught that touchdown pass against Oregon State and beat them, uh," he snapped his fingers, "Twenty-one to seventeen."

"But then you weren't there for your senior year."

"Got beat up. Injury—left ankle. Good thing or I would have tried to turn pro. And then I would be brain-dead. So I went on to law school instead. And guess what?"

"What?"

"After law school and five years in JAG, I *am* brain dead." He laughed.

There was more to it than that, but Jerry decided to let it drop. "How reassuring."

Carmichael's eyes narrowed. "Do you understand the charges against you?"

"In theory. Practically, it's all crap."

"Actually, I agree. Otherwise I wouldn't be here. Okay, here's the scoop. I am prepared to defend you against this Article 133 hearing. It's doable, all right. But the Navy has to put up a big show. The State Department is all over this with a guy named Barton Seidman leading the charge."

"I just heard he's been fired."

Carmichael stopped his cup in mid-sip. "How do you know that?"

Jerry had heard it two nights ago from his father. But he didn't want to let on, so he said, "Grapevine. I think Mike Quinn let on just before I shoved off."

Carmichael said, "I'm pretty sure they'll hog-tie Seidman and send him to the stockyards."

"I hope so. He was an embarrassment to the United States."

"Actually, this makes things look a little better for us. There goes the Rugani family's basis for suing. And there goes the State Department's push for Italian justice."

"Okay, now can we countersue?"

"Yes, but we have to take care of the Article 133 first. Tell me, where is your wife?"

Jerry spread his hands. "She ran."

"What?"

"Quinn told me she booked a flight to Rome, and from there she boarded TWA for Mexico City. That tells me she's run home to Vera Cruz." Jerry filled in details about Rita's parents and her success in New York.

Carmichael steepled his fingers. "Um. Then she can afford lawyers?"

"The best of the best. Killer New York lawyers when necessary."

"Um. Extradition would be tough."

"Very...plus..."

"Go ahead, Lieutenant."

"I have a feeling it would be better for her to stay out of this."

"Speaking of feelings, do you still have feelings for her?"

"I don't..."

"It's okay. We'll come back to it."

Jerry blurted, "I never got a chance to speak with her. I just wish I had."

"Um. Let's put it this way. Do you want the marriage annulled?"

"I...don't know. What I can tell you is that she may be pregnant."

"By Rugani."

"Well, no. By me. Probably. Although the doctors have been flaky about their diagnosis."

"You? Rugani? You're saying you don't know who the father would be?"

"How the hell do I know?" He fairly roared.

"Jesus. This is like an Italian opera."

"And now Rita is hiding behind a grape shed and there's no way to get help from her."

Carmichael drank coffee and then said, "Okay. First we get the Article 133 removed. After that, hell, I don't know. A lot depends on Rita and whether or not she stays hidden."

"Okay, so the pressure's off?"

"No. As long as the Rugani family pursues this along with the Italian government it's still serious. And we have to respond."

"By doing what?"

"Well, like Rita, we need you *in absentia*."

"Hell, I'm halfway around the world. How much more absentia can I get?"

"That's true. You're halfway around the world. So it's tough for people to catch up with you. Phone calls across ten–twelve time zones makes it even tougher."

"Yes." Jerry had a feeling he wouldn't like what was coming.

"But mail, bullshit orders, correspondence, radio messages can catch up with you. Make you do things. Worse, if the Italian or American press gets ahold of this, it may become front-page smut."

"I suppose so." Jerry folded his arms. *This is definitely not going my way.*

Carmichael pulled a package from the folder and plopped it before Jerry. "Lieutenant, ever hear of Operation SWAPOUT?"

"No, sir."

"Well you have now. Read that stuff. It'll tell you all about it. Renewed liaison between the submarine and aviation communities. You'll learn a lot."

"Learn what?"

"The elegant solution, Lieutenant. We put you aboard the USS *Wolfish* for forty-five to sixty days. All this will have blown over by then. And look at what you'll have learned about Ivan and his nukie subs."

"*Wolfish*? To sea? I hate submarines."

"I'm sure you'll get over it."

"No way."

"Well, here are your orders."

Carmichael pushed over a stack of papers. Atop was a set of orders signed by Captain Fowler. It hit Jerry that Captain Fowler was most likely climbing into his P-3 about now. With that came the cold realization that they had him completely cornered. He felt as if an undertaker had sewn him up in a canvas bag with fifty pounds of lead weights and was poised to toss him over the side.

"Lieutenant, I can tell you that you have better than a sixty-forty chance of beating this rap. All we need to do is keep you out of reach."

"Don't know if I like those odds."

"It's all you have. And be assured that Mike Quinn is working the other end."

"When does the sub shove off?"

Carmichael sighed. "She's in for some serious yardwork. Maybe three weeks or so, then she's out of here. You will be assigned to the *Wolfish* with BOQ privileges while in port and not on the watch bill."

"Impossible. I have plans."

"Talk to the skipper. Maybe he'll give you a hall pass."

Jerry fumed and drummed his fingers.

"It's the Navy way, kid."

"I hate submarines."

"See you in forty-five days, Lieutenant."

PART II

On Godless Men

They are clouds without rain,
blown along by the wind;
autumn trees, without fruit and uprooted—twice dead.
They are wild waves of the sea,
foaming up their shame;
wandering stars,
for whom blackest darkness has been reserved forever.

—Jude 1:12–13

21

24 February 1968
Five Palms Hotel lobby
Boca Del Río, Vera Cruz, Mexico

Giorgio Michelleti squirmed in the wicker armchair. The afternoon rain had raised the humidity, making the lobby feel close and airless. His tan sport coat was a little small, the sleeves too short for his thick forearms. His dark brown slacks and white polo shirt felt comfortable enough, though. The Five Palms Hotel, part of the Rugani family's holdings, was colonial with the original trappings of the Zapata Gardens built here in 1879. But it had been modernized with new plumbing, electrical wiring, and air conditioning in 1962, elevating it to five-star status. The white wicker furnished lobby was long and narrow, the floors a glistening white granite where every footstep echoed from end to end making one wonder about ghosts from the past. Voices also echoed, making Giorgio cautious as he spoke to the man in the squeaky armchair next to him.

Pietro Salazar was a second cousin to Doneto Ugolini, a Sicilian mafioso and former U.S. citizen who once operated in Cleveland, was deported as *persona non grata*, and now plied his trade in Palermo and greater Sicily. Ugolini had sent Pietro to Mexico six months ago to look into possibilities for the drug trade. This was a fool's errand, Giorgio knew. The drug trade was a young man's game reserved for those who could move fast, kill quickly and silently, identify opportunities, and most important, be able to run when the pressure was on from rivals or the police. Pietro, on the other hand, was in his sixties, and his wrinkled face showed the demands of time. He was very thin and, except for a graying thatch on his forehead, had lost most of his hair. But he still played the part wearing a white suit, Panama hat, and immaculate blue-and-white spectator shoes. His voice was a husky, deep, baritone, and belied the age on his face. "I think it's her father."

"Are you sure?"

"I'm not sure it's the same family," he said, flicking ashes off a long, thin cigar. "There are so many Hernandez' around Vera Cruz." He waved a hand. "In all of Mexico."

"Mr. Salazar," replied Giorgio. "We need to know if—"

"That's why I'm having great difficulty finding your Rita Hernandez."

"Damn it. The address must be accurate. We think the information is good. But we've been calling and writing. However there's no response."

"My best guess is these are her parents, all right. But I still have to find out if she is there."

Giorgio was becoming frustrated. He'd been at this for fifteen minutes with Salazar. Salvati family or not, he needed results, and Salazar was his only contact in Vera Cruz. "All right. How much?"

"Signor?"

Giorgio made a beckoning sign with his fingers. "How much to verify if this is where Rita Hernandez lives?"

Casually, Salazar looked over his right shoulder, then over the left. When he looked back, his brow was furrowed, his thin lips compressed. "It might be the place. This Hernandez family lives a secluded life up in the hills. They have a vineyard..."

"Yes, go on."

"I will ask a friend for details. But he is expensive."

Here it comes. But Giorgio took into account Pietro Salazar's family connections. One didn't fool around with the Ugolinis. Their tentacles stretched worldwide. Otherwise, he would kill this little gnome sitting beside him. "How much?"

"Five hundred, American."

Not bad. He'd thought it would be more. "Too much. My expenses are limited."

"I am sorry, my friend. That is what it takes for this man to open up."

"Too much."

Salazar raised his hands and then dropped them, his eyebrows raised. A minute passed.

"All right," said Giorgio. "Half now. Half when I get the information."

Salazar made a show of being in deep thought. At length, "*Si.*"

Giorgio drew out his wallet and began counting. "When?"

"I have to make some phone calls. Can you be back here in an hour?"

"One hour." He handed Salazar $250.

"*Gracias.*" Salazar stood and walked out.

On a whim, Giorgio insisted that Salazar go with him. He wanted the company, and he wanted Salazar's local knowledge in case something went wrong. Also, he'd noticed Salazar carried a small automatic pistol in a shoulder holster. A .32 caliber perhaps. *Efficient. Salazar knows how to take care of himself. Yes. Insurance.* That cost him another $200. *Worth every penny.*

Giorgio drove and Salazar rode shotgun while calling directions from a map. According to the map, the Hernandez vineyard was thirty kilometers east in the foothills. On Salazar's advice, Giorgio rented a Jeep four-wheeler. And he was thankful he had as they encountered more pot-holed roads the further they drove inland.

The storm blew itself out, leaving the skies clear, crisp, and sunny. The foothills glistened from the recent showers, scrub and oak trees damp and drying in the sun among cinnamon-colored boulders. The higher they climbed the better the view of Vera Cruz and the Gulf of Mexico beyond. After two hours, the Jeep labored up a steep grade and drew up to a large open gate with a sign overhead that proudly announced *Viñedo de Roja.*

Behind the gate the land leveled off to a sun-drenched, undulating hillside with beautifully coiffed vineyards laden with deep red grapes. It was clear how the vineyard had gained its name. He wondered what variety they grew. Something robust, a cabernet perhaps? Or possibly something lighter, like a rosé? He smacked his lips and reminded himself to ask. A group of white-clothed workers tended the vineyard about fifty meters off to his left.

At the top of the slope was a long, single-story tile-roofed house surrounded by eucalyptus and fruit trees. A cluster of garages and utility buildings stood off to the left. To the right was a small chapel featuring a steeple atop a bell tower and gothic stained-glass windows on either side of the door.

They drove up a paved driveway to the front of the house and pulled up behind a midnight blue Buick Roadmaster. "Brand new. The Hernandez' must be doing all right," said Giorgio.

"*Si*," said Salazar nodding toward a man riding up on horseback. The rider drew up, dismounted, tethered the horse to a rail, and walked over. "*Buenas tardes*," he called. Under a large, floppy sombrero was a long, thin face and a droopy moustache. Like the peons tending the vineyards he was dressed in white. Except this one carried a revolver cowboy style in an ornate gun-belt and beautifully tooled holster. The pistol gleamed with nickel plating. Giorgio guessed it was a .45 long Colt.

Salazar called back, "*Buenas tardes*." Under his breath he murmured, "I'm betting he is the *jefe*, the ranch supervisor. "See that cannon?"

"How can you miss it?"

"He looks capable. We should watch our step."

"Hello?" Another man had emerged from the house and stood on the porch above them. Dressed in immaculate dark brown slacks, alligator skin loafers, and sport shirt, he was stocky with a slightly wrinkled face and a full head of flowing salt-and-pepper hair. He smiled and in flawless English asked, "What occasions this visit?"

This is what Giorgio had been waiting for. He switched off the engine, stepped from the Jeep, and called up, "Greetings, sir. I am Augustine Carrera from *La Ronde* magazine. I have travelled all the way from Paris to speak with Rita Hernandez."

"Ah." The smile disappeared.

"And you are, sir?" asked Giorgio.

"Sssssst," said Salazar quietly. "Never do that."

The foreman moved closer to them and stood slightly behind, his leather belt squeaking.

"I am Francisco Hernandez," said the man. "And please say hello to my right-hand man, Antonio Herrera."

Giorgio turned to Herrera, who merely nodded, unsmiling, his thumbs hooked in his squeaking gun-belt. Giorgio nodded back.

"What makes you think Rita Hernandez is here?" asked Don Francisco.

Giorgio flashed as many teeth as he could and said, "We've tried everywhere else. All over the world. We'd like to ask your niece to do a spread. We have the services of Carminate Herranza." An Argentinian, Herranza was a photographer known worldwide. Giorgio didn't know if the name would mean anything, but he was going for authenticity.

"And who is this with you?" asked Hernandez.

Giorgio started, "This is my guide who—"

Salazar stepped from the Jeep. "Good to see you again, Don Francisco."

Don Francisco pointed to the main gate. "That man is not welcome here. Make him wait outside."

It became quiet. A circling hawk screeched high above. The horse grunted and Herrera's belt squeaked.

Giorgio broke the silence. "Go, Pietro. Wait outside the gate. I'll call for you."

"This is shit," muttered Salazar.

"Go."

"*Si.*" Salazar nodded. He walked around the Jeep, started it up, and drove off.

Don Francisco said quietly, "I will ask again, señor. What is your business here?"

Giorgio spread his hands. "It is like I said, Don Francisco. I would like to speak with Rita Hernandez about a major photo opportunity."

"What makes you think she would like to—"

"It's all right, Father. I can speak with him." Rita Hernandez Ingram stepped out onto the porch. Giorgio barely withheld a gasp. She was more beautiful than he remembered. Rita wore a full-length muumuu, its colors in blacks and fiery burnt orange. Her glistening black hair was drawn back into a defiant ponytail, and she wore no jewelry except for cat-eye sunglasses. "What do you want, Giorgio?"

Don Francisco gave a thin smile. "Giorgio? Giorgio? So where is Augustine Carrera?" He made a show of looking around.

Giorgio straightened up. "Rita. Thank you for coming out. I'd like to speak with you for just a moment. Then I will be on my way."

"About what?" she demanded. "I'm getting tired of this."

Giorgio held up a hand, screening the sun from his face. "I am sorry but I forgot to bring a hat for the heat of the day, which is..." He let it trail off.

"Very well. You may come in, but only for a moment." Rita turned and walked inside.

Don Francisco said to Herrera. "Stay here and watch that man out by the gate. I don't trust him."

Herrera said, "Are you sure you don't want me to—"

"That man carries a gun, did you not see?"

"I did, Don Francisco. I will stay with him."

"*Momentito, Antonio.*" Wait. Don Francisco said to Giorgio. "Are you armed?"

"No, Don Francisco." Giorgio stretched his arms parallel to the ground while Antonio patted him down. He stopped at the breast pocket and pulled out a half-pint bottle. "What's this?" He read the label.

"Tequila," said Giorgio. "Green Dragon. Not the best. Actually, I prefer gin but when in Mexico ..."

"*Sí*," said Antonio, handing it back. He shook his head then stepped back, and mounted his horse.

Don Francisco beckoned, "You may come inside."

The airy parlor was not large, but it was furnished magnificently in dark Victorian furniture. A Steinway baby grand piano stood beside a large bay window that gave a commanding view of Vera Cruz and the Gulf of Mexico. The floor was terra cotta tile with Persian rugs scattered here and there. Several paintings hung in the room, all portraits of be-medaled men on horseback in fine clothes. Giorgio thought of the Salvati family and their meager beginnings. Here there were traditions and riches going back centuries.

Don Francisco stood by his daughter before the fireplace. He did not invite Giorgio to sit.

Rita asked, "I have a feeling you have a message for me, Giorgio."

Don Francisco gave his daughter a quick glance but then skewered Giorgio with his eyes. *Hurry up and get out of here.*

All right, no more games. Giorgio turned to Rita. "Michelangelo sends his greetings."

"How touching."

"You have not replied to his letters."

"I burned them."

"They tried the phone."

"I don't answer it."

It struck Giorgio that this was going to be more difficult than the Ruganis had predicted. He pressed on, "Michelangelo is very concerned about your well-being."

"I'll bet," said Rita.

"Indeed he is. He would like you to join him again in—"

"Not on your life," Rita growled. She pointed a finger at him. "That stupid ski bum doesn't care one iota for me. Do you realize he was trying to rape me?"

Don Francisco gasped. "No." It was obvious he was hearing this for the first time.

She turned to him. "I'm sorry, Father. That's what happened. We drank too much and then…" she shrugged, "and then he tried to rape me."

Don Francisco took her hand. "*Mi pequeño bebé.*" My little baby.

Giorgio was taken aback as well. This was not the way he'd heard it. Michelangelo Rugani had told him, his parents, and his lawyers something far different. Nevertheless, he pressed on, "Signora, I repeat. Michelangelo Rugani intends nothing but the best for you. He is very concerned, as indeed is his father, Rudolpho."

"Concerned about what?" Rita fidgeted and looked at her father.

With the subtle mention of Rudolpho Rugani, father of Michelangelo and chairman of the Enzio Fragrance Empire, Don Francisco realized far more was at stake than Michelangelo's desire to see Rita. *Why*?

"Why should Rudolpho be concerned? I've never met the man," said Rita. "It didn't take me long to realize that I was just a dalliance to Michelangelo. Why can't he just go find another...dalliance...and rape her." Her voice rising she continued, "How many women has that beast raped before?"

Giorgio knew of at least three. He had straightened them out and paid them off handsomely. But here, things had taken a bad turn. He looked about the room. Just the three of them. *Good.* They were five steps away. He moved closer.

Don Francisco raised a hand. "Please, señor. No farther."

"No, I am sorry," said Giorgio. "The Foreign Office of the United States—"

"The State Department," corrected Don Francisco

"Yes, last week, in response to the botched investigation into this affair, they fired Barton Seidman, the chargé d'affaires in Rome, and brought in someone new. This has complicated things with our government and placed pressure directly on the Rugani family. We need someone to promote our cause, someone like Rita Hernandez, an American citizen, a top model married to a U.S. Navy pilot. Her blessing would stand as evidence of our good intentions."

"I doubt we'll be married much longer. I can well imagine what that scene looked like to my husband."

"People don't know that yet." He stepped closer.

"You want someone to get you off the hook and hide your corruption," spat Rita.

Don Francisco turned to Rita, "Please, *mi corazón*. None of this is necessary. Why don't you go to your room? I can work with this man."

"Please keep in mind that we can pay," said Giorgio.

"Take your money and stuff it," Rita hissed. "I will not be intimidated by you, you pile of shit. Tell your Don Rudolpho that I have lawyers, good New York lawyers, who are more crooked than you people. They can rake you and your stupid peasants over the coals and make you wish you'd never come here. Never been born."

Giorgio reached in his breast pocket and pulled out the half-pint bottle of Green Dragon Tequila. Casually, he held it out and examined it. Giving a half smile, he said, "...distilled in Mexico. Very nice." Then he uncapped it and, raising his eyebrows, waved it at Don Francisco and his daughter. "Please return."

Don Francisco rocked back on his heels. He chuckled and said, "Is this a joke? We don't drink that trash. Now, I must ask you to—"

Giorgio took two steps forward and backhanded Don Francisco. Surprised, the man stumbled back. His knees gave way. He grappled for the pistol in his coat pocket but Giorgio got there first and knocked it away, the pistol sliding on the tile. Then he backhanded Don Francisco again. The man fell over to his side, blood trickling from his mouth.

"You bastard," screeched Rita. "Get out of here." She moved to claw Giorgio's face.

Giorgio snatched the pistol off the floor. "Enough, bitch," he yelled. He whipped the open Tequila bottle across Rita's face, the contents splattering her.

Rita looked up in surprise. Then she reached for her face and screamed. "What have you done? Aiiiieee."

She snatched up a shawl draped over the sofa and dabbed at her face, crying and screaming.

Don Francisco looked up from the floor, his eyes wide. He began struggling to his feet and growled. "*Hijo de puta!*" Bastard.

"You've been warned," shouted Giorgio. He backed away, pointing the pistol at Don Francisco. "Don't make me use this."

Someone yelled from behind Giorgio. He spun to see a powerfully built young man clad only in a tee shirt and white shorts charging at him.

"You asshole," the man yelled.

Giorgio aimed at the man's chest and pulled the trigger. Nothing! The safety was on. *Shit*!

Yelling, the man was on him instantly, knocking away the pistol and grappling for a death grip.

Giorgio deftly parried the man, turned him around and wrapped his left arm around his neck in a choke-hold.

Blam! An antique chair crashed over Giorgio's head. Rita sobbed and fell to the floor. Giorgio squeezed harder. He grunted. *Just a few more seconds.*

Savagely, the man thrust upward with his left palm. He connected solidly underneath Giorgio's left elbow, breaking the death grip and shoving it away. A surprised Giorgio couldn't help it as the man turned a quarter turn to his left and rammed the point of his left elbow just under Giorgio's heart, cracking the sternum.

Giorgio gasped and wheezed horribly for air.

The man completed the turn, again ramming his right open palm, this time flat, against Giorgio's nose. The bridge of Giorgio's nose cracked. Like a knife, the whole section of broken nose bone was savagely shoved deep into Giorgio's brain.

"Ernesto?" mumbled Don Francisco.

"Papa...you okay?" Panting hard, Ernesto Hernandez bent to help his father to the couch.

"Uhhhh."

Rita! Crying and shaking, she lay face down on the carpet among wood splinters and pieces of the broken chair. He turned her over, finding the dark glasses askew on her face. She yelled and choked on her spittle.

"Relax, Sis, it's Ernie." She looked awful. Big red welts were forming on her face. "What the hell happened?"

She sobbed, "He threw something at me, acid maybe. Jesus, it hurts."

Ernie spotted the half-pint tequila bottle lying on its side by the wall. The contents had run out onto the red tile floor, which was bubbling up and turning to ooze.

Acid! "Water!" Ernie ran for the kitchen. In less than thirty seconds he was back with a quart pitcher of water followed by Delores Hernandez, his mother, and Carmelita Gonzalez, their cook. It was easy to see the family resemblance in normal times. But right now all were in near panic as Carmenita handed over a package of baking soda.

Ernie fumbled at it and shouted, "Hand towel, quick."

Delores grabbed Rita and took her into her arms, sobbing softly. Don Francisco crowded in, reaching for Rita as well.

Ernie dumped baking soda into the water just as Carmelita returned with a clean washcloth. "Okay." Ernie carefully removed the dark glasses from

Rita's face. Then he sloshed the hand towel in the quart pitcher, wrung out some water, and began dabbing at the red welts.

Rita moaned and tried to shove Ernie's hands away. But he kept at it, dabbing and dabbing and dabbing.

"Will that help?" asked Don Francisco.

"Don't know," muttered Ernie. "High school chemistry. An acid, most likely, hydrochloric or sulphuric, can be neutralized by a base with lots of water. Or just plain water, I imagine. It should help." He turned to Delores. "Mamá. Gather some things together for her. We've got to get her down to the hospital, chop, chop." He reached down and carefully capped the nearly empty tequila bottle. "Better take this so we know what we're up against." To Don Francisco he said, "Can you get Antonio?"

"Of course."

Don Francisco stumbled to the front door and yelled.

Soon Antonio ran through and into the parlor. "*¿Qué pasa, patrón?*"

Ernie explained briefly as he gathered Rita up into his arms, then said, "Help me get her into the car."

"What about him?" Antonio pointed to Giorgio.

Ernie reached down to check Giorgio for a pulse. "Dead."

Hell of a fight.. McGrody, his gunny Marine instructor at Quantico, would be proud.

He silently thanked God that he'd come home on leave before reporting to a USMC helicopter detachment in Da Nang. He'd barely had time to say hello to his parents and change out of his khakis when he heard the ruckus in the living room.

Some R&R this is turning out to be. Never mind. "First we load Rita," he said in rapid-fire Spanish. "Then you get that jerk out there in the Jeep and take this guy out in the weeds and bury him, deep. Make him dig the hole."

"I wouldn't have it any other way, Señor Ernesto."

Ernie frisked the corpse, found a wallet with cash and credit cards, a long stiletto knife, and a small derringer two-shot tucked in an ankle holster. "Tell that guy we'll kill him if any of this gets out."

"You mean Señor Salazar?"

"Exactly. Tell him that if he leaves the country and goes back to Sicily we'll be waiting for him. I know SEALs over there who would love nothing better than a little training exercise. Whether it's him or the Ruganis or the Salvatis. They would love the challenge."

"He should understand that, Señor Ernesto."

Ernie said, "Let's get Rita to the car." He kissed the top of Rita's head. "Come on, Sis. We're going to fix you up."

Rita wailed, "What did that bastard do to my face?"

"Shhh. Nothing serious. Come on, we gotta go."

"Get me a mirror."

Delores held her close, "Soon, *mi amor*, soon."

"I want to see," she wailed.

"Everything will be fine," soothed Don Francisco. The three of them worked Rita to her feet.

"Please, please, let me see."

22

16 February 1968
Sochi International Airport
Sochi, Adler District
Krasnodar Krai, USSR

The crystalline blue sky formed a marvelous backdrop for the snow-capped Caucasus Mountains now looming in the distance. They drew closer as the Aeroflot Ilyushin-18 descended over the Black Sea to a straight-in approach to Sochi International Airport. When he stepped off the plane, Eduard Dezhnev was greeted with a balmy 23 degrees. He peeled off his overcoat, happy to be free of Sevastopol's dreary downpour.

But even Sevastopol was a welcome relief from Leningrad, where he'd taught a variety of political courses at the M. V. Frunze Higher Naval School, a good cover for his spying activities for the United States and Oliver Toliver, an old friend from his San Francisco days. And then recently he'd brought off the impossible dream: he'd transferred to the Nakhimov Black Sea Higher Naval School in Sevastopol where he taught Fleet Leadership to young first- and second-rank captains. The title was misleading because the course was, as everyone knew, indoctrination into a command profile suitable to the government—that is, suitable to the Communist Party.

But he'd brought it off. Sochi was only an hour's flight away; Sochi and Roxana. He'd been seeing her a lot, and once again he felt like a teen-ager with the prospect of a weekend with her. But things turned a bit sour when Dezhnev walked out of the airport to hail a cab and spotted a four-door Lada with a dirty windshield parked across the street. All he could see through the dirty windows were two hulking shapes, dressed in coats and ties. On the way to Roxanna's house he looked back twice, and both times saw the Lada following at a discreet distance.

Thoughts of the Lada disappeared when Roxanna opened the door and jumped into his arms. They slammed the door shut and hugged mightily. Next came a glass of wine, then long, slow lovemaking. Pillow talk took them through sundown, and they decided to go out for dinner. He was first into the shower. Twilight fell as he waited for Roxanna to finish dressing, and he napped in the dark for a bit, the drapes still open. When he turned over to look out the window it was still there. *That damned Lada.*

With the lights off, he rose on an elbow and took a closer look. The Lada was parked across the street. An overcoated man leaned against the fender, smoking a cigarette. Another cigarette glowed inside the little sedan. *At least two men.* They weren't being careful. They didn't seem to care and most likely were taunting him.

Something gnawed deep in his stomach. The years swept through his mind. He made his decision. *The hell with it.*He called, "Utochka?"

She popped around the bathroom door, backlit against the bathroom light with her wet hair wrapped in a towel. "You called, sire?" Even after more than twenty years she still looked spectacular with that lanky, athlete's body. Were it not for those people outside he would have pulled her back into bed.

"Please come in, my love. I have to tell you some things."

"Can it wait? I'm in the process of removing twenty years from my face."

He glanced out the window. "Better be now."

Wrapped in a towel, she walked in and sat beside him. And he told her.

Her fist went to her mouth. "You've been working for them how long?"

"Since 1945 or thereabouts. Twenty-three years roughly."

"But why? Why do such a thing?"

"I'm tired of thugs running our country. So many innocent people have died. Millions. Look, I'm in what they call deep cover. I only report things when I believe it's necessary. I only speak with Toliver when necessary." He didn't add that he'd slipped a message to Toliver recently about the American KWR-37 coding machine. Somehow the KGB must have gotten wind of it.

"Who is Toliver?"

"Oliver Toliver. I met him in 1942 during the war. When I was serving in San Francisco. He and Todd Ingram. Remember?"

"I remember you speaking of Ingram. Wasn't that the great atomic spy scandal?"

It had become public knowledge. The USSR had recruited several young American nuclear physicists, Julius and Ethel Rosenberg being among the most notorious. The Rosenbergs, along with some others, had been caught and executed.

In San Francisco, Dezhnev had been caught red-handed by FBI agents as he tried to contact Todd Ingram, who at the time was in disguise as a nuclear physicist from UC Berkeley. Dezhnev and his associates from the San Francisco Russian consulate were rounded up and unceremoniously deported from the United States.

"And now, here I am in the soup again." He slowly shook his head. "Just yesterday I was in Sevastopol meeting a contact."

Her brows knit.

"No, I can't say who, but he gave me a message from Anoushka."

Roxanna smiled. "How is she? I miss her."

"She's well. As active as ever." He nodded toward the street. "It seems that about three weeks ago, idiots like those tried to kidnap Toliver. On American soil. In Hollywood at a public event. An incredibly stupid move."

"What did they do to the kidnappers?"

"They didn't catch them, but the Americans know what's going on. So it's heads up for us all."

"Then you should get out." She palmed his cheek.

"That's what my contact told me. And so," he took a deep breath, "I want you to come with me."

"Where?"

"America."

Slowly, she shook her head." I can't do that. I have my..." she waved around the room.

"Your school?"

She nodded.

"But I love you. I want you to come with me and live in America."

Roxanna dropped her head in her hands trying to take it all in.

The room grew silent.

He wrapped an arm around her, feeling closer to his Utochka than he'd felt in years. He had so much to make up to her.

He would not tell her that his contact was Colonel General (three star) Maxim Yusopov, a high-ranking member of the Soviet Energy Institute, synonymous with the American's Atomic Energy Commission. The Soviet Energy Institute was responsible for the development and distribution of the USSR's atomic weapons.

Maxim Yusopov had earned his first star in the Great Patriotic War commanding tanks, most notably in the bloody battle of Kursk. As a colonel general he was on solid ground with his military career. But his personal life lacked the sort of discipline expected of a three-star general. Yusopov, with his athletic build and good looks, was known for his womanizing. He played the field, winning victory after victory with extraordinarily beautiful women. At times Maxim's life as a lothario conflicted with what should have been a more serious political persona. After serving with Maxim's son, Vladislav, on that death trap the *K-12* six years ago, Dezhnev often wondered how a man with such great abilities had produced such a lazy and inept son.

If militarily he was on solid ground, politically Maxim Yusopov's position was somewhat precarious. He had aligned himself with his old school chum from Ukraine, Nikolai Viktorovich Podgorny, who was close to the top as chairman of the Presidium of the Supreme Soviet. The trouble was, Podgorny was in open competition with Leonid Brezhnev for the position of Chairman of the Communist Party and overall leader of the Soviet Union.

The two hated each other, and insiders knew they were headed for a clash somewhere down the road. And Dezhnev realized the outcome would affect a lot of people. *Maybe me.*

He wondered if that was what suddenly made him want to defect. To leave his homeland and live a decent, unthreatened life with Roxanna in the United States. They would doubtless give him some sort of menial job; something like setting bowling pins in Jefferson Corners, Nebraska, or dog catcher in Sheboygan, Wisconsin. Fine. He could think of nothing better than a simple life.

He reached over to the dresser and picked up a gold-plated Alcatraz buckle. "Remember this?"

"Yes, I've seen it."

"Before all that atomic spy business, Toliver gave this to me. In San Francisco." Dezhnev carried it always, but as a good luck charm, not a buckle. He flipped it in the air with his thumbnail like a coin. "He was on medical leave and we had a real night on the town—drunk as lords, we were. Dinner at the Top of the Mark; he paid. Later, we stumbled into this little shop in Chinatown and found this. I liked it. He paid for that also. It was expensive. I thought they were screwing him. I had it appraised later. It's fourteen-karat gold. But it didn't matter. Toliver comes from a wealthy family. He always had a lot of spending money, and since he thought he was going to die in the war he spent it freely; he just didn't care. Neither did I, for that matter. He bought it without haggling with the owner. He wanted me to have it. He thought it would outlast all of us through the war." He sighed. "I've had it all these years, and it's seen me through some pretty sticky times." He held it to his lips then looked up to the sky. "Thanks to you, Ollie. It may be time for me to come over."

He turned to her. "You would love him. Ollie married a cute Chinese girl who adores him. His rich parents disowned him for that. So he stayed in the Navy and eventually joined the CIA. He's my control.

"His parents disowned him for marrying a Chinese girl?"

"Second-generation American. And a graduate of Stanford University, too. That's a top university in the States. His parents thought he would leave her and come back for their money. But he didn't."

"This sounds like a Puccini opera."

"Or maybe Russian, like Glinka."

"Yes, tragic."

He shrugged. "Perhaps." He pitched a hand toward the window. "And out there are a couple of damned fools singing the chorus to me—to me and you. They're probably waiting for the right moment to pick me up."

She stood and walked over. "Where?"

"Across the street."

"Show me."

He stood and stepped beside her. The Lada was gone.

"Maybe they got hungry."

They walked to Bublicthki's, a big underground restaurant that passed itself off as Gypsy. But underneath, Bublicthki's had strong Yiddish roots. The atmosphere was rich with dark wood and candlelight, thick cigarette and cigar smoke, and robust food. He forgot all about the Lada as Gypsies danced and swayed to violins and castanets, their shadows flickering over the walls.

They dawdled for two hours over a good meal and were ready to leave when a hand slapped Dezhnev's shoulder. He looked up to see Captain First Rank Vladislav Yusopov grinning down at him, a glass of vodka clamped in his hand. Dezhnev stood and took the hand. "Vladislav, I haven't seen you for years. Wasn't it the *K-12*?"

Yusopov gave a lopsided grin. "Maybe so, maybe so."

There was someone else with him. Roxanna squealed with delight. "Vladimir!" She jumped up and threw her arms around her son, who looked handsome in his navy leytenant's uniform. Dezhnev was filled with pride that this handsome young man, his son, looked so much like him, down to the close-cropped dark red hair and medium athletic build. But unlike him, this doppelganger had both legs. To top things off, he also had a glass of vodka and seemed to be well on his way to being drunk.

Dezhnev said to Yusopov, "You know each other?"

"We're posted to the same submarine," said Yusopov. "And apparently, you know each other as well."

"That's right," Dezhnev said, "this young man is our son."

Dezhnev introduced Roxanna to Yusopov, who sat at their table without asking. He teetered in his chair for a moment and said, "You have a fine son, Roxanna Utkina."

From the corner of his eye, Dezhnev studied Yusopov. Unlike young Vladimir Utkin, Vladislav Yusopov could not claim the good looks of his father, Maxim. His dark, curly hair was already receding, and his cheeks, once sunken, were puffy. His torso was pear-shaped and his shoulders were rounded with poor posture. It seemed he was drinking too much vodka and getting too little exercise.

Vladimir politely shook his father's hand. But Dezhnev clapped his son on the shoulder and pulled him into a hug, saying, "You look marvelous, Vladimir. Congratulations on getting into the fleet so quickly." Once something of a delinquent, Vladimir had turned his life around and had graduated from the Frunze Higher Naval School with near-perfect grades. And now he had done very well in nuclear power school.

"Thank you, sir."

"Oh, Vova, don't be so formal," pouted Roxanna. "Sit down with us so we can talk."

"Yes, ma'am." He sat and waved toward the bar for more vodka.

"What boat are you on?" Dezhnev asked.

Vladimir mumbled something.

"What?" asked Dezhnev.

"*K-129*," said Vladimir.

Dezhnev looked from Vladimir to Yusopov. He'd heard that the *K-129*, homeported at Rybachiy Naval Base near Petropavlovsk, had just returned from a patrol and was being quickly turned around and sent back out to the North Pacific to replace the aging *B-62*, which had serious engine trouble. Plus, the *K-129*'s missile system was far advanced over the *B 62*'s. The *K-129* could shoot missiles from underwater, up to thirty meters deep, while the *B 62* carried only surface-launched cruise missiles and needed precious minutes to prepare and launch them.

He'd also heard there was something odd about the *K-129*'s crew. With almost half of the regular crew on leave or in school, they'd pulled men in from other commands to round out the complement, some of them scientists. It sounded like a real cock-up. "Is she ready?" Dezhnev asked.

Yusopov rolled his eyes. "I wish she wasn't. I just got back from a scary mission, I'll tell you."

"What was that?" asked Dezhnev.

"North Korea," blurted Vladimir. "You should hear what he did."

Yusopov shook his head, "I'd better not."

"They stole an American ship!" said Vladimir.

"Shhh," said Yusopov. "It's top secret."

"It was crazy," laughed young Vladimir.

Yusopov nodded, "Maybe. All I can say is that a bunch of idiots put them up to it. Now these same crazies are going to do something with the *K-129*. It's going to be a real mess, I'll tell you."

"And you're now chief engineer, I suppose."

"Oh, nothing like that. They made me the *zampolit*. Can you imagine?"

Dezhnev almost laughed. It was perfect. From failed strategic missile launch officer to failed engineering officer to political officer. But then what Yusopov had just said hit him. A coldness clamped around his stomach. "What kind of mess?"

"I can't."

Vladimir took a long swig of his vodka and said, "It would be good to know. You haven't even told me yet."

Yusopov pursed his lips and shook his head slowly. "Better not."

"Who are these crazy people?" demanded Dezhnev.

Yusopov swayed in his seat. "Uh-uh." Again he shook his head.

An exasperated Dezhnev turned to his son, "What's your billet, Vladimir?"

Vladimir said quickly, "Operations department, communications officer, right, Mr. Yusopov?"

Yusopov threw a hand out grandly. "Communications officer, yes." He nodded across the dance floor. "See those two over there?"

Dezhnev sat back with folded arms, realizing Yusopov was changing the subject. He looked across to see two women, one older than the other. Both wore 1940s hair-dos, bobby socks, and thick lipstick. They waved.

Yusopov waved back. "The Luzhkov sisters. Sofia, the one on the left, is mine. And your son is dating her younger sister, Yana."

"Oh."

"Let's get together." Yusopov thrust his hand back in the air and waved them over. "Yoo hoo," he called in a falsetto.

Dezhnev looked over to Roxanna.

She gave an eye-roll.

He tried, "Well, we should be..."

But the two women had jumped to their feet and were walking over, carrying drinks. As they drew close, Dezhnev saw that Sofia, Yusopov's date, had two silver-capped teeth in the center of her smile. And she was chewing gum like Americans in their movies.

Yana, on the other hand, was rather attractive except for that ratty hair. With a proper coiffure she could have been a knock-out. And she had straight, white teeth. And deep blue eyes. Dezhnev decided his son had good taste, the ratty hair-do notwithstanding.

It was obvious the sisters were well lubricated as they sat and began blabbing at Yusopov at the same time.

A foot nudged Dezhnev under the table. Roxanna. She arched an eyebrow, excused herself, and walked off for the ladies' room.

Dezhnev kicked his son and nodded in the same direction. "Excuse me, please." He stood, grabbed Roxanna's purse and coat, and walked off while Yusopov and the Luzhkov sisters roared with laughter.

Twenty paces away he turned to see his son had followed. Vladimir half-smiled, "Sorry, Father, they're sort of worked up."

Dezhnev said, "Enough vodka fumes at that table to run a T-34. I hope Vladislav is paying."

Vladimir laughed, deep and rich. "I'll say he is. Every ruble."

Dezhnev envied this young man. He wanted to be this healthy young Vladimir, to have his opportunities, his future, not to have wasted his life facing death against Nazi hordes.

Vladimir waved at the room. "Do you think I could afford all this on my pay?"

They laughed.

Dezhnev threw an arm around Vladimir's shoulders. "I miss you, son. Look. Are you in town for very long?"

Utkin straightened. "I'm sorry, but my leave is up. I'm on a plane tomorrow for Rybachiy."

Dezhnev asked. "And the *K-129*?"

"Why do you ask?"

"Equipment problems, I've heard. Poor maintenance. The word around the fleet is she's an accident waiting to happen."

Vladimir stiffened. "Thanks for your confidence, Father. I suppose you've sailed on the *K-129*?"

"One just like her. The *K-12*. They're slapped together with chewing gum and wallpaper paste. A horrifying ride. Made me shit my pants every time we dove."

Vladimir looked off into space.

Dezhnev growled, "There's more. Rumors have it that a group of GRU idiots are tied to the *K-129*, people loyal to Podgorny. Have you heard that?"

"It's not a rumor, Father."

Dezhnev's stomach churned. Suddenly he was stuck between what Maxim Yusopov had told him and his son's confirmation. It all sounded frightening. "Then get off the damn thing."

"I just got there. Hell, this is my first posting. Do you want me to snivel like a baby and just walk out?"

Vladimir had a point. Dezhnev spat, "All these damn politics. This isn't the Navy. There's too much going on for a young leytenant."

"Politics? Yusopov is the *zampolit*. And he's as far from politics as the man in the moon."

"I wouldn't say that. His father, Maxim Yusopov, is a very powerful man. He is close friends with Podgorny, I'm told."

"So I've heard."

"I don't trust those people, Yusopov included." Then Dezhnev said suddenly, "I can get you transferred."

"Why? This doesn't make sense. Besides, it's kind of fun being close to the seat of power."

Dezhnev blundered on, "Transfer. I know people in Vladivostok who can take care of it."

"Father. I'm under orders. I've been sailing on her for two months. She's a good ship. What would you do?"

Dezhnev had to give him that. His son was a patriot and was willing to do his duty. He looked down and nodded.

Vladimir waved toward the dance floor, "And Vladislav Yusopov, despite all his seeming mishaps, is a good officer. I'm learning a lot."

Dezhnev bit his tongue. He didn't want to share what he knew about Yusopov. He patted Vladimir on the shoulder. "Any word on your mission?"

"Usual stuff. Get under way. Dive. Clear baffles. Make sure there are no Yankee surprises back there. Full power run. Drills and drills, I'm told. Simulate torpedo attacks. Simulate communications exercises. Except I'm the communications officer and we'll be doing very little communicating. Just surfacing every twenty-four hours to receive traffic as we head into the mid-Pacific. Check navigation. Simulate missile launches. Check the Perimetr system. Run damage control drills. Do flooding—"

"*Perimetr* system? You have a *Perimetr* system?"

"Yes, we do."

"Good God."

"What's wrong with that?"

"It's a stupid system. It's what got your boss fired from the Strategic Rocket Forces. Once it's activated there's no way to stop it. Every missile in the Soviet Union would be launched at America."

"Dad?"

Dezhnev liked the sound of that. "Yes?"

Vladimir looked from side to side. "Keep a secret?"

"Of course."

"The coding in *Perimetr* is child's play. I can disarm it in fifteen seconds."

Dezhnev stood back. "You're screwing with professionals. From what I've learned, that system is foolproof. By definition, it has to be."

"There's a back door."

"What do you mean?"

"Those people at the computer labs are idiots. I can..."

Roxanna walked up. She accepted her coat and purse as if it had been preplanned. "My lovelies. I have a terrible headache." She kissed her son on the cheek and gave him a big hug. "Will I see you tomorrow?"

"I have a ten o'clock flight," he nodded east, "for back there."

She threw her arms around him. "So sad. Always, you are on the move. Next time stay awhile." She brushed him on the jaw. "And next time call ahead so we can plan something."

"I will. I'm sorry, Mother."

"Well, at least you had time with your father." She kissed him again and stroked his cheek. "When do we see you again?"

"Sixty days, more or less. I can—"

"Vladimir!" Yusopov roared at them, waving a bottle, gesturing for their return.

Dezhnev said, "Well, even this is special, Vladimir." He hugged his son. "Please convey our apologies to your friends over there. Your mother gets these migraines and—"

"I know, I know. You two take care also." Utkin slapped his father's arm, kissed his mother, and said, "It's good to see you two enjoying yourselves."

He started to walk away. Dezhnev grabbed his arm.

"What?"

Dezhnev dug in his pocket and pulled out the Alcatraz belt buckle. He slapped it in Vladimir's hand.

"What the hell is this?"

"For good luck."

"You're kidding."

"It got me through the Great War. Plus, it's gold. Fourteen karat."

Vladimir grinned. "I like those odds." With his thumbnail, he flipped it in the air.

Just like I do. Amazing.

"Thanks Dad." Vladimir slapped his father on the arm and walked off.

23

19 February 1968
***K-129*, moored at Rybachiy Submarine Base**
15th Submarine Squadron
Abacha Bay, Petropavlovsk Oblast, Siberia, USSR

The odor of canned salmon, their noon meal, lingered in the officers' berthing area, also known as the aft battery. Vladimir Utkin was back at his desk, picking his teeth and poring over an electrical schematic on the Perimetr *system*, when someone knocked at the entrance.

"Yes?"

Lutrov, a senior seaman wearing duty belt, cap, duffle coat, and sidearm, looked in. He was the messenger of the watch topside. Snowflakes clung to his fur cap and coat, courtesy of a winter storm. No doubt Lutrov was happy for a chance to dry out and warm up down here.

Lutrov was an easygoing engineman apprentice of nineteen, known more for clowning around than for the skills he was supposed to be acquiring with the ship's machinery. His capacity to make people laugh was phenomenal, but his superiors shook their heads when reviewing Lutrov's comprehension of the *K-129*'s three two-thousand-horsepower diesel engines. Right now, Lutrov's face was serious as he drew to attention and announced stiffly, "Two civilians to see you, sir."

"Where are they?"

A man of enormous proportions suddenly filled the doorway. His long, dark overcoat and fur cap were also covered with snowflakes. He had a broad forehead, a small mouth, and tobacco-stained teeth. He took a half step inside the little three-bunk stateroom, casually checked inside a curtained-off area for hanging uniforms, then looked deep into the space, his eyes missing nothing. Satisfied, he turned and called over his shoulder, "*Da*."

Another man stepped around the giant and walked in. "Leytenant Utkin?"

"Yes."

"My name is Zubov, comrade. Please don't get up. Where is your roommate, please?" He eased past Vladimir and sat on the lower bunk.

Vladimir stood anyway. "My roommate is on watch in the control room. Who the hell are you?" He looked around the large man and saw Lutrov paw the deck with his boot. He caught Lutrov's eye and waved him across the passageway to a little machinery nook filled with valves and gauges. Lutrov nodded, stepped across, and blended into the shadows.

Zubov took off his cap and unbuttoned his overcoat, shaking off snowflakes. He had thin, sandy hair atop a long face with a pair of gold-rim glasses carefully balanced on his aquiline nose. The lenses weren't thick, but they emphasized Zubov's ice-blue eyes. He took out a key-chain and waved a badge: KGB.

What the hell?

"Sit, please, comrade." Zubov nodded toward the large man occupying the doorway with arms crossed. "Comrade Nikulin is my partner." He nodded toward the desk chair and Vladimir sat.

Zubov glanced at Lutrov across the passageway in the nook. "He is a messenger, is he not?"

"Sometimes. Actually, he belongs topside now. But I keep him here to escort you back."

"Can you please send him to locate Comrade..." he pulled a dark leather-bound notebook from his inside coat pocket and flipped it open, "...umm, Comrade Yusopov."

Vladimir was getting angry. *What the hell does the KGB want with us?* But he pushed it aside and said, "Lutrov. Please go forward and ask Captain Yusopov to join us. I believe you'll find him in the officers' mess."

"Yes, sir." Lutrov walked away.

The giant KGB agent moved into the room and looked over Vladimir's shoulder.

"Do you mind?" Vladimir said sharply. The *Perimetr* schematic was stamped MOST SECRET. He folded it shut and tucked it beneath a large technical manual.

Expressionless, Nikulin took a step back, again filling the doorway.

Vladimir turned to Zubov, "Please tell him to stay back. This is classified material."

"Then you should put it away, comrade," said Zubov.

"I just did. Now, please, what can I do for you?"

"All right, when was the last time you saw your father, Eduard Dezhnev?"

Vladimir sat back. No one was supposed to know Dezhnev was his father. "My father is Ilya Gurov and I haven't seen him in years."

Zubov ignored Vladimir's attempt at diversion and consulted his notebook. "February sixteenth. Three days ago. Does that sound right?"

Yusopov burst in and brushed past Zubov. Vladimir nodded Lutrov back into the machinery nook.

Zubov's eyebrows went up, expecting an answer.

"Sochi. We were both in Sochi. What do you want?"

Zubov looked up to Yusopov. "Please, sit." He waved to a space beside him on the bunk.

"What is this?" demanded Yusopov, sitting on the bunk.

"I think you know." Zubov waved the key chain.

"Let's see your orders," said Yusopov.

Zubov gave a long sigh, pulled a page from his coat pocket, and handed it over to Yusopov.

Yusopov read. His eyebrows went up. "Good God! Second Directorate. What does internal security want here?"

"That's what we're here to find out." Zubov pointed with a large, stubby index finger. "Now, do you see the part right there where your commanding officer has approved our visit?"

Yusopov read and nodded glumly.

Zubov actually smiled. He turned to Vladimir. "You were telling me about your father?"

Yusopov's eyebrows shot up.

Vladimir's skin felt clammy under his collar. "Yes, February sixteenth sounds about right."

"In Sochi?"

"Yes."

"What did you talk about?"

"Well, he—"

"Aww, shit!" Lutrov shouted from across the passageway.

Vladimir yelled back. "What is it?"

The PA system crackled. A man's voice bellowed, "Attention, attention all hands. Fire. Fire in the aft battery. Close all watertight doors. Put on your emergency breathing apparatus immediately. This is not a drill." He repeated the message.

They heard a loud roaring from beneath the deck.

The watertight doors clunked shut at either end of the compartment.

"I'm sorry." Lutrov ran forward out of sight.

Zubov's eyes bulged. "What's going on?"

"Quick!" shouted Yusopov.

Beneath the deck, gas roared loudly.

"My God. The LOKh," said Vladimir.

"The what?" demanded Zubov.

"Must...hurry." Vladimir jumped up to reach the overhead locker. He grabbed a large plastic handle and broke a soft-leaded seal. Quickly he untwisted the guard-wire, undoing a small latch. A canister fell into his arms.

Zubov jumped up. "What the hell are you doing?" he barked.

Nikulin stepped close to Zubov as Vladimir reached in the canister and pulled out two emergency breathing kits. He tossed one to Yusopov. "No time to explain. Have to get you an OBA." He turned to exit the stateroom. Nikulin blocked his way.

Vladimir smelled Nikulin' s garlic-laden breath. He shouted, "Move, dummy, or you're going to die." He pulled the oxygen apparatus over his head and twisted the valve. Faintly, he heard a reassuring hiss. From the corner of his eye he saw Yusopov do the same.

Vladimir struggled to get past Nikulin and into the passageway. But the man's massive paws held him in place.

Then Nikulin' s grip lessened and his eyelids drooped, and he seemed to weave in place.

The grip on Vladimir's shoulders became weaker. Vladimir glanced at Yusopov. Zubov clawed at Yusopov's mask, trying to yank it off his face. But Yusopov stood back, wrenching his head to and fro, parrying Zubov's hands.

Nikulin's hands went to Vladimir's throat. His chest heaved in massive gasps. Then his hands dropped to his side, and his mouth opened to an O. He toppled backward against the sink and crashed to the deck with a groan. Zubov struggled to his feet. He made one last frantic swipe at Yusopov's mask then pitched over and fell atop Nikulin.

Lutrov stood in the doorway, his mask on. In his hands were two emergency breathing apparatuses. Stepping across Nikulin and Zubov, Vladimir reached over and grabbed them. Then he bent down to pull the mask over Zubov's head.

Yusopov brushed Vladimir's hands aside and took the mask. He reached down and felt for Zubov's carotid artery. The man's face was chalk white, his ice-blue eyes open to large discs, and his mouth gaped wide like he was a goldfish dying on a dry kitchen floor. At length Yusopov nodded. "Okay, you can put it on now."

Both men were obviously dead.

Through his mask Vladimir said, "What have you done?"

"It looks like I've done you a favor, you damn fool."

Vladimir Utkin decided Rybachiy was the coldest of the near-frozen Soviet submarine bases scattered around the northern Asian continent. The Polyarny shipyard in Kola Bay where he had initially trained in submarines was a close second. But here, volcanic peaks surrounding Avachinskya Bay stood as macabre cone-shaped sentries giving a somber greeting to whoever ventured out-of-doors.

Wintertime was the worst, with the continual overcast and the bay often frozen over. The Pacific was nearly fifty kilometers distant through a narrow entrance, and the only way for submarines to escape was often behind an icebreaker.

Vladimir, Yusopov, and the crew of the *K-129* had scrambled topside an hour ago in a near panic. But the clean, oxygen-rich air calmed them and the biting cold silenced them to the point where conversation was almost nonexistent. The temperature dockside was -11° Celsius where they stood in the partial shelter of a storage shed. It was still snowing and the silently floating flakes blocked all sound, amplifying the men's senses of remorse and danger. An emergency team of firefighters had boarded twenty-five minutes ago and was finishing rigging emergency hoses and blowers, ensuring the boat was secure. Aside from that, no one else was permitted aboard—until now.

Four medical examiners scrambled down the aft hatch. Their ambulance, red and blue lights blinking and blazing, sat at the foot of the gangway, its rear doors gaping wide open. Sequestered on the dock with the rest of the crew, Utkin and Yusopov fidgeted and paced as they drank weak tea laced with vodka.

The *K-129*'s commanding officer, Captain First Rank Vladimir Kobzar, and executive officer, Captain Second Rank Aleksandr Zhuravin, argued and spat with investigators as more and more officers in long overcoats showed up in cars with sirens blaring. It seemed as if everyone on the base wanted in on this, with people from every military division and subdivision of the Soviet armed forces demanding to be permitted aboard.

The group of unwelcome visitors swelled to about thirty and were forced off to one side and cordoned off by a special KGB detachment organized by Kobzar and Kontr Admiral Boris Ditrilov, the base submarine detachment officer and well-known KGB lackey. As in other military operations, ordinary chains of command were followed aboard the *K-129*... except ... when it came to the personnel selection, loading, off-loading, maintaining, targeting, and firing of missiles. Then, it was the KGB. And there were six of them here now, trudging back and forth, making veiled threats to Kobzar and his officers.

Off to another side, a wide-eyed Senior Seaman Yuri Lutrov stood with his back to the shed. He was nose-to-nose with the chief engineer, Captain Third Rank Nikolay Nikolayevich, and two senior starshinas off the *K-129* trying to explain his actions as Nikolayevich and his men hurled question after staccato question.

Aboard the *K-129*, a man crawled awkwardly up the aft hatch wearing a white hazmat suit and breathing apparatus. But his hood and OBA hung off to one side and he carried a red plastic toolbox. He nodded to the quarter-deck watch, then walked over the gangway and down to Captain Kobzar on the pier. With Zhuravin, the three stepped over to a snow-caped bollard at the pier's edge and stood talking.

Suddenly there was more commotion at the aft hatch. Three of the medical team emerged with some line and a series of pulleys. They rigged it to the hatch, locked it in the open position, and then began hauling. A black glistening body bag slithered up, feet first. It must have been the giant, Nikulin, because the proportions were enormous. The three white-suited men were having difficulty hauling the load all the way up. The men on the quarterdeck were summoned and, grunting and cursing, they worked Nikulin's body over the lip of the hatch and onto a gurney.

Zubov was next. No trouble this time. It took only three men topside to wrestle the earthly remains of Yakov Zubov over the hatch lip and plop him onto a gurney. Then the four medical examiners carefully worked both gurneys down the gangway, the body bags jiggling and bumping as the gurneys' wheels jostled over the wooden treads.

Finally, it was done. Kobzar pushed Zhuravin toward the ambulance, where he met with one of the examiners. Zhuravin signed a few papers then stepped away. The medical examiners jumped in the ambulance. Its doors slammed shut and they drove away.

Zhuravin pressed two fingers to his lips, whistled, and waved a hand over his head. "Back to work," he shouted. Reluctantly, the *K-129* crew lined up at the gangway and began tromping back on board.

Zhuravin and Kobzar were joined by Nikolayevich, and the three walked over to Vladimir and Yusopov. Kobzar, a mild-mannered Ukrainian with light brown hair, said, "Looks like you're in the middle of this one, Utkin. Do you know why the KGB wanted to interrogate you?"

The question was like a slap in Vladimir's face. "Interrogate?"

Kobzar stepped close. "Leytenant. I asked you a question."

Stupid. "Sorry, Captain. I have no idea. They had just begun asking questions when the fire alarm went off."

"Nothing at all?" demanded Kobzar.

"Well, sir, they seemed to be interested in my father."

"What about him?"

"His name is Eduard Dezhnev."

"Really?" said Yusopov.

Kobzar said, "I know him. We served in the *K-12*. What did they want to know?"

Utkin gulped. "Well, they wanted to know when I last saw him."

"And what did you tell them?"

"The last time I saw him was in Sochi about three days ago. I was on leave there with Captain Yusopov."

Yusopov said peevishly, "You don't need to bring me into this."

"It's complicated. You see, he and my mother were divorced and I kept my mother's name. That's what those two were asking about."

Kobzar stroked his chin. "Ummmm."

Utkin nodded. "And then the freon started blasting." It was quiet for a moment, so Vladimir asked, "What happened, sir? Why did the LOKh go off?"

"We forgot something," said Nikolayevich.

"Forgot what?" asked Vladimir.

With a furtive glance at Kobzar, Nikolayevich explained, "We forgot to tag out the control block."

"Tag it out? Why?" asked Vladimir.

Nikolayevich said, "It looks like Lutrov was puttering with the Freon control block. The system had been disabled for maintenance this morning and then put back on line during the noon watch while he was topside. Thinking it was still disabled, he was fiddling with the valve controls while he waited for you. But he didn't know it was reactivated. He just started pushing buttons."

There was a sinking feeling in Vladimir's stomach as he realized what had happened. Each compartment had large bottles of compressed freon gas stored beneath the decks. If the compartment temperature rose above a certain setting, the system, thinking there was a fire, would automatically activate the LOKh (*lodochnaya obyemnaya khimischeskaya*) fire suppressant system, and discharge R 114 freon gas. The gas quickly removed oxygen, which fed fires, but it also snuffed out the oxygen that sustained life. Thus the need for OBA hoods.

"But wasn't the control block tagged out?" asked Vladimir.

Nikolayevich looked away.

Kobzar tamped tobacco into a pipe. "And you know what? They're hauling me, you, Zhuravin, Nikolayevich, and Captain Yusopov here, in addition to the star of the show, Seaman Lutrov, before a special investigation board. And they still expect me to get underway inside of two weeks. But then it may not be my concern. I may be sacked before that and someone else may whisk you off to glory for the Rodina."

"I'm sorry, sir," said Vladimir.

"Zero eight hundred tomorrow morning, Leytenant. You will be there?"

"Do I have a choice?"

They exchanged glances. Zhuravin snickered. Nikolayevich looked away. Kobzar said, "All right. Those two men were pigs. I think we all agree on that. Nobody seems to be crying over their shrouds. We just have to get our stories straight about the LOKh foul-up so we can sail through and get this ship as ready as she can be." He turned to the executive officer. "What do you think, Alek?"

Zhuravin said, "We, uh, need to, uh, show them that the installation was faulty even though our procedures were proper. Leytenant, you said that you attempted to provide masks for them?"

"Yes, sir."

"And that the big one kept you from leaving the compartment?"

"Yes, sir. I had masks for myself and Captain Yusopov, and that was the extent of them in my stateroom. I attempted to go forward to retrieve some from the next stateroom and he wouldn't move out of our way."

Yusopov said, "Those two signed their own death warrants, then. The big man, uh… I don't think I heard his name."

"Nikulin," said Zhuravin.

"Nikulin. He wouldn't let us move. He held us tight to the spot. We tried to reason with him but he was too scared to do anything. And then he just fell down. By then it was too late for us to do anything."

Kobzar tapped his pipe tobacco down and puffed a bit. "We may be able to get away with that, but you can bet they'll have somebody from the UKB-16 design bureau there doing his best to turn the facts around and lay the blame on us. Finger pointing; it'll be a pissing contest."

Zhuravin nodded sagely. "Umm. Maybe a whole legion of engineers, chemists, experts, commissars, paid lackeys, and who knows who else stacking the deck against us?"

Kobzar said, "Maybe, Alek. Maybe not. There may not be enough time. My sense is they really want us under way. That the purpose of our mission may outweigh all that."

Yusopov said, "I think so too, Captain. If we just stick to the truth and prove our procedures were correct, then I believe we'll be okay."

Kobzar actually laughed. "The truth? Now there's a quirk of fate."

"What about Lutrov?" asked Vladimir.

Zhuravin exchanged glances with the other two and then said, "Once this is over he will be transferred, of course. To the surface fleet. The less people talk, the better."

Kobzar turned to Nikolayevich and said, "What do you think now about the freon R 114, Nikolay?"

Nikolayevich said, "We just don't know enough about the stuff. And the whole system stinks. I'd say, get rid of it until something better comes along. At least for now purge all the bottles. We already have enough chemicals with these damned rockets."

Kobzar nodded, "I think you're right." He turned to Zhuravin. "Alek?"

Zhuravin said, "Well, this is the first time the three of us agree on something. Amazing. Yes, get rid of the stuff." He chopped a hand through the air.

"Done." Kobzar turned and nodded to Nikolayevich. "Purge the damn bottles."

"Yes, sir. First thing tomorrow," said Nikolayevich.

"Good." Kobzar clapped Nikolayevich on the shoulder.

Vladimir asked, "May I ask, Captain, why they wanted me?"

Kobzar said, "You don't know?"

"Outside of what they asked, I have no idea, Captain."

"They told me Eduard Dezhnev has suspicious contacts with the West."

Vladimir was jolted. "He what?"

"Leytenant! Remember where you are," barked Zhuravin.

Vladimir braced to near attention. "I'm sorry, Captain. I'm surprised. Do you mean they think he's a spy?"

"They're apparently worried."

"But why? Why would he do such a thing?"

"You are in a better position to tell me and," Kobzar nodded to where the ambulance had been, "to tell them. Are you close to your father?"

Utkin felt as if he'd been kicked in the stomach. "No, sir."

"Well, it won't stop with those two idiots. I'm thinking that if you go ashore they'll grab and hold you someplace. And I need you here."

Vladimir knew anything was possible here in Rybachiy, where there seemed to be more KGB agents than mess cooks. He looked Kobzar in the eyes.

Kobzar said, "Let's try this. Pending the results of the board meeting, we sail within two weeks, no later than the end of the month. It's simple, Utkin. Except for the investigation board, we'll restrict you to the ship. And you'll be under guard, our guard, going and coming."

Vladimir looked up into the night sky to watch snowflakes float down. It didn't really matter where he was. He knew the KGB could get him if they really wanted him. Still, he seemed safer aboard the *K-129*. "All right. Thank you, Captain," he said.

Kobzar continued, "We can hope things will have changed upon our return and that those ghouls won't come back."

24

20 February 1968
BOQ, Naval Air Station, Barbers Point
Oahu, Hawaii

With many of the officers on leave or in school, Jerry was put to work—physically. In the mornings, he ran up and down the *Wolfish*'s hatches, going ashore now and then on various errands and drawing supplies.

After today's lunch he had stood the afternoon quarterdeck watch under a hot sun. But at 1600 he had the night off and returned to the sanity of the BOQ. He had a quick meal, tromped to his room, ignored Cedros, and took a long, hot shower. He flopped exhausted into bed and slept as if never before, dreaming of...scratching. He swam back to consciousness. There *was* scratching; it was at the door, where a bit of hallway light leaked through. He focused on his watch; the radium dial showed it was 0422. Then his eyes acclimated to the dark and he saw it. An envelope had been shoved under the door. He whipped back the covers and retrieved the envelope. In the weak light he saw it was a telegram addressed to him. He went back and sat on the edge of his bed. Flipping on the light, he ripped it open.

JERRY

YOU'RE HARD TO FIND. VERY IMPORTANT AND VERY, VERY SECRET. CALL ME SOONEST, INTERNATIONAL OPERATOR #252. ASK FOR CALLER 0-215-263-1145, PERSON-TO-PERSON COLLECT. VERY IMPORTANT. I'M WAITING.

ERNIE HERNANDEZ

The date/time code indicated the message had been sent two hours ago. Not bad. He put on his khakis and eased out the door. Taking the elevator down to the lobby he found the place empty. So were the two phone booths in the corner. He eased into one, closed the accordion doors, dropped a quarter in the slot, and dialed the international operator.

After a series of clicks and voices demanding numbers a phone rang, the connection surprisingly good. It was then that he learned he was being connected to an operator in Vera Cruz. His heart raced.

"Yes?" It sounded like Ernie.

The international operator cleared the charges with Ernie on a credit card and checked out. Ernesto Hernandez spoke up. "Jerry?"

"Hi, Ernie. Good to hear your voice. What's up?"

"Jesus. Everything."

"Ernie, for cryin' out loud, it's four in the morning here. I'm in the BOQ lobby freezing my ass off."

Ernie snorted. "Freezing your ass off in Hawaii? Tough duty."

"Okay, I should have said, 'spit it out before the ice in my mai tai melts.'"

"That's better." Ernie paused and then said, "Look, I have to tell you about something that happened here. And it's not pleasant." Then he told Jerry everything about Giorgio Michelotti's acid throwing and Rita's subsequent hospitalization. Except he toned down the acid part and the damage to Rita.

Jerry found his heart racing, his breathing shallow and quick.

"Jerry? Jerry?" said Ernie. At length he shouted, "Jerry!"

Jerry shook himself. "Sorry, this kind of hits low."

"Maybe you should get a lawyer or talk to ONI or the FBI or something."

"Giorgio is dead, you say?"

"Buried out in the jungle."

"Jeez. Maybe it should be you who calls the FBI."

"I've thought about that. To tell the truth, it's my mom and dad I worry about now. That those goons, whoever they are, will send more goons."

"I don't think so, Ernie. We've got them surrounded on at least three sides. You say that Barton Seidman was fired?"

"That's what Giorgio said."

"Good. The Ruganis had him in their pocket. Make that surrounded on four sides now. They don't have a lot of wiggle room. Especially with your threat about SEALs. Come to think of it, my attorney threatened the same thing."

"What the hell happened in Sigonella?"

Jerry said, "This may not go over so good."

"Jerry, I know my sister. She's been in hot water before. But nothing like this."

"Okay." Jerry explained the whole incident about Rita's tryst with Michelangelo Rugani, the fight, and the subsequent threats from the Italians and Barton Seidman.

"So all you have to do is ride it out."

"Maybe, but I've got an Article 133 hanging all over me right now."

"So go flying."

"I'd like nothing better, but right now they have me grounded."

"That sounds stupid."

"Yes, all in the name of international diplomacy and the people-to-people program."

"So, what happens next?"

"I have an attorney handling it from Sigonella. And I have another one here who seems pretty good."

"Are they JAG?"

"Both of them. And I have to say the one in Sigonella did a good job. He's still cleaning up crap with the State Department, the Italian government, and the Navy."

"So far, so good."

"Maybe so, but tell me. You sort of glossed over what happened to Rita. And where in the hell is she now?"

Ernie took a deep breath. "This is not easy."

"What is it, damn it?"

"The doctors did what they could. We have a pretty good burn center here, but they couldn't get it all."

"All what? What the hell was it?"

"Hydrochloric acid. Concentrated, I'm told."

"Son-of-a-bitch!" Jerry shot to his feet, his fist doubled.

"Her face on the right side took the worst of it. They were able to save her eyes because she had dark glasses on. But her right cheek and lip are ... are..." Ernie paused and drew a breath.

"I don't believe this."

"Well here's something else that may soften the blow."

Jerry exhaled loudly. "Go ahead."

"She says Rugani was trying to rape her. That they got drunk all right, and that's when he went after her."

"Holy shit!"

"I'll say."

"I'll kill the son-of-a-bitch."

"I'd hold off on that, old friend. At least until you get your own situation squared away."

Jerry took deep breaths.

"You okay? Hello? Jerry, Jerry?"

"Yes, I'm okay."

"Take some deep breaths."

"I'm doing that."

"I'm sorry, Jerry. But I thought you should know."

"You were right. You're a good friend and a good brother. Thanks for being there and taking care of things. It must not have been pleasant for you or your folks."

"Well, we're getting over it."

"Any idea of what's on Rita's agenda?"

"It's going to take surgery—lots of it—to get her anywhere near normal."

"Damn. Her looks are everything to her. Where is she? Can I speak with her?"

"I wish I knew."

"What the hell?"

"She checked out of the hospital early this morning. Chartered a jet. Gone.

"To where?"

"I found the charter company and traced the flight. It was to Phoenix. After that, the trail disappears."

Jerry sat slowly. "Incredible."

"She may try to contact Mom and Dad. Outside of that, I don't know."

"What can she do?"

"She has plenty of money. She can do anything. Certainly the best of doctors. That's what I think she's doing, anyway. So does this mean you haven't heard from her?" Ernie asked.

"Not a peep. She probably thinks I'm really angry at her."

"You should call the FBI in case those goons come after you."

"Not right now. This place is locked up tighter than a drum."

After a long moment, Ernie asked, "You okay, Jerry?"

"I don't know. But I owe you a world of thanks for tracking me down and letting me in on this."

"You have every right to know."

"My poor Rita. She must have been in a lot of pain."

"It was pretty ugly for a while. But the doctors got all that stabilized after a couple of hours. And she was drugged up, too."

"Is there anything I can do?"

"For right now, I don't think so. Rita has gone underground. And I'm still here supposedly enjoying sun, sand, and vintage red in old Mexico."

"You're a good man. Where are you stationed?"

"VMA 69."

"Where's that?"

"Helicopter unit in Nam."

"Jeez, what are you flyin'?"

"UH-34."

"A dog?"

"So far, it seems pretty rugged. I'm satisfied."

"Mine goes faster."

"Mine can hover over your ass and squash it like a grape."

"Okay, okay, if you're satisfied then so am I. Bad news over there."

"Not pretty. It's serious war, I'll tell you."

"So I've heard."

"Look. Do you have my folks' address in case something turns up?"

"I do. And I'll let you know if something does. Anything else?"

Ernie sighed. "I saved the best for last."

"Nice. Can you let me in on it?"

"The doctors discovered Rita is pregnant; a couple of months at least."

25

24 February 1968
***K-129*, moored Rybachiy Submarine Base**
15th Submarine Squadron
Abacha Bay, Petropavlovsk Oblast, Siberia, USSR

The icy blue-green waters of Guba Avachinskya stroked the *K-129*'s casing while snow swirled about her upperworks. After lying dockside for so long, she had a heavy white coating and was nearly invisible against the surrounding docks and buildings. Contrasted on the white-dusted black conning tower were the white numerals 722, her fleet designation.

At 1236, Captain Third Rank Nikolay Nikolayevich rolled the submarine's middle engine. It had been warming for the previous hour and caught immediately; the two-thousand-horsepower diesel rumbled into what was otherwise a silent darkness. The two outboard diesels likewise caught immediately, all three exhausts now ripping at the night.

Wearing parka and cap, Captain First Rank Vladislav Yusopov stood dockside watching electricians and machinists disconnect shore-side power cables and hoses, snaking them off the ship and coiling them near junction terminals on the wharf. Beside Yusopov were the *K-129*'s skipper, Captain First Rank Vladimir Kobzar, and executive officer, Captain Second Rank Aleksandr Zhuravin.

An engine roared in the distance, and through swirling snow a command car crunched up to the gangway and stopped. It was a Dodge WC 6, one of 18,000 half-ton vehicles that had begun life as a weapons carrier. Built in Auburn Hills Michigan, the rugged four-door Dodge was shipped under the Lend-Lease program to the Soviet Union in 1944 via the Murmansk run. After the rout of the Wehrmacht in 1945, the Dodge was shipped on to Kamchatka for life as a combination weapons carrier and command car, one of the world's first crossover vehicles, so to speak. This four-wheel Dodge was open with just a canvas top and no canvas sides.

The Dodge stood quietly, its engine ticking over. Eventually, the driver jumped out and lit a cigarette. In back, a guard sat in shadows, the butt of his PPSh-41 submachine gun jammed on his thigh, the barrel sticking up in the air. Both driver and guard were naval infantry functioning as part of the KGB home guard.

Leytenant Vladimir Utkin was seated beside the guard, a large double-locked leather pouch slung over his shoulder. He rose and stepped from the Dodge to join Kobzar, Zhuravin, and Yusopov.

Zhuravin motioned with his hands, *Gimme*.

Utkin transferred the pouch to Zhuravin. "Damned thing's heavy." He dug in his pocket, pulled out a key, and dropped it into the exec's hand.

Immediately, Zhuravin adjusted the burden, turned, mounted the gangway, boarded the *K-129*, and disappeared down the forward hatch.

Kobzar turned to Utkin. "How was your night ashore, Leytenant?" On a lark, Kobzar and Zhuravin, after having restricted Utkin to the ship for the past two weeks, had sent him over to pick up the last-minute security mail, just to give him a last taste of land before they got under way. Under the protection of an armed driver and guard, he'd been off the *K-129* for fifteen minutes. Now he was back.

"Not much time to chase girls, Captain," said Utkin.

"Plenty of time for that when we get back. There was a message a few minutes ago that we go into dry dock upon our return. So budget your time. I'm sure your calendar will be full." He nudged Utkin with an elbow.

"Yes, sir. Thank you, sir," said Utkin.

Yusopov leaned forward and tipped two fingers to his fur cap. "And now, Captain, permission to leave the ship?"

Kobzar nodded, "As long as you're back by 0200, Vladislav. Otherwise, we'll be gone and you'll be feeding seagulls."

"Well before that, Captain. Thank you, sir." Yusopov bowed to the others and walked over to the waiting command car. He pounded the hood, a summons, and climbed aboard while the guard in back drew to a semblance of attention.

The driver, a beefy man with blond hair, expertly flicked his cigarette five meters over the seawall and into the icy water. He eased himself in and said, "Yes, sir?"

"Club Rigoletto."

The driver stomped the floor-mounted pedal. With the engine still running, the starter engaged the spinning flywheel, making a shrill grinding noise. "Sorry sir."

"How long have you been driving?"

"Long enough to know better than that. It won't happen again, Captain." He shifted into low and said, "Club Rigoletto, yes, sir."

Captain Third Rank Akim Motorin, a naval architect, had designed the newer buildings at the Rybachiy Submarine Base. Along with upgrading the shipyard facilities and the various trade shops needed to keep the submarine fleet at sea, Motorin also designed and supervised the building of the common mess hall, hospital and dental facilities, gymnasium, theater and meeting hall, and the senior officers' quarters. The latter was where Yusopov was headed. Formally Building 404, to those assigned to Rybachiy the heavily guarded building was called Club Rigoletto due to Motorin's passion for Italian opera. During the three years he oversaw the completion of his projects, Motorin lived in one of the fourteen suites designed for travelling flag rankers. For hours and hours at a time, opera music cascaded from Motorin's suite, most often his favorite, Giuseppe Verdi's *Rigoletto*, hence the building's nickname. Some of those staying in the officers' quarters next door loved it and languished in the arias. Other's damned the screeching and demanded the music cease immediately. Still others, in a convoluted sense of fair play, forced Motorin to play Tchaikovsky, Rachmaninoff, and Prokofiev as well.

Rigoletto.

In the bleak winter snow, Building 404 looked more like the Lubyanka than the Lubyanka itself. It was the windows. Like the rest of the architectural design in Rybachiy, the windows looked as if they were ready for bars and conversion to prison cells. Perhaps that's what Motorin had in mind. No one knew.

"There." Yusopov pointed. The driver pulled the Dodge into a parking space posted with a red flag with the three stars of a colonel general. "Keep warm. Don't switch off the engine. Take turns waiting in the lobby. They should give you coffee." The sailors grunted thanks and Yusopov got out and walked into the building. Unlike the stark exterior, the lobby was done in warm dark woods. Paintings of colorful country scenes decorated the walls. A man sat behind the counter on high chair. In fact, his chair was higher than Yusopov was tall: meant to intimidate. Another man stood opposite near a fireplace in the lobby. Like the driver and guard outside, both were KGB border troops.

Yusopov walked up to the man at the counter. "General Yusopov, please."

The man was bald with hooded eyes. He looked at Yusopov for a moment and said, "It's late." He looked at his watch to emphasize the point.

Yusopov had been through this many times. Instead of raging at the man, he crossed his arms and let his eyes drift around the lobby.

At length, the counter clerk gave a long sigh and asked, "Who is calling, please?"

"I am Captain First Rank Vladislav Yusopov."

"Ah, my apologies, Captain. One moment, please." He picked up a phone and dialed a number. It was answered right away. The clerk nodded and hung up. "Yes, sir. They're expecting you. Right down that hall. Room 107."

They? Who the hell are they? "Thank you." Just then, the command car driver trudged in and let the door close behind him. Yusopov said to the clerk, "He is with me. There's also a guard out in the car with the engine running. Do you have something hot for them?"

"Coffee, sir."

"Very good. I shouldn't be too long." Yusopov nodded to his driver and then turned and walked down the hall, his boots sinking into the thick white carpet. The wainscoted walls, light green on top and white beneath, were decorated with battle flags and photos of famous soldiers of the Great Patriotic War and later. One was the oft-posted photo of Yuri Gagarin, the first human in space. The rest were mostly Army officers. *No Navy. Interesting.* Then he realized that the men in uniform were mostly KGB, GRU, the military intelligence arm of the Red Army, and Strategic Rocket Forces men. Together the three groups had developed the targeting codes for the R-21 missiles now aboard the *K-129*. They also developed and enforced firing procedures, personnel selection, and promotion of senior officers in the submarine fleet.

The entrance to room 107 was nestled in an alcove. A heavy-set man with large jowls, an oily face, and close-cropped hair sat next to the door, chair tilted back against the wall, reading a magazine. He wore a shiny blue suit with a solid dark blue tie. Casually, he stood and sidestepped before the door, his face like gun metal. "Yes?"

Yusopov recognized him. "Good evening, Oleg."

The man's face brightened a shade. "Ah, Captain Yusopov. We're expecting you." Oleg Caroni had been Maxim's batman and friend for many years. Born of an Italian father and Russian mother, Oleg was a former Spetsnaz officer. He had mangled his leg on a low-altitude night parachute jump and was about to be forced out of the service after eighteen years, but Maxim kept him on doing odd jobs so Oleg could accumulate his twenty years and retire. That was twelve years ago, and they were still together and fast friends.

"The general is expecting me?"

"Indeed he is, sir; please go right in." Oleg pushed the doorbell button then stepped aside. It rang, a pleasant, muted chime like that of an exclusive residence.

The door opened with Maxim Yusopov filling the entrance. "Vlady!" His father opened his arms and enveloped his son in a bear hug.

Yusopov went along with it, trading back slaps and grunts. Soon they parted with Maxim running his eyes up and down his son. "You look magnificent."

"Thank you, sir." Yusopov stripped off his fur cap and overcoat and dropped them in a chair.

"Come in, come in. What can I get you?" Maxim steered his son into a drawing room furnished in period French.

Yusopov couldn't tell if it was authentic but it definitely had the feel—especially since no electric lights were burning. A fire crackled in a two-meter-wide fireplace with an ornate mantle. Faded wall tapestries and sconces with lighted candles gave the place an eighteenth-century aura. Maxim prided himself on his expensive foreign sound system. His prized Akai Japanese phonograph played the Prelude and Good Friday music from Wagner's *Parsifal* through an RCA receiver and Telefunken speakers. Not a scratch, not a pop. Perfect. Soothing. Yusopov had heard the Prelude many times. He loved it almost as much as his father.

Maxim pointed to a deep sofa and picked up a large crystal flask. He swirled it, his brow furrowed.

Yusopov sat with a sigh. "You wanted to see me, Father?"

"Have a brandy, son. Relax for a moment," Maxim said expansively.

"Did you say brandy?"

"Alita."

Yusopov smacked his lips. He loved brandy, especially Alita, brewed and bottled in Riga. But then he thought of the fire before him and this wonderful sofa and brandy and getting too comfortable. "No thanks, Father. We sail within the hour and I'd better not."

"Ah. I'm sorry. Good thinking, though. If you will forgive me?"

"Of course."

Maxim poured brandy into a crystal tumbler then sat beside his son.

Yusopov took in his father. At seventy-two he was still a striking man. His once coal-black hair was salt and pepper now but still abundant and spilled over his forehead. Smooth olive skin, steel blue eyes, and his mouth lined with perfect teeth under a full moustache. His open shirt and dress trousers and white socks didn't mask the powerful body, now at rest and relaxed.

Father.

Maxim sipped and in the silence both men focused on another crystal tumbler sitting on the coffee table before them. It was half full with a lipstick smudge on the rim.

Maxim gave a sheepish grin. "My assistant, Iliana." He nodded toward the hallway.

"Ah, yes." No doubt the "assistant" was another of Maxim's string of bimbos. Quite frankly, he was surprised. Maxim had very specific tastes when it came to women. Where would his father find a good-looking woman in Rybachiy? Since returning here three weeks ago, he hadn't seen such a person. Maybe this was a travelling bimbo. Plus, he missed his Sofia, silver-capped front teeth and all. She had a wonderful sense of humor and was the only woman he knew who could hold her liquor and keep up with him. He looked at his father.

"She's gone to bed."

"I see." Yusopov tried to imagine the twenty-five-year-old half-naked bombshell who undoubtedly awaited his father in the bedroom.

Maxim lowered his voice to a near whisper. "Look, my boy. I'll be honest. A man of my age must be careful. You can't lose your edge. With me, for whatever reason, being successful with women is most important."

Yusopov sat up straight. This was getting interesting. He grabbed a glass, poured brandy, and drank, savoring the fire as it burned its way down.

"That's more like it." Maxim nodded. He continued. "This is the last time I'll speak to you about such things. After this you are on your own."

Yusopov gave a smile. "Yes, sir." Maxim often prefaced his maxims, as he called them, with that same phrase. But it was never really the last time. Still, Vladislav found his father's advice good most of the time. He ventured another sip.

"In the beginning, I'll tell a lady that I've lost it. That my desire and ability to perform have dried up. That I just can't do it anymore."

Yusopov nearly choked on his brandy.

"And you know what I've learned?"

Yusopov shook his head.

Maxim grinned but kept his voice low. "It's abject disbelief. Women can't wait to disprove it. It drives them crazy. They come after you like animals. It's amazing." He tossed a hand in the air and gulped brandy.

They laughed.

Maxim sat back and swirled his brandy for a moment. "I asked you here to speak to you about your voyage."

The Wagner finished and a new record dropped with a soft click. Smetana's *Moldau*.

"Yes, sir."

"Has the contingent reported aboard?"

"Yes, sir. About half an hour ago." It had been strange. Eleven men showed up on the dock, ranking from kapitan leytenant to starshiy second class. "Do you know about this?"

"Yes. Was their paperwork in order?"

"Yes, all signed by Admiral Dygalo."

"Ummm." Maxim nodded and poured another dollop of brandy.

"Is there something you want me to do?"

"Give them every assistance they need."

"Why are they there? We're fully manned already, and this puts a burden on our ship."

"How so?"

"Well, for one thing, we don't have enough bunk space."

"So hot-bunk them."

"That grows tiring after thirty days. Men get irritable. Tempers flare. Fights break out. And besides that, there is the issue of food."

"You'll get by. We checked. You should have enough food."

Yusopov set aside his glass. "Well, aside from food and berthing problems, there is the mission itself. They all seem to be either KGB or rocket specialists or both. And their orders are nonspecific. Why do we need these men?"

"Captain Kobzar has a special set of orders that he'll open in three days."

"Is there anything else you can tell me? At least I can soften the blow."

"Only this. You may be coming home in thirty days."

Yusopov sat back. "What?"

"That's all I can say. Look, I want to say this. While you're out there, your vision, your worldview, may be challenged."

"Who is going to do that?"

Maxim growled. "Shut up and listen." He steepled his fingers and looked down. "Times are trying now. Nikolai needs us desperately."

By that Yusopov knew Maxim meant Nikolai Podgorny, chairman of the Presidium of the Supreme Soviet, who was supposed to support Leonid Brezhnev, general secretary of the Soviet Union. But too often the two were at odds, arguing openly before senior politicians and officers, who stood by in embarrassed silence. Now, the two were engaged in a full power struggle, with Podgorny gradually losing but still hanging on. Podgorny had recently appointed Maxim to the governing board of the Soviet Energy Institute, the public name for the USSR's nuclear weapons administration. It was a gamble. Yusopov was well aware that if Podgorny went down, Maxim would go down with him.

Yusopov felt stupid. He had no control over this. "What can I do?" he said stiffly. His eyes flicked to his watch: 0132.

That wasn't lost on Maxim. "Right now, all I can ask is for you to do your duty. You'll know when the time comes."

"On this trip?"

"Ummm."

A vague answer. He didn't understand. He checked again: 0133.

Suddenly, Maxim's eyes ripped into his son. "Let me put it to you this way. If the leader is filled with high ambition and if he pursues his aims with audacity and strength of will, he will reach them in spite of all obstacles."

Another maxim. "Who said that?"

"Von Clausewitz."

Silence. With a forefinger, Yusopov moved his sleeve up his wrist: 0135. He stood. "I'm sorry, Father. I must leave or miss movement."

Maxim stood with him and flopped both hands on his son's shoulders. "Be brave, my boy."

"Are you speaking of war?" Yusopov blurted. He stepped over and began putting on his overcoat.

Maxim shrugged. "War is regarded as nothing but the continuation of state policy with other means."

"Von Clausewitz again?"

"Of course."

"This is stupid."

"We're warriors. This is what we do. When the time comes, you'll do what you're expected to do."

"When the time comes?"

"I know you'll do your duty."

Yusopov finished buttoning his coat. He put on his fur cap, adjusted it, and turned to his father. Tipping two fingers to his forehead, he said, "Thank you for the brandy, sir."

" I'm not finished."

Yusopov checked his watch. "Father, I'll be late. We shove off at 0200. And Captain Kobzar said—"

"Kobzar is an idiot," hissed Maxim.

Quiet. Wood crackled in the fireplace. Yusopov clasped his hands behind his back. "Yes, sir?" *Thirty more seconds then I walk out whether he likes it or not.*

Maxim knocked back his brandy and seemed to weave in place. "You did well in North Korea. I'm proud of you. It's obvious you have overcome the problems of the past. But Korea was a test. Here is where you really earn your rubles." He faked a laugh.

"What can I do, Father?"

"Take care of those men to your utmost. Do whatever is required. It's extremely important. My future and the future of the Rodina are at stake."

"I will, Father. You can count on me." *I have no idea what he's talking about.*

Maxim's eyes became unfocused. Then he bear-hugged his son and stepped back. "Be well, my son."

"Thank you, sir." Yusopov walked out.

26

24 February 1968
***K-129*, moored Rybachiy Submarine Base**
15th Submarine Squadron
Abacha Bay, Petropavlovsk Oblast, Siberia, USSR

The Dodge WC 6 sped through slush at sixty kilometers an hour, throwing mud and snow, nearly careening into a fuel truck. With the engine growling and horn honking, the command car bounced onto the dock, the driver wheeling between oil drums as if he were on a tank obstacle course. Yusopov checked his watch as they ground to a halt opposite the submarine's gangway. The *K-129*'s engines rumbled as steam rose from the exhaust pipes. A mobile crane was alongside the gangway, its driver taking a strain on the cable. Yusopov leaped from the Dodge. "Wait!"

The driver, a cigarette dangling from his lips, didn't seem to hear. The gangway popped loose and rose a half meter.

Yusopov shouted, "Wait, you fool." He leaped on the gangway and ran across. The moment Yusopov stepped aboard the *K-129*, the crane operator reengaged the hoist and the gangway rose high in the air and away from the submarine.

Yusopov stood breathless for a moment, his hands on his knees as the stern lines were taken in, then the bow lines. Soon they were free and backing slowly from the dock.

Fog swirled. Yusopov looked aft and could hardly make out three figures atop the sail. One was Kobzar, he knew, but he couldn't identify the others.

"You pushed it too close, Vladi." Zhuravin, the executive officer, frowned at him.

Yusopov stood up and flashed his watch. "One fifty-five, damn it. I was on time."

"Maybe you were on time, my friend, but the *General Kluska* is ahead of schedule."

They headed for the hatch to the forward compartment. "Who the hell is *General Kluska*?"

"Tsk, tsk," clucked Zhuravin, his dark eyes flashing as he clambered into the hatch and started down. "I see you didn't read the op order."

"I did, too," protested Yusopov as an ancient C-2 cargo ship materialized from the fog just one hundred meters off their port bow. He pointed. "*General Kluska*, right?"

"Very impressive," Zhuravin's voice echoed up the tube. "Now tell me something else about the *General Kluska* and I'll give you liberty ashore tonight."

Yusopov watched as thick fog swirled around the old ship. Condensation and rust ran down hull plates dished in by countless storms over the years. The black hull contrasted with the deeply rusted white superstructure, which glared in the early morning light. A peacoated figure stood on her bridge wing peering over the gunwale, a lone sentinel for their voyage into Guba Avachinskya, through the fog-shrouded strait, and finally into the Pacific. As clapped out as the rusty old hulk appeared, Yusopov knew the Polish-flagged freighter was fitted with the latest radar to lead them safely.

The classified op order also stated that the 9,000-ton freighter was laden with 12,000 cases of AK-47 rifles, ammunition, hand grenades, and 10 artillery pieces all bound for Hanoi and the North Vietnamese now embroiled in the Tet Offensive with the Americans in the South.

The *K-129* vibrated and rattled for a moment as Kobzar put on an ahead bell to kill sternway. Then he called for slow ahead, delicately maneuvering to fall in behind the *General Kluska* for their trip to the open ocean.

Yusopov grabbed the rungs and followed Zhuravin down into the forward torpedo room. Men were everywhere, shouting, stowing gear, slamming lockers closed. From a Japanese tape recorder Otis Redding crooned "Sittin' on the Dock of the Bay" as two young sailors swung pillows at one another. Ten or so others lay in bunks reading or turned on their sides trying to sleep. Someone noticed the two officers and gave a shout. The men drew to attention as Zhuravin and Yusopov edged between them, including a half dozen Yusopov didn't recognize. He stopped before one of them, a giant of a man with red hair and a beard, and opened his mouth to speak.

"Later," said Zhuravin. "Let them get organized."

"I suppose so." Yusopov moved on past. He had organizing of his own to do.

They moved aft and soon found themselves in the control room. Harbor stations were manned with men standing before instrument panels or large valves or large wheels. Gauges, dials, electrical cable, and gleaming tubes ran everywhere. Watch-keepers wearing headphones made entries in logbooks and clip boards.

Nikolayevich stood peering through one of the periscopes. He saw Zhuravin and Yusopov, flipped up the handles, rolled his eyes, and said, "Can't see shit. I hope they know what they're doing up there." As chief engineer, Nikolayevich was the control room officer for harbor stations.

"How about radar?"

Nikolayevich shrugged. "Eh, it's okay. We painted the *Kluska* five minutes ago, and now, here she is." He leaned over a sailor sitting before a large cathode ray tube. The radar rendered a view of Avachinskya Bay with contacts showing as large blobs. He pointed almost directly ahead, "Right on time."

Yusopov relaxed. They'd practiced this many times. It should go without a hitch. And tonight was the payoff. To foil the American SOSUS system, they planned to stay as close as possible to the *General Kluska*, the sound of their diesel engines mixing as one, until they were several kilometers off the coast and ready to dive.

Hopefully.

As if on cue, the diving klaxon sounded. Hatches thumped shut. More submariners piled into the crowded control room.

"Dive, dive," the PA announced. "Prepare to snorkel."

Kobzar, an enlisted watch-stander, and Vladimir Utkin slid down the ladder from the sail, their peacoats and binoculars dripping with condensation from the wet night air. The conning tower hatch slammed shut. Utkin raised his binoculars strap over his head and handed them off to a quartermaster. Looking at Yusopov he gave an eye-roll.

Kobzar called out. "This is the captain. I have the conn." He stood next to the attack periscope, nudging Nikolayevich aside. "Pardon me, Nikolay."

"All yours, Captain," said Nikolayevich, moving over to become diving officer and OOD.

The chief of the watch announced, "Boat secure, sir."

"Very well, make your depth ten meters."

"Ten meters, aye," responded Nikolayevich.

"Secure port and starboard engines, make your rpm zero-five-zero for five knots."

"Secure port and starboard engines, zero-five-zero for speed five," repeated Nikolayevich. He cranked the ship's engine room annunciator and flipped gauges for corresponding rpm.

A little bell clanked indicating the engine room understood the order. The rumble and vibration ceased as the two outboard diesels were shut down.

The conn became quiet as they motored ahead on the center engine. Men in the overcrowded control room stopped talking with the realization they were about fifty meters behind the old freighter and sailing right in her wake. Visons of the *General Kluska*'s massive bronze four-bladed propeller chopping the water, and possibly them, came to more than one of the men in the control room.

Only the *K-129*'s periscopes and snorkel mast were visible during their silent journey. And in this fog it was nearly impossible to sight the freighter's ancient superstructure. Yusopov's skin became clammy, and the cabin temperature seemed to shoot up. He suddenly felt the press of people and bulkheads closing in, something he hadn't endured since he first began sub school and went to sea in a leaky old training submarine. He found himself jammed up against the fire-control panel where four rather than the customary two men were seated. And all four were part of the eleven who had boarded earlier. The four men worked the fire-control board, pushing buttons and pulling levers. Red, green, and yellow lights flashed on and off. The board answered back with bleeps and buzzes.

They looked up at him, glaring.

Men of inferior rank, every one of them. Yusopov had had enough. "What the hell are you looking at?"

"Sorry, sir," said the closest.

"It's just that—" This from a man at the other end of the control panel. His forefinger was pressed to a column in a thick procedure manual.

"What!" demanded Yusopov.

"You're sitting on the firing key."

Yusopov shifted his weight off the board. "That better?"

The man, short, squat, and balding, gave a half yawn. "For now. Thank you, sir."

Insolent. "What is your name?" demanded Yusopov.

"Gurin, sir, Starshiy Leytenant Gurin." The man was thin, had a Van Dyke beard and a curiously chipped front tooth.

"Where are Rabiloff and Kupinsky?" These were the regular men on the firing panel.

"Bunkroom, I suppose. They walked aft."

"And who authorized this?"

"Why Captain Zhuravin, sir, of course." The man's eyebrows were up as if Yusopov should have known all along.

Yusopov looked for the exec. Only three meters away, he was impossible to approach through the sea of humanity crowding the control room.

Instead Yusopov's eyes found Utkin nearly beside him, still in his peacoat. They caught each other's glances and nodded.

Yusopov began squeezing his way aft.

"Where you going, Vladislav?" asked Utkin.

"Out of this mess, to my bunk to compose myself," said Yusopov quietly.

"Sorry."

"Sorry, what?"

"We've been kicked out. These new people. Our stateroom has been turned over to them."

"Where do they have us?"

"Forward torpedo room. Aft bulkhead. One of the preferred spots, I'm told. You and I are hot-bunking."

"The hell you say!" Yusopov shouted.

From across the control room, Kobzar bellowed to the overhead, "Do you have a question, Mr. Yusopov?"

"No, Captain. Sorry, sir."

Kobzar went back to peering in his periscope. "We're nicely on station, Alek. Why don't you take her for a while?"

"Love to, sir. Thank you." Zhuravin stepped to the periscope and called out, "This is Mr. Zhuravin. I have the conn."

"That's right, Alek. Keep us tucked in behind the *Kluska.* Just don't overrun him and get our nose chopped off."

"Wouldn't think of it, sir."

Kobzar raised his voice and said, "Well, then, if Mr. Yusopov has no objection, I believe I'll go forward for a cup of tea."

27

25 February 1968
BOQ, Naval Air Station Barbers Point,
Oahu, Hawaii

Jerry was about to shove the key in the door when it opened to reveal Cedros, walking out. The young blond navigator said, "Good news. They've assigned me to a plane."

"Wonderful."

"And the better news is that I'm moving into a house with two buddies."

"A snakepit."

"Well…I wouldn't go so far as to…"

"When do you go?"

"Checking out now. Pick up my gear at the end of the day." He grinned. "You won't have to put up with my snoring."

"Gee."

They shook hands. With sincerity, Jerry said, "Good luck with your plane, Paul."

"Can't wait to get settled. By the way, someone's been calling for you. The number is on your bedside stand."

"Okay. Thanks."

"Adios." Cedros walked through the fire exit door and was gone.

Jerry walked in and sighed when he saw Cedros' clothes, underwear, and shaving gear scattered about the room. The bathroom floor was littered with towels and smelled of cheap aftershave.

He spotted the note Cedros had left. Penned out in his neat hand was a ten-digit phone number. Area code 213. What? He sat up straight; 213 was the area code for the Los Angeles, California, area. He picked up the phone, got the operator on the line, and put through the call, station to station.

It rang three times and then a woman with a deep, well-smoked voice answered, "Yes, hello?"

"Hi...er...my name is Jerry Ingram. Someone called here and left this number."

"One moment." A hand covered the mouthpiece. He heard muffled voices on the other end. Finally, "Hello?"

Rita! Thank God.

"Hello? Jerry?"

"Rita," he sputtered. "Where are you?"

"With friends."

"What happened? I...mean, Ernie told me—"

"I just talked to him. He gave me your number. You've been doing a bit of travelling."

Her voice sounded even, determined. Not like the carefree, slightly ditzy girl he married. Yes, mature. And intelligent. "Well, yes. Hawaii, now."

She continued, "Look, I called to say I'm sorry. I got the shock of my life, and it's made me think."

"Ernie told me some of it. How...do you...do you have any pain?"

"Just about gone now. But I'm still on painkillers. May take another week or so."

"And your...you know, your face where..."

"Jerry, I look like Frankenstein times six. Little kids would run if they saw me."

"Jesus, I'm so sorry, baby."

"Well, we all got our licks in on Giorgio. First you, then Ernie. Even me. I popped him over the head with a chair. And now he's paid his dues."

"Not sorry about that."

"Me neither. That guy was a creep."

"So I noticed. Look, what can I do to help?" He wanted to know more about her face and about the rape, but that was a conversation for later.

"I'm in a clinic. They tell me they can get rid of the Frankenstein look. But that will take time. Lots."

"Days? Weeks? Months?"

"Could be years. I'm trying to read between the lines with what these guys tell me. If I understand them right, I might be able to get into a church potluck dinner after they're done. But no way will I be walking down the runway again."

"I'm sorry..."

A moment passed, then she took a deep, gasping breath. "Look, something is really important to me right now."

Here it comes, the pregnancy. He didn't know how to handle this. "What is it?"

"Can you ever forgive me?"

"Aw, Rita." He found he'd been standing. Now he sat on the bed. "Of course. Yes. Don't worry about it." She needed to hear this.

There was silence. Then she took another breath. "You mean it?" she squeaked.

Reaching deep, he grasped for sincerity. "Of course I do."

"That son-of-a-bitch tried to rape me."

Jerry's fist doubled. "Yes, Ernie told me."

Her words tumbled out. "It was my fault. We drank too much wine. The next thing I knew he had thrown me over his shoulder and walked in the bedroom. He...he tore off my clothes...the bastard...he was going to..."

"It's okay, honey."

"But he couldn't, didn't...because you walked in."

Once again, Jerry doubled his fists. "They tell me I broke his nose and four front teeth."

She wailed, "Jerry, I'm so sorry. I let him go too far."

"And a couple of ribs for good measure."

She sniffled and the line became quiet.

"Rita?"

"I'm sorry."

"Don't worry, baby. It's done. Over."

"Thank you. I believe you. It's all I have to hold onto."

"I do mean it." He really did. "When can I—"

"Did Ernie tell you about the other part?"

"About the little surprise?"

"Yes. That's the one. Just so you know, the doctors tell me he's doing fine. There was no damage."

Jerry's heart jumped. "He?"

"I don't know. I just said that."

"How did they miss it before?"

"Doctor says it happens all the time. I was still having periods and things looked normal. Sometime the tests are inaccurate. And the stupid rabbit doesn't always die when he's supposed to. So, here we are pregnant again."

"How far along is he?" Jerry stumbled on that. Here he was calling the baby 'he' like Rita.

"Two and a half, maybe three months, the doctor estimates."

"So where do we go from here?"

"Well, they tell me I can travel soon. Maybe look all right except for bandages that have me looking like the phantom of the opera. And a fat, pregnant one at that."

Jerry let out a chuckle. "That I gotta see." Then he asked, "Where are you?"

"A clinic in Los Angeles. They cater to the movie crowd. I was lucky to get in. But they have satellite clinics. New York, Paris, Miami Beach, San Francisco and..."

"You're kidding."

"You guessed it, Honolulu."

"You can come out here?"

"I think so. If you'll have me."

"In a heartbeat." Jerry felt like soaring. "This is great. But can't you tell me where you are now?"

"I'm not supposed to."

"I have the phone number."

"It's a relay. They change it every so often. They're really tight on security."

"Shit. I'm under way tonight," he checked his watch, "in three hours."

"What does that mean?"

"It means I'll be gone for forty-five to sixty days." He gave her details.

"Call me when you get in? I'll be through the initial treatment."

"Then maybe you can come here?"

"I think so, if they'll let me. So, you'll call me?"

"First thing number one line hits the dock."

"Jerry?"

"Yes?"

"Do you really forgive me?"

28

24 February 1968
Berth S-1B, Quarry Loch
Pearl Harbor Naval Station
Pearl Harbor, Hawaii

A man and a woman sat huddled in the gray Ford pickup truck. Both doors were stenciled USN with long serial numbers beneath. They were parked under a tree in shadows made darker by a storm lingering overhead. The outline of the now-dark Admiral Lockwood Officers Club hulked in the distance. The submarine *Wolfish* was moored portside to the pier about fifty yards away, her sail with the numerals '562' jutting above a stack of two-inch pipes between them.

He was in working khakis, windbreaker, and garrison cap, his face in deep shadow. Even so, it was easy to spot the three stars on his cap and collar points. By contrast, his wife's olive skin blended into the darkness, and she had drawn a shawl over ebony hair pulled into a saucy ponytail. Streaks of silver here and there added to her aura of maturity and wisdom.

Rain plinked on the Ford's thin roof while Ingram wondered, as he had since he first met her so long ago on Corregidor, what made Helen's eyes seem to glow when everything else was dark. As always, her vitality came from within even on this dismal night, making him ponder what miracle made her look so utterly composed and in command.

Especially now, with all this turmoil in the Far East and the North Koreans getting away with stealing the USS *Pueblo*. It constantly gnawed at his liver, and he was glad to be out here with her for a few stolen moments, even if only to secretly watch their son shove off.

Sitting in this old pickup sure beat sitting in that dark, smoke-filled situation room listening to terse reports from frustrated frontline units watching the Communists' taunts and jabs as they consolidated big and little victories up and down the coasts of Asia. His staff pestered him for decisions he wasn't authorized to make. The worst of it was making recommendations to the Pentagon or the State Department and waiting for answers that never came while the North Koreans and Russians tightened their strangleholds.

The *Wolfish*'s Fairbanks Morse 38D8-1/8 diesel engines bellowed into the evening as Sailors, mere silhouettes, stepped carefully about the rounded casing singling the mooring lines, pulling them in, and stowing them in lockers. Now the submarine waited to take in the rest of her lines and get under way. Two tugs were made up on the starboard side: one at the bow, the other near the stern. But they waited, and for the time being everyone was idle. Sailors called back and forth from the dock to the submarine over the engines' mighty rumble: an off-color joke, a promise to pay a loan; from the few women standing across on the pier, a pledge to write often, ironic because it was impossible to write a Sailor living five hundred feet or more beneath the sea.

Ingram checked his watch again: 2105. "Where the hell is he?" he muttered.

Helen reached for his hand. "Shhhh. It's not as if he's had a lot of time to get ready for this, is it?"

"It's the Navy way." He looked at her with a soft grin. "Threw it all at him with no time to duck."

"And you expect him to be organized for a, what, a forty-to-sixty-day trip after just a few days?"

"It's been nearly a month."

"Has it? I barely got to see him."

Ingram looked at his watch again then nodded toward a crane that wheeled up to the submarine's brow. Sailors jumped around and began hooking it up.

Ingram shook his head, muttering.

There was a knock at the window. An officer in a garrison cap and light windbreaker grinned from outside. Commander's silver oak leaves glistened from his collar points and rain dripped down his face.

"I'll be damned." He turned to Helen. "It's Tony Wade. *Wolfish*'s skipper." Quickly, he cranked down the window, oblivious to the warm rain that spattered in.

Wade, a thin dark-haired man with a freckled face and an infectious grin, reached in. They shook.

Ingram said, "Hi, Tony."

"Good evening, Admiral."

Wade tipped two fingers to his garrison cap and bent down. "Good evening, Mrs. Ingram."

Helen leaned over. "And a good one to you, too, Captain."

Ingram said, "Nice of you to come over, Tony. How did you spot us?"

"Well, sir, we have this really cool gadget called a periscope. My ops officer was scanning the pier when he saw you two hiding back here like a couple of Commie spies. I thought I'd better check it out." His face grew serious. "I'll bet you're worried, Admiral."

"I was kind of wondering, Tony."

Wade nodded back to the *Wolfish*. "We just got word from the main gate. Snafu up there. Oil truck had a flat right in front of the guard kiosk. Traffic's backed up for two blocks. So your boy is stuck back there in a cab along with my comm officer and the guard mail. They should be along any moment. I'd ask you aboard but I understand this is all on the QT."

"It is. He mustn't know about it. Not even you. How did you figure it out, anyway?"

Wade looked away for a moment. "One of my officers was a year ahead of Jerry at the Academy." He leveled his eyes at Ingram. "He recognized the name."

Ingram sighed. "The underground telegraph."

"Don't worry. We'll keep him occupied and take good care of him. Quite frankly, I can use him. I hear he's a damned good pilot."

Ingram grinned. "So he loves to tell me, a lowly surface squid."

They laughed. "I know for a fact that—oh. Looks like this is him."

Wade nodded toward a yellow taxi racing down the pier, rainwater spewing from its tires. He said, "Let's hope we have two for the price of one."

Wade's wish was granted. The taxi pulled up and two khaki-clad figures jumped out. One had a thick briefcase and was first over the brow, saluting. Just behind him was another officer.

"Glad he made it," said Ingram offhandedly.

Helen said, "I forgot to pack a peanut butter and jelly sandwich for him today."

"Don't worry about that, Mrs. Ingram," said Wade. "He's pretty aggressive at the wardroom table. He'll do just fine."

Ingram added, "Yeah, too much peanut butter means too many zits."

Helen slapped his shoulder.

"Don't worry, Mrs. Ingram. We'll make a good bubblehead out of him."

Ingram said, "If you don't, just be careful next time you go flying. One can never tell who the pilot will be."

"I'll be sure to watch for that," said Wade. He stepped back and with a salute, said, "Time to shove off, Admiral. Mrs. Ingram."

Ingram returned it. "Thank you, Tony. Have a safe journey."

"You can plan on that, Admiral." Wade turned and walked into the mist. He must have been the last aboard because once he was over, the crane took a strain and the brow was lifted clear of the submarine's foredeck and gently dropped ashore.

Helen's grip tightened when, three minutes later, a figure joined two others atop the sail. "Is that our boy?"

"Mmmm. Most likely Tony Wade. Jerry's probably down below soaking in the hot tub."

"I'm sure."

To Ingram it seemed like milliseconds, but it actually took twelve minutes for the *Wolfish* to take in the rest of her lines and breast away from the dock. The tugs hooted and chugged, whistles blew, and men waved to each other through the warm Hawaiian downpour. Fifty feet off the dock the *Wolfish* engaged her engines, wound up turns for five knots, and crept away into the mist.

"Where are they going?

Ingram saw no reason not to tell her. "Central Pacific. Quiet zone. Nothing to worry about."

With the *Wolfish* about three hundred yards away, they got out and walked toward the pier watching the 1,600-ton submarine begin her journey.

"Piece of cake?"

"Mmmm, more like piece of apple pie."

She gave a long exhale. "So, how do you feel, Sailor?"

"Never stops, does it?"

The *Wolfish* disappeared into the mist.

Gone.

She sighed. "That's life, I guess. Two things, though."

His arm went around her. "Two things?"

"I have you and I have a pot of spaghetti waiting for us at home."

"Now you're talking."

29

24 February 1968
USS *Wolfish* (SS 562)
Berth S-1B, Quarry Loch,
Pearl Harbor, Hawaii

The OOD on the quarterdeck, a silver-haired chief engineman, logged Jerry in and sent him to the forward hatch. With that, he slammed his logbook closed, turned, and saluted the bridge. When they waved back, he followed Jerry.

As Jerry descended, his nose confirmed he was once again aboard a U.S. Navy ship. The bittersweet aroma of hydraulic fluid, the signature lifeblood of a submarine—or any ship, for that matter—wrapped itself around him.

By the time his feet landed on the polished green linoleum deck he was feeling at home. He looked forward toward the *Wolfish*'s business end. Six torpedo tubes were arranged with an electrical firing board mounted on the port bulkhead. A dazzling array of pipes, air ducts, cables, and junction boxes ran overhead. Behind him, torpedoes were neatly secured throughout the compartment with bunks above and below. Sailors' personal gear was cast about the bunks and being stowed as they chattered and joked, oblivious to the officer who edged his way among them. A portable radio played loud music, something from the Captain and Tennille.

Beneath his feet, the ship vibrated just a bit, telling Jerry they were indeed under way, most likely headed toward the main channel, past Hospital Point, and out toward the sea buoy and the Pacific.

The Sailors kept up their chatter as Jerry moved toward an oval hatch on the aft bulkhead. He stepped through the hatch and once again bumped his head. "Shit, I hate submarines," he said softly as he entered the midships passageway. It was narrow, perhaps three feet wide, the deck also covered with shiny green linoleum.

"What was that, Sailor?" An officer stood before him, a large grin on his round, chubby face. Like Jerry he was a lieutenant (j.g.), but about six inches shorter and very stout.

Jerry rubbed his head. The damn thing hurt, but there was no blood.

"Hello? Jerry?" The man leaned close and waved a hand in his face.

He knew that voice. It belonged to—

"That's right, dunderhead. Phil Saltzman. I used to kick your ass at the Academy." He stuck out his hand. "Congratulations on making it through flight school."

They shook. "Phil! I'll be damned. So you got back in time to get under way." Saltzman had been a year ahead of Ingram at the Naval Academy and had borne down hard on Plebe Ingram during his freshman year when, at times, he became truculent. But Jerry pulled through and they became good friends.

Saltzman's grin widened. "Here I am, just to make sure you don't screw things up. And guess what?" He looked from side to side and spoke softly. "They had the poor judgment to make me operations officer."

Jerry was already aware of this. But he played along. "Jeez, how do I get off this death trap?"

"Don't worry; I'll make sure you have plenty of popcorn when things get dull."

"I can't wait."

"Trouble is; it never gets dull. We're always tripping over Communist submarines or running into uncharted mountain peaks. So most of the time you'll be having fur ball breakfasts."

"How reassuring."

"That's the spirit. Here, here's where you bunk." With the back of his hand he swept aside a green curtain. "Take a look at your new palace."

Jerry stepped into his stateroom. He'd moved his gear in a week before, but stayed away because the overhead was ripped up with pulling cable and ducting. This was the first time he'd seen it functional. It was a small stateroom with three bunks fitted into the starboard curvature of the submarine's hull. Each bunk was equipped with a reading lamp and a small bookshelf. A small metal desk, lamp, safe, and overhead bookshelf were on Jerry's right. Beside that was a metal chest of drawers. A washbasin, towel rack, and small curtain-shrouded hanging closet were mounted on the forward bulkhead.

"Yours truly gets the lower bunk."

"How nice. What else must I have to put up with?"

That earned a sour look from Saltzman. "Mitchell Cunningham, our main propulsion assistant, resides in the middle rack. He's on watch now with sea detail back aft. You, of course, have the bunk with the best view in this high-rent district." He sat on the lower bunk. "Have a chair."

Something moved behind Jerry.

"Ten-hut!" called Saltzman, springing to his feet.

Jerry turned to see a full commander standing behind him. He snapped to attention.

The two looked each other over.

The commander said, "At ease gentlemen. As you were." He wore a rain splattered foul-weather jacket, and his freckled face was dotted with raindrops. He whipped off a garrison cap, revealing dark, curly hair. He gave a broad grin as he extended a hand. "Welcome aboard, Mr. Ingram. Your humble commanding officer Anthony Wade at your service."

They shook. Jerry said, "Thank you, Captain. I'm glad to be here. I hope I'm the one who's at your service."

"And my apologies for not being here when you first reported aboard. But I'm told you did a great job on cumshaw and chasing parts in general."

"It was a real challenge, Captain."

"Bullshit," said Saltzman. "First thing I heard him say was, 'I hate submarines.'"

Jerry turned to protest, but then he caught Saltzman's eyes crinkle in the corners. He turned to see Commander Wade's doing the same. *They're screwing with me*. He waited.

Wade laughed; Saltzman joined in. Soon all three were chuckling. Ingram added, "All right. I admit it. I'm a zoomie, a duck out of water. I just hope that—"

"I don't blame you, Mr. Ingram," said Commander Wade. "The Navy shanghaied you, but quite frankly it's good to have you aboard. We deal with the aerial community a lot, and I'm glad to have an interpreter." He steepled his fingers. "In the meantime, here's what we'd like to do. Mr. Saltzman here is the senior watch officer and will be assigning you to your various watch bills. I'd like to start you out on the diving stations so you get a feel for the ship. After that, we'll get you as close to qualifying as an OOD as we can. In the meantime, if we have any events with air ops, you'll be pulled away to coordinate. Does that make sense?"

"Yes, sir, it does."

Commander Wade waved around the stateroom. "This isn't exactly the Royal Hawaiian, but..."

"It's perfect, Captain. I was worried I'd be sleeping between torpedoes.

Wade turned to Saltzman. "XO is taking us to sea. I'd like to attend to those dispatches..."

"Got 'em right here, Captain." Saltzman heaved a leather pouch from the desk and unbuckled it. He rummaged for a moment. "Just got it with the guard mail. Here we are. 'Eyes only.'" He handed over a heavily wrapped packet of four or five manila envelopes, all of them heavily stamped in red.

"Sign for me please, Skipper?" He handed up a ballpoint pen.

Wade leaned over and signed. "Very good, thank you, Phil." Wade nodded to them both and left the stateroom.

Saltzman raised his eyebrows.

"What don't I get?" Ingram asked.

"That was a bit unusual, don't you think?"

"I don't know what to think on submarines."

"I've been on this floating turd for eight months and I've never seen that level of secrecy."

"Maybe they're tired of your bullshit."

Saltzman sorted through the rest of the envelopes in the pouch. All were stamped SECRET or TOP SECRET. "Let's see..." he tossed them on the desk. "This is a bill for fuel oil at least six months past due. Um...here's one for water-blasting the sanitary tanks...okay ... this is a bill for my annual dues at the Central Communist Party. Uh..."

"I get it, Mr. Saltzman. Thanks for the welcome aboard party. Now, request permission to hit the sack?" Jerry took off his jacket.

"No, not at all, Mr. Ingram." He checked his wristwatch. "Oh— whoops."

"What?"

"It's now 2247. That gives you time for about a half hour of sleep."

"What?" Ingram's hands went to his hips.

"You have the midwatch in the control room. They'll come to wake you in about thirty-five minutes."

A wave of protest rose through Jerry, but he suppressed it. Better here than some Sicilian jail. "Okay, Phil. I get it. Okay."

"Seriously, Jerry. We'll be diving at around one or two o'clock. I wanted you to be in on it from the beginning."

Jerry sat in the chair and yawned. "Makes sense to me. Thanks."

"And a word of advice?"

"Please."

"The Captain hates ass-kissers."

"Pardon?"

"Why did you drag your folks into this?"

"What are you talking about?"

"I saw them waiting for you out in the parking lot. You were late so you missed them. But the skipper went out there and put them at ease."

"Huh? How did you know?"

"Hourglass liberty on the periscope. I saw the admiral and the missus snuggled in a Navy pickup under a tree in the parking lot waiting for you."

It hit Jerry. Saltzman came from a lumbering family in southern Oregon. He was a rough-hewn guy who had often worked in the woods with the lumberjacks. During their three years at the Academy together Saltzman had dealt harshly with midshipmen born to privilege. Especially those who put on airs or peddled influence. And now Jerry realized this whole thing had the stamp of his father. That would really burn up Saltzman. Actually, it made perfect sense. How could they proceed against him with an Article 133 while he was deep under the ocean? Except he hated submarines, and now Rita had reentered his life. Ingenious? Maybe so. Maybe not. *Shit.*

"I had no idea."

"Ummm."

Jerry turned and drilled Saltzman with his eyes. "I said, I had no idea they were out there or that anything else was going on. As far as I'm concerned, the deal is I'm here as ordered. You're the ops officer. That means when you say shit, I squat in the corner, drop my pants, and let it fly."

"No need to get worked up."

"I work for you and the *Wolfish*, nobody else. Okay?"

They held a stare for two seconds. Saltzman's eyes softened just a bit then he said, "Okay." He reached for a stack of books. "I drew these for you."

"What?"

"Submarines. All the stuff you need to know to become a submariner and an OOD." He passed them over. There must have been ten or so, some very thick.

"Will I get my dolphins?"

"Probably not."

"Where do you suggest I start?"

30

25 February 1968
Fleet Operations Control Center
Kunia Regional SIGINT Operations Center (KSOCK)
Level B, Room 2506
U.S. Pacific Command, Kunia, Hawaii

Arnold Zook was a sonarman second class rotated in from the Pearl Harbor–based destroyer fleet (Pineapple Fleet) to Ingram's watch team. Normally, new watch-standers were given menial tasks like making coffee and sweeping the massive floors in the operations center while they learned their jobs. But Zook was a popular kid. With his butch haircut, trim athletic build, and ability to play a beautiful guitar, he'd made a hit in KSOCK with officers and enlisted. Especially when Ingram let him play his guitar on slow watches. People would tilt back in their chairs, put their feet up, blow smoke rings, and listen to Zook as he strummed through an extensive repertoire.

But not this morning. Things had gone wrong from the very beginning. To begin with, the phone rang at 0534 reporting Adm. Alexander Corrigan had been up all night with nausea. Would Admiral Ingram mind returning and taking his regular watch session after all? After muttering "yes," Ingram tumbled out of bed with a raging case of heartburn. He'd slopped up Helen's spaghetti last night, heavily sprinkled with freshly grated Parmesan cheese. Then there were seconds and whatever was left on her plate. Plus her special garlic bread and Caesar salad. Basically, he ate everything in sight along with guzzling that bottle of basket-wrapped Chianti. After they killed that they went to bed, making long and marvelous love.

Holding his head, Ingram stumbled to the bathroom seeking Alka-Seltzer. After gulping that, he groaned, looking longingly at the bed. And for sympathy. But Helen was merciless. With one eye open, she said in a low, husky voice, "You could have retired two years ago." Then she rolled over and went back to sleep.

Suck it up. Yes, you are roped in on what is supposed to be your day off when you looked forward to sitting on the beach with Helen and recovering from this horrible hangover.

Trouble struck again just after Ingram reported in and relieved an exhausted Jack Collins standing an extended watch. The USS *Razorfish* (SS 556), normally stationed forty miles off Petropavlovsk, reported she'd suffered a casualty—a valve bonnet had blown off one of her diesels, seriously injuring two Sailors. Worse, with fuel gushing about, a serious fire started taking twenty minutes to quell. The aft three compartments were full of smoke and the *Razorfish* had to surface to ventilate the ship and deal with the fire damage. With just two out of four diesels available, she abandoned her station to limp to the closest friendly port: Yokosuka, Japan.

And now, things were going from bad to worse. People were shouting updates at him. The tote board scribes furiously dashed off numbers and symbols on their plots. Something was up. But the *Razorfish* was gone and they had lost their ability for close-in verification of activity coming in and out of Petropavlovsk.

"Zook!" He shouted.

"Yes, sir." Zook shot to his feet. He'd been sweeping paper chads from under a card-punch machine.

"Get over here and put on the headphones. Everybody!" he shouted. "Let's run a quiet ship. We're losing the picture."

With a lopsided grin, Zook dodged desks, chairs, and portable file cabinets like a tailback charging the line. He blasted onto the chair beside Ingram, let it spin once, then stopped and jammed on a set of headphones. "All set, Admiral."

Ingram jabbed a finger at one of the tote boards. Something didn't seem right about the contact entries for Skunk Bravo three-one. He snatched his hand telephone from its bracket and called over to the station five operator two rows down.

"Yes, sir," Lt. Scott Trinkle, answered. Ingram could barely see him hunched over his glowing CRT, adjusting the picture.

"What do you have, Scott?"

"We did have what looked like a Russian merchie coming out of Petter, Admiral." Trinkle used submariner's vernacular for Petropavlovsk.

"And then what? The contact report is vague. Is it a skunk or a goblin?" Ingram was asking if the contact was a surface ship or a submarine.

"Well, sir, SOSUS Delta two-one reports what sounded like a steam plant and a diesel." Station two-one was a SOSUS listening station in the Aleutian Islands.

"And then?"

"And then we still have the merchie with the steam plant. Definitely a noisy surface ship." Trinkle paused for a moment. "A Russian freighter headed south, maybe Hanoi." He stopped talking.

This is gonna be bad news. "Go ahead, Scott. I'm not going to kill you. Not yet anyway." Ingram decided to tread softly. Trinkle was a submariner out of University of Washington, where he'd rowed number six on the varsity crew.

Trinkle cleared his throat. "Yes, sir."

Silence.

Ingram said slowly, "Maybe I will kill you now."

"No, sir! Sorry, sir." He laughed. "I'm trying to read between the lines, that's all."

"That's what we're getting paid for, son."

"Okay, Admiral. The way I see it, we have a goblin, a diesel boat most likely, trying to sneak out of Petter under the belly of a freighter, or maybe snorkeling in his wake but closed up really tight. Right now, we're not sure. The contact drifts in and out. And Adak has difficulty evaluating the contact, if indeed there is one."

Adak, Alaska, was one of several naval facilities (NAVFACs), ringing the Pacific and Atlantic basins. Each NAVFAC was connected by submarine cable to bottom-mounted hydrophone arrays for the monitoring of Soviet submarines. A TOP SECRET project, the entire system, beginning in 1951, became known as SOSUS.

Trinkel added, "They're still working up the LOFARGRAM, Admiral."

"Do tell." Ingram thought it over. The Russians had done this before. He said, "But you think it's valid."

"If I were to stick my neck out, sir, I'd say it's a Commie submarine; especially when you consider the freighter and then when we plotted his position at lost contact."

"Where was that?" Ingram guessed what was coming.

"We lost contact at the fifty-fathom curve. That tells me he secured his diesels and dove."

"Makes sense to me, Trinkle. Let's cut to the chase and designate him as..."

"That would be goblin Juliette three-zero-five-five, Admiral. I would classify it as probable submarine."

"Okay. Make it so. Juliette three-zero-five-five it is. Stay close to Adak and see if we pick up any more noise. And those things are noisy. I'm told Ivan cleans his false teeth with ball bearings. We should be able to track him fairly easy."

"We'll stay on it, Admiral—whoops."

"What?"

"Just received a confirming report from NAVFAC Midway Island. And NAVFAC San Nicholas Island is getting murmurs. They'll be back soon."

"Meaning we're getting close to a positive submarine contact?"

"I believe so, Admiral. I'll let you know."

"Please do." Ingram hung up. He glanced to his right, surprised to see that Rusty Fletcher had quietly pulled up a chair. "Where'd you come from?"

"I was out and about. Heard the commotion."

"Heard?"

"Admiral, come on. This place has a personality all its own. You can tell when something is up."

Fletcher was doing what good operations officers do. Taking care of the boss.

"Okay, Rusty. I'd like a P-3 on top of that contact as soon as possible. We gotta see where he's headed."

"Yes, sir. We'll get one out of Adak." Fletcher rose to walk over to the air controller's station.

"And Rusty."

He turned. "Yes, sir."

"I'd like some more help from our bubble-headed friends. What assets do we have out there?"

They both looked at the tote board. What few submarines they had were tracking other targets. The *Razorfish* had been their only hope. And now...

They looked at one another. "Never mind," said Ingram.

"Maybe...," Fletcher posed.

"What?"

"The *Wolfish*?"

The *Wolfish* had been in the back of Ingram's mind but he had compartmentalized the idea and not let it out, essentially pushing it into a corner. With a sense of guilt, he said, "Of course, she's just under way."

Fletcher looked away.

He's being kind to me. Ingram went on, "Yes that's right. Get on the phone to SUBPAC and draw up an op order for *Wolfish* and a change of plans. Yes, send her up to Juliette 3055's datum to join the hunt."

Fletcher gave a crisp, "Yes, sir."

No sooner had he hung up than the phone buzzed. He yanked it from the bracket. "Ingram."

"It's Trinkle again, sir."

Ingram looked over two rows down to see the young lieutenant wave his hand over his head.

"What do you have, Lieutenant?"

"A BORESIGHT intercept, Admiral."

Ingram sat up. "And we have..."

"A squirt transmission from a Soviet submarine. Let's see, ahhh, here it is. Three quarters of a second duration. The transmitter's characteristics are the same as what we have for the *K-129*. And she is based in, guess where?"

"Trinkle!" Now Trinkle was being smug. The kid, as good as he was, could be aggravating at times.

"Sorry, sir. Rybachiy, Admiral."

"So you conclude that this intercept is our goblin?"

"A BULLSEYE reading is what we're waiting for. Oh, one more thing, Admiral."

"What?"

"The *K-129* is a Golf II class, a boomer. Carries three R-21 missiles."

Ingram felt butterflies in his stomach. And this, he knew, was not from last night's spaghetti. "That's not good news."

"No, sir. Wait one. The BULLSEYE report is coming in now."

The two systems usually went hand-in-hand. BORESIGHT, an advanced radio recording and control system, had the capability to compare the intercepted radio transmitter's characteristics against a secret U.S. Navy library and identify the transmitting station, in this case, the *K-129*. BULLSEYE was a series of powerful radio receivers linked together to provide a fairly accurate line of bearing to the transmitter.

"And here it is, Admiral." said Trinkle. "We have a line of bearing that lies about thirty miles below Petter."

"Fifty-fathom curve."

"I'd say so, Admiral."

"I would, too. Okay, add to goblin Juliette three-zero-five-five ID characteristics that she is a probable sierra-sierra, the Soviet *K-129,* a Golf II class."

"Will do, Admiral."

Ingram punched his switchboard.

"Fletcher."

"Rusty. We have BORESIGHT/BULLSEYE confirming goblin Juliette three-zero-five-five as the Soviet *K-129*. It's a boomer out of the barn, a Golf II. Add that to your messages."

"Will do, Admiral." Fletcher hung up.

With his crew working up the contact information, Ingram reached for his recognition manual for Soviet submarines. Flipping pages, he finally came to it:

. . .

Builder:Komsomol, Amur

Completed:1960

Displacement:2,700 tons

Length:328 feet

Beam:28 feet

Draft:28 feet

Propulsion:3 diesel engines, 2,000 hp each, 3 shafts

Speed:15–17 kts surface

12–14 kts submerged

Endurance:70 days

Complement:83 men

Armament:Missiles

D-4 launch system: 3 R-21 missiles

NATO: R-21 equals SS-N-5 Serb missile with 750–900-mile range

Warhead: 1 megaton each

Torpedoes

533 mm SET—53 and SET—53M

533 mm SET—64 nuclear tip

There it was. He'd read it often over the past few years. Nuclear-tipped torpedoes. All Russian submarines carried at least two of them; it was their policy. And now they were deploying this Golf II–class submarine. The submarine was technically backward, noisy, and easily detectable, but she carried three of the Reds' newest missiles: the R-21, each carrying a one-megaton payload, fifty times more powerful than the Hiroshima bomb; enough to wipe out any major American city. He drummed his fingers wondering if the *Wolfish* would be enough. Could she get there in time to intercept? Should he recall the *Razorfish* as wounded as she was?

Fletcher was back at his desk, watching. "It's okay, Todd. We'll have a P-3 on top within a couple of hours, well before the watch is over."

"I know."

"And that thing is a piece of crap. You can hear it in a trombone factory."

"I know."

"You want some coffee?"

"No thanks, Rusty."

Fletcher sighed and turned to his desk, signing papers. The room became quiet. The IBM computing machines whirred down to standby, the cathode ray tubes glowed a soft green, and the tote boards remained alight. Worse, the reports stopped coming in.

Zook picked up his guitar and began strumming a tune he'd never done before: "Amazing Grace."

"Zook!" barked Ingram.

"Yes, sir?" Zook stopped abruptly.

"Never mind. Keep going."

"Yes, sir. Thank you, sir."

31

25 February 1968
***K-129*, underway, Pacific Ocean**
52 nm southeast of Abacha Bay
Petropavlovsk Oblast, Siberia, USSR

Dr. Ivan Sudakov considered himself fortunate. They'd let him board the *K-129* with his brand-new Japanese tape deck. It had been smuggled in from North Korea and sold at black-market rates at the naval retail center in Petropavlovsk. A beautiful unit: a portable, battery-driven Akai. The deal closer was that the retail center had a Stas Namin tape, a rarity in Soviet Siberia. Stas Namin and his Flower Rock Band was one of Ivan Sudakov's favorite avant-garde groups.

He'd lugged the machine over to Rybachiy, where the gate guards spent more time going through his luggage than examining the Akai. Same thing at the *K-129's* gangway. He wasn't sure it was the *K-129* at first. The hull number on the submarine's sail read 722. But then he put that down to the Navy's disinformation campaign he'd read about.

Sudakov had been motioned into a line with several other men at the head of a gangway, all waiting to board. Intermittent snow flurries swirled as the deck watch examined their personal gear. But more time was spent looking over their orders by flashlight, vowel by vowel, it seemed, as the men on the pier stomped their feet for warmth.

Finally, it was Sudakov's turn to clump up the gangway and onto a makeshift wooden platform that served as the quarterdeck. The Akai was ignored as the guards rattled his papers and shot questions at him. Then it was over. The officer of the deck nodded him through. A messenger was assigned to carry his suitcase and the Akai—very nice. But when Sudakov stepped off the platform, he stopped. He'd made the mistake of looking down to the black icy waters on either side of the slender submarine.

The officer of the deck had seen it many times with newcomers, especially civilians. "Go," he shouted, "and don't look down. Better not fall, because we can't get to you in time. You'll sink to the bottom before you can take a breath."

Others laughed.

Sudakov gulped.

"I'm right here, sir," whispered the messenger with the Akai. He was close behind.

Sudakov heaved a lungful of sharp Kamchatka air, gritted his teeth, and began walking. The torpedo room hatch was twenty meters away and he was terrified of every step. But he made it. Warm air and the odor of hydraulic fluid wafted up to greet him from what was to be his home for the next thirty or forty days.

Sudakov was a semi-retired recluse living in Amur with his second wife when he was summoned. His entire career had been with the Strategic Rocket Forces in eastern Russia, and later in Soviet Siberia. But he didn't mind. He loved Helena, his wife of fifteen years, and the two children that she'd presented to him: a boy and a girl. The boy, Yuri, looked just like his father, even at the age of eleven. His blond hair was already thinning, and one knew he would be bald by the age of twenty-one. Indeed, Ivan Sudakov had gone bald at age twenty-three and now had a prominent girth that ran the scale up to a 120 sumptuous kilograms.

Quiet and reclusive by nature, Dr. Ivan Sudakov looked forward to spending a lot of time on this submarine listening to his Akai through his

Bose headphones. People scoffed when he listened to the Flower Rock Band, a raucous group featuring five musicians and the raspy, guttural voice of the garish front man, Stas Namin. From time to time Dr. Sudakov hummed and sang along with Namin's Western-style protest songs.

Recently, two officers of the KGB had come to call. Somehow they'd learned of his infatuation with Stas Namin and Western singers. They strongly suggested that Sudakov step away and return to Tchaikovsky and other good Russian composers. It was only after their second visit that Dr. Ivan Sudakov revealed his employer—the Strategic Rocket Forces—and told them he was working for the KGB's Third Chief Directorate, the technical division. Had they been able to look further, the two investigators would have learned Sudakov was a fuels expert who specialized in hypergolic fuels for rockets. Not that they would have known that hypergolic fuels are a binary system in which the fuel is stored in two separate components. In this state, the fuel is considered stable. Ignition is achieved when they come in contact with the other. However, the two compounds are very sensitive to corrosion and mishandling, with that, it can ignite by itself—tricky stuff

The *K-129* was not yet under way when Sudakov crawled into the hastily made up middle bunk in the tiny stateroom. He was curled up almost fetal with his back against the cold bulkhead doing his best to keep clear of his two new roommates, who were in the process of kicking out the two former occupants. As it turned out, one of the previous occupants was the ship's *zampolit*, and that gave Sudakov's stomach an uneasy turn.

Sudakov reached for the Bose headphones, plugged them in, and pulled them over his ears. Then he shoved the Akai against the forward bulkhead and made room for a pillow. Plumping it up, he energized the machine then reached for a tape in his pocket. He found the right one and seated it in the tape deck. Stas Namin came to life drowning out the sounds of the haranguing.

One of the stateroom's occupants, in the process of clearing out a drawer, leaned in. "Is that a Stas Namin tape? Where in the world did you get that?" It was one of the stateroom's former occupants, clearing out a drawer.

"I...I...in town. Is that all right?" Sudakov removed the Bose headphones to study the young leytenant. He had dark red hair and an athletic frame, along with the most penetrating and intelligent eyes. Most of all, his tone of voice was not demanding like so many of these submarine thugs; it was friendly and disarming.

"Of course it's all right. It's wonderful. I wish I had bought it. But then I would have needed a tape deck to play it." He nodded. "Hello. I am Vladimir Utkin, and I have no idea why we're being kicked out."

He had an easy tone and a half-smile. Sudakov rose on an elbow. "I'm Ivan Sudakov with no idea why I'm here."

The leytenant extended a hand. "Welcome aboard." He rolled his eyes.

They shook and laughed. Sudakov felt immediate trust for this young officer half his age. He nodded toward the Akai. "Please. You can use it anytime."

"Thanks," said Utkin. "I may take you..."

He was drowned out by Yusopov arguing with one of the newcomers. "Damn it. You'll listen to me. I am the ship's political officer."

"Who cares about *zampolits*?" said one of the newcomers who wore the badge of a starshiy leytenant. "We have a mission. Are you aware of our mission?"

His suitcase was on the deck next to the washbasin. Utkin sneaked a look at gleaming gold letters beside the handles: GEORGI VITALI GURIN.

"As far as I know, you're American spies! Show me your orders," growled Yusopov.

Gurin said flatly, "I've already presented my orders to Captain Kobzar. We are directly from Strategic Rocket Forces. That's all I have to tell you. Now will you please leave so we can get to our jobs?" He moved in close.

Utkin flattened himself against the bunks to give Yusopov and his adversary, Starshiy Leytenant Gurin, room to jockey. But Yusopov stood his ground and puffed out his chest. He wouldn't yield.

It was then that the third new man in the compartment, a veritable giant, stepped between the two officers. He turned and steadied his gaze on Yusopov, blocking his path, effectively pinning him against the desk. His unkempt hair was red, much brighter than Utkin's, and he had a long red beard to match. He was of an enormous girth and weighed at least 124 kilograms. His face was marred by acne scars, and his eyes were so close together that they almost combined into a single blazing eye.

Terrified, Utkin squeezed into a corner. He was reminded of the thug who'd come aboard a few weeks back and was killed by the gas. He wondered if there was a way to summon it up again. He darted a glance at Sudakov. The man's spectacles were pushed askew, his eyes were like saucers, and the Bose earphones had moved around his face. They were now clamped over the back of his head and his forehead.

Yusopov grabbed the compartment phone. "Executive officer, quickly. Yes, yes, this is Mr. Yusopov." He turned to the man confronting him. "Stand back, Igor."

Gurin peeked around the giant. "His name is Luka...Luka Sorkin, *zampolit*. You'd be well advised to stay clear of him"

"He's a starshina second class, and I'll bust him to starshina if he doesn't move right now." Yusopov pointed to the opposite side of the compartment.

To everyone's surprise, Sorkin spoke in a meek baritone voice. "Yes, sir. Of course. I was simply worried. I'm sorry." His tone and demeanor were cultured. He moved out of range, leaving Yusopov and Starshiy Leytenant Gurin to once again snarl at each other.

A figure filled the doorway. "What the hell are you doing?" he yelled. It was Zhuravin, the executive officer, still in his foul-weather jacket and headgear.

Yusopov stood aside. "These people are rude. They don't know their place on this ship. They need to be counseled. Closely. They need to be—"

"I'll decide that, Mr. Yusopov." Zhuravin said quietly. "Look. It's only for a few weeks. Then we'll all be home. In the meantime, you and Utkin here get settled up forward. We'll need you on watch soon. And—"

He was interrupted by a loud clanging.

"What the hell is that?" demanded the red-headed giant, his eyes darting wildly.

Zhuravin shrugged.

Yusopov picked up the phone, listened, and hung up."Engine room. Changing out an overboard discharge valve. Frozen in place. Apparently they had to break the sea chest to get it out of there."

"Any Americans nearby?" asked the starshiyi leytenant.

"We're listening on all bearings. Nothing. No Americans apparently."

"Apparently," said Utkin. They all shot scathing looks at him. All but Sudakov. From the corner of his eye, he noticed the Akai-toting civilian's eyebrows raised and the trace of a smile on his face. The sarcasm had just slipped out. He hadn't intended it to be heard. But now he looked the fool. And he felt like a fool. He wished he could tie a string to the remark and yank it back.

Zhuravin jammed his hands on his hips. "We're getting nowhere here." He looked at Yusopov. "How soon to clear out your stuff?"

"Five minutes, sir."

Zhuravin nailed Utkin with a stare.

"Five minutes, sir."

"Good." Zhuravin dropped his arms and straightened up. "Good," he repeated. "Hurry it up, gentlemen. Meeting in the wardroom in fifteen minutes." He turned and was gone.

32

5 March 1968
USS *Wolfish* (SS 562)
North Pacific Ocean

With her 287-foot length and 27-foot beam, the *Wolfish* had a pronounced beam-to-length ratio. Like most submarines, she was very narrow and had no bilge keels to dampen the wave motion, causing her to roll in any kind of seaway. Tonight the sea was calm and she did that now with hardly any white or even green water washing over the deck. Behind, *Wolfish* drew a long white phosphorescent wake of about four hundred yards, very straight due to concentrated steering by Higgins, a torpedoman first, on the helm down in the control room.

The captain had called a meeting yesterday afternoon in the wardroom. He'd disclosed their mission upgrade: they were now hunting for a Soviet submarine out of Petropavlovsk. *Razorfish* was supposed to cover the sub's exit, but she blew a valve bonnet and had to retire to Yokosuka for emergency repairs. Meanwhile, the Soviet submarine could be headed their way since there had been no further contact reports either near the Asian mainland or in the western Pacific. Commander Wade had emphasized quiet ship, quiet running, and overall stealth. He intended to find this bastard.

On the bridge, Jerry Ingram wore working khakis and a light windbreaker with a bright, cartoonish USS *Wolfish* patch over the left breast. Binoculars dangled around his neck. He saluted Lt. (j.g.) Mark Shelby, a dark, ghostly figure standing before him, barely distinguishable in the light of a quarter moon, and said, "Course three-one-zero, speed fourteen knots, engines one and three on line. Engine two on battery charge. Captain's night orders are to dive at zero-four-fifteen but to notify him first. I relieve you, sir." He whipped off his garrison cap and stuffed it in his belt, letting his light brown hair ruffle in the light breeze.

"I stand relieved." Shelby's teeth briefly glinted in the moonlight as the *Wolfish* rolled easily through a nearly flat sea. "Sack time," he added, and turned toward Lt. Phil Saltzman, "I have been properly relieved as JOOD and the conn by Lieutenant Ingram and request permission to lay below, sir."

Saltzman said, "Granted, Brian. Coffee's pretty good. Hollingsworth just whipped up a new batch. Doughnuts, too." Saltzman had relieved the previous OOD, as had the two lookouts now up in the periscope shears.

"Now you're talking," said Shelby with a grin. "You guys have a marvelous time. Keep an eye out for the dancing girls." He stepped in the hatchway, onto the ladder, and was gone, swallowed by darkness as he skillfully descended twenty-five feet to the control room.

Saltzman muttered something.

"Pardon?" asked Ingram.

Saltzman cast a glance up to the two lookouts strapped to the periscope shears. With powerful binoculars pressed to their eyes, they stood back-to-back, each silently scanning a 180° sector, one to port, the other to starboard. "Did I hear somewhere that you're married?"

Ouch. Jerry hadn't thought about this. He raised his glasses and began scanning over the starboard quarter to the southeast. In the past few days, he and Saltzman had renewed their friendship, but now the operations officer was latching onto something he hadn't thought about. On the other hand, it would be interesting to know how much Saltzman did know and whether his adventures in Sigonella had leaked out. "Yes, I am."

"Who's the lucky girl? I mean is it someone I might have known from Annapolis?"

"No, I met her at a party out on the Hamptons."

Saltzman faked an accent, "Oh, rah-thah."

Jerry pressed on. "Yeah, it was right after we graduated from flight school. Sad Sack Mason, remember him?"

"I do. Who could forget that crazy nut?"

"Yeah, you remember he was born to the purple. His folks live out there. They trotted us out for a summer party wearing whites and our shiny new wings."

"Sounds like the perfect time to make points."

"We got drunk instead."

Saltzman chuckled.

Jerry continued a slow sweep to the south. Then he stopped...there was something. "We barely made it through. But Sad Sack's mom was an okay gal—"

"What do you see?"

A pinprick of light.

"Contact." Jerry said evenly. "Bearing one-six-five, range approximately six miles."

Saltzman whipped around and spotted it. "I think...I think..."

"What?"

"There. See his navigation lights? Looks like he's crossing left to right across your radio dial."

Jerry adjusted his binoculars a bit. The contact snapped into tighter focus. He saw the lights. "You're right."

"Okay, very good, Jerry," he said softly. Then he shouted up to the starboard lookout, "Ryder, what the hell are you doing?"

"Sir?"

"What is that almost directly aft?"

Ryder twirled to his right and found the target. "Oh, yes, sir. Sorry. Contact, one-seven-zero, estimated range seven miles."

Before Ryder was finished, Saltzman leaned over and keyed the 7MC. "Control, bridge."

A tinny voice replied, "Control, aye."

"Weaver, wake up down there. We have a contact almost dead aft. Looks like he's drawing left. What the hell are you guys doing? Who is on the radar?"

"Rafferty, sir."

"Well, tell Rafferty next time he misses a contact, he'll be Electronics Technician Third Class Rafferty."

"Yessir."

"Good. Come on, what did the skipper say? Vigilance. Now get with it. Bridge out." Saltzman flipped off the switch.

After a moment of quiet he said to Ingram, "You don't fool around when you chase Communist submarines. Do you realize those bastards are armed with at least two nuclear-tipped torpedoes?"

Jerry knew this from his P-3 training. "I do."

Ingram and Saltzman checked aft for the contact. The light had blinked out. "Gone. Over the horizon," Jerry muttered.

"Good." Once more Saltzman keyed the 7MC. "Control, do you have that contact, yet?"

"Yes, sir," came the report. "Desig, contact Oscar. Bearing one-seven-two true; range eight point two and opening; course two-five-five, speed twelve."

"Very well. He's out of sight up here. Now keep a vigilant watch."

"Yes, sir." They clicked off.

Saltzman returned to their subject. "Well, who the hell is she and why wasn't I invited to the wedding?"

Jerry laughed out loud. He was getting ready to respond with an inflated tale when...what was that? With quiet seas, he had no trouble holding his glasses steady. He steadied up on a glint he thought he saw on the horizon.

There.

"Phil, he's back."

"Huh?" Saltzman spun to look in the same direction.

Both lookouts shouted, "Contact dead aft, sir. I see side lights."

"Bridge, Control."

Saltzman bent to the 7MC. "Bridge aye."

"Our contact has reversed course and is back for an encore. Bearing one-seven-zero, range seven point nine."

Saltzman punched the lever. “Bridge aye. Ahhh...how do you know it’s the same contact?”

The answer came right back, “To tell the truth, Phil, we’re guessing down here. But he has the same characteristics as the previous contact, and since this is such a large, empty ocean, I’d bet it’s the same one bringing us a box of red roses.”

“Well, okay but—”

“Hold on, Bridge. Two things. First ECM just copied a squirt radio transmition from him, or at least a ship on that bearing, and...”

“What? Damn it, go ahead, control.”

Weaver said softly, “Captain’s on his way up.”

“Oh...thanks, Bridge out.”

Even when asleep, skippers have an uncanny sense when their presence is needed; often without being summoned, they are up and on their way within seconds.

The bridge area was small. Two men could stand there easily. Three was a squeeze. There was movement at the hatch. In a moment, Cdr. Anthony Wade stood among them. “Morning, gentlemen.”

“Morning, Captain,” repeated Saltzman and Ingram.

“Whatchagot Phil?” asked Wade.

Saltzman pointed aft. “Contact, Captain. About eight miles away now. We first picked him up about ten minutes ago. He was on course two-five-five and drawing right. But now it looks like he’s on our tail or at least sniffing at us.”

Wade had binoculars, too. He raised them and studied the contact’s lights, now much brighter including her red and green side lights. He turned to Jerry. “Getting closer, you think, Jerry?”

Jerry said, “I’d say so, Captain. When we first saw him he passed us astern and went over the horizon.

“But then almost right away he changed course and is coming straight for us.”

Wade kept his binoculars planted on the target. “Uh, huh.”

Jerry glanced at Saltzman then said, “And if you heard the control room on your way up, ECM just copied a squirt transmition from a ship on that bearing.”

"Yup. What do you think, Phil?"

Saltzman said, "My money says it's a trawler, Captain. Although we haven't had time to examine the R/F characteristics of the transmition I'll bet he's a Soviet AGI. And he's got a three-to-five-knot speed advantage on us, so he'll overtake us in about ninety minutes or so."

"Yup," said Wade, studying the contact.

In the darkness, Jerry and Saltzman exchanged shrugs.

"Secure the radar, Phil," said Wade.

"Yes, sir." Saltzman flipped the switch. "Weaver, secure the radar."

"Control aye. Secure the antenna?"

Saltzman looked to Wade, who nodded.

"Affirmative, Larry. Secure the antenna."

Jerry glanced up to see the radar antenna sliding silently down into its housing in the sail. *He wants to dive.*

Wade peered again at the contact. "You're right, Jerry. He is a little faster than us."

"Sniffing us out, Captain. But so far all he can see is our stern light."

"For sure he's sniffing like a tall dog. And if he has radar, which I imagine he does, he's pretty well painted us and has an accurate picture." Wade clamped Jerry on the shoulder. "What's the battery charge, Jerry?"

Just then the 7MC chirped. "Bridge, Maneuvering Room."

Saltzman keyed the box. "Bridge aye."

"Battery charge complete. Request permission to put engine number two on propulsion."

Saltzman looked to Jerry, who grinned at Commander Wade with, "Full can, Captain."

"Very well. We can dive the boat now. Make your depth one hundred feet. I'll be in the control room." Commander Wade stepped into the hatch and disappeared.

Saltzman turned back to his 7MC. "Maneuvering, Bridge. You can secure the main engines. We're diving."

Jerry keyed the 1MC public address and said, "Now dive, dive the boat." The diving klaxon sounded as he shouted over his shoulder, "Lookouts down!"

With all the antennae masts sliding down, the two lookouts needed no urging. Quickly, they unbelted, scrambled onto the bridge, and then zipped down the hatch.

Saltzman tipped two fingers to his forehead and said, "Good luck, kid." Then he disappeared down the hatch.

It was Jerry's first time as conning officer on a dive. Yet here he was with all sorts of things happening, 99 percent of them someone else's responsibility, thank God. He felt worldly standing there alone on the bridge in what was about to become a hostile environment. He took a last look at the Soviet AGI. *Closer.*

The vents opened and air blasted from the ballast tanks with a hideous shriek. *Get the hell out.*

"Adios, world." Jerry stepped into the hatchway, pulled the hatch closed over his head, and secured it. Then he found his handholds and began sliding fireman style down the tube.

The remainder of Jerry's watch turned out to be a nonevent. The Soviet AGI inexplicably reversed course and disappeared south. There was an hour of darkness remaining, so Wade surfaced the *Wolfish* and resumed course three-one-zero with Saltzman and Jerry returning to complete their watches on the bridge.

But the captain reduced their speed to seven knots. This meant they had shifted to hunting mode, slowing down so the sonar could be more effective and listen without noise interference from the hull and the water. It would be this way from now on, seven knots or so surfaced, less when submerged as they listened for their quarry.

After their watch, Wade, XO Frank Hill, and Saltzman crowded around the plotting table in the control room. Everyone seemed to be talking at once. Jerry was too tired to linger. He'd find out later. He walked forward to his stateroom and stepped inside, leaving only the red lights on. He removed his clothes down to his shorts and climbed into his rack, the upper, expecting to fall asleep quickly. Instead, he lay there for ten minutes, eyes wide open as he stared at the curved overhead sixteen inches above.

There was a dream out there. Elusive. A recollection; it wouldn't let him sleep. And it wasn't the Soviet trawler that swirled through his mind. Flipping on his reading light, he fumbled along a small shelf above his rack. He found the Philips portable eight-track tape player and lay it close by. The night before, he'd been listening to *La Mer*. He ejected Claude Débussy and slid in a tape he thought he'd never play again. He turned off the bunk light and eased the earphones over his head, then flipped the play switch. The melody in all its subtleness came to him and filled him and made him tingle and feel alive. At the same time, it was soothing with promise and hope.

There must be a way, a path to a life together again.

He relaxed and closed his eyes.

Happy Together.

33

7 March 1968
K-129
39°59'5" N; 178°57'2" E
North Pacific Ocean

They played Utkin's tape on Sudakov's Akai. The selection was a special Archiv recording of Mikhail Glinka's great choral, *A Life for the Tsar: Glory, Glory to the Great Nation*. It was after the evening meal and they were huddled in Sudakov's stateroom, formerly Utkin's, both swept up by Glinka's powerful harmonics. But Yusopov cautioned them to keep the volume low lest others conclude the two were fomenting a revolution; after all, it was well known that Glinka's magnificent chorale was dedicated to the Tsar and his family, a faded bloody memory.

Glinka, Tchaikovsky, Stas Namin, or even Yuri Bedelvadich, a Stas Namin sound-alike, all seemed to run together as they swapped tapes with the crew, keeping the Akai running almost full time.

With the machine spewing Glinka, Sudakov sat at his desk poring over schematics and engineering logs while Utkin lay in the bottom bunk reading a manual on fire-control procedures.

Since they'd been under way, Utkin had noticed that most of the "add-on" crew were up at all hours routing cable, working computer code, troubleshooting electrical circuits, or poring over fire-control and navigation procedures. For the past two days, they'd been running simulated launches with the ship at battle stations. The most difficult times were the meal hours. The cooks couldn't keep up and kept running out of whatever was on the menu. The executive officer and supply officer were forced to ration the food, and that made both officers and crew unhappy.

And Sudakov seemed to have changed in the last day or so. Before, he would sit with his Akai, sometimes with Utkin, dreamily listening to music. But now he was preoccupied, even agitated, sitting at that small excuse for a desk whipping through charts and diagrams, sometimes groaning, sometime muttering, "Oh, no."

The K-129 proceeded to her destination under simulated wartime conditions, or so Kobzar said, for training purposes. That meant very little radar transmission and no running lights at night. Further, she was on a severely restricted EMCON schedule with just one squirt radio transmition allowed every forty-eight hours for position reporting. She submerged during the day but ran on the snorkel half the time, charging batteries. At night she was always on the surface.

Surfaced or submerged she'd headed directly south until three days ago. Then she came ninety degrees left and headed directly east, something Utkin found curious, especially when he discovered they now sailed tightly fixed to the fortieth parallel.

"Why is that?" he muttered absently.

"What?" Sudakov shot back.

"The fortieth parallel."

"What about it? Last I heard it is just above the thirty-ninth parallel."

Utkin didn't bite. "Our course. We sail exactly on the fortieth parallel. Why is that?"

Still distracted, Sudakov flipped pages and said, "No fly zone."

"Speak Russian."

Sudakov lay his book down and said, "The Americans. They have a no fly zone."

"I'm still not with you."

Adjusting spectacles on his nose, Sudakov said, "American antisubmarine patrol planes that fly out of Adak, Alaska, fly as far south as the forty-first parallel. From Hawaii, they fly north to the thirty-ninth parallel. In an effort to avoid collisions, they don't venture toward the fortieth parallel." He waved a hand, "The road is all ours, you see."

"Oh." Utkin wondered how his government had learned this. But it did make things convenient.

Sudakov returned to his logbook and suddenly jabbed at an entry. "Shit!"

"What is it?"

"Damn it!" He threw down a pencil, reached in the small closet, and drew out a pair of overalls and a work shirt. Utkin watched with mild interest as Sudakov reverted to his distressed state. He reached in a drawer and pulled out a flashlight, a large one powered with three batteries. Then he turned to Utkin and gave a twisted smile. "Do you mind being my scribe?"

Utkin half-rose and yawned. He'd been planning to snooze before going on watch at midnight, when another exercise was scheduled. "Scribe?"

Sudakov said, "Please, it's for the Rodina."

What? The irony was not lost on Utkin. The *Rodina*, the motherland; this with Glinka vomiting music about the royal family. *What's going on?* "You mean take notes or something?"

Sudakov looked tired and drawn. "That's all I'm asking. I can't do two things at once."

Utkin pushed aside his manual and turned to peer at his friend. Sudakov's voice was raspy. Normally reasonably well kept, he smelled heavily of body odor, his hair was messy, his clothes wrinkled. But somehow he looked better as he stepped into work clothes. "Of course. What's wrong?"

"Maybe nothing, maybe a lot."

"Like what?" Utkin stood.

His next move surprised Utkin. Sudakov reached for the phone, rang the control room, and said, "Yes, it's Ivan Sudakov. I need to see Comrade Yusopov right away. He...what...yes, put him on." Sudakov leaned on the desk and massaged his temples.

Finally, "Ah, Captain Yusopov. Thank you. It's Ivan Sudakov. Yes. See here. I have a matter that requires your attention. No...no, it has to do with the security of the ship and the security of our mission. Yes, can you? I'll be in my stateroom. Thank you." He hung up, giving Utkin a sidelong glance.

Utkin said, "Everything all right? You want me to clear out?"

"No, I'd like you to take notes. Sort of record this conversation. Do you mind?"

"All right."

Yusopov burst in. "So here I am." He pulled the curtain closed behind him, eyeing Utkin. Then he reached over and switched off the Akai. "You don't mind if Mr. Glinka beats a retreat as we discuss mission security?" He folded his arms and settled back. His eyes said, *this had better be good.*

Sudakov closed his eyes for a moment, then opened them with, "This mission is in jeopardy."

"So you implied. What is it?"

Sudakov waved at diagrams. "A lot. Maybe a little, but it looks like a lot."

Yusopov stepped close. "Damn it, little man. Out with it."

Sudakov said, "The maintenance logs. Somebody has been faking them."

This was not news to Yusopov. The ship's maintenance logs were faked all the time. They were simply too short of qualified personnel. And well over half the crew had been rotated out since the *K-129* had returned from its last patrol. There just wasn't enough time to train new men. It was the way the Soviet Navy did business. "Show me."

Sudakov picked up a grease-smeared journal and flipped pages. "This is the log for the UDMH transfer valves. Look at the signatures all dummied up in the inspector's column, the supervisor's column, and the approving authority's column. It's all in the same pen, the same hand."

Yusopov leaned over to examine the log. It was pretty obvious. "Uh-huh."

"So we need to look at these valves now."

"Why?"

Sudakov pointed, "See? Right here. It looks like the last *legitimate* inspection took place seventeen months ago. That's way too long."

Utkin reminded, "Comrade. It is nighttime. We can't get to the missile tubes without reasonable light."

Sudakov turned on Utkin. "You don't think I know that? So let's poke a flashlight or two into this junk pile and see what's going on."

"What's UDMH?" asked Yusopov dully.

Sudakov's eyes snapped back to Yusopov, "Unsymmetrical dimethyl hydrazine. It's one component of the hypergolic fuel."

"Plain talk, damn it."

Sudakov said, "And it's the same for the dinitrogen tetroxide transfer valves. All twenty-four of them. One speck of grease or rust and we all go up." He snapped his fingers. "Vaporized in seconds."

"What the hell? Why?"

Sudakov took a deep breath and said. "The rocket fuel. It's hypergolic, which means it needs no ignition source. The rocket engine fires when the two components come in contact with one another. Also, they are extremely sensitive to outside contamination. Dirt, rust, anything could set off what we call an auto heat condition. At that point you can't stop it. It all explodes."

"Jesus. What idiot thought this up?"

Sudakov stood straight. "That idiot would be me."

Yusopov grimaced. "Oh."

"Look, these are very reliable systems. Our spacecraft use them to great effect. You can throttle the rockets, no need to set off ignition, and you can restart anytime you want. Besides that, the thrust-to-weight ratio on hypergolics is much higher than monopropellants, meaning kilo for kilo you get greater thrust and you have very clean burns."

"I see. Reliable as hell," said Yusopov dryly.

Sudakov grew red in the face. "When properly maintained. But if not, terrible things can happen."

"Calm down, you little twit," growled Yusopov. He checked his watch: 2225. "No satellites."

Yusopov scratched his chin. "It's a full moon out there."

"That'll help accessing the missile silos. But once inside, it will be all flashlight."

"How long will it take?"

"About five minutes per tube. Only if everything is all right. Otherwise, I may have to do some valve adjustments and wipe-down. And that's dicey. Could take up to a half hour."

"Let's see what the boss says." Yusopov grabbed the phone and pushed a button. Soon, Aleksander Zhuravin, the executive officer, came on the line. "Alek? Alek, wake up, damn it. I need you back here. The skipper, too. What?...We have a situation with the R-21 maintenance. No...the damn things could cook off in their tubes. And that means roast us all for fish food. I'm with Sudakov back in his stateroom. I recommend we meet here. I don't want anyone else overhearing this, especially those renegades. Okay?...Good. Can you bring the skipper too? It sounds serious."

Five of them were squeezed into the tiny stateroom now. Sudakov sat at his desk. Yusopov sat on the bunk beside Utkin, who scribbled notes. Kobzar and Zhuravin stood over Sudakov, their arms crossed. But Zhuravin looked more out of sorts than Kobzar, who sipped tea from a mug and smiled from time to time, his brows knit in thought.

Yusopov said, "Okay, Ivan, it's your show."

Sudakov sat up straight and said, "Gentlemen, as you know, I worked on this system—"

"And you did a very good job," interrupted Kobzar. "From throughout the fleet, I've heard many good comments on the R-21 and work you've done previously. So, you mustn't worry about your status. You're tops in my book."

The curtain rustled. A slender man eased in. He had a sharp, mousey face with eyes close together and slick brownish hair that grew halfway down his forehead. A scar ran up the right side of his chin. He wore the collar tabs of a kapitan leytenant. They knew him as Aleksey Logonov, leader of the new complement. "Excuse me gentlemen," he said. "Should I be here?"

Zhuravin shot a look at Kobzar as if to say, *who invited him*?

Kobzar defused the situation by opening his arms expansively and saying, "Please, come in Alex. We all just got here."

Zhuravin eased over to the bunk and squeezed beside Utkin while Logonov moved next to Kobzar.

"Everything all right?" Logonov checked his watch. "Everything all set for the exercise?"

"We're just finding that out," said Kobzar. He waved a hand at Sudakov. "Please, begin."

Sudakov stood with difficulty, the space being tight, then turned and faced his audience. "Gentlemen, I'm concerned with the maintenance of the R-21 rockets, specifically the fueling transfer valves for each one." For five minutes he went into specifics, with Utkin writing furiously. He finished with the series of fuel transfer valves, the Lokset series of valves, eight in each rocket. "The maintenance is shoddy. We need to examine them now."

"Right now?" demanded Zhuravin.

"Yes, before the exercise. I don't want to take any chances."

"Who's responsible for this?" asked Logonov.

Sudakov picked up the logbook and handed it to Kobzar. He ran a finger down the columns, nodded, and then handed it around. All could see that the handwriting was the same in each of the checkoff boxes.

Zhuravin said, "I remember this man. It's Ednik Nerntski, a missile specialist."

"Get the bastard in here," growled Logonov.

Zhuravin lighted a cigarette and shook his head. "He transferred off thirty days ago, right after our last patrol."

Logonov said slowly, "Send me his particulars. We'll give him some nice vacation time in the Lubyanka."

If the *K-129* officers gathered in that stateroom had any doubt about the backgrounds of the last-minute crewmembers, they were erased now. Everyone knew about the KGB's feared Lubyanka prison in Moscow. Too many people had been dragged within its fortress-like walls, often before sunup, never to be seen again.

Kobzar defused the situation by asking, "Comrade Sudakov. Do we need to be completely surfaced for you to do your inspection?"

Sudakov stroked his chin. "I suppose not. If it's calm, we may be able to do it with decks awash." He rubbed again. "No, no. On second thought, I think we should be completely surfaced."

"All right," Kobzar said slowly. "You're sure."

"Yes, sir."

"Very well. But at the slightest provocation I must dive."

The hot stateroom seemed to turn suddenly cold. One by one they all looked at Kobzar, who was saying that he would dive the boat if an enemy blundered onto the scene. Anyone in the sail inspecting the rocket fuel transfer valves would either be trapped in the confined sail inspection compartment or washed overboard into the cold North Pacific as the *K-129* dove beneath him.

Sudakov's eyes grew wide and he gulped.

"Is it necessary to do this inspection?" asked Zhuravin gently.

Sudakov squeaked, "I wish it were not, but yes, it is necessary."

Kobzar nodded. "If we must, we must. So we should do it quickly, gentlemen. Are you ready to go Comrade Sudakov?"

Sudakov Adam's apple bounced up and down. "Yes, sir," he gasped.

"Do you wish to take anyone with you up there to assist you?"

"N–n–no, sir. It's not necessary. In any case there's only room for one inside the access panel."

Kobzar exhaled loudly. "This hypergolic fuel, it's tricky stuff, eh?" His eyes pierced Sudakov.

Sudakov stammered. "I beg your pardon?"

"The fuel. We must be careful."

"Yes, sir. Some call it the devil's venom."

Kobzar repeated it slowly, "devil's venom." He gave a slight shake of his head and said, "Very well."

He turned to Zhuravin. "Let's get this over with."

34

8 March 1968
40°12'4" N; 179°15'6" E
***K-129*, North Pacific Ocean**

A thin fog clung to the ocean's surface; the ceiling hung a mere twelve meters above. The air was damp, the ocean flat, otherworldly, and mirror-smooth under the filtered light of a full moon. As if seen through cheesecloth, the *K-129* ghosted along at three knots trailing a thin, bubbly wake. Her diesels rumbled softly, as if they too held their breath while Sudakov poked and tampered among the missile tubes in the sail.

It had taken twelve precious minutes to remove the inspection plate, actually a door, for the tube access and for Sudakov, wearing foul-weather parka and warm, fuzzy boots, to squeeze inside.

Two meters above, Vladimir Utkin sat precariously on the edge of the cockpit acting as Sudakov's scribe along with handing down tools and speaking with him on sound powered phones. Connected on the same circuit was Aleksandr Zhuravin, standing the OOD watch while the crew down in the control room prepared for the upcoming exercise.

For safety's sake, Zhuravin positioned himself right behind Utkin, one hand firmly gripping Utkin's collar lest he tumble off the sail and into the Pacific, whose somber gray waters slid past at a bone-chilling 7.2° Celsius. The ship was on EMCON with the radar secured. Two lookouts stood in the upperworks scanning the horizon, but their binoculars were useless in the hundred-meter visibility. Kobzar had set battle stations as a safety precaution. It was intensely quiet throughout the boat. People were on edge, sniping at each other, while topside Sudakov performed his wizardry.

Utkin squeezed his eyes open and closed trying to rid himself of the vison of an enormous white seventy-thousand-ton cruise ship blasting through the fog at twenty knots; her half-asleep deck watch and drunken passengers barely noticing the dark mass they were just running over. Automatically, he reached in his pocket for his father's good luck charm, the gold belt buckle of Alcatraz Prison in San Francisco Bay. It had always given him comfort. But he'd forgotten it today. It was among his things in his bunk in the forward torpedo room.

The phone crackled in his ear. "Utkin, damn it, can you hear me?"

Utkin pushed the button. "I'm here, Ivan."

"Send down a number eleven wrench."

"Number eleven on its way." Utkin fished the wrench out of the bag and tried to snap on the alligator clip, but his hands shook from the cold. The clip slipped and the wrench flipped from his hand, spinning down the sail. It bounced on the pressure hull with a small clang and plopped into the Pacific.

"Shit!"

"Not another one?"

"Afraid so."

"Look, Vlad, this is the third one. Maybe you're not cut out for this?"

"I can handle it," Utkin nearly cried.

"Alok?" called Sudakov.

"I'm here," replied Zhuravin.

"Look. Utkin's a little nervous. Could you get a machinist's mate up there or maybe a shipfitter?"

"How about a torpedoman?"

"That's the stuff."

"Thirty seconds."

"Excellent." Sudakov raised his voice. "Sorry, Vlad. I don't think you're qualified to pass tools. Working the fire-control console maybe, but not passing tools."

Utkin was too frustrated and too angry to respond. He stood seething while the XO called up to one of the lookouts. "Ovinko, get down here."

It *would* be Ovinko, Utkin grumbled to himself. A starshina second class torpedoman, Ovinko was built like a Yeti and strong enough to rip telephone books in half.

Within two minutes Ovinko, a heavily bearded man, had clambered down from the periscope shears while a replacement climbed up and took his place. Carefully, Ovinko donned the headphones and checked in with Sudakov. Now he was passing down a new number eleven wrench, grunting occasionally into the mouthpiece.

Zhuravin clapped Utkin on the shoulder. "You may as well get below. They've decided to add a live fire drill. Maybe you can learn something."

"A live fire drill? Does Sudakov know?"

Zhuravin shrugged.

Ovinko yelped as Utkin pulled off the headphones. "Sudakov, you hear me?"

"What the hell? Are you still on the bridge? I thought for sure you'd be playing cribbage with the mess cooks or something by now."

"Do you know they're conducting a live fire drill in the control room?"

"What?"

Utkin repeated it.

"Okay. Zhuravin, are you there?"

Zhuravin bent down to his phone. "Go ahead."

"Look. I recommend you stop the live fire exercise until I finish in here."

"Can't do that. Gurin and the captain planned this. And what you're doing fits right in."

"Fits right into what?"

"A casualty. And how to work around it."

"Jesus, Alek," shouted Sudakov. "You want to blow us all up? Maybe the whole damned world, too?"

"They're not that stupid, Ivan."

"Yes they are! They're all a bunch of corrupt politicians with fancy titles.

Look, I had to disconnect the safe settings on the fueling system so I could work the valves up here. It's the only way. This is not good. Shit! Can you get down there, Alek?"

"Everybody is assigned to something down there. And Utkin is not qualified to stand a bridge watch."

"Okay. You there, Vlad?"

"Y–yes."

"Get down there now. Take your regular station but make sure they don't activate the fueling panels. You got that?"

"Fueling panels," repeated Utkin. "I'll do it." He pulled off the headphones and handed them back to Ovinko. Then he headed for the hatch.

"And Vladimir," said Zhuravin.

"Sir?" called Utkin.

"After you're settled down there, could you send up some more tea? It's colder than Solzhenitsyn's ass up here."

Standing halfway down the hatch, Utkin managed a grin and tipped a salute with two fingers. "Don't I know it, sir? Right away."

It all happened so quickly. Jerry was on watch in the control room as, of all things, the diving officer in training while Phil Saltzman stood quietly by as OOD, watching everything as *Wolfish* poked along submerged at one hundred feet.

And there had been plenty to watch. Ten minutes ago, Harrison, a sonarman second class, had clamped his hands over his headphones and put his head down—a sure sign for others to shut up and knock off idle chatter. Cautiously, Harrison tweaked dials and moved cursers. Like a bloodhound sniffing live bait, everybody knew he was onto something.

Harrison turned to see Commander Wade leaning over his shoulder.

Crowded around Wade were Lt. Cdr. Frank Hill, the executive officer, Lieutenant Ganz, the weapons officer, and Torpedoman Chief Petty Officer Gilbert Freeman. They were watching three cathode ray tube displays of the PUFF—Passive Underwater Fire Control—system, part of the BQS 2 passive sonar detection suite in the *Tang*-class submarines. The key word was *passive*;

no active pinging or energy emanated from *Wolfish* lest she be detected by an adversary.

And now, on a passive search, Harrison discovered a contact bearing 013°.

With the *Wolfish* running quietly at five knots, Wade carefully slowed to investigate.

"Bearing?" Wade mouthed.

"Now it's zero-three-seven, Captain," said Harrison. "Drawing right. He's running on diesels. I'm betting it's a Russian submarine that just surfaced."

"Why do you say that?"

"Because that bearing was clean until ten minutes ago. Then all of a sudden, boom, here's this junk machine."

Wade said, "Okay, time to get things going. Sound general quarters, Mr. Saltzman. And rig for silent running."

Most of the crew, especially the ones in the control room, had already drifted to their battle stations over the past few minutes. It was so on most submarines. Word gets around; people know they're needed. To save time, they move close and hover near their battle stations as if to pounce on them when the alarm is sounded.

In moments, all had taken their places quietly and efficiently. The talker whispered to Saltzman, who said softly, "Battle stations manned and ready, Captain."

"Very well." Staring at the PPI over Harrison's shoulder, Wade asked, "What's it look like now?"

"Bearing rate opening. I believe he's abeam of us now, Captain." He turned to the BQQ 3 console and flipped switches. "Blade rate...uh, thirty rpm for three knots."

"Mr. Ganz?"

Ganz had taken his seat beside Harrison and was running a plot based on the passive bearings and blade rate. "With three knots speed, best I can come up with right now, Skipper, is course zero-nine-zero, speed three knots. But we need more time for a better solution."

"Very well, Mr. Ganz. Time is on your side," said Wade. Then he muttered, "I wonder if this is our boy out of Petter."

"The fire-control division thanks you for your generosity, Captain," said Ganz. They knew that plotting only with bearing rate and estimated speed was a crapshoot and generating range and an accurate course would take time after many readings. "But I gotta add, Captain, with all we have now and the fact that he's so noisy, he has to be fairly close. Maybe in visual range." He glanced over to the periscopes. "Maybe twenty-five hundred yards."

"I agree, Mr. Ganz." Wade called over his shoulder, "Mr. Saltzman, come right to zero-nine-zero, speed three knots."

Saltzman said, "Zero-nine-zero, three knots, sir."

"And come to periscope depth," called Wade quietly.

As the *Wolfish* began her turn, more than a few faces looked to the captain. Then to one another. The control room became deadly quiet.

Saltzman's men wore deer-in-the-headlights expressions. He snapped his fingers. "Come on, guys. No time like the present."

There was a momentary shuffle as men focused back on their tasks. Among them was Lt. (j.g.) Arrum Fenster, the battle station diving officer who had just relieved Jerry. He turned to the planesman. "Make your depth four-five feet."

Jerry stood back watching, doing his best to hide his disappointment that he hadn't done the maneuver, an opportunity that wouldn't often come his way.

"Ssssst!" Still at the sonar console, Wade waved to Jerry. "Got a minute?"

"Captain?"

"You up for some overtime pay?"

"You bet, Captain."

Wade glanced at the bulkhead-mounted clock: 2358. Then he whispered to the second-class quartermaster at the nav table. "Collins?"

"Yes, sir?"

"What's the picture topside? Do we have any moon at all?"

There was a momentary shuffle. Then Collins said, "Lollapalooza, Captain. Full moon."

"Okay," said Wade to Jerry. "You should be able to see something up there. Weather permitting. I'd like you and Frank to take the periscopes and see what's going on. At the least, you might see a snorkel; at the most, a Commie submarine."

"Time for a little sightseeing." Frank Hill nodded Jerry over to the periscopes. Hill stepped before the type 2 attack scope and reached up to slap the red ring encircling it at the top. Quietly, it hissed up under hydraulic power. Standard procedure was to raise the attack scope first before getting to periscope depth. This ensured nothing was in the way and that once the surface was confirmed clear, it would be safe to raise the other periscope.

Hill bent to ride the scope all the way up. Eventually he said, "All clear...but ..."

"What?" called Wade.

Hill pulled away from the periscope and blinked. Then he pressed his eye to it again. "Fog, damn it," he finally said. "There's light, all right, plenty of it. But I can't see a thing."

"Just in case." Wade called over to Collins. "Collins. Can you rig the camera, please?"

"Yes, sir." Collins bent under the nav table to unbox a large Hasselblad camera.

Hill said, "All clear, Jerry."

"Yessir." Jerry slapped the red ring controlling the type 8B nav scope. It cleared the water, and just as Hill reported, Jerry likewise saw wisps of gray sweeping over a mirror-glass surface. "Pea soup."

"Still want to go with the camera, Skipper?" asked Hill.

"Rig it anyway. You can never tell," said Wade.

"Sure enough." Hill beckoned to Collins. *Get over here with that damned thing.* Soon they were trying to slide the Hasselblad into its bracket. "What's wrong?" demanded Hill.

"Uh. Oh, shit ... sorry, sir. Wrong adapter. Can you hold this, please? Take me thirty seconds."

"Huh?"

Collins dumped the ungainly Hasselblad into the executive officer's hands and dashed over to the camera box at the nav station.

With the camera in both hands, Hill didn't have the means to manipulate his periscope. He growled, "Collins, damn it!"

Collins rattled stuff in the box. Suddenly, he held up a shiny black plastic object. "Got it, sir." He rushed back and began screwing it into place.

Jerry peered unto his periscope and saw nothing but gray wisps meandering over a dead calm ocean surface.

"Any day now, Collins," said Hill dryly.

"Just about got it, sir."

Jerry cranked out the range a bit. Suddenly, the fog cleared. He could see hundreds of feet. He looked up to align the periscope on their new course: zero-nine-zero.

Something black jumped into his lens. He twirled the focus handle. A submarine. Decks awash, stern aspect just as Harrison had predicted. A big fat thing with an ungainly conning tower. "Son-of-a-bitch!"

35

8 March 1968
40°03'7" N; 179°19'3" E
***K-129*, North Pacific Ocean**

The urgency in Sudakov's voice echoed in Utkin's mind as he mounted the ladder. *Get going.*

Utkin slid fireman style down to the control room and plopped on the deck. He was hardly noticed; everyone's face was in a scope or a plot or was talking on a phone.

Three seconds later he'd dashed to his console, glad to find the chair empty. He sat quickly, earning a dark look from the man beside him: Leytenant Nosov, the add-on crew's group commander in charge of missile fire control.

Puffing an American Marlboro, Nosov growled, "What the hell are you doing, junior? That's Kupchenko's station now."

"Too bad." Utkin grabbed the headphones lying atop the console and jammed them on. He punched the keyboard, watching the CRT come alive with white letters and numbers against a jade background.

Just then, Kupchenko, a civilian rocket specialist, walked up carrying a mug of tea. "Hey, that's my seat." He pushed Utkin's shoulder.

Ignoring him, Utkin eyed his control panel. The master display was up. *Good God.* It couldn't have been worse. *Perimetr* had been keyed in and was energized. He looked over to Nosov's display. Shit! The fueling panel was energized.

Kupchenko shoved his shoulder again.

Utkin rabbit-chopped his hand. The teacup fell away, shattering on the deck.

"You ass. Get up!"

Utkin twirled the headphones' barrel switch, hoping Sudakov's line would come up.

It did. He shouted, "Ivan. The fueling panel is energized. Numbers are jumping all over the place."

Sudakov immediately came back with, "Get to Kobzar! Tell him to stop the exercise. And hurry. I'd just removed a valve and now I've got hydrazine pumping all over me."

Utkin looked over. "Those KGB thugs are beside him."

"Get over there."

Just then, Nosov shouted, "What the hell is this?"

Utkin looked over to Nosov's display.

"What is it?" demanded Sudakov.

Utkin stammered, "It…it says 'auto heat.' What's that?"

Sudakov wailed, "Aww, shit. It means those idiots may have killed us. Look. No time. Do you see the fueling panel master control switch on that panel?"

"I do!" shouted Utkin.

"Kill it. Our only chance."

Utkin reached over Leytenant Nosov and threw the switch. The fueling panel went dark.

"Hey, you little shit. What's the idea?" yelled Nosov.

For good measure, Utkin returned to his panel and quickly typed: EXECUTE PERIMETR, DISENGAGE. Then he punched the enter key.

"You're screwing everything up," yelled Nosov. He reached over and tried to hit keys on Utkin's computer.

Utkin slapped his hands away. Nosov wouldn't stop hitting the keyboard. Utkin hit the block-headed Nosov in the head with his fist.

Nosov jumped up with a bellow and bear-hugged Utkin, lifting him from the chair. "You little turd!"

As he was pulled away, Utkin saw his screen flash: PERIMETR, DISENGAGE COMPLETE.

Nosov shouted, "Get this little bastard out of here. He's sabotaging the exercise." He spun and dumped a struggling Utkin on the deck shouting, "Help!"

Someone tried to grab Utkin from behind. Others rushed over. At once he was surrounded by men pulling on him; shoving each other.

"What?" yelled Nosov.

They felt a rumble. Then a roar. Very loud. Intense. Heat, very intense. Intolerable. Utkin tried to scream.

Then, nothing...

36

8 March 1968
40°02'2" N; 179°22'4" E
USS *Wolfish* (SS 562)
North Pacific Ocean

Fire!

A gigantic plume of flame shot from the top of the Russian submarine's sail. The *Wolfish*'s sonarman screamed and ripped off his headphones.

Through the periscope lens Jerry could see two men silhouetted up in the periscope shears. One immediately threw his arms straight out. He stood like a blackened scarecrow for three seconds, then withered to an ebony crisp. The other man stood rigid for a moment then disintegrated into a gelatinous, boulder-sized lump.

Jerry gagged, trying not to vomit, desperately holding it down.

Heads in the control room turned to him.

But he kept to the scope. The submarine seemed to be staggering, listing a bit to port. Belching smoke, the torching flame was down to about half of what it was. Getting smaller. It...

"Jerry, move," Commander Wade shouted.

"Uh, sorry, Captain." Jerry stepped aside and wiped his mouth.

Wade stepped in place and immediately mouthed, "Son-of-a-bitch! Was that a submarine?"

Jerry gagged again but nodded yes.

"Did you see fire coming out of that thing?"

Jerry's stomach heaved but he managed, "Yes, sir."

Someone kicked over a bucket and rag to him. He didn't know who did it, but the unwritten rule in the Navy was, you puke, you clean it up. Fortunately, he hadn't vomited and he kicked it to the bulkhead.

Wade was next to him, oblivious to his erupting stomach. "Mr. Ingram. I asked if you saw fire coming out of that thing."

"A whole bunch. It seemed to shoot straight up, like a torch... like...like..."

"Like what?"

"Like an enormous Bunsen burner. White-hot flame..."

"What the hell? How high?"

"Uh, twenty, thirty feet. Intense. All blue and orange..." He gagged.

"Jesus."

"And there were a couple of men. Lookouts up in the periscope shears, I think. One guy was incinerated right away...just roasted alive. The other roasted like...like a marshmallow. To a black blob."

"God."

"Sorry, Skipper. I can't..." He covered his face with his hands.

Wade grabbed Jerry's sleeve. "Listen to me!"

Jerry looked up.

"And then what happened?"

"And then the damned thing started going down."

Wade nodded. "That's when I got here."

"Did...did you see anything, Captain?"

"Just periscopes and antennae. A bunch of smoke," said Wade. He looked up to Hill. "What about you, Frank?"

One look at Hill told the story. Shaking his head, the man said bitterly, "My hands were full of Hasselblad."

Wade called to Saltzman. "Surface the boat. And then come to all stop."

Saltzman repeated the order. The *Wolfish* began rising. Donning a jacket, Phil started up the ladder, watching the depth gauge. The two planesman who were to act as lookouts followed him.

Wade called after him, "Mr. Saltzman, I want an accurate fix, right now. As close as you can get it."

"You want me topside, too, Skipper?" asked Hill.

"Yes, do it," said Wade. "Look for survivors. I'll join you shortly. Meanwhile, I better get a message off to Pearl."

"Yes, sir."

Wade turned to Collins, the quartermaster. "Be sure to log all this stuff. Especially the time." He checked the clock: 2400 exactly. *Strange.*

"I'm doing it, Captain."

"And Frank."

"Sir?"

"As of now, we're on complete EMCON. Except for my message, nothing goes out without my permission."

Hill wiggled into his parka asking, "What about nav messages?"

Wade said, "That too. Everything. Any outside transmission must have my specific permission."

"Yes, sir."

The *Wolfish* broke the surface. Hill cracked the hatch and made ready to scramble up. "Mr. Hill," Wade called.

Hill leaned down into the control room. "Yes, Captain?"

"Remember, speed zero. Look for survivors or anything else of interest. And then I intend to return to Pearl Harbor by the quickest route."

"Yes, sir," said Hill.

Wade rose and stepped over to Lieutenant Ganz at the fire-control station. "What do you hear, Rudy?"

Ganz turned to Harrison, his eyebrows up.

The sonarman said, "Some machinery noise at first, almost none now. Crunching sounds. Consistent with breaking-up noises." He turned to Wade and pulled a headphone aside. "It doesn't look good, Skipper."

"What's the depth here, Harrison?"

"Permission to key the fathometer, Captain?" asked Harrison.

"Granted. We can use it in our fix as well."

Harrison turned to the fathometer and flipped switches. Thirty seconds passed. Harrison's face turned white. He ran his hands over it.

"Harrison?" Wade asked gently.

Harrison's adam's apple bounced up and down. He tried to form words but nothing came out.

Ganz leaned over and looked into the fathometer. Then he turned to Wade. "It reads a little over sixteen thousand feet, Captain."

Her position was 40°06' north, 179°57' east. The time was exactly 0000 mike when flames first shot from the *K-129*'s sail. That's when her number one R-21 missile, mounted with a one-megaton nuclear warhead, ignited in its tube for a programmed ninety-six seconds. Due to Utkin's desperate last second keyboard-jabbing, the missile did not leave the launcher and was held in place. The rocket's intense heat exceeded five thousand degrees. With nowhere to go, the rocket cooked off, burning through the tube and eventually the bottom of the hull. The heat and gases killed the control room crew right away. With the hull penetrated by the blowtorch-like rocket blast, tons of water cascaded in, compromising buoyancy and causing the submarine to stagger.

Her snorkel mast had been raised, meaning all hatches were open for maximum ventilation. The rest of the *K-129*'s crew died soon after, killed by the intense heat and rocket gases. With hatches clipped open, the entire submarine was open to the sea. Through the control room, she flooded massively and began her last journey, this one to the ocean floor sixteen thousand feet below.

Precisely six minutes after the first explosion, as the *K-129* was descending through three hundred meters, the number two rocket fired. This indicated that the D-4 automatic fire control system had been activated; that everything was in automatic. But this second rocket, another one-megaton-loaded R-21, also remained in its tube and cooked off. Like the first rocket, the burn time was exactly ninety-six seconds.

The third rocket did not fire.

The *K-129* descended at a rate of about twelve knots and, fifteen minutes later, hit soft clay on the ocean floor five thousand meters down. Landing on a slight slope, she slithered down about thirty meters and jerked to her final stop amidst a cloud of muddy water and tiny spine fish.

PART III

We win here or lose everywhere; if we win here, we improve the chances of winning everywhere.

—General Douglas MacArthur

37

11 March 1968
USS *Wolfish* (SS 562)
Approaching Berth S-1B
Quarry Loch, Pearl Harbor, Hawaii

"See anything?" asked Phil Saltzman.

Jerry, bent at the periscope and said, "Still murky. It's overcast. No moon." He twirled a handle, running the scope's elevation down to where he could see the submarine's deck with the crew standing sea detail for entering port. They had retrieved the mooring lines from lockers beneath the outer hull. Now the lines were flaked down on the casing ready for sending ashore.

"Okay. Let me..." Saltzman nudged Jerry aside from the attack periscope to watch the last phase of their approach to Berth S-1B.

Cdr. Anthony Wade and Lt. Cdr. Frank Hill were on the bridge hovering over Lt. Rudy Ganz, who stood as OOD. Jerry felt sorry for Ganz. As weapons officer, Wade and Hill had pounded him to document every nanosecond, it seemed, of their approach to the Russian submarine, the actual moment of contact, Jerry's account of what happened to the submarine, and acoustic reports as she disappeared and sank to the bottom. After three drafts, Wade signed the report, and now, boosted by two tugs, the *Wolfish* was being shoved into her berth, starboard side to, with what seemed a sluggish dread.

Jerry checked his watch: 0146. They'd made landfall off Oahu at a little after 1600. But then orders came through for *Wolfish* to stand off until 2300 before beginning her entrance to Pearl Harbor. Someone wanted secrecy for their arrival.

Jerry felt a jerk as the submarine thumped against the camel lying against the pier. She was motionless as the mooring lines snaked ashore and secured to bollards then doubled. The order came down and was relayed on the 1MC. "Now the ship is moored."

"Holy shit," said Saltzman.

"What?"

"They got all the king's horses and all the king's men out there."

"Huh?"

"Take a look." Saltzman stepped aside and let Jerry move in. It took a moment for him to pick out objects. Actually, the resolution was pretty good. He could see buildings, some bright lights in the distance. Cars on the pier. A lot of them. A gathering of men dockside. "Jesus."

"You noticed."

"Uh-huh." One of the cars was a long black sedan, a Buick. At this time of night, everything looked naturally black out there. But this car had flags mounted in the front fenders. Large, dark flags with four stars. "Holy shit." Jerry looked up to Saltzman. "That has to be Admiral Hyland, CINCPAC himself."

"Yessiree." Saltzman whistled across the control room to Lt. (j.g.) Karl Rader, the heavy-jowled supply officer. "Hey Karl. Better check the wardroom for extra chairs and plenty of coffee. We got some heavy-duty brass coming aboard."

Rader stood leaning against the chart table, his arms crossed. "How heavy?"

"CINCPAC, other admirals, captains, a whole pot load along with some ass-kissing sycophants. Got it?"

"Holy cow. Got it." Rader waved over his head and walked forward through the hatch.

Saltzman said, "I guess the skipper's message was a wake-up call, all right.

"I'll say." Jerry bent to the scope again. Several men were crowded around the Buick's hood. It was still warm outside even at one in the morning. Everyone wore working khakis with short sleeves and garrison caps. And there was a lot of collar glitter. Three or four looked to be admirals with gleaming stars. In fact—"Shit."

Saltzman grinned. "Your dad?"

Jerry nodded.

Saltzman said, "Don't worry. I don't think he's here to roast you. It's part of his job, don't you think?"

Jerry sighed. "I guess." He bent back to the lens, focusing on Admiral Hyland's party. He counted three admirals, three captains, four commanders, and various other minions. What discouraged him were their faces. Their mouths were set. Usually, the norm at ship arrivals was lighthearted conversation and bantering.

Not this group. They looked grim and kept to themselves, checking their watches and watching the deck crew secure the *Wolfish* to the pier.

"Aside from all this, you about ready, Jerry?"

Saltzman had put Lt. (j.g.) Jerimiah Ingram on the watch bill as the in-port OOD. Which meant he would soon go topside and stand at the gangway as Admiral Hyland's party boarded the ship. As such, he wore pressed working khakis and shirt with military pleats and garrison cap. Jerry replied, "Can't think of anything else. You sure you want me up there?"

Saltzman slapped both hands on Jerry's shoulders. "You bet. You're the star of the show. Might as well get used to it. They're about ready to put the brow over, so get up there. I'll send Rader up to relieve you when they call for you in the wardroom."

"I can hardly wait."

"Rudy will come down from the bridge to back you up. The captain and exec will also be standing by to formally welcome them aboard. But you'll be first to greet them. Make sure you check their IDs. Every last one. If you don't, we'll all be in deep, dark brown smelly stuff."

"Any chance of me being in there first?"

"At the slightest provocation they'll toss you in and throw away the key. And don't forget to salute properly. Otherwise, it's the shit can for sure."

"Side arm?"

"Just your watch messenger. And here, you may need this." He handed Jerry a long naval telescope.

"Oh, no."

"Smack 'em over the head if they get out of line."

"Yeah, maybe my dad." He tucked the telescope under his arm, stood to attention, and clicked his heels with a mock salute.

"That's the spirit."

Jerry asked, "Should we gong these guys aboard?"

"Not at two in the morning. You want to wake up the seagulls?"

"Not necessary," said Ingram. "Okay." He looked around the control room and said in a loud voice. "Nice knowing you all. Don't forget to send the comic books and doughnuts to me in Leavenworth." Then he walked for the forward hatch.

Adm. John J. Hyland was the first to walk up the gangway. He threw a smart salute toward Lieutenant Ingram standing right at the gangway's edge. Lined up four feet behind Jerry were Commander Wade, Lieutenant Commander Hill, Lieutenant Ganz, and Lieutenants (j.g.) Saltzman and Rader, all five standing at stiff parade rest on the *Wolfish's* rounded hull.

They all heard Hyland call loudly with the traditional, "Request permission to come aboard, sir."

Ingram stood up before Admiral Hyland, returned his salute, and said, "Permission granted."

But the admiral did a double take when Ingram said, "May I see your ID sir?" He remained standing before Hyland, not letting him step off the gangway.

It was nearly two in the morning, and the group moving up the gangway heaved a sigh of disgust. Indeed, a bit of bother flashed across Admiral Hyland's face. But he reached for his wallet as others gathered up behind him.

Admiral Hyland's aide, a young blonde crew-cut lieutenant wearing aiguillette and aviator's wings, was right behind carrying a stuffed briefcase. He leaned around and whispered loudly, "Hey bubblehead, do you know who you're screwing with?"

Admiral Hyland caught Commander Wade's eye, his own eyes barely crinkling.

Wade gave an eye-roll.

Junior officer wars.

Ingram squared up and said, "And you, Lieutenant, are tampering with Navy Regulations. I'll see your ID next or you won't be allowed on my ship."

"That's enough," snapped Hyland. "Butler, show him your ID." With a grin, Hyland whipped out his own ID.

Ingram bent down with a flashlight and examined it closely. Finally, he said, "Thank you, Admiral. And welcome aboard, sir."

"Thank you, son. Nice to be here." With an index finger he tapped Ingram's wings. "Refreshing to see another flyer." His voice dropped to a whisper. "We're the only sane ones in the Navy." He gave a slight grin.

Jerry's eyes flashed over the decorations on Hyland's left breast: aviator's wings were positioned above the Navy Distinguished Service medal with gold star, the Silver Star, the Distinguished Flying Cross with two gold stars and the Air Medal with four gold stars. World War II stuff. *Wow.* He took a chance. Dropping his voice to match, he said, "I'll say, Admiral. These guys are driving me nuts."

"Don't worry. Your secret is safe with me." This time he grinned and continued, "What are you flying?"

"P-3s, Admiral."

"What squadron?"

"VP 72, sir," Ingram shifted his weight, feeling nervous.

Hyland said, "Good. Hope to see you back in the right seat soon. We need every one of you." He stepped off the brow and walked over to Commander Wade. "Tony, how are you?" They shook hands and then Wade escorted Hyland down the line introducing his officers.

Hyland's aide walked up with Jerry blocking his way.

With eyes like slits, the lieutenant eased his briefcase to the gangway and pulled out his ID.

Ingram took a half-step back, shrugged, and then stood at attention.

"What the hell's wrong, bubblehead? You got what you want."

Ingram whispered loudly, "Aren't you supposed to say something?"

The man behind the Lieutenant was Vice Adm. Todd Ingram. He leaned toward the lieutenant's left ear and whispered, "You're being had, Butler. Ask for permission to come aboard."

"Damn it," muttered Butler. He drew to attention and asked loudly, "Request permission to come aboard…sir."

Others snickered as Ingram returned the salute and said in an exaggerated, baritone, "Permission granted. And welcome aboard the *Wolfish*, sir." He stepped aside letting Lieutenant Butler pass. Ingram added, "And I'm not a bubblehead."

Butler spun around, "What do you mean?"

"I'm a zoomie, like you."

Butler bent to examine Jerry's wings. With an exaggerated eye-roll, he wailed, "Oh, my God. They'll let anyone in."

Jerry had a retort on the tip of his tongue when he heard a familiar voice, "Permission to come aboard, *sir*!" Todd Ingram, resplendent in a uniform with five ranks of ribbons and three glittering stars on his collar, glared at his son.

Jerry gulped and returned the salute. "Permission granted."

With impassive face and lips pressed together, the admiral presented his ID to the officer of the deck, his son.

Jerry stooped, looked at the ID, and counted to five. How could he not feel intimidated by this man who outranked him in every category? His father was so visible in the Navy. And here in this extremely pale light Admiral Ingram was stone-faced with the overwhelming command presence Jerry had always admired.

Jerry stood straight and said, "Welcome aboard, Admiral."

Ingram stepped off the gangway and offered his hand. "Thank you, son, nice to be here." They shook. Then he walked over and extended his hand to Tony Wade.

Jerry welcomed seven or eight faceless people. He was trying to hustle them through quickly when the next in line, a crew-cut blond look-alike of Lieutenant Butler, drew up before him and snapped to attention with a Hyland salute. He said, "Permission to come aboard, sir?"

Automatically, Jerry said, "Granted," and then examined the man's proffered ID. That voice...he looked familiar.

Meanwhile, the man said. "Submarining seems to agree with you. I never would have believed it."

Jerry sputtered for a moment. The man's eyes crinkled as Jerry struggled to make the connection. Finally, "I'll be damned. Ron...er, Commander Carmichael. How are you?" It was his JAG attorney.

They shook. "Fine, Jerry." Carmichael lowered his voice. "Maybe we can talk later."

"Sure thing." Jerry felt a pang. Things were happening too fast.

Jerry stomped his feet and walked up and down the hull to relieve the boredom. It was very dark on the pier. Still overcast and no moon. The only thing to watch was Admiral Hyland's driver over on the pier chain-smoking cigarettes beside the Buick. From the corner of his eye, he followed the two sentries out on the pier. Stiffly, they marched up and down, M-1s slung over their shoulders.

In a way, Jerry couldn't wait to get down below. The admiral had called for doughnuts thirty minutes earlier and sent the Buick after them. The driver had returned with eight boxes, the odor tantalizing as the boxes were handed down the hatch. Jerry overcame his dread of facing the admiral as he thought about the doughnuts sitting on the wardroom table: glazed, chocolate covered, cinnamon, cherry in the middle. He wondered what was worse: feeling utterly alone up here while thinking about those beautiful doughnuts or getting skewered by the admiral's panel.

There was a rustle behind him. Rader. "Okay, Jerry. They're down there with formaldehyde and sharpened knives. I think they've decided to embalm you."

Jerry groaned. "Have you been in there?"

"No. Phil came out and sent me up."

"How's he look?"

"Couldn't read him. But he was serious. Not screwing around." He looked about. “But that admiral. He’s a regular guy. He sent two boxes of doughnuts to the control room and two more to the crew’s mess.”

“That should be a hit.”

“I’ll say. Okay. What have you got?”

Jerry said, “Ship’s all secure. Everything shut down. We’re on shore power and auxiliaries. Sounding and security watch just reported all secure. Also got the word stores are scheduled for delivery at 0900 tomorrow morning. I guess we’ll be afloat for a while.”

“Very well. I relieve you, sir.”

“I stand relieved.”

“And Jerry...”

Jerry stood in the hatchway, ready to descend. “Yup.”

“Good luck.”

38

11 March 1968
USS *Wolfish* (SS 562)
Moored starboard side to Berth S-1B
Quarry Loch, Pearl Harbor, Hawaii

Jerry rapped twice and entered. The room and its occupants were even more intimidating than he had imagined.

The baize-covered wardroom table was littered with coffee cups, water glasses, and ash trays, a few of them full. Two doughnut boxes were shoved aside, empty except for one miserable stale doughnut. All the chairs surrounding the table were occupied. Elsewhere, more men stood pressed against the bulkhead.

A blue-black death fog of tobacco smoke hung over the table, the exhaust vents barely maintaining life for the officers and men therein. Jerry counted at least twenty people jammed in here: the three admirals plus a mixed bag of captains, commanders, a few lieutenants, and a few chiefs and petty officers. Ranging among them were the officers and men of the *Wolfish* who had been on watch in the control room that night. A stenographer sat in a corner huddled over his machine, tapping away.

Jerry was surprised to see Wade seated in his usual place: the captain's chair at the end of the table. He looked at ease. Before him was an unlighted fat stogie still in its wrapper, something he smoked only after the cooks served a fine dinner on a Saturday night. Seated to Wade's right was Admiral Hyland, who had allowed the commanding officer his prerogative, the chair at the head of the table. But Jerry also realized it was a gesture of respect on Hyland's part. Many four-star admirals would have kicked the commander out of his chair and taken over.

Seated behind Admiral Hyland was Lieutenant Butler, his aide, rummaging through papers in that briefcase, which seemed thicker than when he'd dragged it aboard. Vice Adm. Todd Ingram sat to Hyland's right. A balding Navy captain sat to Ingram's right. At the far end of the table sat Lieutenant Commander Carmichael. He and Jerry nodded at one another.

The chair to Wade's left was empty.

The room fell silent. With a nod from Admiral Hyland, Wade looked up at Jerry. "Relax, Lieutenant. We've decided to let you live."

Jerry replied, "Thank you, Captain. I enjoy doing that."

Nobody laughed, but somehow, Jerry felt the joke hadn't fallen flat.

Wade gave a thin smile, then waved to the empty chair. "Please." When Jerry was seated, he said, "Okay, Lieutenant, we speak informally here, so don't worry. Relax."

A quick look in the corner at the stenographer madly smashing his keyboard told Jerry just how informal this get-together was. That was confirmed when Wade said, "Kindly state your name, Lieutenant."

Instinctively, Jerry looked to Carmichael, who gave the slightest of nods. With that, he said, "Jeremiah Oliver Ingram, Lieutenant junior grade, United States Navy."

"And your duty station?"

"Pilot with VP 72, Barbers Point, on TAD to the USS *Wolfish* for ASW orientation."

"Wade said, "You mean submarine orientation."

"Well, that, too, Captain."

Smiles flashed around the room. Even Wade. But not Jerry's father. He looked even grimmer. This was supposed to be serious business.

Wade cleared his throat and said, "Thank you for the clarification, Lieutenant." He continued, "We're all trying to figure out what happened. That's why so many people are here—to save time." He pointed to a balding captain sitting across beside Vice Admiral Ingram. This is Captain Hudson Fletcher, who works at KSOCK. Are you familiar with KSOCK?"

Every head in the room turned to stare at Jerry, their faces saying *the kid sure as hell should know what his old man does.*

"Yes, sir. I'm familiar with it," replied Jerry.

Wade said, "Very well. I'll return this meeting to Captain Fletcher, who has been appointed to coordinate these proceedings. So, back to you, Captain."

Jerry stole another glance at his father sitting to the right of Admiral Hyland. Todd Ingram was impassive, poker-faced.

Fletcher folded his hands and cleared his throat, "Good morning, Lieutenant."

After a pause, Jerry replied, "Good morning, Captain."

"How are you?"

"I'm well, Captain."

"And you've enjoyed your time aboard the *Wolfish* as part of Operation SWAPOUT?"

"Operation what?"

"You know, Lieutenant. SWAPOUT. A program exchanging pilots and submariners...ah, a familiarization program between the aviation and submarine communities to learn more about associated tasking."

"Associated tasking," repeated Jerry.

"To learn how the other operates. SWAPOUT. At least that is what your orders read. Do you care to look at them?"

Jerry stole a glance at his father. His hands were folded on the table. He looked up to the overhead almost as if he were nonchalantly whistling, "Yes, sir. I remember now. I just didn't focus on that term."

"Very well. What do you think—"

"And yes, sir. I've enjoyed my time and learned a lot aboard the *Wolfish* as part of Operation SWAPOUT."

Fletcher stopped and stared at Jerry. Ten seconds passed.

Wise-ass.

Again Jerry looked at his father. The muscles in his jaw flickered and he ground his teeth. From boyhood, Jerry knew that look. Todd Ingram was getting irritated. Time to run and hide under the bed. "Uh, sorry, sir."

Fletcher cleared his throat loudly, then said, "That's okay, Lieutenant. We'd basically like you to tell us in your own words about what happened on the night of March eight and nine."

Jerry had met several times with Wade, Hill, Ganz, and Saltzman, in addition to Arrum Fenster, the quartermaster on watch that night. They'd all worked hard to complete the captain's action report. A copy lay before Captain Fletcher, opened to a page with several penciled notes. *In my own words, he said. I sure as hell can't tell it in somebody else's words.*

"Lieutenant?"

"Oh, yes, sir. Sorry, sir. Ah, yes. That night. It's really gross," he cautioned.

Fletcher waved around the room. "We're grown men, Lieutenant."

Jerry shrugged. "It's pretty much what I've stated in there." He pointed to the report. Then he went on to describe exactly what he had seen. All eyes were fixed on him as he worked up to the final time he placed his eye to the periscope. "Flames shot in the air. They were—"

"How high?" Fletcher interrupted.

"Uh, a good thirty, maybe forty feet. Like an enormous Bunsen burner. It was—"

"What color?"

"The flames?"

"Yes, Lieutenant. What color were the flames?"

"Yes, sir. The flames were blue-white, like I said."

"And you saw men?"

"Yes, sir. Up in the periscope shears. They looked like lookouts. Facing opposite directions scanning the horizon with binoculars."

Fletcher flipped a page in the report. "You didn't mention binoculars here."

Jerry glanced around the room. They all looked at him with more than mild interest. "You're right, Captain. I just remembered. They had binoculars and were scanning the horizon, facing opposite directions."

"And what happened?"

Jerry swallowed a couple of times. Glasses and a full water jug stood in the middle of the green baize–covered table. He reached over and filled a glass. After downing half, he said in a loud voice, "The flames blasted out, and right away, these guys were reduced to nothing more than a dark mass, like marshmallows. And then—"

"Can you tell us what they were wearing, Lieutenant?"

"Bulky duffle coats, I'd say. Foul-weather gear. Just like the guy who flew out of the conning tower."

"Whaaat?" asked Fletcher.

Wade leaned forward and said, "What guy, Jerry? You didn't say anything about another guy."

Jerry stammered, "It…it just popped into my mind. I remember, now. Jesus. A guy flew out of the side of the conning tower. His hair was on fire. So was his coat." Jerry raised the glass and gulped water.

"Flew out?" asked Fletcher.

"Yeah…er, yes, sir. Like he was ejected. He shot out about ten, fifteen feet from the submarine and fell into the water. This is when the conning tower was all aflame."

Fletcher drummed his fingers for a moment. "What side?"

"Sir?"

"What side of the conning tower did he 'fly out of' as you say?"

"Port side. We were behind the Russian submarine. Target angle of zero, zero, zero. There was sort of a hatch; it looked flimsy. It slammed open. I don't think it was watertight."

Fletcher shook his head. "I don't know. Who ever heard of someone…?"

A chief warrant officer leaning against the bulkhead raised his hand. "Pardon me, sir."

"Yes, ahh, Chief…"

"Latakos, sir, Sándor Latakos." The chief's olive skin and curly black hair bespoke his Eastern European heritage, and he spoke in a beautiful, rumbling baritone.

"Do I know you?"

"Yes, sir. I just reported to KSOCK yesterday. Previously from the Washington Navy Yard, sir."

Fletcher and Todd Ingram glanced at one another. Then Fletcher turned back. It hit him. "Admiral Moorer's staff." Adm. Thomas H. Moorer was the Chief of Naval Operations.

"Yes, sir," said the chief warrant officer, who looked more like a brute from an East German Olympic wrestling team. "Special projects."

There was a collective intake of breath. Admiral Moorer, a highly decorated World War II flyer, was known for running a tight ship in his department. "Special projects" could mean anything. Latakos had four rows of ribbons and silver submarine dolphins. Fletcher recalled now that the man was an expert on the *Voyenno Morskoy Flot*, the Soviet Navy, especially submarines. He'd been sent to KSOCK to beef up efforts to counter the great proliferation of Soviet submarines in the Pacific. Many were now patrolling along the U.S. West Coast and around the Hawaiian Islands chain. "Yes, go on please, Chief."

Chief Latakos said, "I agree that we're dealing with a Golf II submarine here."

He paused. Fletcher waved around the group. "Yes, Chief, I believe we all agree on that."

Latakos said, "Yes, sir, the evidence is very good. My comment is on Lieutenant Ingram's testimony."

Bits of Latakos' background popped up in Fletcher's mind. He'd glanced over his service record yesterday. Latakos had a BS in naval architecture from University of California, Berkeley. Yet the man had refused offer after offer for a commission, saying he preferred the freedom of an enlisted man and not being encumbered by ridiculous paperwork and, some suspected, close oversight. Fletcher motioned, "Yes, please go ahead."

"It's entirely logical that a man, most likely a technician, was in the conning tower at that moment. Most likely he would have been working on the fuel transfer system of the rockets, which as you know, are hypergolics."

"Hyper what, Chief?" said Wade. "Please help me. I'm just an old diesel jockey."

Latakos spread his hands, "As rudimentary as it is, the Golf II Soviet submarine is classified as an ICBM submarine. It carries three R-21 rockets nested in the latter section of the conning tower."

"Yes," said Wade. "I understand that."

"The Russians are known for taking great chances. In this case they use hypergolic fuels as propellants, a combination of hydrazine and a saturated solution of dinitrogen tetroxide."

"I think I heard something about that in high school," groaned Wade. He picked up his cigar and stuffed it back into his pocket.

Chuckles ranged around the table.

Latakos kept a straight face. "Nevertheless, that is what the Russians do. Separately, the components are very stable. But when they combine? Boom." His hands wiggled out an explosion. "Our scientists learned long ago that there are serious problems with hypergolics, especially in the transfer or even the storage stages. They become unstable with the slightest bit of impurities or dirt or rust. It causes an irreversible condition of what we call auto heat. It will eventually go off. So they must be very careful.

"Accordingly, I believe what Lieutenant Ingram saw is highly plausible. The poor fellow was in there doing something to ensure the transfer lines were not contaminated. But the auto heat was already in progress. It was just too late. The whole system went off when he was in there. He was ejected."

"But inside the conning tower?" Fletcher asked.

"Oh, yes, sir. There's a crawl space inside that barely allows a man to squirm and wiggle among the pipes and tubes. He must have been trying to fix something before it went off. For whatever reason, he didn't get to it in time. Must have happened quickly. Those rockets burn at five thousand degrees. And it most likely burned through its tube, venting all its smoke and heat inside the boat. "It's curious, though," Latakos stroked his chin. "Normally, the hold-down lugs should have unlatched, releasing the missiles. But apparently, they didn't. The missiles remained in their tubes, and that's why they cooked off and killed everyone in the submarine. Death must have been almost instantaneous."

"Instantaneous," repeated Fletcher.

"Yes, sir."

Nobody dared look at anyone else. Eyes found separate objects: cableways overhead, an ash tray, the painting on the opposite bulkhead, that one lonely doughnut.

Fletcher asked. "And a door?"

Latakos nodded. "Twenty-two-millimeter steel. That's, uh, equivalent to a little over zero point eight-eight inches of their QT-28 nickel steel alloy. Also used in the pressure hull. All of this inspection area is free flooding underwater. And the door is just an inspection plate on hinges, really. A small latch and six screws to secure it at sea." He looked at Jerry, "And you're correct, Lieutenant. The door is located on the port side."

Fletcher looked around the table. Nobody could think of a reason to ask Latakos how he knew so much about the inside of a Golf II's conning tower.

"Anything else, Chief?"

"Not at the moment, Captain."

Fletcher scratched his jaw. "Well then, I guess—"

Todd Ingram shoved a note across the table to Fletcher.

Fletcher picked it up and quickly read it. He turned back to Jerry. "One more thing, Lieutenant."

Jerry reached for the water glass, decided against it, and said, "Yes, sir?"

"How is it that your memory is so selective, that you remember all this just now?"

"I wish I knew, Captain. It just popped into my mind. I'm sorry."

"Well, then, we'll have to keep tabs on you for further testimony."

"Yes, sir."

Fletcher looked at Jerry and was poised for another question when—

"Sir, if I may?" Lieutenant Commander Carmichael, the JAG lawyer, spoke from the end of the table.

Fletcher nodded. "Of course, Commander."

Carmichael introduced himself and said, "Lieutenant Ingram's sudden recall is not unique. We see it in court from time to time. Especially with traumatized witnesses. People just don't remember everything all at once. Their minds don't work that way, especially when there has been a horrific scene. Details are forgotten or even suppressed and don't come out during the relative quiet of the deposition process. But then testimony in court sort of bumps it out of them. Accordingly, this is not surprising."

Fletcher said, "I see." With a glance toward Admiral Hyland and Vice Admiral Ingram he said, "I believe that wraps it up for now. Except, I believe Admiral Hyland would like to close."

Hyland sat back and steepled his fingers. "Gentlemen, first, I want to thank you for your time putting this little event together." He turned to his aide behind him, "And to you, Lieutenant, well done gluing all these factions together on such short notice." He reached back and slapped Butler's knee.

"Thank you, sir," Butler said softly.

Hyland raised his voice. "We've all learned a lot this morning. I'm glad we were forced to meet at this time. And with none of the usual interruptions that screw things up. I can't wait to see the transcription and digest what's going on. Also, there are other sources we're pursuing aggressively. Satellite coverage, for one. SOSUS recordings, for another, which should provide some confirmation as to the location. Also, KSOCK tells us the Soviets are going nuts. Ships, submarines, aircraft are pouring out of their Asian facilities, mostly from Petropavlovsk and Vladivostok. We've had reports that Soviet submarines are unabashedly pinging on sonar, obviously looking for something. But so far they haven't been to the area where *Wolfish* saw the submarine, which we now believe was designated the *K-129*, even though she carried the side number seven, two, two, on her sail."

He turned to Jerry, "By the way, there has been no testimony. Did you see those numbers on her sail?"

Jerry said, "I'm sorry, sir. It was too dark for that. Besides, we had a stern aspect."

Hyland nodded. "Very well." After a pause, he went on. "This is still developing, especially with the Soviets. I imagine they'll be pounding on our door soon, claiming we rammed one of their submarines and demanding retribution. The White House, State and Defense Departments, SECNAV, CNO, and appropriate type and area commanders have been alerted. It's all classified TOP SECRET, and I must instruct you not to discuss this among yourselves or to speak to anyone of this beyond these walls...er, bulkheads."

Silence. The bulkhead-mounted Chelsea clock chimed seven times: 0330. The joke having fallen flat, Hyland turned to Captain Wade. "You and your crew are quarantined for the next few days until we sort this out. No liberty. I'm sorry. We'll trust you and make it quarantined to the base. But that's it for now. We'll try to sort this out as soon as possible and let you know when we lift the restriction." He turned to Butler. "Right, Lieutenant?"

Butler said, "Yes, sir. We'll make it happen."

"That's the spirit."

Wade said, his eyes wide. "Everybody?"

Jerry smiled inwardly at the astonishment in Wade's face. The man had every right to feel indignant about this. Yet Jerry knew, and Wade knew also, that it was the right thing to do for the moment, that nothing lasts forever, and that this would blow over, except for those poor Russian sailors at the bottom of the Pacific and their loved ones. At the same time, he felt as if a great weight had been lifted. Now apparently out of the spotlight, he was like anyone else aboard the *Wolfish*, just another Sailor waiting in line. Nice.

Hyland replied, "I'm sorry, no exceptions. As for the rest of you, I want you to keep quiet about this. That means keeping your mouths shut. Anyone who does otherwise will be dealt with to the full extent of the Uniform Code of Military Justice. Do I make myself clear?" He looked around the room.

"Very well. Any questions or activity on this subject will be conducted with me, Admiral Ingram, or my aide, Lieutenant Butler. Is that understood?" Again he stared around the room. "This is a very sensitive time. For obvious reasons, we don't want the Soviets pinning this on us, which they're prone to do and will try to do. Worldwide, our relations are on such thin ice that any public knowledge of this could send up the balloon. Very well, gentlemen. Again, thank you for your great efforts getting here. You may all leave. Except I would like Admiral Ingram, Lieutenant Ingram, Captain Wade, and Commander Carmichael to remain, and of course Lieutenant Butler."

Well, here it was at last. *This has to do with the Ruganis.* He wondered if they'd caught wind of what happened to Giorgio. Moments before he'd felt relief. And now...

Admiral Hyland said, "Very well. Secure."

39

11 March 1968
USS *Wolfish* (SS 562)
Moored starboard side to Berth S-1B
Quarry Loch, Pearl Harbor, Hawaii

As everyone filed out, Hyland ordered a hot pot of coffee to be sent up for the quarterdeck watch, and specifically his driver, still waiting on the pier. Since the wardroom needed to be cleared for the morning meal, the rest trooped across the passageway to Ward's stateroom.

Jerry hung back staring at the empty wardroom table: coffee cups, glasses and ash trays. When they were gone, the silence embraced him. He wished he could stay. Instead, he was back in the soup. This time his father waited in Wade's stateroom. Maybe to cart off his remains.

The boat felt strange as Jerry crossed the midships passageway, now red-lighted for nighttime. Except for those in the captain's stateroom, the only ones awake were a dozen or so watch-standers. As the crew slept, the ship's silence seemed louder than the noise and angst of underway activity.

He knocked on the bulkhead and swept aside the dark green curtain.

Admiral Hyland was seated comfortably in Wade's desk chair. Admiral Ingram, Commander Wade, and Commander Carmichael sat on the bunk while Lieutenant Butler leaned against a bulkhead, his hands in his pockets.

Jerry took a spot at the bulkhead opposite Butler and nodded to Admiral Hyland. "Sir."

After glancing up to Jerry, Hyland looked at Wade. "Where's your scotch, Tony?" He started opening drawers. CINCPACFLT during World War II was the storied Chester Nimitz, who insisted on meeting and getting to know all the skippers under his command. It seemed to Jerry that Hyland must be following the practice and had gotten to know Wade pretty well.

Wade spread his hands. "Why, Admiral. On an American man-of-war? I wouldn't think of such a thing." With his foot, he eased open the bottom desk drawer.

Hyland leaned over. "Uh-huh. Just as I thought. Look at this, gentlemen. With great panache he pulled out a pint of Johnnie Walker Black.

"Medicinal purposes only, Admiral," said Wade with a poker face.

"Well, I guess that's all right. Otherwise I'd have to throw the book at you." He raised the bottle to the light. "Hmm. Unopened. Why, that's terrible."

"Yes, Admiral, it is just awful, I admit. We do have an active investigation under way. In the meantime, we keep this one, uh, sample here for emergencies...and as I said, for medicinal purposes."

"I see. Well, we'll have to test this *sample* for quality of content." Hyland grabbed a glass from over the sink and poured a generous dollop. "Anyone else?" Hyland waved the bottle.

They politely shook their heads.

Hyland gulped his scotch. "Ahhhh, that lights me up. You sure, anybody? Last chance. Otherwise Commander Wade will slop it all up."

Silence. They shook their heads.

"Well, you may all change your minds." He capped the scotch and kicked the drawer shut. Then he put the glass aside and beckoned with his fingers.

Carmichael pulled a sheaf of documents from a folder and handed it over. Admiral Hyland turned to Jerry. "You've been at sea, so I doubt if you know what this is."

"No, sir, I don't," said Jerry.

Hyland said, "No, I wouldn't think so. Okay, here it is in black and white. I've been aware of your situation in Sicily all along, even before you landed here. I have to say the whole thing was an absolute cock-up from beginning to end. And for good measure, we get that State Department jerk— what's his name?" He looked over to Carmichael.

Carmichael checked a document. "Seidman, Admiral, Barton Seidman, State Department chargé d'affaires in Palermo."

"That's it." Hyland snapped his fingers. "Seidman. That idiot was on the take. We got him fired. He's been recalled and I hope they throw his ass in jail." Hyland raised a glass to Jerry. "As for you, young man. There will be no Article 133 hearing. That's the biggest bunch of nonsense I've ever heard. Waste of our time. Case dismissed. You're free to go, except I need you and many more like you in P-3s. So, you're going back to Gregg Fowler and VP 72."

Jerry gasped. "They can do this?"

Hyland said, "*I* can do this. RHIP. Get used to it. And you're welcome."

"You, sir?"

Hyland pointed to the four stars on his collar. "Yes, I gladly did it. My call. So, don't let me down. Okay?" He reached.

Jerry shook his hand. "Thank you very much, Admiral. You don't know what this means to me."

"I think I do, son. Congratulations. And that was a nice job in there." He nodded toward the wardroom. "It's obvious you're like your old man. During the war he stepped in shit all the time, but he always did a magnificent job getting out of it. And so have you." Jerry stole a glance at his father and noticed a flash of red zip across his face. He'd never seen his father blush.

Hyland stood. "Unfortunately, that doesn't lift this restriction. You're still restricted to base, in this case Barbers Point and VP 72."

The rest stood with him. As they did, Todd Ingram leaned over and said quietly, "Congratulations, junior."

"You owe me a spaghetti dinner."

"First thing when the restriction is off." The admiral threw a fist at Jerry's shoulder.

Ron Carmichael walked up. "How about that, kid?"

"I still don't believe it," Jerry said.

"You lucked out. Not many four-stars would put it on the line for a jay gee. "Here." Carmichael pulled a folder from his briefcase.

"I still don't get it," whispered Jerry, "He can overrule the rest of the Navy?"

"It's his prerogative. An admiral's prerogative. Irrefutable. Here." He lifted out a document. "This a JAG release. Print your name here, date it, and sign on the bottom. Keep the copy. And you're free to go."

"Thanks, Ron. You did a great job."

"You're welcome. Just call next time you need a ticket fixed. Charges are low. Only twenty-five thousand dollars plus court fees."

Butler walked close. "Congratulations, you lucky stiff."

"Thanks."

Wade stood with them and extended a hand. "Congratulations, Jerry. I can imagine what it feels like to have all this lifted off your shoulders."

Jerry said, "I'll say, Captain. It's just catching up to me. Maybe we should hike over to the O club and let me buy everybody a round."

"Some other time, Jerry." Wade waved a hand. "Meantime, go aft and clock some solid sack time. Your orders will be ready after you're up and have had breakfast. You can detach then." He added, "I gotta say you did a good job aboard the old *Wolf*. Thanks for everything. Come back anytime and we'll make you a proper bubblehead."

"Afraid I'd stick the thing in the mud, Skipper," said Jerry.

"Can't blame me for trying, can you?"

Hyland parted the stateroom curtain and called over his shoulder to Butler. "Speaking of transfers, that goes for you, too, Noah. Like I said, I need P-3 jockeys. You're going to VP 72 as well, as soon as you can scrape up your replacement."

"Huh?" Butler's jaw dropped.

"And I expect you to do that chop, chop, Mr. Butler. And make sure it's not a flier. I need every one of those guys in the air. Maybe a submariner this time. Come to think of it, look over the fellows here. Seem like a decent bunch."

"Yes, sir. My pleasure," said Butler.

Wade groaned.

Jerry waited until the last official car had pulled away and disappeared between the buildings. There. Across the pier he spotted his destination. A dimly lit telephone booth. But right now, Phil Salzman was in it, hunched over the phone. Behind him were Commander Hill and two other *Wolfish* sailors. No matter. He jammed on his garrison cap, saluted the OOD, and walked across the brow.

The men waited quietly, patiently. They all knew one another and there was no bellyaching. Finally, it was Jerry's turn. He slipped in and was surprised to see four more men behind him, including Commander Wade.

Fortunately, he had a good supply of quarters. They clanked their way down, then the connection was made with all of its clicks, static, and beeps.

Finally, a voice came on the line. A man. "Yes?"

"Rita Hernandez, please."

"Who's calling?"

"Her husband, Lieutenant Gerald Ingram."

"What?"

"You heard me. Lieutenant Gerald Ingram."

"Buddy, do you know what time it is?"

Jerry checked his watch and did the math. Close to one o'clock in Los Angeles. "Yes, I do. Now put her on the line."

"All right." His tone was that of *it's your funeral.*

Fifteen seconds later. "Jerry!"

He began humming "Happy Together."

"Stop it, you idiot. There are people around me."

"Okay. Sorry. It's what men do, like howling at the moon."

She laughed. "It's good to hear you. I thought you were going to be out longer."

"Back sooner than anyone expected."

"I've been worried sick. Are you all right?

"Never better. And guess what. I'm back on flying status. They've dropped all charges and I'm like a regular guy again."

"Oh God, Jerry."

They were silent for a moment. Someone tapped on the glass behind

Jerry. Now the line was ten men deep. "Look, honey, I gotta go. Just wanted to check in and say we're back. I'll call tomorrow. Now..."

"Wait."

"Yes?"

"Turns out the clinic in Honolulu has an opening. I could transfer there. Is that all right?"

"Jeez, yes! Get it going," he fairly yelled.

She giggled. A wonderful sound. Like the Rita he once knew.

Someone tapped on the glass again. A faceless officer.

"Gotta go, honey. I love you. I'll call tomorrow. By the way, how's Junior?"

"Oh, Jerry. He's doing fine."

Jerry slept until 1030 and awoke refreshed. After a shower and breakfast, he packed and said his goodbyes to Commander Wade and Lieutenant Commander Hill.

Saltzman walked him off the ship to a taxi waiting on the pier. They shook, with Jerry saying, "It was a nice ride, Phil, except for all that..."

Saltzman shook his head. "I imagine they'll be pulling us through the wringer for the foreseeable future."

"What a bunch of crap, huh?" Jerry tossed the bag in the front seat, then climbed in the back and rolled down the window.

Saltzman grinned, "See you in the next lifetime, huh?"

Jerry said, "I hear Admiral Hyland is looking for a new aide."

"What?"

"How would you like to wear an aiguillette?"

"Not me. I hate ass-kissing."

Jerry slapped the front seat. *Go!*

The driver gunned the engine and eased out the clutch.

Jerry called out the window as the cab pulled away. "That's great. I'll let him know you're interested."

40

13 March 1968
Building 404, Senior Officer's Quarters
Rybachiy Submarine Base
Abacha Bay, Petropavlovsk Oblast, Kamchatka, USSR

Iliana's crossed legs were provocatively exposed beneath her white silk robe. Abundant blonde hair tumbled in defiant curls to her shoulders as she sat on the couch, occasionally checking her lipstick in a small compact. Beside her sat an incredulous Colonel General Maxim Yusopov, who had just been dragged from his bedroom by three heavyset KGB goons. At three in the morning he'd been completely surprised at the raid. They handcuffed him, shoved him onto the couch, and told him unceremoniously to shut up. Maxim wore only his nightclothes—a tee-shirt and white knee-length drawers.

Breathing heavily, Maxim desperately tried to catch Iliana's eye. But she wouldn't cooperate. Instead, she sat there pouting and bouncing an exposed leg.

Oleg Caranni, Yusopov's batman, sat opposite, uncuffed, on a matching eight-foot couch not caring about eye contact.

Iliana sat and drummed her fingernails, crossing one leg over the other and back again.

The raid consisted of five KGB men. All wore dark suits and solid-color ties. One stood guard at the front door, now barely hanging from its hinges, while the rest went about their business.

After relieving Oleg Caranni of his pistol, they had kicked in the front door, tossed Oleg inside, and sat him down with a guard. The others woke up Maxim and Iliana and dragged them into the living room. Three withdrew to search the two back bedrooms and bathroom while a man named Dmitri, who appeared to be the leader, searched the living room.

He had just pulled out a desk drawer and held it sideways when Iliana asked, "Can I go?"

Dmitri stood straight. "Madam?"

"Go. You don't need me anymore. I've done what you asked. I'm tired. I want to go."

Dmitri, a thinnish man with slick-backed patent leather hair, dumped the drawer's contents atop the desk and ran a hand through them. "Soon, Mrs. Kwolochek, soon."

"But—"

Dmitri turned quickly, his coat swirling up to expose a holstered pistol. He leaned in and snarled, "Shut up. Or you'll get duct tape over your mouth, your tits, and everything else."

Iliana Kwolochek sat back, crossing her arms.

Dmitri eyed her once and, flinging the top drawer onto the floor, went back to tearing apart Maxim Yusopov's desk, drawer by drawer. Soon the contents were out of all the drawers and strewn across the desktop, some spilling down on the floor. He began shoving the drawers to the floor. But he stopped. He picked up the top drawer, a narrow one. "What do we have here?" He flipped it over, examining the edge. With the flat part of his palm he smacked the bottom. It flew apart in two main sections and shattered pieces of wood. Papers fluttered. They had been sandwiched between the two sections. He bent over and picked up the papers muttering, "Yes, yes." He gathered the papers, about eleven in all, and jogged them into a neat pile.

The desk chair had been upended. Absently, Dmitri leaned over while reading one of the sheets and picked up the chair, setting it upright. Still reading, he sat and scratched his head. After a bit, Dmitri leaned over and said to Maxim Yusopov, "You know, Maxim, it's been a while since we heard from the *K-129*?" He looked over.

Maxim fixed his gaze on Iliana's legs.

"She's missed several required communication and location checks, you know."

Still silence from Maxim.

"And now we have this." He tapped a sheet with the back of his hand. "Who are these people?"

Maxim did not stir.

Iliana lit a cigarette and blew smoke toward Oleg. Oleg waved his hands through the fog and gratified her with a spasmodic cough.

The corners of Dmitri's mouth raised a bit as he read. Then he said, "Here. Luka Zotkin. I know this man. We were in a refresher class two summers ago. KGB, Ninth Directorate, technical operations, right?"

Maxim grunted.

"Big fellow. Red hair. Red beard. Rasputin personified, right?"

Maxim looked up. Dark circles hung below his eyes, and creases lined his face.

"One stupid son-of-a-bitch, yes?" Then, "Come on, Maxim. Zotkin's an expert at yanking fingernails. Won a contest somewhere doing that. Can you imagine the screams? But nothing else. He has the mentality of a walnut."

Iliana blew smoke on Maxim, who accepted it stoically. After it cleared, he said to her, "Iliana. Truly, I've appreciated everything you've done for me. But now, your ticket comes due. You're going nowhere except to an airport to board a plane for the Arctic Circle and Chukotka. Maybe from there you'll get work at Kolyma Gulf cleaning fish." He slowly shook his head. "Otherwise, my dear, the end will come quickly."

Iliana stopped bouncing her leg. But she again inhaled deeply and blew smoke at Maxim.

Maxim said, "I'm sorry, my dear. But you see, they think you know too much. Believe me, you'll be lucky if they let you clean fish."

Iliana stubbed out her cigarette and looked up at Dmitri. "Please, may I go?"

"In due time, my dear, in due time." Dmitri turned to Maxim. "This is the list of last-minute people who boarded the *K-129*. Yes?"

Maxim knit his brows. That list was already on file with the Fifteenth Submarine Squadron Headquarters. He saw no problem in denying it. "Yes." He heaved his chest. *Tired extremely tired.* "Really, I've had no sleep. May I go to bed for a while, please?"

Dmitri sat on the coffee table. "You'll get your sleep after we get our answers." He raised his voice. "What was the purpose of bringing these people on board?"

"I don't know. Except to say that the Fifteenth Submarine Squadron might have believed they needed backup. That the performance of the *B-62* was so piss-poor that they wanted real experts in there. Not a bunch of tired clods who would steal your mother's breakfast."

Maxim saw something in Dmitri's eyes. A hint of victory, maybe. He realized he'd said too much. He'd given Dmitri an opening. "They're doing that throughout the fleet," he added gamely.

Dmitri rose and circled the couch with exaggerated steps. "Thank you for that, Maxim. We'll have to check the other manifests."

"Do as you wish."

Dmitri was on his second circuit around the couch, now behind Maxim. Suddenly, he leaned down from behind. "Do you know we have Eduard Dezhnev, too."

Maxim gave an involuntary start. "Who?"

"You know, Dezhnev. His son is aboard the *K-129* with your son. Vladislav? Isn't that your son's name? Maybe they're friends, yes?" He walked around the couch and faced Maxim. You must be worried about Vladislav, no?

Maxim waved a hand. "I've not heard of Dezhnev or his son."

Casually, Oleg stood. He drew an eight-shot Tokarev automatic pistol from an ankle holster and stepped behind Dmitri. Placing a sofa pillow against Dmitri's back, he shoved the Tokarev into it. There was a loud pop. Dmitri's mouth flew open. His eyes like saucers, completely surprised. Another pop as Oleg squeezed off a second round. That shot blew out

Dmitri's spine. With a gasp, he spasmed to his tiptoes, then crumpled to the floor, groaned, and lay still.

The man at the door was reaching for his pistol in a hip holster. But it had happened too fast. Oleg had him covered.

"Please." The man slowly raised his hands over his head.

"Gun on the couch, there." Oleg pointed. "Slowly, now."

The man slowly complied, picking up his pistol with two fingers by the grip.

Oleg stepped to the doorjamb leading to the back hallway. "Now, call the others."

The man shook his head.

Oleg walked back, picked up the pillow and approached him.

The man called loudly, "Leonid, Mikhail, Nestor."

Their crashing noises stopped. "What?" They echoed.

"We need the three of you out here for a moment."

Dutifully, they trooped in, one by one. Seeing Dmitri's corpse, they spun to see Oleg, his pistol leveled on them.

It was tense. Slowly the three began to move apart. Then the fourth.

"I'm not messing with you people," said Oleg. He raised the pillow, jammed in the Tokarev and pulled the trigger.

Pop! One of the men went down clutching his leg.

Oleg pointed. "You! Uncuff the colonel general. The rest of you throw your handcuffs on the couch.

Under Oleg's watchful eye, handcuffs clanked on the couch while one of the KGB men uncuffed Maxim, dropped the cuffs beside him, and stepped back with the others.

Maxim struggled to his feet. "Well done, Oleg."

"Thank you, sir. But this is as far as I've thought it through."

"We go. That's what. And we're taking Iliana."

She sat up straight, incredulous. "What?"

Maxim nodded to her. "Yes, dear. You know too much. They would have killed you or ordered you killed as soon as you arrived in Chukotka. Now help Oleg cuff these men while I get dressed." With a nod to Oleg, Maxim rushed into the bedroom.

Oleg stood before them. "You, take off your belt, and tie a tourniquet around this man's leg." That done, he had them empty their pockets and weapons on the couch. Not surprisingly, he found two pistols on three of the men, three on another.

Then he had them lay on their stomachs. Iliana did the dirty work of handcuffing them all together, their arms and legs intertwined. Oleg was surprised to see two of them looking fearful, far unlike the stereotypical KGB agent so willing to lay down his life for the *Rodina*. Even so, he plastered duct tape over their mouths. Essentially, they couldn't move at all, especially Dmitri, who lay dead among them.

Maxim rushed out, dressed in civilian clothes and carrying a suitcase. "Take Iliana back there, get her packed. Pack your stuff and we'll get out of here. The sooner the better. And watch her every move. She may try to bolt."

"So, why not let her?" asked Oleg.

Maxim turned to Iliana. "Is that what you want? On the run in Petropavlovsk?"

"I don't know," Iliana fairly sobbed.

"I can tell you this. If you stay here, they'll find you in two hours and pull you through a knothole. Maybe pull a few fingernails, too, just to hear you scream. If you don't want that, then you can come with us. I have a bolt-hole halfway around the world and the means to get there. You're welcome to join us. Otherwise, I'll cuff you with these monsters and you can take your chances."

Iliana sat on the couch and put her head in her hands, blonde hair cascading over hands and arms. "I don't know."

Maxim said, "Oleg, leave her here."

Oleg made for the hallway.

"No!" she said. "I'll go. I'll go." She rose and squeezed past Oleg down the hallway.

Oleg raised his eyebrows. "Are you sure?"

Maxim replied, "Like so many young people, she drifts with the wind. But she's from good stock. She'll catch on. Now go."

"Very well." Oleg leaned over to Maxim and whispered, "She makes one false move and I'll kill her. Our lives are at stake."

Maxim waved a hand in agreement. "As you wish."

With a grunt, Oleg disappeared down the hallway.

Maxim walked over to the junk littering the top of his desk. The papers Dmitri had uncovered were still there in a neat stack. He grabbed them and shoved them in his vest pocket.

Yes. The ornate ivory telephone was still in place, the receiver on the hook. He picked it up and dialed a series of numbers. For thirty-five seconds it clicked through a system of relays. Twice he had to enter a numerical code. Then static and clicking again.

Finally, the connection went through. It rang. "Hello?"

"It's me. *Aida.* I'll tell you once more. *Aida*. Goodbye."

It was 0446 and the *Maria Adonar* was still docked in downtown Petropavlovsk. Her mooring lines were singled up. A crane stood ready to take in the gangway, and men slouched at the bollards ready to throw off the lines.

Originally, the *Maria Adonar* was christened the *Gary A. Lisotto*, a World War II Liberty ship of 13,900 tons and 450-foot length. The U.S. Navy had put her to great use during the war. She'd been damn near sunk by a mine at the invasion of Lingayan Gulf in the Philippines. But she survived and plodded on, her hull plates more and more dished in with advancing years. As war surplus, the *Lisotto* was sold to Cuba for a song in 1952 and renamed the *Maria Adonar.* Now, sixteen years later, the *Maria Adonar* still plodded the oceans at fifteen knots, staying afloat by guess and by intense prayer from her chief engineer.

And now, the *Adonar* was supposed to have sailed at 0430, but Carlos Velázquez, her captain, had agreed to wait. He tromped back and forth from bridge wing to bridge wing pulling the lapels of his peacoat tighter against this damned Siberian freeze. Their destination was Valparaiso, Chile, to deliver the rest of his cargo of sugar and fine Cuban tobacco, and he looked forward to that. He couldn't wait to get there.

His crew didn't understand the delay; nor would they be told. The reason was that Velázquez had accepted a bribe of US $5,000 to be at the narrows at 0515. And if he didn't get under way in the next five minutes he wouldn't make it, and there would be hell to pay. Maybe his neck. One didn't fool around with the Russians, especially when money changed hands. They all knew what the Russians were doing. He had joked with other merchant ship skippers: screening Soviet submarines. And Americans were listening, he knew, as they boasted about the extra money in waterfront bars.

Tires screeched. A taxi lurched between the warehouses and bounced to a stop right before the gangway.

At last. Here comes another US $20,000.

Carlos braced his hands on the bulwark and leaned over watching three people jump out.

Each with a suitcase, they ran up the gangway to the main deck where they were met by the second mate. He held them at bay and picked up a sound-powered telephone. Then he turned and looked up to an agitated Carlos Velázquez four decks above, staring down from the starboard bridge wing.

Velázquez picked up his phone. "Who are they?"

The mate answered, "Two men and a woman. She's not bad looking, either."

"Get on with it."

"Their IDs say they are the Gutiérrez family; two brothers and a sister."

"Yes, that's them."

"Their Spanish isn't too good."

"Did you hear me?"

"*Sí, Capitán.*"

"Allow them on board, and I want you to escort them to their cabins. But first, call away the gangway. We're getting underway as of this moment."

"*Sí, Capitán.*"

41

12 March 1968
Room 202B, Nakhimov Black Sea Higher Naval School
Sevastopol, Crimean District of Ukraine, USSR

It was drizzling outside and otherwise a deep, overcast day. The Sevastopol townspeople hadn't seen the sun for two and half weeks, and this day, a Tuesday, was just more of the same; dismal and wet, the semitropical climate notwithstanding.

Dezhnev had just finished teaching his Fleet Leadership class for young first and second rank captains. There was very little leadership taught and a great deal of party propaganda, the object being to mold them into a command profile suitable to the Communist Party.

The classrooms were empty, and nobody else, student or teacher, was in sight, which was not unusual. Nobody lingered around the institute unless it was absolutely necessary. Most went downtown looking for action. Dezhnev put away his teaching materials and made ready to leave town. He was going to Sochi and his Roxanna. They were getting close, very close, and he couldn't wait to see her. Maybe get things going.

The phone rang. Five instructors used this phone. The call could have been for any one of them.

On a whim, he picked it up. "Hello?"

It was a scratchy connection. He waited a moment, then heard a voice he barely recognized, "It's me. *Aida.* I'll tell you once more. *Aida*. Goodbye."

Dezhnev sat heavily in the squeaky wooden desk chair listening to the dial tone.

Aida.

In recent weeks he'd half-expected to hear that word. But nevertheless it surprised him. *Aida* didn't mean the opera; it meant "get the hell out, now." And Dezhnev knew Maxim Yusopov wouldn't have sent that message on a whim. He had to be serious. Which meant Maxim was also on the run right now and unreachable.

He looked out the window at the receding twilight. It still drizzled out there and his mind raced with options. *To run or not to run.*

That one was easy. Yes. Run. He'd been living on the edge for so long. *With Yusopov's disappearance, they'll be after me.* Maybe they had already caught Yusopov. *Then I'd really be in the soup.*

But he had an appointment at the Sochi clinic tomorrow at nine-thirty. They were to give him a new prosthesis. He'd grown out of the current one; it hurt too much. And he wanted to grab Roxanna, no matter what. Plus, he had some bad news to tell her. She had to know that her son was aboard a submarine that was overdue and might well be lost. Quite naturally, she would balk as any mother would. But in which direction?

He'd made Aeroflot reservations for six this evening. It was a one-hour flight and he would be there at seven. Fortunately, his bag was packed. He hadn't planned to return to his apartment here. But what about the airport?

Not now. Too chancy. They'd watch the airports. And the train stations. No buses either.

Motor pool.

He picked up the phone and reserved a Moskvitch, a small sedan. He asked for civilian markings, but there was no guarantee. He picked up the phone and dialed again: Roxanna's number. It rang six times and the answer machine came on with her voice. Yes, she was still teaching a class downstairs. At the beep he said, "I'm delayed. Won't be able to get there after all.

But keep your bag packed. I'll call back with instructions." That sounded so cryptic, but he didn't know who might be listening.

He hung up and waited for the Moskvitch to be delivered. They'd said ten minutes. He looked at his watch: five minutes to go. It could be the longest five minutes of his life.

Three minutes later the car drew up in the parking lot. A Moskvitch 412 painted light green. Good. Civilian colors just as he'd asked. A military-looking vehicle would have been conspicuous.

So far, so good.

He walked down the back stairs as fast as his gimpy leg would allow. The knee joint became painful as he pushed open the side door and stumbled his way across the parking lot to the waiting sedan, white vapor rising above its tailpipe. Just as he opened the door, a black Lada pulled up to the front door. Two overcoated men got out and walked inside.

Dezhnev got in the Moskvitch. The driver was a thin, hawkish man in an oversized garrison cap. "Captain Dezhnev?"

"That's right."

He handed over a clipboard and ballpoint pen. "Very good, sir. Sign there, there, and your initials, please, in the space on the bottom. And date all three, please." He flipped the car into low and eased out the clutch. Dezhnev slid down a bit and turned away as the driver did a U-turn and cruised right in front of the Lada's grille and its glaring headlights.

Damn it. Through the windshield splotched with rivulets Dezhnev saw a third man at the wheel. But he appeared distracted, looking down as he held a microphone to his mouth; he barely noticed the Moskvitch.

They turned onto the main road, and Dezhnev made a show of reviewing the checkout sheet. One item called for destination. He scrawled: "Taking three faculty members to dinner meeting in Yalta."

"Sir?" The man had shifted into high gear. They were two blocks away and headed toward the motor pool, the tires hissing in the drizzle.

"What?" Dezhnev looked back. Nobody following. *Thank God.*

They drove into the motor pool lot. The driver stopped and pulled the emergency brake, leaving the engine running. "Anything wrong with the checkout sheet, Captain?"

"Full tank?"

"Yes, sir."

"Very good. But it seems the pen ran out of ink." Dezhnev clicked it a couple of times. He'd been holding his breath. Now he exhaled and took a deep breath. He felt a bit lightheaded.

"Oh, sorry," The driver reached into his pocket and produced another pen.

Moskvitch translates to "native of Moscow," began production in 1946. The design was based on the German Opel Kadett. After the Soviets invaded Brandenburg, Germany, in the latter stages of World War II, they took over the Opel plant there. They forwarded the design specifications back to Moscow and began manufacturing almost immediately. The Moskvitch-Opel was a surprisingly well-built car and became popular in an export version all over Europe. This 1968 Moskvitch 412 had a forty-nine-horsepower engine with overhead valves; it was simple and reliable. A good wet-weather car. Dezhnev felt warm and comfortable.

He called her from a grocery store in Novorossiysk, about halfway to Sochi.

"Are you all right?" she asked.

"We have a situation," he replied.

"Ahhh, yes. I've been wondering about this. Does it have to do with your friend with the belt buckle?"

Amazing. She was way ahead of him. But now, listeners would be alerted that something was going on. He couldn't stop it now. "Most definitely."

"What do you want me to do?"

"Meet me tomorrow as planned."

He repeated, "As planned." He hung up realizing listeners, most likely the KGB, would be alerted something was up. But they hadn't said when or where. It was still a guessing game.

42

13 March 1968
Community Hospital No. 14
Sochi, Tsentralny City District
Krasnodar Krai, USSR

Dezhnev ditched the Moskvitch in a theater parking lot and walked in pain two blocks to the hospital.

He was mildly surprised to see Roxanna standing by the door to the prosthetics ward. She looked spectacular in white slacks and dark blue top. He pecked her on the cheek, but as he held the door for her she was noncommittal, her face expressionless. It gave onto a large lobby with rows and rows of squeaky wooden chairs. The windows looked out onto green lawns. Palm trees lined the circular driveway and the main thoroughfare outside. Blooming flowerbeds added color to clear skies of a beautiful morning.

Nobody was there, so he kissed her on the cheek again and went to hug her. But she wiggled away. "What's the situation?"

"What?"

She looked at him directly. “You said there was a situation. It must be serious for all this,” she waved at the hallway, “skulking about.”

He went to an inner door and made to open it. “In a minute.”

She pushed the door closed. “Tell me now or I’m walking out. I’m tired of all this.”

“Not here. Look, I—”

The door opened for a baby-faced twenty-five-year-old wearing round wire-rimmed glasses with thick lenses. He had shoulder-length blond hair and wore an overly starched white lab coat over a checkered blue shirt and yellow tie with gravy stains. A Bakelite nametag on the top pocket read PUCHKIN. “Captain Dezhnev?”

“That’s right.”

“Good. You’re on time. We’re busy today. Come in, please.”

Dezhnev looked at Roxanna and said, “Utochka?” He bowed deeply, waving her inside.

She threw him a *we’re not through* look and walked in.

The prosthetics ward looked more like an auto repair shop than an examination room. Cabinets were mounted on the opposite walls, some open to reveal bits and components of artificial limbs. Like wheelchairs and pitchforks in a general store, artificial arms and legs dangled from the ceiling in a bizarre jumble. A long workbench was built into the wall across from the windows. Above it hung a large photograph of Leonid Brezhnev, premier of the Soviet Union, who glared at them as if daring them to steal a loaf of bread. Gleaming tools and fasteners were scattered about the workbench. Doors led to other work areas on either side.

One would wonder why this room was so active in such a small hospital. But during the Great Patriotic War, this ward, and many others in the region, served thousands of unfortunate soldiers of the Red Army who had been chopped up in the murderous battles ranging from Moscow to Berlin. Sochi was well isolated from the many fronts and served the Red Army not only for medical help but because its Mediterranean climate made it a pleasant place for rest and recreation. Long after the war, Community Hospital 14 remained a favorite of the Soviet high command.

“Sit there, please.” The therapist waved to a gleaming stainless steel table. And roll up your pant leg, please.”

While doing that, Dezhnev remembered this kid. He had the finesse of an orangutan. "We've met before, Mr.—"

"Puchkin, Captain. Anatoliy Puchkin." He pointed to his nametag and then pulled a strap on Dezhnev's prosthesis. "And its Doctor Puchkin. I passed my exams two months ago."

"You? An MD?" Dezhnev asked incredulously.

Puchkin yanked a strap. "That's right." He reached into a refrigerator mounted under the table and drew out a can of Seven-Up. Opening it, he poured it into a gleaming beaker. Raising it to his lips he gulped twice, Seven-Up dribbling down his jaw. "Ahhh." He wiped his face with his lab-coated arm and asked. "Would you like some?"

"No, thank you, I—"

Puchkin pulled a strap on his artificial leg.

"Ouch, damn it."

"You must have it on wrong, Captain. Here, let me..."

"Arrrgh. Shit. What are you doing?"

"Just readjusting things, Captain."

"Forget this one. Just give me my new one and I'll be on my way."

"Well, that's what I'm trying to tell you, Captain. You see, we can't give you a new prosthesis yet."

"What?"

"They're saving money. Cutting back. They've asked us all to do our bit, and that means getting along with what we have." He gulped more Seven-Up.

Dezhnev taught this Communist cost-cutting crap at the Nakhimov School. And now this kid was shoving it back down his throat. "What do you mean cost cutting? Your department said my new prosthesis was approved and ready."

"Well, Captain. We   "

"Do I have one or do I not?" He was tired. He'd slept only two hours in the car in the theater parking lot. Now he was getting heated.

"I'm sorry, Captain. They've put it off for six months. The expense, you know." He pulled two more straps and buckled them. "There."

"No, I don't know!" He sat up straight.

"Ah, one more thing. You see, Captain, you have an American prosthetic."

"That's right." He almost added *the quality is better.*

Puchkin said, "...and it's constructed in English units. All I have are metric tools. Please bear with me. I can adjust this for you so it will be like new."

"That's what I'm afraid of."

Puchkin yanked another strap.

Dezhnev yelled.

Roxanna laid a hand on his arm. "You baby."

His face grew red. "Damn thing hurts."

Puchkin said, "Almost done, Captain. We'll have you out of here in no time."

"I'm too old for this." Dezhnev said in resignation. Then he glanced out the window. He sucked in his breath.

"What?" asked Roxanna.

He pointed. A dark blue Lada sedan was parked across the street. It was covered with dust and the windshield wipers had been used to clear a streaked path through grime.

"How much longer?" he asked, his mind racing.

Puchkin clanked his tools. "I found the American wrenches. Almost done."

Roxanna draped an arm around him and bent close, her voice low. "Those people? What's with them?"

He whispered, "Same guys as last time. I think they mean business."

Her eyes narrowed. "Are you sure?"

"Well, I'm certain that they—hello, what's this?"

Two men emerged from the car. They wore dark suits and, standing tall, looked capable. A trunk-secured whip antenna at least three meters in height, sprang into the air, see-sawing back and forth.

One of the men, average height and broad shoulders, reached through the driver's window, pulled out a microphone on a long cord, and began talking.

"Russia's finest," said Dezhnev.

"Oh, dear."

An ambulance roared by, thumping over potholes. It downshifted and turned for the emergency entrance, its siren spooling down. The other man, tall and nearly bald, stood back for the ambulance to pass, then walked around the Lada and bent close to the other, listening.

Dezhnev's heart beat quickly. *They've found me. How the hell did they do it so quickly?* In minutes it would be off to the Lubyanka, most likely. He kicked himself. A number of opportunities had arisen over the years, mostly from Toliver: go to the other side, to the West and freedom. But always his response was no. He was too much of a patriot—like his son. And his Utochka didn't know about that, yet. *How the hell to tell her?*

His breathing became quick. He felt clammy.

Quick exit? Community Hospital Number 14 was just a simple two-story building. He could dash out the back. "This does not look good," he muttered, his eyes darting about the room.

"Nonsense, you're being paranoid," she said. "They're just...just men. Don't worry."

She's in denial. "You sound so convincing." He turned to Puchkin. "Go, please."

The kid was adjusting a pair of gleaming vise grips. He looked up. "Just a couple of more minutes, Captain. All I have to do is—"

"'Go,' I said. Now." He pointed at the door. "I have to do something. Please wait outside."

"But—"

"Damn it, get out!" Dezhnev stood and again pointed to the door.

"Well, if that's the way you feel..." Puchkin rose and shuffled out.

Another Lada pulled up behind the first. Two more men in dark suits got out. A third Lada pulled up alongside the first. The four gathered around the third Lada for a moment. Then it drove off and screeched around the corner.

Damn it. They're covering the rear.

The four men squared their shoulders, fanned out, and began walking toward the hospital.

Roxanna turned to him. "Do you think...?"

"This is it, all right." He turned and held her by both shoulders. "Look. We have maybe fifteen seconds. Will you come with me?"

"Come where? To Moscow? To prison? To Dzerzhinsky Square?" She shook herself free and took a step back.

"I'm getting out. To America. Right now. But there's no time to go home and pack. It must be right now!"

She jammed her hands on her hips. "What about your dream for the *Rodina*? Answer me that."

"I...I've lost."

"Yes you've lost, you damn fool. Not that you could have done much, anyway. You're like Don Quixote tilting at German tanks. You never had a chance. But not me. I don't share those dreams. I'm a citizen of the Soviet Union. And I live in Sochi. And my little dancers are out there making big names for themselves."

"They know we're together. They'll make it hard on you."

"Hmmmfff." Another step back.

"That's why I'm here, damn it. *I love you, Utochka.*"

Her face softened.

"I really made a botch of things. I shouldn't have let you go the first time. That was incredibly stupid. But I'll be damned if I will let you go a second time."

"I..."

"Please, I need you. Come with me." He walked to a large cupboard and began rummaging.

"You haven't said that in a long time."

"I'm sorry. I've been thinking about this, about us. That's why I came here so suddenly. I want to marry you."

"You idiot!" she yelled. Her fists doubled. "You want to get married just before the KGB hauls you off to pump a bullet into your head?"

"I can get us out if we hurry."

"You're crazy! You want me to flush all my work down the drain?"

He found surgical gowns. Scrubs, boots, masks, and all. He tossed a set to Roxanna. "Put these on."

"Absolutely not!" Letting them fall to the floor, she marched to the other side of the room and folded her arms.

There was a knock. The door opened softly. The bald man from across the road walked in. He drew something from his top pocket, a gleaming KGB badge. "Captain Dezhnev?"

"Yes?" Dezhnev backed against the opposite wall.

Another man walked in. His hand was jammed inside his coat against a bulge under his armpit. Slowly, he side-stepped around the room, past Roxanna toward Dezhnev.

The bald man held out his hands, palms up. "It's all right. We just want to ask a few questions."

Maneuvering between the two men, Dezhnev found his voice. "I don't understand. I'm a naval officer on leave. That's all you need to know."

The bald man said, "I wish it were up to me. But you see..."

Dezhnev took a step toward the bald man.

The other man pulled his pistol from his shoulder holster, a Makarov PM. He waved it at Dezhnev. "That's far enough. Turn around."

Dezhnev stood his ground. *Where are the other two?*

"I'm sorry we have to do it this way." The bald man unhitched a pair of handcuffs from his belt and walked toward Dezhnev, reaching for Dezhnev's wrist. "And I'm sorry about your son," he said.

"What about his son? Our son?" Roxanna's voice was low and husky.

The bald man's mouth drew to a solicitous grimace. He turned to Roxanna. "I thought you knew."

"You bastard!" Roxanna grabbed Puchkin's Seven-Up and pitched it into his face. "What about my son?"

The bald man yelled and wiped at his eyes, dropping the cuffs. "The stupid son-of-a-bitch is dead!"

"No! Impossible! Dirty bastard," Roxanna yelled again. She picked up a lab stool and brought it down on the man's head. It shattered on his head and shoulders. Blood splattered. The man sank to the floor with a groan.

The other man had stood watching in open-mouthed disbelief, but now he raised his pistol and pulled the trigger. *Nothing*. The safety was on. In panic, the man lowered his pistol and threw the safety.

Three steps. Not enough.

"Uhhhhffff." The KGB man stumbled, his eyes bulging. He half-turned and saw Roxanna had hit him on the head with a prosthesis, an artificial leg —white gym sock topped with blue and red stripes, white tennis shoe, and all. She swung again, hitting the man in the same place. The Makarov twirled on his trigger finger and clattered to the floor. He went down with a groan and lay still. Dezhnev leaned down and picked it up, thumbing off the safety.

Dezhnev turned, finding the bald KGB man still conscious. With blood running freely down his face, he wobbled to his knees, eyes wide in terror.

Dezhnev drove a fist squarely in the face. The man's nose crunched. He crumpled onto his back and was silent.

Dezhnev found words. "Good God." He locked eyes with Roxanna for five whole seconds. They looked at what once had been an orderly repair station, now converted to an abbatoir. Two wounded men were splayed on the floor amidst shattered glass and splintered wood.

And blood had splattered Roxanna's white slacks. She looked down and clapped a hand over her mouth. She shook her head slowly. Then she began shivering. "Why, why?"

"More guts than I ever had." Dezhnev went to her and wrapped his arms around her.

"I didn't mean to..." She looked up. "Vladimir? Is what he said true?"

Dezhnev struggled for an answer. A day before he'd gone on the run, General Yusopov had told him that the *K-129* hadn't transmitted position reports for the past several days. Now there was general panic with Admiral Dygalo and submarine headquarters sending nearly every ship out to look for her.

"Vladi?" she repeated.

Lost? The last time the *K-129* sent a position report was about ten days ago. Now they believed she was lost. He couldn't tell her that. But what? "I'm sorry to tell you this. The *K-129* grounded on a reef in the Philippines," he lied. "I was going to let you know at a better time."

"My God." She lay her head on his chest. "But surely they can be rescued."

"They're not sure. Problem is, the reef is off Zamboanga, that's the big island of Mindanao populated with Moros. They're Muslim, savages. They behead intruders."

"Eduard," she shrieked

What a terrible lie. But better than what really happened. "As long as they stay with the ship, they'll be all right. They're sending rescue ships now."

She sniffed. "How long?"

"Don't know. As long as it takes. Days, maybe."

The door squeaked open.

Dezhnev whipped up the pistol.

It was Puchkin, his eyes wide as saucers.

Dezhnev barked. "Robbery attempt. You have poor security here."

"Uh, huh." Puchkin nodded.

"Quick! To the lobby. Call the police."

"Wha-what?"

"The police, you dolt. Now go." He waved the pistol at him.

Puchkin ran out.

Dezhnev flipped on the safety and stuffed the pistol in his belt. He felt stupid for lying to her but he couldn't think of anything else. He moved close and caressed her cheek. "Utochka. You're very brave."

She stammered, "I just couldn't let it happen. I saw that"— realizing the artificial leg was still in her hand she tossed it on the workbench among the tools. Then she slapped her hands to her face and began shaking. Dezhnev walked to the cabinet and pulled out two more sets of surgical scrubs. "We don't know where the other two goons are." Throwing a set to her he said, "Hurry."

"Eduard ... I ..."

"Now, damn it." He stepped over to her. "Look at these men. I think that one's dead. Those two outside will be on us soon. And when they do, they're going to figure it out. You'll be shot alongside me. Your only chance—our only chance—is to get the hell out of here and run."

Something flashed in her face. Like a light going on. "Okay." She began peeling the starched surgical robe apart. Dezhnev did the same. That done, he pulled the two KGB agents in a corner behind a screen. There was a ripping sound. He emerged with a bloody rag.

"What?"

Dezhnev said, "Your friend's shirt." He dabbed it against her surgical gown, smearing blood. Then he dabbed blood on his gown. "How do you like that?"

"I feel like vomiting."

"Me too. But I have these." He raised his robe to display two Makarov .38 caliber pistols stuffed in his belt. "And unlike that idiot, I know how to use them. Got their wallets, too. Enough money to get us to where we have to go."

She shivered again and hugged her hands to her shoulders.

"No time for that. Let's go." He grabbed her hand and walked to the door. Tying up his mask he barked, "You too."

She did so saying, "Do you really think the blood is going to work?"

"Maybe not. But I'm hoping for the shock value will get us to the emergency room. Come on." He opened the door and stepped into the hall.

The other two agents stood in the hallway: one leaned against the opposite wall, reading a newspaper, the other talking to the blond therapist. They paid no attention to Puchkin across the hall, frantically calling for police.

Dezhnev nudged Roxanna's elbow. *Walk.*

She walked.

Puchkin saw them, his face registering mild surprise. But he said nothing.

Dezhnev nudged her again. Four meters ahead an overhead sign pointed to the emergency room. He said softly, "Turn right."

"Yes."

They were there. They turned and whipped around the corner.

One of the goons shouted, "Hey!"

"Go," Dezhnev urged. She ran. He stopped and pulled a gurney across the hall right at the corner. Two men walked in the other direction, surprise and consternation registering on their faces.

Dezhnev ran and heard a great clatter. Glass tinkled. Men cursed. Risking a look back, he saw the gurney laying on its side, the two goons on the floor kicking and struggling to disentangle themselves while yelling at the two passers-by.

Roxanna waited at the emergency room double doors.

Dezhnev ran through and grabbed her arm, dragging her along. The doors swung shut and they found themselves in a large ward sectioned off by curtains. Medical equipment was strewn about. Some of it bleeped. Doctors and nurses dressed like Dezhnev and Roxanna walked back and forth or stood at patients' bedsides. Some wore masks, others didn't.

"Let's go."

"What?" Her eyes darted about. She looked crazed.

"Quick. Our only chance is out there." He pointed toward the exit doors, grabbed her hand, and said quietly, "Walk."

They moved into the main passageway and weaved their way among stumbling patients and medical staff.

They'd almost reached the exit when the door opposite blasted open and the two KGB agents rushed through. One held up his badge and yelled, "Nobody move."

A man in scrubs and mask walked up to one agent. "What the hell is this? Can't you see some of these people are critical?"

"Silence." The agent yanked off the man's mask and examined him, discovering an angry doctor. The KGB agent shoved him aside and shouted, "Everybody stand where they are. Do not move." They waved their pistols and began yanking off people's masks. Shouts of protest were greeted by a hard slap in the face or a shove in the chest.

Dezhnev made ready to bolt. Just then, the outside emergency room doors banged open. Four medical technicians pushed in a gurney with a patient. It held a woman covered with a dark blue blanket. Her mouth sagged open and she was very pale.

One of the men shouted, "Car accident. Severed artery, she needs blood, type O negative." He looked around seeing everyone backing away from the two goons. "What the hell is wrong with everybody?"

A doctor broke ranks and rushed up. Then a nurse. Dezhnev pushed Roxanna around them and they dashed through the door.

The ambulance sat there, backed right up to the emergency room, its doors open and empty. The engine ticked over.

Roxanna needed no cue. She ran for the right door. Dezhnev slammed the rear doors shut and ran for the left. Jumping in, he kicked off the emergency brake, ground it into gear, and hit the accelerator. They shot out. Roxanna found the siren as they rounded a corner and roared down the back alley.

She gasped when she saw the two KGB agents standing beside their Lada. Politely, they stepped aside as the ambulance aimed for a narrow gap between the Lada and the hospital's brick wall. Dezhnev didn't let up on the accelerator and at nearly fifty kilometers per hour screeched through to the next intersection and turned right.

43

13 March 1968
Highway A 148
Sochi, Tsentralny City District
Krasnodar Krai, USSR

The ambulance, a converted wartime Zil, coughed and sputtered each time Dezhnev shifted gears. They had raced away from town and were now on a two-lane asphalt highway with little traffic. With steep foothills on both sides, the Zil rattled and belched as they headed east up a long slope into the Caucasus.

He checked the rearview mirror. "I think we're okay for the time being."

She bit her thumbnail. "How reassuring."

"Turn off the siren."

She flipped the switch. "Any idea where we're going?"

"None at all."

"They'll find us. This thing is too obvious." She looked up for helicopters, and then scanned the roadway. Then she frowned and let out an exaggerated sniff. The ash tray was overcrowded with cigarette butts. She cranked down the window, pulled out the ashtray, and emptied the contents into the wind.

"Nice," he said.

They soon paralleled a river fed by runoff from the snow-capped mountains. It's cold, frothy waters cascaded past, crashing over boulders.

"Umm," she cooed.

"You know this place?"

"Mzymty River. We come up here in the summers to picnic. It's a beautiful place to camp."

"I didn't know you went camping."

She gave a short laugh. "I talk a good game, but actually, I hate camping."

"I don't understand."

"The ground is hard, there are too many bugs, and the night is cold and black. And I need my coffee in the morning without waiting for someone to start a fire and rattle around with pots and pans."

"Not at all civilized."

"And after that you get to crawl out of your warm sleeping bag and tromp off somewhere to find a log to sit on, drop your pants, and go wee-wee, while freezing your buns off."

"Sounds awful."

"Travelling with the Kirov did have its benefits."

"We should all join the Kirov."

"The main benefit was that my husband didn't go with me."

"Mmmmm?" Dezhnev's brow went up, clearly amused.

"He hated it more than I did." She faked a yawn. "Yes, my concept of roughing it is poor room service."

"I wish I had your sense of self-sacrifice."

She chuckled and then asked, "Where are we going?"

Dezhnev checked the rearview mirror again. "We're about thirty kilometers out of town. And I don't know where we're going, but we need to get under cover. Helicopters will be looking for us, and this thing really does stand out. Might as well paint a bull's-eye and sign on the roof saying 'Aim right here.'" He slowed and looked up a dirt road. But it dead-ended at the river. The next two roads ended the same way.

"Take them at least two hours to mount a concentrated search."

"Less than that, I think. We should—ah." He slowed and turned onto a dirt track that crossed the river via a rickety covered bridge. They rattled over the bridge and bounced in ruts and potholes on the other side at a slow speed.

"Eduard?"

"Yes?"

"I'm scared."

"Don't be."

"I can't help it. What will they do when they find us?"

He reached over and took her hand. "They're not going to find us."

"What if they do?"

"I'm the one they want. Not you."

"I'm the one who konked that guy over the head. They'll be after me as well."

"Nonsense."

"Tell me about our Vladdie."

He shrugged. "You know as much as they know. That the *K-129* is propped up on a reef."

"Can't they go after it?"

"They're doing that. It's like an international manhunt. Except the Philippines are tricky. Basically, it's an American protectorate and fortress right now. And worse, Zamboanga with its Muslims and Moros are dangerous to Filipinos and Americans alike. We're going to have trouble negotiating with them."

"Don't they have signals and radios and stuff like that?"

He faked a yawn. "Ummm. They do. But that's only good if ...if..."

"What?"

"If they can use them."

She thought about that. "Oh."

He didn't want to add about the political contingent that boarded the *K-129* at the last minute. That they may have become a rogue crew. What good would it have done to go into all that now?

They came to a rutted path and jiggled along for a kilometer or so. At length, they pulled into a dense grove of mountain cedars, and boxwoods, the canopy overhead masking them from the early afternoon sun.

He felt it before he heard it, the *whack-whack-whack* of a helicopter. Soon he heard the whine of the twin turbos. Though the overhead canopy they saw a Mil Mi-8 helicopter flash past, flying low to the ground as it followed the highway up the valley. It looked like a deadly green grasshopper. "It's a gunship," said Dezhnev.

"That's not good," muttered Roxanna.

Dezhnev said, "Lucky we ducked under." Then, "Let's keep going." They bounced and jerked on the road for another five minutes. Then it petered out when they came to a clearing against a steep cliff. But there was still plenty of canopy overhead. Dezhnev stopped and switched off the engine. It was quiet. Wind flowed gently through the boxwood leaves overhead. The river raged in the distance.

The doors squeaked as they got out. Leaning against the fender, Roxanna hugged herself. "Brrrrr." She shivered and her teeth chattered. Yet the sky above the canopy was clear blue, the temperature a gorgeous 24° Celsius. *Hug her, you idiot.*

He walked around to do it but instead came face to face with a boy about three meters away at the edge of the clearing. He had coal black hair, was dressed in pantaloons, vest, and boots, and looked to be about ten or eleven. He stared at them fiercely, as someone five times his age might have done.

Roxanna found her voice, "We...we must look like fools in these surgical gowns."

"Right." They stripped off their gowns, booties, and face masks, and pitched them through the ambulance's open windows.

The boy's eyes narrowed as he focused on Dezhnev's naval uniform. He took a step back.

Dezhnev stood to stiff attention, leaned a bit forward, clicked his heels, and saluted the boy. With deep formality he said, "Good day to you Comrade Brezhnev."

The boy said nothing and took another step back.

Dezhnev saluted again. "Comrade Brezhnev?"

"I think he's a Gypsy," said Roxanna. "Maybe he speaks Romani."

"Ah," said Dezhnev. "If we—"

The boy reached behind his back and whipped out a pistol, an eight-shot Makarov PM. Aiming it at Dezhnev's chest, he said, "Don't move."

"I'm sorry, little fellow. I didn't mean to—"

"On your knees, both of you," he said in a reedy voice. With the pistol, he gestured them to the ground.

Holding his hands in the air, Dezhnev took a step toward him. "Look. We're out of the city and trying to—"

The Makarov cracked. The round blasted a tuft of dirt between Dezhnev's legs. Week-kneed, he fell to the ground. "Sorry, what can I do to—?"

"That's enough, János," called a voice from the boxwood grove. A man separated himself from the shadows. Another smallish man with a heavily tanned face walked out from behind the ambulance. A third, with swept-back silver hair, stepped out from the other side of the clearing. The first thing Dezhnev noticed was that all three carried World War II Mosin-Nagant five-shot bolt-action rifles. And they held them ready for immediate action. Each was dressed like the boy except in varying colors. The closest, who had an enormous handlebar moustache, said, "You are right about the Romani, madam. But don't attempt to curry his good graces. He's a Magyar. Red soldiers killed his mother and father as they were escaping from Hungary." The man drew up before Dezhnev. "And you look like one of them, except you are Navy instead of the border troop."

Then the man looked over at the boy. "Give János a good reason not to put a bullet in your head, right now."

"I...we..."

"He yearns to do it, to kill you. Just like your comrades did to his mother and father. János got away and saw it from a distance. The guards showed no mercy. Both parents were made to kneel. Then just two rounds. No one was allowed to bury them. Their bodies rotted out there."

"I'm not a border patrol guard."

"János' mother was...my sister."

"I'm sorry. But look. I'm not even in the infantry."

The moustached man nodded to the short Gypsy. "Check him."

The short one stood his rifle against the ambulance and stepped over to Dezhnev. Raising a hand, he said, "Up."

Dezhnev raised his hands while the man patted him down, coming up with the two KGB Makarov pistols. He handed them over to the moustached man. "Hmmmmm."

"What?" said Dezhnev.

"These are rigged for silencers. Hard to find this model. Do you plan to 'silence' somebody anytime soon?"

Dezhnev kept quiet.

"How did you get them?"

Where is he going with all this? Dezhnev said nothing.

At a nod from the moustached Gypsy, the short one turned to Roxanna.

"You better not, you snake," she growled.

Both were spun around, held fast by their hands, and bent over the hood of the ambulance. Dezhnev struggled, but a pistol jammed against his head settled the matter. Roxanna yelped a couple of times while she was searched. Then they were released and allowed to turn around.

Dezhnev said to the little man. "Was that fun?"

"Eh." The man tipped his hand from side to side and walked over to his rifle and picked it up.

"The moustached man said, "Yes, I see you're not in the infantry. You're in the Navy. Submarines, it looks like. Where's your cap?"

Dezhnev patted the top of his head and realized he'd left it at the hospital.

"I don't have it."

"Then you're out of uniform. Why?"

"I left it at the hospital. We had to get out in a hurry."

"Why?"

"The KGB came to arrest me. They marched right into the room while I was having my prosthesis adjusted." He raised his pant leg and waved his artificial leg.

All three men stepped close to examine Dezhnev's leg. "How did that happen?" asked the ringleader.

Dezhnev shrugged and dropped his pant leg. "German E-boats jumped me from out of a fog. Three against one. They chopped us up. Only four of my fourteen men survived."

Roxanna stepped close and wound an arm around Dezhnev's waist.

The man said, "You survived. My sister did not."

Dezhnev stood to his full height. "You damn fool. Do you know what it's like having three 37-mm and nine 20-mm cannons blasting at you from close range? To be showered with your men's blood and body parts? I still dream about it and often I wish I were with them." By now, he was yelling. "Your brother got it easy. My boat sank beneath us. Almost every night I see my men's faces, their grins and their girlfriends and their drunken boasting. And then I see their arms, legs, and intestines flying through the air through smoke and muck!" He took a step forward. "That's how I lost this."

The Gypsy with the handlebar moustache met him face to face, centimeters apart. "Why does the KGB want you?"

"I can't say."

"Tell me or I'll turn you over to János."

"Then you'll be doing me a favor, you stupid son-of-a-bitch. It'll be much easier than going to the Lubyanka."

"Eduard," said Roxanna. "Can't you tell him something?"

The Gypsy leader seemed to relax. "Eduard? You are Eduard Dezhnev?"

Inside, Dezhnev felt a jolt. Outwardly he fought for control, hoping he didn't show it. "Yes. How did you know?"

"You left your hat at Hospital 14 on Slotsky Boulevard?"

Dezhnev nodded.

Roxanna said, "How did you know that—"

Dezhnev pinched her.

The man held out his hand. "Please show me your ID."

Seeing no reason not to, Dezhnev whipped out his wallet and flipped to his Navy ID.

The man took it and examined it closely. The other two Gypsys stepped near and looked over his shoulder. They looked at one another and nodded just as another Mi-8 *whacked* its way up the valley.

The leader said, "They have FLIR equipment, do they not?"

"Some of the newer ones, yes."

"Then we better get inside." The man extended his hand. "I am Orbon Dráfi." They shook hands and he nodded to the boy. "And you have met my nephew János Dráfi."

"Nice to meet you, son."

The boy looked away.

"And these are my cousins, Lázló Boeri," he gestured to the shorter of the two men, "and Tomás Botos," he nodded to the wizened-looking man with the silver hair.

The other two shook hands as well. Dezhnev said, "and this is my wife to be, Roxanna Utkina."

"Your fiancée," declared Orbon.

Roxanna bowed her head.

Dezhnev looked down to her. "Yes?"

She cupped her hands over her face.

Dezhnev dropped to his knees, looked up to her and gently pulled away her hands. "Marry me, please?"

Her voice was barely a whisper. "These people, these men. I don't know who they are."

"It doesn't matter. Please, Utochka. I'll say it again. I was a damn fool to let you go the first time. I'm not about to do it again." He held her hands tightly.

"They could kill us."

"Better to die with you than live without you." He looked up into her face. Tears streamed. "Please."

"Get up," she said.

Dezhnev rose.

She nodded.

"I can't hear you, Utochka," said Dezhnev.

"Yes, yes, you damn fool. I will marry you." She threw her arms around him. They kissed.

The Gypsies shoved Dezhnev aside and each ceremoniously kissed her twice on each cheek. That done, Roxanna slumped against the ambulance's fender, a bit flushed.

Dezhnev said, "What is it?"

She put her hands to her face. "Many times I've been kissed by foreign diplomats, generals, artists, politicians, and even once by Nikita Khrushchev. But this is the first time by smelly men armed to the teeth with guns, knives, and ammo belts."

They laughed, then Dezhnev turned to Orbon, "How did you learn so much about me?"

He gave a slight smile. “The KGB thinks they own the public airwaves. They talk too much.”

“Pardon?”

“We have an American-made scanner, built by Radio Shack. We monitor their broadcasts. Our survival depends on it.” He picked up his ear. Another helicopter *whacked* in the distance. “Their FLIR will eventually find you, you know.”

Dezhnev tried to be silent. Eventually he nodded.

“What do you plan to do?”

“I had no plans this morning except to go shopping with my fiancée. And now,” he waved toward the helicopter, “I’m just not sure. They’re on to me. I… I’ve been lucky over the years. Actually, there were several occasions when I thought they would arrest me. But it didn’t happen, and I dropped my guard and got lazy.

“Years?”

“A long time. I’ve been a damned fool. I’ve always thought there was hope for our Russia, our *Rodina*. But Podgorny and Brezhnev and their idiots are screwing it up, just like Stalin and Beria did.” He shook his head. “Such corruption. Such waste. I don’t see any hope.”

“A patriot.”

“Not good enough, I’m afraid.”

“Let me ask again. What do you plan to do?”

“Now? Get married and get out fast.”

Orbon chuckled and twirled his moustache. “Again I ask. How?”

Dezhnev straightened. “We must get to the West.”

“Easier said than done.”

“Actually, I do have a plan. All I need to do is get to Trabzon.” Trabzon was a coastal port in Turkey on the Black Sea about 280 kilometers due south.

“How?”

“I was thinking of the auto ferry.”

Orbon snorted. “Very dangerous. You could easily be captured.”

“Airport? Road blocks? Far worse. No. the auto ferry is our only hope.”

“What’s in Turkey?”

Dezhnev said, “I can’t say much, except it’s a way to the West.”

"How far?"

"All the way."

Orbon's eyes narrowed. "Can you pay?"

"Depends."

"I mean a great deal. We may have something for you."

"Yes, We…I can pay. But only if we get to Trabzon."

"I see." Orbon rubbed his chin.

They looked up. The helicopter was returning.

Orbon said, "We better get inside before his FLIR starts bleeping or whatever it does."

"Inside where?"

44

13 March 1968
Four kilometers north of Highway A 148
Caucasus foothills
Krasnodar Krai, USSR

They piled into the ambulance with the old man, Tamás Botos, driving. Lázló Beeri rode in the passenger seat, occasionally jumping out to clear brush. Dezhnev, Roxanna, Orbon, and János Dráfi rode in the back. Tamás carefully eased the old Zil around trees, through dense groves of cedars, and once, by mistake, into a deep mudhole where the five got out and pushed with Roxanna at the wheel. Half an hour later they pulled into a thick grove where one could hardly see the sky overhead. Dezhnev looked, out realizing they were again at the face of the cliff.

Tamás and Lázló jumped out and began pulling aside brush. At length, they came to a set of large boulders. One tugged while the other pushed and the boulders swung out, as if on greased skids. Inside was a large cave with bright light spilling out.

Dezhnev's jaw dropped. "How did you do that?"

"Fake boulders; papier-mâché, really. We airbrush them with paint to match the boulders.

Tamás eased the Zil inside. Orbon sent young János off to cover their tracks, and the boulder assembly was swung shut.

Dezhnev looked about. The large cave, about the size of a very large basketball court, was well lighted with fluorescent lights overhead. The central and left portions were given over to a garage and what looked like vehicle overhaul and restoration. A machine shop occupied the center of the cave. Automobile components, fenders, bumpers, windshields, and engine parts were organized into bins.

Two beautifully kept automobiles stood before them. One Dezhnev recognized as a 1967 Mercedes Benz 280 SL roadster in light green livery. The other was a 1965 Lancia Flavia sport Zagato, a machine far too rich for the common man's blood. One man was deep under the hood working on the engine. Another sat on the floor banging a dent out of the left rear fender. Further to the left against the far wall was a full-sized ventilated auto-spray booth. Somewhere off to his right Dezhnev heard the ticking of an electric motor, presumably driving the ventilator for the booth. In shadows at the back he spotted an ancient MTZ-2 four-wheeled tractor out of the Minsk Tractor Works in Belarus. But it had an enclosed cabin that seated four, and the tires looked all new. Beside it was a double-wheeled dolly and a hay wagon.

What looked like living quarters lined the right wall. There were six tent-like structures with blankets stretched across the doorways. They were arranged three on each side of a galley with two long crude wooden tables with benches before it. Behind the tables, three women stood around a large kettle suspended over a fire. One stirred with a large wooden paddle. Another peeled carrots and tossed them in while a third threw in spices.

Dezhnev turned a circle, his hands on his hips. "Amazing." He looked at Orbon. "Why haven't they found you?"

Orbon shrugged, "These mountains are riddled with caves. They finally gave up looking."

"But one would think they would have been on to you a long time ago."

"As long as we stay out of their hair, they stay out of ours."

"So, you restore cars?"

"Yes. And that way we don't need to steal food. We're now pretty self-sufficient."

"Where do you get the cars?"

Orbon twirled his moustache and gave a thin smile.

Dezhnev pressed. "A beautiful setup."

"Depends upon how you look at it. Yes, we live our own lives in here and contact with the outside world is minimal. We're pretty self-sufficient. Aquifers give us plenty of clean, potable water. Much of our food we get from the forest. Christians hid here in ancient times." He waved a massive hand," You should see the wall carvings. And there are at least two escape routes we've discovered."

"More room?"

"Yes, but we seldom go back there. One can fall down a hole and disappear forever."

Dezhnev looked toward the rear of the cave and shuddered.

"Come," said Orbon. He waved toward one of the tables. "Business."

Dezhnev looked back to Roxanna. "You coming?"

"What is this?" she demanded.

"Getting us out of here."

"How? Where?"

"To the West."

"What?" She drew up at the bench.

"Please sit," Dezhnev said.

Orbon's eyes clicked between the two.

Roxanna sat with an exaggerated sigh.

Orbon began, "There's a chance."

"For what?" asked Dezhnev.

"We may be able to get you to Trabzon."

Dezhnev leaned forward.

"We do you a favor. You do us a favor."

"What choice do I have?"

Orbon smiled. "You see that car over there?" He nodded toward the Lancia Zagato.

"Ummmm."

"Normally, we have our, ah...merchandise sold in advance with our money in hand before delivery. But this time there are special expenses attached to getting it to the ultimate buyer, a Greek textile executive."

Dezhnev nodded. This was getting interesting.

"There are cousins and uncles in the, ah, distribution system who will assemble this transaction."

"Baksheesh."

"That's a very crude word."

"How much do you need?"

"For the both of you? Two hundred thousand, American."

Roxanna gasped.

Orban sat back and twirled his moustache. "The border guards cost the most."

"Nonsense." Dezhnev doubled his fists.

"You are easily worth it. An escaped fugitive. Your fiancée, a once-revered ballerina. Yes, worth every penny."

Dezhnev reviewed his options. One hundred thousand for him was possible. But Roxanna? He wasn't sure if Toliver would approve that. Or even try to secure approval. "How can this be done?"

"Obie!" It was one of the women at the kettle. Dark-haired and slender, she moved with grace as she stirred stew with a wooden paddle.

Orban sniffed. "Ah, my wife. Dinner is ready." He called over to her. "One minute, Iva."

She scowled. "Hurry up. We're ready to sit."

Orban chuckled, "What did I do to deserve you, my sweetheart? What about our guests?"

"They will have full bellies. You will starve."

"So be it," said Orban. He winked at Dezhnev and Roxanna.

The other two women walked over and put plates and two large baskets of bread on the table. With the women came the odor. Dezhnev sniffed. Some sort of meat dish. *Not bad*. He looked toward Roxanna, who returned his look with one of indifference. *Not good*.

He said to Orbon, "How can you do this?"

"With the car."

Roxanna shook her head.

Dezhnev squeezed her hand.

"I'm sorry," she said softly.

"Orbie!"

Orban said, "Come. We'll talk after dinner."

The fluorescent lights were doused as Orban explained the danger of light leaking outside after dark. It was just too much of a risk. Everybody sat at the two tables, their only light the bonfire used to cook the stew. They ladled it on their plates and ate with their hands. Silently and with gusto.

Roxanna refused to eat this way, so Iva handed her a small wooden ladle. With that, Roxanna spooned over a large portion and dug in.

Dezhnev said, "This is really good. Where do you get it?"

Orban swabbed his plate with bread, "It's not *dugo* (roadkill) if that's what you're worried about."

"I meant no such thing."

Orban said, "We haven't had to resort to that. However, one of Comrade Lutrov's cows is missing. But he has a fairly substantial herd, so he may not realize it yet. And with our new investments, we'll be able to eat well for quite a while, so we won't have to resort to Comrade Lutrov's generosity."

Dezhnev understood. *Investments* meant him. Also, it meant Roxanna and the Lancia. He said, "Please convey our thanks to Comrade Lutrov."

"Of course."

Their meals finished, the others stood and wandered over to the galley fire. At a prompting from Lázló, János threw a couple of logs on the fire. The wood must have been dry, for it flared up almost immediately, the flames casting flickering shadows on the cave walls. They sat in ones and twos. One or two read; the rest stared into the fire. At length, Lázló grabbed a violin case, snapped it open, and began tuning and picking it. Dezhnev and Roxanna were surprised when János sat beside him with a guitar and joined in. They played a slow, mournful tune in a minor key with low notes and yet a distinctive tempo.

Dezhnev looked at Roxanna. She shook her head no; she didn't know the song either, but it was clear from her face that she enjoyed it. At length, she asked Orban, "What's it called?"

"Woman in Shadows," he answered.

"It's beautiful," she said.

"Yes."

"Comrade Dezhnev?" Orban raised an eyebrow. "I need an answer. The ferry sails tomorrow night at eight o'clock and there are arrangements I have to make tomorrow morning."

Dezhnev looked at Roxanna. She seemed to be ignoring them. But then, as the music played, she said, "That's beautiful. I must have that music."

Orban said, "Talk to Iva. She wrote it."

"She's very talented. Do you suppose she would give it to me?"

"Talk to her," said Orban.

Their shadows flicked across the wall in tempo to the music. Roxanna took Dezhnev's hand and said, "Yes, you damn fool. I'll go with you."

"Yes!" Dezhnev jumped up. She stood and they kissed across the table.

"Hoo-rah!" Orban stood and ran toward the wall. He picked up a guitar and joined the other two, shouting for a robust piece. They strummed a new tune and played fiercely. Iva walked among them smacking a tambourine. Julia, one of the cooks, jumped up and began dancing before Lázló.

Roxanna smiled wistfully. "Young lovers." She clapped to the music as Iva began singing "Woman in Shadows." To their surprise, young János walked beside her with his guitar and joined in with near perfect harmony.

Roxanna clasped her hands. "It's so compelling, so spontaneous."

Dezhnev moved close and wrapped his arms around her waist. "I'm tired. Let's go to bed."

45

14 March 1968
Sochi, Tsentralny City District
Krasnodar Krai, USSR

Orban drove the MTZ-2 tractor with Iva seated beside him. It was cramped in the enclosed cabin with Dezhnev and Roxanna wedged on a little bench in back. They wore Gypsy clothing belonging to Iva and Orban. And they smelled like goats because the clothes hadn't been washed in a long time; maybe ever. Making matters worse, Iva and Julia had fashioned a full beard and sideburns for Dezhnev. It looked convincing, but his face and neck itched. It was hard to keep from scratching. And the odor of feces on his clothes assaulted nearly his every breath. Roxanna had trouble with it too. She kept squirming. He understood. He couldn't wait to get outside either.

She squirmed again.

He grabbed her hand, "Not much longer, baby."

She threw an eye-roll.

He couldn't blame her. It was miserable back here. They were trapped and helpless if trouble should arise.

The tractor towed a ramshackle trailer carrying three large, grimy crates packed tightly together and marked "farm machinery." It was a strange contraption. The outside looked dirty and ramshackle. The Lancia was mounted inside on the auto trailer.

János straddled the MZT-2's hood acting like a village idiot, his tongue lolling from his mouth. Sitting atop the crates on the trailer were Lázló and his girlfriend, Julia. The old man, Tamás, sat on the back, his feet dangling just above the road.

They were chugging down a broad, tree-lined four-lane boulevard. Most of the leaves had dropped over the winter, leaving the branches to look like dark -gray spiders in the fading daylight. Dezhnev checked his watch: just after five in the afternoon; the sun would go down in about half an hour. The ferry pushed off at six. They were late.

Orban called over his shoulder, "Can you see where we are?"

Dezhnev replied, "The heart of Sochi. Gorkovo Boulevard. Which takes us past the train station. Is that wise?"

"Just to see if there is any unusual police activity, my friend. Don't worry."

Dezhnev fidgeted. "Why are we going so slowly?"

"We're doing forty kilometers now, and that's as fast as I want to go with this old rig. Please relax. We'll be there soon. Another kilometer or so."

"Yes, but—"

Roxanna squeezed his hand, hard. "Breathe."

He'd forgotten the power, the strength, in those hands, in her entire body. Still the athlete. He let out a lungful and took three deep breaths. He smelled shit and gave a polite cough.

"Better?"

"Nice suggestion."

She squeezed his hand.

He checked his watch for the third time in as many minutes: 1306. If he remembered correctly, the auto-ferry lines would be long.

She pulled his coat sleeve back over his watch. "Breathe, you damn fool."

The train station drifted past on their left. The parking lot was about half full. He didn't see any military vehicles or anything else unusual in the lot such as a police or KGB Lada. Still, his heart raced.

"There she is," said Orban. He waved toward the waterfront, now two blocks away. Rising above the tree line was their ticket to Trabzon. The auto-ferry had stubby, rakish lines, and Dezhnev gauged her to be about 80 meters long and 3,000 tons. Her original white paint had faded to a chalky light gray, and rust streaks ran down her sides from hawsepipe and scuppers. Indeed, she looked well used with her plates dished in from heavy seas. Atop her superstructure was a single red stack with a streaking blue star emblazoned on the side, the logo of the Blue Star Line. Her name was at the bow: *Star of Tengri.* She was secured in a Mediterranean moor facing out into the Black Sea, leaving her open stern accessible for the boarding of automobiles.

Orban growled, "Here we are." They swung around a bend to find a military truck blocking the entrance. Several soldiers stood around. One stepped in front of the MTZ, blocking further progress. By his insignia he was a sergeant in the local militia. There were generous rolls around his waist, and his jowls sagged. But an AK-47 was slung over his shoulder, and he looked like he knew how to use it. Two rows of ribbons on his tunic testified that he'd served in the Great Patriotic War.

He hoisted himself up to the cab and rapped on the window.

Orban cranked it down.

"Paperwork, Grandpa."

"Show some respect." Orban produced a large piece of paper.

"Ah," said the sergeant, "a blanket visa. You have tickets?"

"Yes."

"Well, come on."

Orban pulled out a grimy envelope filled with eight tickets.

The sergeant handed them back and held up the visa. "You Gypsies expect so much. You are Orban Dráfi?"

"Yes."

"And," he nodded to Iva, "you are..." He snapped his fingers.

"Yes, Iva Dráfi." She pulled out an ID and handed it over.

The guard matched the card against the blanket visa then said, "Hot stuff."

In the rearview mirror Dezhnev saw Orban roll his eyes as the sergeant returned the ID card.

He looked in back, snapping his fingers but keeping his eyes on Iva, who had hiked her skirt to mid-thigh.

Then the guard sniffed. "Whew. Pig shit."

"Nonsense," said Orban.

The guard snatched the ID cards from Dezhnev and Roxanna and said, "I grew up on a farm. I know pig shit when I smell it."

In the rearview mirror Dezhnev saw that Orban was doing his best to suppress a grin.

The guard asked, "You are..."

"Felix Maga," said Dezhnev.

"And?" The sergeant nodded to Roxanna.

"Marcia Kalucza," said Roxanna.

The guard returned their IDs then stepped down. "I'm so pleased you know your names. I should have them hose down the lot of you just to keep the Turks from sending you back."

Then he walked back checking the IDs of Lázló, Julia, and Tamás. At length, he walked forward, checked János, then handed the visa back to Orban. "Good luck shoveling shit in Trabzon." He waved them through.

Dezhnev felt lightheaded. The ID cards that Orban had faked this morning had worked. So had the disguises, all the way down to the pig shit they'd smeared on his boots.

With a nod to the sergeant, Orban eased the clutch and they moved ahead. He called over his shoulder, "Funny how things work out."

"How's that?" replied Dezhnev.

"That militia sergeant and Tamás were in the same tank unit during the war. In fact, they were in the same T-34, Tamás the tank captain, Sergeant Gurov the loader."

This was beginning to make sense. "How much is he going to cost us?" Dezhnev asked.

"You'll get the bill," laughed Orbon.

Roxanna looked up to him. "Almost there." She smiled and kissed him on the cheek."

Dezhnev mouthed, *Almost there*, and bent down to kiss her.

"Shit!" said Orbon.

"What?" Dezhnev looked up to see an eight-wheeled BTR-60 armored personnel carrier parked right at the stern ramp of the *Star of Tengri*. A half-dozen soldiers stood around. Their shoulder patches showed they were KGB border troops, an outfit to which he once belonged during the latter stages of the war in the Far East...on Sakhalin. "You can say that again."

"Where'd they come from?" said Orban. He checked his watch. "We're due on the boat now. Close to sailing time."

Roxanna grabbed his arm. "What do you think?"

Dezhnev sighed, "Just play it through. That's all. We do some more jumping about."

"Well, I'm not going to sit trapped in the back of this thing while those animals paw at me. Let me out, please."

Orban drew to a stop. "I'm not sure if—"

"Me, too," said Iva. "Come on, Roxanna." Iva yanked the door handle and jumped to the ground. Turning around, she looked up and yelled, "Come on."

Roxanna stepped forward and asked, "Coming Eduard?"

"Sure." He jumped out with Roxanna and stood with Iva and the others as Orban haggled with a Border Patrol sergeant outside the window on the left side. The two women walked aboard. *What the hell*? Dezhnev walked over the stern ramp with crossed fingers. *Amazing*. He stood in the nearly full auto bay and through the deck felt the thump of the *Star of Tengri* 's engines warming up.

He turned to see the KGB guards poking at the three crates on the trailer. One produced a crowbar and began prying up the top. Another guard joined him and they made rapid work, the nails squeaking as they pried and grunted.

"Hey!" Tamás Botos ran up. "That's perishable. You'll ruin it."

Another guard, a beefy one, stood between Botos and the crate while the two guards did their work. The guards and curious passengers stood closer as they pried.

"Hoo-rah!" shouted one of the guards. The two lifted the lid and stood it on end beside the trailer.

A terrible screech pierced the air. People jumped back. Two chickens—a white hen and a dark red rooster—jumped out, their wings flapping furiously. Laughter broke out. The guards looked sheepish as they rummaged through an assortment of rakes, shovels, feed sacks, and other hand tools. At length they shook their heads and lifted the lid back on the crate.

Another guard, a corporal, had caught the chickens and carried them by their feet to the sergeant. They spoke for a moment, then the sergeant nodded. The corporal grinned and walked off with the clucking and flapping chickens toward the BTR-60.

Orban ran after him yelling, "Idiot! Those belong to us."

The corporal grinned with dark tobacco-stained teeth and tossed the protesting chickens in the BTR-60 and slammed the hatch shut, the chickens squawking inside.

"No!" Orban reached for the hatch lever.

"Uh, uh." The corporal yanked out a pistol and jammed it against Orban's temple. "That's contraband, you miserable slob. You could be fined. Maybe worse."

The sergeant walked up. "Get that thing aboard, bottom crawler. God, you stink!" He checked his watch. "Nearly time."

"But my chickens."

The sergeant and the corporal turned and stared at Orban, their fists jammed on their hips.

Orban shook his head. "I hope they shit all over your electronics." Then he walked back to the tractor, started it up, and moved it aboard. He switched off the engine and hopped out, glaring at the two border guards on the wharf as the ship's crew set the stern gate assembly. Still glowering, Orban reached in his pocket and handed over their tickets to a blue-uniformed man standing near the gate.

We're here! The hell with the chickens. What else can happen?

As if in answer to Dezhnev's unspoken question, Roxanna clutched his arm.

The blue Lada with the dirt-smeared windshield skirted the BTR-60 and drove to the wharf's edge. Two men got out. Both were in ties and dark overcoats. Dezhnev recognized one of them by the extensive bandages covering his nose. His face was red and he had two black eyes.

The two KGB officers skirted the stern gate, walked aboard, and began milling among the passengers. They were soon drifting around the MTZ-2. And then the trailer. They lifted the crate lid and began poking down among the tools

A melody drifted out. It was János on his guitar. And then Lázló joined with his violin. Soon, Orban was with them on his guitar. Iva walked up and sang, tapping her tambourine. Right away the crowd was seized by the music and moved in, watching, listening to "Woman in Shadows."

More people pressed in. The KGB border troops stepped aboard and moved close.

The man with the bandaged face weaved through the crowd closer and closer. Looking at faces. A cold wind sliced through Dezhnev. Automatically he reached for his pistol. It wasn't there. It was back in Orban's hideout.

The man stood before Dezhnev, dried blood prominent on his nose bandage. His eyes were bloodshot but his pupils were still an intense blue. His eyes darted about Dezhnev's face. He reached up for his beard. Dezhnev opened his palm, ready to smash the man again.

The crowd gasped. The music suddenly increased in tempo. The beat low, driving, captivating.

Roxanna. She'd hiked up her blouse to just below her breast line exposing belly and navel. The former ballerina had tied on a thin veil, and began weaving and dancing among the Gypsies. A small circle opened for her, and she moved and twirled quickly around, seeming to be everywhere at once, the guitars strumming furiously. Lázló played his violin beautifully as Iva sang and rapped her tambourine. KGB soldiers, passengers, and dock handlers stood closer. They clapped as Roxanna danced faster and faster.

Ever the athlete, she twisted and gyrated into an outright snake dance.

The crowd clapped and roared.

The *Star of Tengri*'s horn gave a six-second prolonged blast that echoed over the waterfront. The music played on. An engine order telegraph clanged through a hatch up forward.

Line handlers lifted the dock lines off cleats and bollards and tossed them aboard the auto-ferry.

But still the music gushed from the Gypsies. And Roxanna, her skin glistening, danced and danced and danced.

"Move!" It was the border guard sergeant.

The music played on as the KGB border troops hopped off the ship's fantail. Again the engine order telegraph clanged. The deck vibrated.

The man with the bandaged face looked back and forth from a still dancing Roxanna to the wharf. Then he looked at his partner realizing the ship was moving. A meter separated ship and wharf and the gap was rapidly growing. They ran and hopped the stern gate. The ship was two meters away when they jumped. Like Olympic athletes, they flew through the air and landed like cats.

The man with the bandage turned and looked back to the *Star of Tengri.* The distance grew to ten meters as he searched the crowd for Dezhnev. But Dezhnev had eased behind another passenger, a large Turk in an overcoat, who clapped and drooled as Roxanna twisted and turned. The crowd roared as she clasped her hands high and gave them all they asked for and more.

One hundred meters. The KGB guards, the wharf, Sochi faded to obscurity. The engine-order telegraph clanged once again. The *Star of Tengri*'s deck shuddered and she picked up speed, cleared the breakwater, and sailed between channel markers.

The music slowed. Roxanna was beside him now, swaying, twisting, her body gleaming with perspiration. The music strummed to a finale and the crowd cheered and danced along with her. She yanked off her veil and threw her arms in the air. Then she bowed deeply with a broad, victorious smile.

"Utochka!" shouted Dezhnev.

"Yes, master?" She twirled before him.

"You are so beautiful. Like the first time I saw you." It was true. Roxanna's face had somehow dropped twenty-two years. She was a radiant nineteen-year-old again, as if she had quaffed liberally from the Fountain of Youth. Her hair was smooth, her face, flushed with victory, was wrinkle free. Her skin was tight and her eyes shone like headlights on a dark night.

She threw her head back and laughed.

"Amazing," Dezhnev laughed with her. "Your finest performance."

"Yes, it's been quite a while."

The overhead lights flicked off. Roxanna flung her arms around him and they kissed.

The *Star of Tengri* worked between the last of the channel markers. Finally, she stood into the Black Sea on a smooth, moonless evening.

"The Woman in Shadows."

46

15 March 1968
CIA Regional Headquarters
West Los Angeles, California

Oliver Toliver was in a meeting with two agents when the door opened a crack. It was Joan Sutton, his secretary.

"Yes?" he asked. He checked his watch: 0922.

"Field telephone."

Toliver sat back. "Red phone? For me?"

"Yes, sir. Call from station agent in Trabzon, Turkey."

"Trabzon? What the hell?" Toliver stood. "Sorry, gents. Sounds like I have to jump."

He walked down the hall with Sutton matching him stride for stride. "Authentication." She handed over a single page.

"Thanks."

She pushed the Down elevator button. "Agent's name is Tommy Venuto. He's from the Bronx, same as me. I know his mother. He served in the Army in Korea. Silver Star, Purple Heart."

The elevator doors whooshed open and Toliver walked in. She reached past him and pushed B. "He was a POW for thirteen months; lost an arm."

Toliver grimaced. He'd nearly lost a leg in World War II. And he still had pain in his hip. Arthritis, he supposed. He took in her knitted brow. "Tough break. I remember Tommy. He's a good man. Thanks, Joan." The elevator stalled for a moment. "I'll let you know."

"Good luck."

He knew what was on her mind. This was unusual. He'd only used the red phone once before. And that was during the Korean War when he'd set up a submarine to extract three South Korean agents from near Wonsan Harbor where they'd blown up a train waiting in a tunnel: an ammunition train. The explosion brought down half the mountain.

Turkey was an area he didn't know well. The Pacific was his specialty. He knew some of the regional staff in Ankara and that was it. But Trabzon: as best he could remember it was a coastal city on the Black Sea. Other than that he drew a blank. *What's in Turkey*?

The elevator doors closed, and fifteen seconds later they opened in the basement.

He walked down a long hallway covered in linoleum. There were no photos or paintings. Just green linoleum, most likely war surplus from a Navy shipyard. He walked around a corner and came to a door marked Authorized Personnel Only. He knocked. A buzzer zapped and he walked in, finding himself before a desk manned by a guard in a dark suit and plain blue tie. Toliver produced his ID. The man carefully examined it, then nodded and buzzed open a small gate beside his desk. "Extension four-two, sir."

"Thanks."

The gate opened to a doorway. The guard buzzed that open and Toliver walked into a plain room, perhaps ten by ten, and swung the door closed. It was heavy and seated with a metallic thud. It should have. The room was lined with lead.

No one else was there. On the far wall were government issue photographs of President Johnson and Vice President Humphrey. The other walls were bare. A plain oak table stood in the middle surrounded by six chairs. A red telephone, a new one with white pushbuttons instead of a rotary dial, sat on the table. Four buttons were arranged along the bottom. One flashed on and off. It was marked with the numerals 9942.

He picked up the telephone and jabbed the button. "Toliver speaking."

"Authenticate, please." The voice sounded gravelly and distant. Toliver wasn't used to these new satellite phones.

He pulled out the single page Joan had given him and read, "Oscar, oscar, figures three, five, one, five, seven."

The response came back, "Roger: romeo, tango, figures six, three, seven, one, six."

It checked. Toliver relaxed. "That you, Tommy?"

"One and only, Ollie. Good to hear your voice."

"You too. What's up?"

"I have a couple of your people here seeking asylum."

Static ranged on the line. Toliver waited then asked, "People? I don't have anyone in Turkey."

They said they belonged to you. "A guy by the name of Eduard Dezhnev." He spelled it out.

Toliver's heart leaped. "Holy cow. Are you sure? I didn't know he was in Turkey."

"He was in Sochi to visit his girlfriend or wife; whichever she is."

"Wife? Girlfriend? The only one I know of is Roxanna Utkina. And they haven't been on very friendly terms."

"Well, Roxanna is with him here now. They say they want to get married. She used to be with the Kirov Ballet. I gotta tell you. She's a damned knockout."

"Wow! That sounds like Roxanna, all right. Where are they now?"

"Right here. Really pooped. Hungry. Been on the run for the past couple of days. Dezhnev says his cover was finally blown and he had to get out. Dragged her with him. And not too soon, either. The signals I get are that the KGB is all over this. They want your boy badly."

"How did they get out?"

"Auto-ferry, disguised as Gypsies."

"Wow. They have ID?"

"Just phony ID supplied by the Gypsies."

"What time is it there now, Tommy?"

"About nine-thirty in the evening."

"Is he there? I'd like to speak with him."

"Asleep. They were dog tired."

Toliver drummed his fingers. "Wake him up."

"He'll bitch."

"Fine. Then tell him to find a ride somewhere else."

Tommy Venuto laughed. "Okay. Hold on. Er...ah..."

"What, Tommy?"

"Ah...how is Joan?"

So that was it. "How long you been in Trabzon, Tommy?"

A moment of silence. "Twenty-six months."

"Tell you what. I can fix it so you can accompany the Dezhnevs here to Southern California. Then you can ask her yourself."

Tommy Venuto exhaled deeply. "I'm for that. Thanks, Ollie. Hold on. I'll get Dezhnev."

Toliver drummed his fingers. Three minutes passed. Then the phone rustled. "*Da*?" He sounded hoarse.

"Ed, speak American, damn it. How are you?"

"Trying to wake up, Ollie."

"Sorry. But Tommy tells me you want to come out."

"I have to, Ollie. They got on to me somehow. We just barely got away." Dezhnev explained their escape from the KGB.

"Whew. Talk about leaving town in a hail of bullets."

"*Da*."

"And now you wish to marry the Grand Dame of the Kirov?"

"As soon as we get settled in the States. Tell me, how is my mother?"

Toliver said, "She's here in town. Rest assured, I'll put a twenty-four-hour watch on her." Then he asked, "What's your status? Are you married, about to be married, or just thinking about it?"

"Engaged."

"Okay, then we can—"

"There's a problem."

"What?"

"I owe the Gypsies two hundred thousand dollars; a hundred thousand for each of us."

Toliver sighed. “Then we do have a problem.”

“What?”

“I don’t think they’d want to pay for a mistress. That would—”

“Damn it, she’s not my mistress!”

“I know, I know. Nevertheless. They would look negatively on this. I could probably do it, but it will take a few days, maybe weeks. But not right away. And my sense is we should get you out now.”

Silence. Then, “Okay, what if we were married?”

“You would be airborne, chop, chop.”

“For two hundred thousand?”

“I’m pretty sure. Look, get a priest, marry that girl, and we’ll pick you up.”

“Okay. Consider it done. There’s something more important.”

“What?”

“I need to speak with Todd. It’s extremely urgent.”

“What the hell? Can’t you tell me?”

“Maybe. But Todd has to know. Right now.”

It struck Toliver that Dezhnev might know about Todd Ingram’s assignment in Hawaii. How did he know that? “Okay, I’ll have you flown out here to Southern California. You two can speak on a secure line. How does that sound?”

“I’d rather speak to him personally.”

“He’s really wrapped up in something now, Ed.”

“I can imagine. And there’s more to come.”

Toliver drummed his fingers. Then he decided. “Okay. Get married in the next couple of hours. If you can’t, too bad. I want the both of you at Incirlik Air Base by noon tomorrow. Come to think of it, forget getting married there. I’ll have the chaplain at Incirlik Air Force Base waiting for you.”

“Okay,” Dezhnev said. Then, “Incirlik. Where’s that?”

“Southern Turkey, about three hundred miles or so if I remember correctly. Tommy will drive you.”

“Is he good at this?”

“Don’t worry about Tommy. Extraction is his middle name. Should be a ten-hour trip.”

“If traffic and road conditions permit.”

"Let's hope. As soon as we ring off, I'm ordering a VC-137 from Ramstein Air Base to come down and pick you up. A courier will be aboard with the money. We'll send him back to Trabzon to pay off the Gypsies. Are they still there?"

"Damn near camped on the front doorstep."

"Okay, and from Incirlik you, your bride, and Tommy can fly directly. I'll set it up so they can tank midair if they have to. How does that sound?"

"Excuse me. I'm a little behind. What's a VC-137?"

"Air Force version of the Boeing 707. You've seen them. Backbone of the U.S. civilian fleet."

"I understand. Okay. Let me wake up Roxanna and give her the wonderful news that she won't be sleeping for a while."

"Once aboard that jet, she can sleep as long as she wants. Should be about a twelve-to-fourteen-hour trip."

"Okay. Thanks, Ollie."

"You're welcome. Now put Tommy back on."

"Okay."

"And I reserve the right to be the first to kiss the bride when you land. And don't forget to name your kid after me."

"We're too old for kids. So, you can kiss my ass." Dezhnev handed the phone back to Tommy.

Toliver stood outside the Robert E. Mason Terminal, a fixed-base operator situated on the south side of the Los Angeles International Airport, enjoying the sparkling 73-degree morning. Runway 25 L, the southernmost of four ten-thousand-foot parallel runways, stretched before him.

Twenty miles to the east, a pair of landing lights blinked on over the San Bernardino Mountains. It was as if two gigantic eyes had flipped open. This pair became the last in a line of six jets on final approach to LAX. Soon, the train of airliners cruised over the sprawling city, bleeding off speed, preparing to land. Hopefully, one of them would be the VC-137 Toliver had been awaiting. The first one drew closer, lined up on one of the northern runways: it was a Flying Tiger DC 8. Next was a Western Airlines 707 touching down on runway 25R. After that was a Pan American 707 and a United Air Lines 727 landing on the two northern runways.

Two to go: the next to last was a Japan Air Lines 707 on 25R; and the last one...indeed, it looked as if this sixth airplane was lining up for runway 25L.

The landing lights glowed brighter as it drew close. Yes, it was definitely lined up for 25L, heading right for them on a straight-in approach. The dark shape began to take form. Yes, this was the one. The jet's livery was the gray-white of the U.S. Air Force. Toliver checked his watch. Dezhnev and his wife had been airborne more than thirteen hours, having tanked once over the Azores.

Toliver hadn't slept in the past twenty-five hours while monitoring their progress. Almost constantly he had phone conversations going with the Pentagon, with CIA headquarters in Langley Virginia, the CIA office in Ankara, Turkey, the latter angry about his yanking Tommy Venuto out of Trabzon. Yes, he'd pulled strings, yelled at subordinates, pleaded with superiors, and called in favors. But he'd brought it off. Here were the Dezhnevs, sauntering in on this four-engine beauty.

Jacked up on coffee, Toliver was having what he knew was one final blast of adrenalin. After that, there was no telling how long he could stay awake before he collapsed, maybe a half hour. Good thing Joan Sutton was with him, her arm hooked through his. She'd agreed to prop him up and drive him home if the situation warranted.

He had no idea what shape Dezhnev and his wife would be in. He did learn that the base chaplain had conducted a ceremony and had married them just before takeoff. The officer of the day had signed as a witness. So far so good.

The VC-137 grew in his vision; lower and lower. At last the Boeing swooped past with full flaps, engines whistling softly. Finally, the large jet flared perfectly; smoke puffing from the mains as it settled to earth, reversing engines and lightly braking on runway 25L.

"I can't believe this is happening," Joan said.

"Me, too. I wonder how many enemies I've made."

She laughed and held on to his arm. "How many of your people have defected before?"

"This is the first one."

"And now you have two for the price of one." Usually quiet and withdrawn, Joan was effusive today. Toliver knew she would be. Tommy Venuto was aboard that VC-137 as he'd promised. And he'd brought Joan along not just to hold him up but as a surprise for Tommy.

It was a gorgeous day for love, Toliver thought, except he needed to put Dezhnev to work right now. Toliver wondered how wide-awake they would be as the stately VC-137 taxied in. The ground attendant waved his wands; the VC-137's nose dipped as it braked to a graceful stop. The engines spooled down, a stair-ramp rolled up to the forward door.

Two figures stepped out wearing khaki flight suits. Dezhnev, in dark amber aviator glasses, looked over and spotted Toliver. Both hands shot over his head with two-finger vees like Richard Nixon. Then he grinned and gestured to the woman beside him. Her flight suit was a little tighter and did her figure justice. She also waved and began her descent to the United States of America. Both reached the ground and made it official by dropping to their knees and kissing the asphalt.

Tommy Venuto, hair in a crew cut and wearing a polo shirt and sport coat, walked out of the hatch, an overcoat hooked over his shoulder. As he descended, he spotted Joan Sutton. His mouth dropped open.

Joan cupped a hand to her mouth and called, "Hello, stranger."

"Good God!" said Tommy, stepping off the last step

The two ran for each other and embraced.

Toliver groaned. It hit him that his chances of a ride home had sunk to minus ten. Also Toliver observed that Tommy Venuto was doing very well hugging Joan with just one arm.

The flight crew descended and surrounded Dezhnev and Roxanna. There were seven, and they shook hands all around. Roxanna kissed each crewmember briefly except for a first lieutenant who held on. At length, he received three kisses from Roxanna. The flight crew gave a *faux* bravado. Then they turned and ambled off toward a waiting bus.

Toliver stepped up and took Dezhnev's hand. "Welcome home."

Dezhnev said, "You are amazing. Everything went like clockwork."

"Glad we pulled it off. It got a little tight for a while. You get any sleep?"

"Off and on. I got four hours straight in one spot. Roxanna slept most of the time."

Roxanna walked up. Even in her baggy Air Force jump suit she was a knockout.

Dezhnev turned. "Please greet my better half, who after all these years finally did me the honor of becoming my wife."

Toliver took both of Roxanna's hands. "I'm so happy for you two. Welcome to America, and welcome to our home here. We're going to take good care of you."

"You are so kind." She raised her head and gave Toliver a kiss.

"Ah, your English is good." Toliver turned to Dezhnev, "You were right. She is a knockout."

"Quiet, you two," said Roxanna.

Toliver said, "I saw you dance once in New York. About ten years ago. It was a beautiful performance. *Romeo and Juliet*, I think. Ed has very good taste."

She leaned close and said quietly, "It was *Sleeping Beauty*. It ran for just two nights then they pulled us out. Fourteen years ago."

Toliver blushed. "You're right. I'd forgotten. But it was still beautiful."

"Thank you for that. But my time is past. And I want to say something to you and hope you are not offended."

"What's that?"

"My husband prefers to be called Eduard."

Toliver looked up. "Eduard. Okay. So it shall be. Thank you for telling me."

"There is something else."

"Yes?"

"Thank you for saving our lives. And thank you for bringing us here." She waved at the blue skies. "This is very beautiful."

"Glad you're here, Roxanna. I believe you'll find you've made the right choice."

"I know I have. Excuse me for a moment, please." Roxanna turned and went over to Tommy Venuto and was introduced to Joan.

Dezhnev clapped a hand on Toliver's shoulder and spoke softly, "Sorry we had to get out so quickly, but they were breathing down our necks. It looked like they were even on to Tommy Venuto's house. He took some back roads and we got out of town just in time."

"Glad it worked out. Look, we're going to give you a couple of days to rest up, buy clothes, and get acclimated. Then we should talk."

"Can we talk for a few minutes now? Maybe get a cup of coffee?"

"Sure, Eduard."

Dezhnev nodded with a slight smile.

"Talk about what?"

"Rybachiy."

"The naval base?

"Yes, Rybachiy Naval Base."

47

18 March 1968
Secure room, Fleet Operations Control Center
Kunia Regional SIGINT Operations Center (KSOCK)
Level B, Room 2506
U.S. Pacific Command
Kunia, Hawaii

This lead-lined secure room was in the basement; it was a hot, humid non-air-conditioned space, a throwback to World War II and Cdr. Joe Rochefort's famous code-breakers before the Battle of Midway. The paint was chipped and the chairs metal. Ingram checked in with the guard, a Marine looking spectacularly ready for inspection, walked in, and closed the door. He flipped the switch on the single fan and pointed it at the red phone sitting in the middle of the table, its light patiently blinking. Beside the phone was a yellow scratch pad and two pencils.

Ingram picked up the phone. "Ollie."

"Todd, I have a surprise for you."

"I hope it's a nice one the way things are going around here.

"Oh, what seems to be the problem?" asked Toliver innocently.

"Nothing that a keg of dynamite and a thirty-second fuse can't solve. What's going on? How's your hip?"

"Hurt's like hell. May have to go back into surgery."

"Ouch."

"Ouch is right. Look, we have a guest."

"You mean a live person? As in someone in the room with you?"

Toliver said, "That's right." Quietly, he said, "Go ahead."

In Kunia, Ingram drummed his fingers.

The voice boomed. "Todd, old buddy, how's your ass?"

Ingram sat up straight. "Ed. Ed?"

"One and the same."

"I thought you were...were..."

"Dead? At times, I thought I was, too. But fortunately, the reports all turned out to be false."

"Good God, how are you?"

"As well as I can be for an old man. How about you? You getting fat?"

Ingram chuckled. "Too scared to get fat. I'm still shaking after that night in Toro."

"Shakhtyorsk."

"Whatever." In December 1945, Ingram had taken a load of Japanese POWS at the Shakhtyorsk air base (formerly known as Toro when garrisoned by the Japanese) on Sakhalin Island aboard the USS *Maxwell* (DD 525) for transfer back to Japan—but only after a shoot-out with the Soviet cruiser *Admiral Volshkov*. Dezhnev helped turn the tables in this duel by capturing a Russian artillery battery and diverting the cruiser's attention long enough for the *Maxwell* to fire a deadly salvo into the *Volshkov*, allowing Ingram, the *Maxwell*, and her load of Japanese POWs to escape into the night. Ingram continued, "You sound well."

"And happy for a change. I'm married. Her name is Roxanna. We met during the war. Off and on. We never got serious about things until now. Ollie got us out in the nick of time." He gave Ingram a rundown on their escape.

"She with you now?"

"Asleep at the hotel. And you are a vice admiral now?"

"Well, poor judgment on somebody's part. They forgot to check—"

"Gentlemen," interrupted Toliver, "we should get on with this. Time later to reminisce. Go ahead, Eduard."

Todd picked up on the *Eduard*.

Toliver helped out. "I was told he likes to be called *Eduard*, now."

Dezhnev laughed.

Ingram said, "Well, I should check with our protocol officer first. Mustn't upset anyone. Might start World War III. Okay, that said, what's the dope, *Eduard*?"

"Okay, I'm concerned about the *K-129*. My son is aboard her and—"

"Son? You have a son?"

"A fine young man. We had him as...as...well, an accident. That was 1946. Roxanna raised him, really. I couldn't get away that much. It got worse. We separated. But I still saw my boy at least once a year. And he turned out nicely in spite of me, did well in school and is in the navy now, a starshiy leytenant in the submarine force." He paused. "His name is Vladimir."

Ingram waited.

"What I'm about to tell you didn't come from him. He—"

"Eduard. I'm wondering. With you and Roxanna having jumped to the other side, isn't he in danger?"

"We worry about that constantly. I tell you, had those KGB thugs not come after me in Sochi I'd still be there. But they did come after me and we had to run. But we've had no indication they're after him. There are no retributions, and they don't seem to want to punish him."

Ingram had a bad feeling about this. He probed, "Anything else?"

Dezhnev said, "That's it, and we're scared. Roxanna doesn't know yet. I told her this big fib about the *K-129* being off on a long secret mission running aground off Zamboanga. But I can't keep that up too long. And before I do anything else, I'd like to see if he's all right and if we can get him out. Can we do that, Ollie?"

"Maybe. If he wants to come," said Toliver.

Dezhnev came back with, "Then there's another complication."

"What's that, Ed, er, Eduard," asked Ingram.

"Last I heard, the *K-129* was out of communication. Maybe even lost. They're going nuts. They're searching for it."

Bingo. The lost Soviet submarine has to be the K-129. Ingram grabbed the pad and a pencil and wrote *K-129*. "Radio glitch, probably. She'll turn up. Where is she?"

"Patrol, central Pacific. You…er…haven't heard anything?"

"Not a thing, Ed. It's quiet out here. Except maybe in Viet Nam. The VC is kicking the daylights out of us."

Toliver interrupted with, "What else can you tell us about this *K-129*?"

"She's a modified Project 629A ICBM submarine. Diesel powered, three R-21 missiles in the conning tower."

"Yeah, we've seen pictures," said Ingram

"Todd!" admonished Toliver.

Ingram said, "Come on Ollie. Ed knows we have photos and we're not that stupid."

Dezhnev said dryly, "Right. You're not stupid."

Toliver groaned and said, "Anything else, Eduard?"

"Something you should know. We ran into my son in a restaurant in Sochi a few weeks back. That's when he let on to us that he was aboard the *K-129*…"

"And?"

"And with him was his immediate superior, also attached to the *K-129*. His name is Captain Second Rank Vladislav Yusopov. They were both full of vodka, and Yusopov was going on about how he'd been to North Korea. They grabbed the *Pueblo*.

"Ballsy move," said Ingram.

"Until a few days ago, his father, Maxim Yusopov was a member of the Politburo and ran the atomic energy committee. In his seventies, he was paving the way for his son to succeed him. The way he did this was to make Vladislav a KGB tool. Trouble was, young Vladislav blundered often along the way and the KGB had to cover up for him or substitute him out to other commands to let whatever it was blow over. But with the *Pueblo* business, it sounds like Vladislav did something right for a change. It seems to me the KGB had the DPRK seize the ship for their own purposes. But for the life of me I don't know why."

Ingram knew all about the intelligence capabilities aboard the AGERs, but he wasn't going to share it. "Sorry, don't know much about that. Tell me, what does your son do?"

"Assistant communications officer. Normally that is a beginner's job, but Vladimir told me they have a *Perimetr* system on board and that—"

"A what system?" asked Toliver.

"A *Perimetr* system," Dezhnev explained, "is a weapons system that, once activated, will launch all available missiles nation-wide, assuming their launch crews are incapacitated or dead and unable to control their weapons. There is no way to stop it once it begins counting down."

"Good God," said Toliver.

It was quiet until Dezhnev said, "But my son is sort of a...a...fruit loop with the computer."

"A fruit loop?" asked a confused Ingram.

"What you would call a nerd. He understands electronics. Anyway, he told me there is a back door."

"What does that mean?" asked Ingram.

"It means there is a simple way to interrupt the program and keep it from functioning. A programming error. But nobody seems to know it."

"And the people General Yusopov is working with?" asked Toliver.

"To be frank, their only objectives are personal power and a return to a Stalinist government. Their initial goal is to topple the Brezhnev regime and put in Nikolai Podgorny. It goes way back, you see. Maxim Yusopov and Nikolai Podgorny have been friends since childhood."

"How can they topple Brezhnev?"

"These people are the worst kind of fascists. And they've infiltrated everywhere. Compared to them, Comrade Brezhnev is a saint. Anyway, I got to know Maxim a few years back, and I learned he was totally against all this." Dezhnev turned to Toliver. "Maxim was my main contact. But with this *K-129* ruckus, Yuri Andropov, the head of the KGB, started looking under rocks. He found out about Maxim Yusopov and followed that trail to me. Just in time, I got word from Maxim to get out, and that he was leaving the country and that I should jump as well. Which is what I did. Just in time."

"Where is he now?" asked Toliver.

"I don't know. The Petropavlovsk airport would have been too risky. The only other way out would be by sea, so I imagine he snuck out on a freighter. If so he could be anywhere—Southeast Asia, India, South America." Dezhnev leaned close to the microphone, "But I do know one thing, Todd. If the KGB really wants him, they'll find him. It may take years, but they'll find him."

"Just like Trotsky," said Ingram.

"That's right," said Dezhnev. "And guess who's next? Me."

Toliver snapped, "That will never happen. You can bet on it."

"I am betting on it," Dezhnev said. "You're our only hope."

Toliver said, "Well, believe this. A large number of your, shall we say 'comrades' have come over to us, many of them very high profile, but we take very good care of them and their families. They live comfortable and happy lives. And they are extremely well protected, day and night."

Silence followed. Then Ingram said, "Ed, would you—"

"Eduard," said Toliver.

"All right, damn it. Eduard, your highness. Would you excuse us for a moment and leave the room?"

On the other end, Toliver said, "It's okay. Do you mind?" He nodded toward the door.

"Okay."

Ingram heard a chair squeak. After a moment Toliver said, "Okay, he's out. What do you have, Todd?"

Ingram told him.

The chair squeaked and Dezhnev said, "Okay, Todd, I'm back."

Ingram said, "Eduard, what I'm about to tell you is strictly between the three of us. Understood?"

"Of course."

"The last time I trusted you with sensitive data, you went over to the other side."

"Hey, come on," protested Dezhnev.

Toliver snapped, "Todd, shit, that's below the belt."

Toliver never swore. He was really angry. Ingram took a deep breath.

"Calm down, calm down, you two. Okay, Ed. Here we go. Grab your armrests. You're going to need it."

"There are no armrests. It's a cheap chair. Ollie has the only chair with armrests. Just like in Russia."

For some reason, that struck a chord. They all laughed uproariously. At length, it was quiet.

Ingram said, "Ed, I'm sorry to tell you this but we have good reason to believe that the *K-129* went down with all hands, that your son is...is...gone."

A heavy silence swept over them.

"I'm sorry, Ed," Ingram said softly.

Dezhnev choked out, "Are you sure? Couldn't there be a mistake?"

"Not with what we've learned," said Ingram.

"From SOSUS?" asked Dezhnev.

Ingram knew the Soviets were trying to lay their own network of underwater microphones. "Yes."

"And that's how you know?"

"Pretty much," replied Ingram.

"Did the *Swordfish* run into her?" asked Dezhnev.

That question took Ingram aback. *How does he know about her*? Well, there was always the truth. "No, Ed, it wasn't the *Swordfish.* She hit an iceberg in the Sea of Japan on March 2. She just put into Yokosuka yesterday. She has a bent periscope and that's it. No major collision damage."

"You're sure."

"I'm sure, Ed. Look I'm—"

"Eduard," snapped Toliver.

"It's okay," mumbled Dezhnev. "Ed is okay among friends." He sniffed and then asked, "Can I tell Roxanna?"

Ingram fielded that one, too. "I'm sorry. Ollie tells me you'll have to wait at least two years on that one."

"But—"

"All I can say is to stretch out the secret mission story as best you can. Look, damn it, we decided to tell you this now only so you'll know the KGB didn't get their paws on him."

"Okay." Dezhnev gave a long exhale. "Todd, you have a boy, don't you? In the Navy?"

"Yes."

"What's he doing?"

"He's flying P-3s and is married with one on the way."

"You're going to be a grandfather?"

"Afraid so."

Dezhnev blew his nose. "That's nice."

48

2 May 1968
Continental Airlines Flight 24
Final approach, Honolulu International Airport

The 707 banked right and settled on a new course. Rita's pulse kicked up when she heard the flaps grinding down. She was in first class and the pilot had just announced they had turned over the Molokai Channel, were down to five thousand feet, and were cleared for a straight-in approach to Honolulu International Airport. She'd been here many times, and the Molokai Channel meant they were indeed close. Ahead, the peaks of Oahu swung into view above the clouds. She sat on the 707's starboard side and soon picked out Diamond Head. Lower and lower. She tried to keep her heart rate in check, but it just didn't work. She'd flown tens of thousands of miles, all over the world, had been to Hawaii often for photo shoots, and was usually able to put a cap on nervousness. But not now. Jerry was down there, waiting.

She inched the black beret further over the right side of her face and adjusted the oversized Audrey Hepburn–style dark glasses. The bandages were still visible, but the worst was covered. At least the man beside her didn't seem to mind—or even to notice. In his forties, he was in a suit, was rather pudgy with a gold ring on his fourth finger, and sat on her left side, her good side. They'd talked amicably when departing LAX, but then he slept for much of the journey and otherwise had his nose in a paperback book. She'd tried sleeping, too, but it just wouldn't come. Too excited. Still, she hoped there was enough of her for Jerry to still love. The nervous excitement generated an unsettled feeling in her belly, and she wondered what to take. She rummaged through her purse, found a roll of Tums, and popped one.

The landing gear rumbled down and thumped in their wells. The 707 wobbled easily in ground turbulence. The pilot came on the PA saying that it had just rained in Honolulu and to expect water pooled up on the runway. That would make the plane look as if it were water skiing; but nothing to worry about.

Oahu, the beaches, rocks, and Waikiki rolled past the right side as they went down. In moments, they flashed over the runway's threshold. The pilot chopped the power. The 707 settled on the runway in a spectacular miasma of mist and spewing water. At length, the jet rolled out, turned, and taxied to a stop at the gate. The pilot shut down the engines, and passengers began deplaning directly onto the tarmac.

The Tums weren't helping. The cheese enchiladas she'd wolfed last night, liberally sprinkled with extra hot taco sauce, must be responsible for the gnawing in her belly, Rita decided. That and two glasses of pinot noir. She admonished herself not to do that anymore. She had to take good care of junior.

She descended the stairway into tropical humidity that reminded her of Vera Cruz. But she looked and felt cool and comfortable in her white, short-sleeved silk blouse and matching white skirt. She walked toward the gate, scanning the crowd for Jerry. It seemed like hundreds of people were milling behind the hip-high chain link fence waving and shouting to the passengers pouring off the 707. Many of the onlookers had leis and carelessly tossed them around passenger's necks with shouts of "Aloha!" Against the terminal wall, a four-piece band on a dais played Harry Owens–style Hawaiian music.

An attendant opened the gate. Rita walked in, among the first to arrive.

Jerry? Where in blazes are you?

She walked over to a clear area, turned, and scanned the crowd.

Come on, Jerry, damn it.

"Hello? Rita? I'm Helen Ingram." A fine-looking woman stepped before her with an outstretched hand.

Rita took it and recognized her immediately, almost exactly as Jerry described her. "A spitting image of you," he'd put it, "ponytail and all." She took Helen's hand. "Mrs. Ingram—"

"Helen, please." She pulled Rita into a warm embrace.

"Oh, thank you for coming. But I can't find..." Rita looked around.

Helen wrapped an arm around her. "It's the Navy way, I'm afraid. Jerry was scheduled to have the day off today and pick you up. But then another copilot got sick and they plugged Jerry into his spot at the last minute. So, our boy," she waved at the sky, "Is out on patrol. He should be back about six o'clock. I'm sorry. I know how you feel, having been through it so many times myself. And Todd wanted so much to be here."

Unconsciously, Rita put a hand to her bandages and said, "I suppose I'll get used to all this."

"This is how we live," Helen said with a smile, "the Navy way."

"I see." Rita fished out a baggage claim check. She felt dizzy.

"You okay?"

"Long flight." The feeling passed.

Helen grabbed the baggage check and hailed a porter with, "You're all set. I have a car right outside." She checked her watch. "Coming up on lunch time. How about a bite to eat?"

Rita still felt woozy. "They fed us on the plane," she lied. "Maybe later."

She waited at the curb, and soon the porter, baggage, and Helen all showed up. With the bags in the trunk, Rita tipped the porter and then stepped into Helen's car, a 1965 pale green Chevelle sedan. Still unused to the extra weight the pregnancy had put on her, she miscalculated and tipped over into the driver's side. Pushing herself upright, she groaned.

Helen slid into the driver's seat. "Honey, are you sure you're okay?"

"Just fine."

"You look kind of pale." Helen reached over and palmed her forehead. "Good Lord! You're burning up."

Rita mumbled, "Planes affect me that way. I'll be okay." She settled back into the seat.

Helen said, "Okay, where are we headed?"

Rita forced a smile, "I'm supposed to go to the clinic, but I booked a couple of nights at the Royal Hawaiian as a surprise for Jerry."

"That sounds good. A hop, skip, and jump from here." Helen started the engine.

"Arrrraaaahhh!"

"Rita, good God. What is it?"

"...I think...I think...," Rita looked down and wiggled her hips. "I think I made a mess. I'm sorry. I...awash!"

Helen switched off the engine and looked at Rita's face. It was paler than before and contorted with pain. "Oh dear. Did...did...?"

"My water broke, I think. Oh, Lord."

"Good God," said Helen. "We'd better--"

A sharp voice echoed from the left side. "Ma'am? Ma'am? You'll have to move the car. Hey there. Can you hear me? Lissen up. Move the car, please. This is a white zone."

Helen spun around. It was a policeman, a traffic cop, a young good looking dark-complected Hawaiian with white teeth. "I'm sorry. I...I," she stammered.

"Move the car, please ma'am."

Rita groaned again. Her lips were drawn over her teeth, her face contorted in pain.

"Say, what's going on?" demanded the cop.

Helen said, "Look, we need your help." She dropped her voice. "My daughter-in-law is just off the plane from LA. She's pregnant and I think her water broke."

The cop's eyebrows went up. "Just now?"

"That's right."

At that moment Rita erupted with another open-mouthed groan.

Helen laid a hand on his forearm. "Look, I'm Helen Ingram, RN, Major, U.S. Army, retired. I've delivered many babies. If you can just call ahead to the Naval Medical Center, Pearl Harbor Naval Station, and have them open the gates for us I can take her straight to ER."

The kid rubbed his jaw. “I’ll do ya one better. I’ll call my dispatcher and have them run up the balloon. You know, clear the way for Pearl Harbor. So, all you have to do is follow me. Okay?” He nodded over his shoulder to a parked motorcycle across the street.

Helen flashed a smile. “You got a deal! What’s your name?”

“Waldo. My friends call me Wally.”

“Okay, Wally. I’m Helen.” She added, “One more thing. Tell them it’ll be a premature delivery. She’s only six months or so along. Come on Wally, let’s hit the road!”

“You bet!” He squeezed Helen’s hand and then sprinted across four lanes of traffic, dodging cars as he went.

Rita said in a clear voice. “We should really go to my clinic.”

“Are you sure? How do you feel?”

“Better, believe it or not. Look, my clinic is the William F. Kane Trauma Center on,” she fumbled a piece of paper from her purse, “...on Kapiolani Blvd. That’s where we should go.”

Helen hesitated. Across the road, microphone pressed to his mouth, Wally kicked his starter twice and the motorcycle roared to life. Still jabbering on the microphone, Wally weaved into traffic, lights blinking, siren bleeping and buzzing. He stopped in the center of the street, blew his whistle, and held out his hand Traffic jerked and screeched to a halt. That done, he waved Helen in behind him.

Rita screamed again.

That’s it. Helen started the Chevelle and pulled out behind Wally. “Honey, I don’t know about your clinic, but the Naval Medical Center has some of the finest doctors in the world. That’s where we’re going.”

Wally looked around.

She waved.

Wally nodded, pumped a fist, turned his siren up to full screech, and pulled out. Helen crossed herself and blasted right behind him.

Rita groaned loudly and then called out, “Jerry!”

“Here, soon, hon. Hang on.” With the accelerator pressed to the floor, Helen shifted into third gear, grabbed Rita’s hand for a quick squeeze, and muttered under her breath, “Navy way, baloney. When the going gets rough, the Navy blows town.”

49

2 May 1968
P-3 flight 49 ROMEO
18°20'46" N; 177°5'44" E
North Pacific Ocean

Noah Butler was flying. Gregg Fowler was standing behind him on a small platform puttering with the radar display. The thing was acting up and he couldn't find targets. Noah was getting frustrated. They were about to overfly datum, and nothing was out here. He kept calling back to Fowler whose answers were more brief and curt each time.

Jerry was perched in the right seat searching outside with binoculars as they cruised on three engines at 2,500 feet. The day wasn't bad. For the past four hours, they'd been aloft in overcast skies that later burned off to broken clouds, the sun peeking through occasionally.

He smiled ruefully to himself. With Admiral Hyland's declaration aboard the *Wolfish*, both Butler and Ingram had suddenly become available to VP 72. One senior, one junior. Fowler built a crew around them and assigned them to a P-3. Today was their third time out, and they were finally getting used to each other with Gregg Fowler along today to see how they were doing. Jerry's admiration for Butler was growing steadily.

Jerry was thankful to be off the shit list. It felt good just to be a pilot again. Or at least a copilot. The rest of the P-3's ten crewmembers had all flown together at some point and joked with an easy repartee. He was beginning to fit in.

Jerry was supposed to have had the day off so he could meet Rita at the airport. But then one of the other copilots got sick and Fowler, in a mad shuffle, reassigned Jerry to his regular flight and posted the guy who was to be his replacement to the flight with the sick copilot. He should have felt screwed, he supposed—denied the chance to meet Rita at the airport and sweep her into his arms. But it was *the Navy way*. Last minute foul-ups. Jerry checked his watch; she was already there. Mom was picking her up. He'd have to wait until late this afternoon to fling his arms around her and take her to the cottage he had rented a block from the beach at Nānākuli. He'd bought some furniture—the essentials: a bed, a TV, a stereo—

Jerry spun to his right. There! Two specs on the horizon. Hull up. He twisted the focus a bit. *Wow! That's it!*

He let Fowler and Butler bitch at each other for another five seconds then said, "Hey guys, over there. Two o'clock."

"Huh?" Butler cranked his head around and spotted the two ships, now above the horizon, definitely their target: an American and a Soviet destroyer close together. "I'll be damned."

Jerry pointed to the radar display. "You forgot to drop in quarters."

"Smart-ass," said Butler.

Fowler said, "Very funny. Now, now get on with it." He nodded for Butler to swing right.

Today, Lieutenant Butler was the pilot and Captain Fowler, skipper of Squadron VP 72, was the patrol plane commander. Fowler was a grizzled amphib jockey from the PBY and P5M days of World War II. He could have sat behind a desk and punched his ticket for retirement. But he loved flying and was happy just to be out with his boys, watching the action. Most times he surrendered the left seat because he wanted his pilots to get experience. Sometimes he rode right seat, insisting the copilot take over left seat and become temporary command pilot.

But this mission was intense. A *Gearing*-class destroyer, the USS *Conrad A. Joseph* (DD 812), had three days previously collided with an oil tanker in a fog. Part of a carrier task group with the USS *Hancock* (CVA 19), the *Joseph*'s surface search radar was on the fritz when it happened. It was at night with both ships on similar courses. The *Joseph* was steaming at ten knots; the tanker, a black-hulled monster with white superstructure judged at ninety thousand tons and possibly Russian, was steaming at an estimated seventeen knots. The tanker overtook the *Joseph* in moments, body-slamming the destroyer's port side, damaging her port screw and shaft. The tanker plowed on, ignoring strident foghorn blasts from the *Joseph,* and disappeared into the mist: a hit and run. The *Joseph* reported no casualties, but several seams had opened on the port side, the largest one over the aft fireroom. With the damage judged not too serious, the task group commander detached the *Joseph*, sending her back to Pearl Harbor on one shaft; the *Hancock* and her brood of seven destroyers continued on to the South China Sea for raids into North Vietnam.

But on the way back the hapless destroyer ran into stormy weather. Twenty-foot seas opened the seam in the after fireroom to twelve inches right at the waterline. Pumps couldn't keep up, and the space flooded in three hours causing the shut-down of boilers three and four, half the ship's main power source. Almost right away, another damaged seam opened on the port side to the after crew's quarters causing that space to flood. It too had to be evacuated and secured.

Six hours later the *Joseph* reported calm seas. She was riding better and things were improving. But then a Soviet destroyer intercepted the *Joseph* and began a cruel game of cat and mouse, running close to her damaged port side and harassing her. The overtaxed *Joseph* was basically unable to maneuver clear.

That's when KSOCK directed P-3 flight 49 ROMEO to break off her submarine search pattern and investigate the two ships just 150 miles north of their position.

Butler twirled a finger in the air. "Restart number one."

"Got it." Jerry reached up to the overhead engine panel and flipped switches. Number one engine, the port outboard, had been shut down to save fuel. Now, it was brought back on line for greater maneuverability.

Butler said, “Jerry, can you tell the fellas what’s going on?”

“Will do.” Jerry dialed the ICS switch and said, “Okay everybody. We found our targets. Dead ahead at about ten miles. We intend to communicate with the *Joseph* and render any assistance possible. Right now, she and the Russian ship look kind of close together, so be ready for anything. Any questions?”

“Yeah, Lieutenant. I just raised the *Joseph* on channel 4425.” It was Lt. (j.g) Ron Bertrand, seated back about ten feet on the starboard side, the navigator/communicator. “They don’t sound happy. And they tell me Ivan is making another run at them.”

Fowler came up on the line, “Well, tell ’em to stand by for a little entertainment, Ron.”

“Wilco, Skipper.”

Jerry signed off the ICS as Fowler said quietly, “You know what to do, Noah?”

“On the deck, Skipper?” said Butler.

“You bet,” said Fowler. “And slow down to 175.” Then he called over, “Ingram?”

“Yes, sir?”

“Sit back, relax, and enjoy the ride.”

“Yes, sir.”

“And keep your mouth shut when we get home.”

Jerry looked over to Fowler. His ice blue eyes were dead serious. No wise-ass answer. Jerry wasn’t going to fool with that. “Yes, sir.”

And then, suddenly, they were on the deck; really on the deck, maybe sixty feet or less with whitecaps whizzing by almost close enough to touch. Jerry had to blink a couple of times to get rid of a dizzy feeling. He glanced at Butler. The man was in control, not a worry, flying like a barnstormer, his eyes occasionally flicking over the instrument panel.

“Lookit that, Skipper.” Butler pointed. The P-3 was approaching the pair of ships. Except they weren’t exactly a pair. The Soviet destroyer had just drawn close and bumped the *Joseph* on her port side.

“Bomb bay doors open!” snapped Fowler.

Jerry reached up to the armament panel and threw the switch. When he looked back, all he saw was the two ships filling the windscreen. They were going to hit in a fiery crash. "Shiiiiiiit," he cried.

At the last second, Butler pulled back on the control column. The P-3 cleared the Russian's mast by ten feet.

"Something wrong, Ingram?" asked Fowler.

"Geeeez...I mean, holy shit. Er...no, Skipper. Everything's hunky dory." Ingram looked over to Butler who slipped him a quick grin, then went back to his flying. This time he threw the P-3 into a right bank, held it for twenty seconds, then changed to a 270° left bank to return to the ships.

Bertrand called, "*Joseph* reports the Commie hit them on their port side, their damaged side. That's the third time, they say."

"Bastards," said Butler.

"Damage any worse?" asked Fowler.

"They're checking now, Skipper."

"Okay, keep us posted."

Fowler called, "Hooper, you got anything on that Russian?" Lt. Garrett Hooper, the patrol plane tactical coordinator, or TACCO, was seated on the port side opposite Bertrand.

"Coming up now, Skipper," reported Hooper, his teletype clacking. "Let's see...okay...she's a *Kashin*-class destroyer, 3,400 tons full load, four gas turbines with top speed rated at thirty-eight knots. Not bad for such a heavy piece of crap—"

"Continue, Hooper, and please don't editorialize," barked Fowler.

"Roger, Skipper. Four gas turbines; crew size can be up to 320 little Communists; and —"

"Hooper."

"Sorry, Captain. Two twin 76-mm guns; two twin GOA missile launchers for thirty-two Isayev surface-to-air missiles; one torpedo mount for five 21-inch torpedoes; two twelve-barrel RBU 6000 ASW rocket launchers, and, finally, two six-barrel RBU 1000 ASW rocket launchers. Plus, two popcorn machines and one substandard vodka dispenser in the officers' head. But then—"

"Hooper! Damn it!!" yelled Fowler.

"Sorry, Captain. I get bored back here."

"Well, your boredom days are over. I got a little job for you."

"What's that, Skipper?"

"I'll put you in for a medal, but for the time being, shut up!"

"Shut up. Yes, sir. Shutting up."

Butler and Jerry traded grins. Then Jerry stole a glance at Fowler, whos face showed a tinge of red. Hooper had pushed too far.

Jerry looked over to the ships. They were separating but not too quickly. It looked as if the Russian was undecided about going back in.

Fowler growled, "Keep her on the deck, Butler."

"You bet, Skipper," replied Butler.

Jerry scanned the instruments. *Shiiiiiiit!* They were about thirty feet off a calm sea, whizzing by the surface at a blinding speed. And Butler edged the plane even lower. Jerry wanted to cross himself. Instead, he held fast to his armrests.

"Garrett! Punch out some chaff over that son-of-a-bitch when we fly over."

"Got it, Skipper. Can somebody call it from up there?"

"Ingram. That's you."

"Yes, sir," replied Jerry. Then he called on the ICS, "TACCO, it's third pilot."

"Any time, Jerry."

"On my command." Jerry judged the distance. God, they were close. He looked up at masts and radoms and surprised faces on the two bridges. That damned Butler was going to fly *between* them. There wasn't enough room. He opened his mouth to warn Butler and said instead, "Now! Punch it out, Hooper!"

The P-3 was on them. Men dove for safety on both ships. Butler put the P-3 into a slight right bank, enough to tilt the left wing up and over the *Joseph*. With no room to spare they shot between the two ships. Jerry got a look at the Russian ship. A fist was shaking at them. They flashed past.

"Yah hoo!" shouted Fowler. He pounded Butler on the back. "Not bad."

"Thanks, Skipper. Learned from the best," shouted Butler. He pulled up on the control column to gain altitude and waggled the P-3's wings, a signal to the *Joseph*.

"You okay, Ingram?" asked Fowler. "You're lookin' kinda peaked."

"Shit my pants, Skipper."

They laughed.

"They didn't teach us that in flight school," added Jerry.

"Don't forget what I said. 'Keep your mouth shut.'"

"Count on it, Skipper."

Fowler keyed his mic again, "Hooper, you ready?"

"Ready for what, Skipper?" replied Hooper.

"A little supervisory duty on the SAR package."

"Jesus! We doin' that, Skipper?"

"You bet. Now get back aft and let me know when the package is ready."

"Why me? I did it last time."

Fowler grinned, "Because you get the wise-ass of the month award. That's why. And make sure you take a good set of headphones. I could hardly hear you last time. Okay?"

"Okay, Skipper."

"And sound off when you're ready," said Fowler.

Fowler spoke again, "Kingsford, can you make a SAR package ready?"

Xavier Louis Kingsford (he went by Louie), a tall, thin aviation ordnanceman first class, had been with Fowler since the Korean War. "I figured you'd want that. It's almost ready, Skipper."

"Hooper's on his way aft to supervise. Don't dump shit on him this time."

"Who, me?" protested Kingsford. "That was an accident."

"Okay, okay. Just be careful. I wanna hit this Commie with everything we've got."

Hooper came up on the line. "Okay, Skipper, I'm here. Looks like Kingsford has it all ready. Okay to open the hatch?"

Fowler keyed his mic, "Are you strapped in, Gary?"

"All three of us are, Skipper."

Fowler Looked at Butler, who gave a thumbs up.

"Okay, permission granted to open the hatch."

Butler had the P-3 cruising at about 1,500 feet in a slow circle around the ships, now roughly six miles distant. But the Soviet destroyer still was close to the *Joseph*, maybe making another run.

Fowler was shouting over his shoulder to Bertrand, something about gaining radio contact with the Soviet destroyer.

Jerry leaned over and looked at Butler and mouthed, *what gives*?

Butler said, "Search and rescue; you know, SAR."

"I got that. But what's going on back aft?"

"Well, in a SAR exercise, we open the back hatch and toss out rescue packagers like life rafts and medical supplies."

"Right."

"Well this time we fill a ten-gallon trash bag with shit from the porta-potty."

"No shit?"

"Lots of shit. Then we toss it on Ivan." Butler grinned and made a pushing motion with his hands. "That's what they're doing back there. Safety straps connected to hold them fast, they push the shit out on our command. We try to aim for the bridge."

Jerry definitely had not heard of any of this. "You've done this before?"

"All the time. And Fowler's one of the best."

"Good God."

"The Commies are getting used to it. They turn fire hoses on us."

"Yeah?"

"We fly right through it."

"Amazing."

Ingram looked back to Fowler. He'd been listening. Slowly and deliberately, he said, "Not a damned word, Ingram. You got me?"

"You bet, Captain. I'm right with you."

"Good." Fowler looked at his watch and then his eyes flicked over some instruments. "Getting low on loiter time. Let's get the show on the road, Noah."

"On the way." Butler drew back on the power levers, dropped altitude, and circled in, heading toward the Soviet destroyer's bow from about seven miles out. He looked back, "What do you say we close the bomb bay doors, Skipper?"

"Do it and make your speed 250 knots," said Fowler.

At a nod from Butler, Jerry reached up and closed the bomb bay doors.

Butler inched up the power levers a bit. "Two-fifty it is, Skipper."

Jerry asked, "Why?"

Fowler rubbed his chin. "I'm looking at his fire-control radars. They've been tracking us. Best solution they had before was when we passed over them. Our speed then was 175, right?"

"Right."

"Let's hope they get lazy and don't get a good solution at first. May give us a chance if they start shooting." Then Fowler keyed his ICS mic, "Hooper, the pooper bomber. You ready?"

"All turds armed and ready, Skipper."

"Okay Garrett. About four miles. Stand by."

"Standing by."

Bertrand, the navigator/communicator came on the line. "Russian destroyer attempting to contact us, Skipper. Plain English. Do you believe it?"

"No kidding. Plain English?"

"Yes, sir."

"Tell him to go fu— go jump in a lake."

"What?"

"And if he grumbles about that, tell him I've got two Bull Pups to shove up his ass if he wants to do something about it."

"Sir..."

"Do it, Ron. We're almost out of time. Just tell him. See what he says after we pass over," shouted Fowler.

"Yes, sir."

Fowler slapped Butler on the shoulder. "Okay, Noah. Heading looks good."

Butler called over his shoulder, "I'll pull up at about three hundred yards Skipper."

"That's when we go," said Fowler.

Jerry found himself jammed in his seat again, gripping the armrests for dear life. The Soviet destroyer filled his screen, closer than before; and closer and closer.

The ship leaned slightly to starboard, a sure sign she was turning to port. At the same time, Jerry noticed the *Joseph*'s five-inch battery had swung to port and was trained on the Russian.

"He's turning, Skipper," said Butler.

"Stay on him."

"Now," shouted Butler. He pulled back on the control column.

"Bombs away," yelled Fowler.

Once again the Russian destroyer zipped beneath. Fire hoses were on, but they were aimed in the wrong direction. One stream did arch up to them and they flew right through it.

Bertrand started giggling, then cackling, then roaring with laughter.

"What?" demanded Fowler.

Bertrand had to catch his breath. Finally, "Skipper. Ivan is angry. He's threatening to open fire. You should hear him sputter. Russian mixed with English. It's like something from Abbot and Costello."

Butler banked right and they looked back. The Soviet destroyer was heeled over in a left turn and headed away from the *Joseph*. Smoke belched from her twin stacks meaning they were speeding up.

"He's calling us, Skipper. Do you want to respond?"

"Patch me through," said Fowler.

"Here we go, Skipper," said Bertrand.

The line squeaked. They could all hear it. "American aircraft, do you read me?"

"Loud and clear, Boris," said Fowler.

"My name is not Boris."

"Too bad. Now what do you want?"

"You just committed an act of war."

Fowler's voice raised a notch. "You mean deliberately ramming a U.S. Navy ship is not an act of war?"

"...ship...that...in our way. We had to respond. And now we feel we have every right to shoot you down."

Fowler said slowly and deliberately, "Go ahead, Boris. And if you put your glasses on us, you'll see not one but two Bull Pups drop off our wing pylons. Those warheads are 250 pounds each of happiness headed your way, Boris. Maybe right into your precious little JP 5 tank, huh? Won't that make for an interesting party? How's that for starting World War Six? Plus, my colleague, the USS *Joseph*, has its entire battery of five-inch guns trained on you. That's another three hundred pounds of happiness coming to you, Boris."

"My name isn't Boris."

"Tell you what, Boris. You light us up with your fire-control radar and your ass is grass."

"My ass is what?"

Fowler clicked off. "Asshole."

Butler had the P-3 at three thousand feet in a slow orbit around the Soviet destroyer still visible on their right side. The destroyer was still headed north and away from the *Joseph* at high speed.

Jerry saw it first. Fire hoses were trained on the pilothouse, three of them. He tweaked the focus. "Jesus, looks like we hit it right where it counts. The trash bag is stuck to a port hole."

Fowler motioned with his fingers. Jerry handed the binoculars over. Fowler's lips drew into a grin. "I'll be damned. We hit it smack on." He looked at Ingram and made to speak.

"I know Skipper. Not one damned word," said Jerry.

They had another two hours to go to Barbers Point and things were quiet. Jerry was flying. Fowler had unfolded a portable desk and was scribbling an action report. Butler was asleep, his chin on his chest. Very quiet.

Jerry was content. He was sorry to miss Rita's arrival, but that's the way things go sometimes. *The Navy Way*.

Almost there. He looked over to Butler—someone he'd initially disliked and resented when he boarded the *Wolfish* as Admiral Hyland's aide. But now, he realized the man was a genius. He only wished he could be half the pilot Butler was when he was a full lieutenant.

Hooper interrupted his musing. "I'll be damned."

Jerry looked back. "What?"

Hooper walked forward with a radio-flimsy. "This is for you, Pop."

"Huh?"

It was a radio message addressed directly to him.

BT

UNCLAS

. . .

TO:INGRAM, JEROLD O., Lt. (jg) USN

FM:C/O VP 72, BARBERS PT.

INFO:C/O KSOCK, KUNIA

1.BE ADVISED MRS RITA INGRAM LANDED SAFELY HONOLULU INTERNATIONAL AT 1146.

2.ARRIVING FORTY-FIVE MINUTES LATER WAS A BABY BOY BORN TO MRS. INGRAM AND WITH MRS. INGRAM (SR) ASSISTING AT NAVMEDCNTRPEARL.

3.THE LAD WAS PREMATURE, BUT HE IS IN AN ISOLETTE. DOCTOR REPORTS HE IS HEALTHY AND THE PROGNOSIS IS GOOD.

3.MOTHER, GRANDMOTHER ALSO DOING WELL. REQUEST YOUR PRESENCE ASAP.

4.ALSO REQUEST NAME SUGGETION

J . F. CHILDS

BY DIRECTION

BT

"Hey," Ingram yelled and thrust a fist in the air.

Butler groaned and turned away. "Shaddup, will yeah?"

"Yeah, keep it down, okay, hotshot?" said Fowler. He pointed to the four pages he'd written. "I still have a lot to go."

A grinning Bertrand clapped him on the shoulder. "Congratulations, Pop. What are you going to name him?"

"Working on it, Ron, working on it."

"Okay, Dad. Your turn to buy at the O Club." Bertrand walked away and it was quiet again.

The Navy Way. Jerry snugged his seat belt and ran his eyes over the instrument panel. All okay.

Then he sat back and read the message—three times. He smiled that he'd been snookered twice by *the Navy Way* today: once early this morning when they posted him on the flight line, and now this. A well-known ghost citation had long ago been posted in Navy Regulations:

While it is necessary for the father to be present for the laying of the keel, it is not necessary for him to be present for the launching.

That must have been one hell of a flight to send her into labor. But Rita, he was learning, was made from tough stock. She did her job well. Thanks be to God.

And the kid's name?

He looked over to the man beside him. That brave pilot; scrunched in his seat on his left side; fast asleep.

Noah.

EPILOGUE

God and the soldier
We like adore
In times of danger
Not before

The danger past
And conflict righted
God is forgotten,
The Soldier slighted.

Attributed to
Francis Quarles, 1592–1644
Of Common Devotion

31 July 1976
U.S. Naval Submarine Base
Point Loma, San Diego, California

The Defense Department in cooperation with the U.S. Army and the U.S. Navy, had finally determined that Helen Z. Durand (Ingram), Major, U.S. Army (Ret.), should be awarded the Silver Star because of her contribution in uncovering top secret Japanese studies on American torpedoes and their major faults. Additionally, she discovered a top secret operating manual on the Japanese Type 93 torpedo.

Trapped behind enemy lines in the Philippines in 1942, Helen was masquerading as a Filipina charwoman aboard a Japanese work barge in Nasipit, Mindanao, to avoid capture. While there, she snatched the operating manual for the Japanese Type 93 torpedo. Weeks later she escaped via submarine and delivered the manual into Allied hands.

Helen was a hero, but they swore her to secrecy. Not that it mattered. She married Todd Ingram, rose to the rank of major, served the rest of the war as a nurse at the Fort MacArthur Infirmary, mustered out in 1946, served in the Reserves until 1960, had two children, and kept the family together during Todd's absences. With the passing of her parents, Frank and Kate Durand, Helen inherited their ranch in Ramona, and in 1969, settled there after Todd put in his papers.

At first, Helen was reluctant to participate in the award ceremony. But Todd sternly reminded her that she was lucky to have lived and owed it to those that didn't come back. And heroes these days were in short supply. Especially with all that had gone on in Vietnam.

Thus influenced, Helen convinced them to have the ceremony at the submarine base out on Point Loma at the entrance to San Diego Bay. Up until the end of the Pacific War it had been known as Fort Rosecrans, a large Army base for major costal defense artillery, much like Fort MacArthur in San Pedro where she'd been permanently stationed. On occasion, she'd been sent to the Fort Rosecrans infirmary to fill in for the busy times when World War II wounded were returning.

It was a brilliant Saturday morning, and they wore their uniforms. Helen still looked smart as an Army major, her husband looked equally elegant as a vice admiral in summer khakis. Their son, Cdr. Jerry Ingram, also wearing summer khakis, was there with his wife, Rita and ten-year-old son, Noah. Daughter Kate, Helen's doppelganger, was there with her husband, Navy lieutenant Frank Murphy. Oliver Toliver, now retired from the CIA, showed up on crutches with his wife, Suzy. Old friend Jerry Landa, still a senior Los Angeles harbor pilot, was there in slacks, sport coat, and tie. With him was his wife, Laura, now retired as a TV game show hostess and a full-time Beverly Hills philanthropist. Still flashing that ear to ear winning smile, Landa had lost weight and looked sharp in the pork-pie hat he wore to cover his baldness.

The ceremony was at the flag pole parade ground down the hill from the old Army headquarters building, now becoming the Navy's new submarine base at Ballast Point where Point Loma juts southward into the Pacific.

Philip Ledbetter, brigadier general (MC) U.S. Army (Ret.) Helen's commanding officer at Fort MacArthur, conducted the ceremony. Long retired and now practicing as a doctor at the Long Beach VA, Ledbetter was attended by a platoon of soldiers. Since Corregidor and the Philippines were part of a Navy Pacific campaign, Ingram was able to scare up a platoon of Navy Sailors from the Naval Training Center. That and a fifteen-piece marching band.

Helen stood dutifully at attention as Ledbetter read the citation and then pinned the Silver Star on her. After that she was ready to march away and be done with it. But then Ledbetter called everyone back to attention. He read a second, unexpected citation. Helen was being awarded the purple heart for wounds suffered at the hands of the *Kempetai*, the Japanese secret police, on Marinduque Island in the Central Philippines before her time on Mindanao.

Ledbetter pinned on the medal and then stood back to salute. But uncharacteristically, Helen's composure evaporated. Her lip quivered and she had difficulty raising her right hand. Suddenly, both hands went to her face. She covered her eyes and silently began to sob.

Ingram stepped over and ran his left arm around his wife's waist. There was a perceptible gasp from onlookers as he slowly, like a Marine, raised his right hand, ... *one thousand and one, one thousand and two, one thousand and three* ... and returned the salute for her.

Ledbetter snapped off his salute and, not wanting to extend things, declared the proceedings completed. The band played "God Bless America" as family and friends swarmed to Helen, now smiling sheepishly, dabbing her eyes with a handkerchief, shaking hands, giving air kisses.

The night was moonless. Innumerable stars carpeted a clear sky overhead. Unsullied by city-borne pollutants, the sky shouted at them, admonishing them to ponder endless ages and a universe so incredibly large and that they were so incredibly small, and what their existence meant in all this. They were in Ramona, about fifty miles' northeast of San Diego, in California's once forgotten back country, now coming alive with vineyards, avocado and citrus groves.

Todd had stepped easily into a rancher's role after his retirement, riding horseback and tending the land. But like his neighbors, he had trouble making ends meet when a virulent root-rot disease killed many of his avocado trees. Fortunately, both he and Helen had their service pensions to help. That and a small stipend Ingram received from the Obsidian Corporation, a think-tank in La Jolla doing classified projects for the U.S. Navy.

But no worries about that tonight. The entire Point Loma entourage had driven out for a barbeque after the award ceremony. A surprise guest was there as well. Furnished by Oliver Toliver were Roxanna and Eduard Dezhnev, both looking every bit of California vibrant. They were all sleeping over thanks to accommodations Todd and Helen had added in the little-used bunkhouse behind the main house. Not a four-star hotel, but there was room and privacy for everybody and a large coffee pot for the morning.

Everyone gathered around two stout wooden picnic tables with checkered table clothes under a darkening sky. Helen and Kate served Caesar salad, corn on the cob, and garlic toast. Ingram, Jerry, and Rita cooked and served restaurant-quality steaks.

Rita was still a fetching woman, but she would never again be drop-dead gorgeous. Her right eyelid and a corner of her mouth drooped a bit, and under a certain combination of light and shadows gave her a sinister look. But after nine surgeries, each successive one giving less return, Rita had decided enough was enough. She took cooking classes at the French Culinary Institute in San Francisco, graduated, and became a certified chef. After that, she went back to her Mexican roots. Her four *Rita's* restaurants had become all the rage in Riverside Country, the most recent in Palm Springs.

Lively talk ranged among the guests about the USA's recent bicentennial, the Montreal Olympics now under way, and the upcoming presidential election between Jimmy Carter and Gerald Ford. Roxanna picked up a guitar and played and sang old Russian folksongs. Among them was "Woman in Shadows," its significance known only to a smiling Eduard Dezhnev seated close by. A piano was out for Laura and she picked up the tune right away, the two harmonizing as if they'd sung together for years.

With nightfall completed, crickets fell into perfect accompaniment to their singing. Helen still had a gray tabby cat, this one named Luther instead of Fred, and it was crashing among the bushes, chasing field mice. With just candles and the stars to light their faces, they talked and wondered up at the sky, the same brilliant sky Todd had first seen when he drove down here from San Francisco in 1942.

Ingram strolled among their guests, all of them people who really mattered, giving thanks that they could all be here enjoying this day and tonight's spectacular setting. He stopped for a moment looking down at Jerry Landa. His World War II skipper had fallen asleep, his pork-pie hat pitched over his forehead onto his nose, bald skull gleaming. Jerry Landa: Ingram's brave, fighting commanding officer, now passed out under the stars with a half-finished bottle of Coors carelessly jammed under his chin.

Gently, Ingram pulled away the Coors, set it aside, and moved on. Soon, he found Toliver and Dezhnev on a swing set, their feet propped on a table.

He sat in a chair opposite. "You guys all right?"

"For cryin' out loud, Todd," said Toliver. "What could be better?"

Dezhnev spread his arms to the sky, "This place is amazing. You've got it all."

Ingram nodded, "Have to admit, we're pretty lucky."

A silence followed. Toliver picked up on it. "What is it?"

"I'm going to say something, and I'm going to give Eduard something." He pulled his chair closer.

Toliver sensed it. He grabbed a crutch and pushed himself to an upright position. "Oh yeah?"

Ingram spread his hands, "Keep your seat, Ollie. He has to know."

Toliver said, "If you're going where I think you're going, then I'd better leave." He made to push up on his crutches.

"Come on, Ollie. And to hell with the Official Secrets Act. He and Roxanna have a right to know."

"Todd, damn it. I—"

Jerry stepped up, a bottle of Coors in one hand and a towel in the other. With Noah, Kate, and her husband, he'd been swimming in the pool the Ingrams had had built two years before. "Water's fantastic. You should give it a try."

Ingram looked up at his son, now a P-3 squadron commander at Moffett Field near San Francisco. He was still wet and his body glistened in the soft light. He thought ruefully, *the kid made commander before I did.*

Reluctantly, he gave Jerry a look known throughout his childhood. *This conversation is confidential.* "Maybe later son, thanks."

"Damn fools." Jerry walked off.

The three looked at one another. Their eyes twinkled.

"Fine boy," said Dezhnev.

"Thanks." Ingram dipped his head for a moment, then looked at Dezhnev. "We found the wreck of the *K-129,* at least the forward section of it."

"Good God!"

"Don't ask me how, but we raised that section off the ocean floor and now have it for examination. There was a lot of stuff in the forward torpedo room. This was part of it." He reached in his pocket and flipped the Alcatraz belt buckle on the table. "Among other things we've learned is that your son was instrumental in avoiding a major calamity."

Dezhnev turned the buckle over and over in his hand. "I never would have ever imagined..."

Jerry went to turn in a little after eleven that evening. He looked out the window and saw the three men still out there in the darkness, the candle long since burned out.

Rita joined him, and they watched in silence. Finally, she looked up at her husband, her eyebrows raised.

"Those guys go way back. They have a lot of ground to cover."

"So be it." Rita walked to the main house, and six minutes later emerged with a large pot of coffee and cups on a tray. Silently, she set it before them then plugged in a fresh candle and lit it for them. With that, she stepped back to return to the bunkhouse. But not before Todd jumped up and gave her a hug. Then she came back to her husband and settled beside him in bed. Soon, they fell asleep.

Jerry was up once more at about one-thirty. He peeked out the window. They were still out there, heads close together, still talking, a tall long-necked bottle between them; it looked like brandy.

AFTER DUNKIRK by Lee Jackson
Book #1 in the After Dunkirk series

From the beaches of Dunkirk to the codebreakers of Bletchley Park, from Resistance bombings in the south of France to the machinations in the basements of MI-6.

"Lee Jackson embeds you in the peril of war-torn France in the aftermath of Dunkirk."—**Buzz Bernard, author of MWSA finalist *When Heroes Flew***

Winston Churchill called it Britain's finest hour. The Royal Navy evacuated 330,000 soldiers from Dunkirk. But more than 200,000 were left behind.

On the beaches, Jeremy Littlefield hides for his life. His path home will draw him through the iron will and the unbreakable heart of the French Resistance.

Only a few miles away, his brother, Lance, rallies fellow soldiers to start a trek that will take them across Europe, sabotaging the Germans in a mission tantamount to suicide.

Back in England, their sister Claire works at Bletchley Park, cracking the codes that could save the lives of her brothers, and thousands of their comrades.

Finally, there is Paul, the cerebral eldest son, working for MI-6, who always knows more than he is able to tell his beloved siblings.

***AFTER DUNKIRK* is a panoramic tale of war, love, courage, sacrifice... and betrayal. A family scattered across Europe, doing their duty for king and country while war rages.**

NEVER MISS A NEW RELEASE

Sign up to receive exclusive updates from author John J. Gobbell.

Join today at SevernRiverPublishing.com/John-J-Gobbell

ALSO BY JOHN J. GOBBELL

The Todd Ingram Series

The Last Lieutenant

A Code For Tomorrow

When Duty Whispers Low

The Neptune Strategy

Edge of Valor

Dead Man Launch

Other Books

A Call to Colors

The Brutus Lie

Never miss a new release. Sign up to receive exclusive updates from author John J. Gobbell.

SevernRiverPublishing.com/John-J-Gobbell

ACKNOWLEDGMENTS

As always, I've had incredible counsel from people from many walks of life. Without their help it would have been impossible to write this book, and to them I am forever indebted. From the military, they are: the late Capt. Randall J. Lynch, USN (Ret.); Capt. Daniel Truax, USN (Ret.); Cdr. George Wallace, USN (Ret.); Maj. Will Coe, USMC (Ret), Maj. Robert J. McGrody Jr., USMC (Ret.); Lt. John Preis, USN; John's sister, Lt. Annie Preis (JAG), USN; and Capt. Richard Bertea, USMC (Ret.). Medical commentary was provided by: Dr. Steven Daines, Dr. Greg Di Rocco, Dr. Robert L. Jones, and Dr. Russell Striff. Along with this I received great help from: Justice Robert Mallano, Messrs. Lou Carrier, Frank Daniels, Terry Miller, and Roger Pechuls. Thanks also to Anna Journey, Ph.D., at USC's Dornsife School. Last, a massive bundle of appreciation to Mindy Conner, my copy editor, who did an outstanding job on this work, as well as its predecessor, *Edge of Valor*.

Most of all, my love, appreciation, and admiration go to my wife, Janine, who never varies in her support of my fiction and is a great mechanic when it comes to proofreading. Well done, Janine.

I must never forget you, my readers, who send appreciative comments and gentle suggestions, along with one or two not so gentle. All are welcome with the realization that it can only improve the work or at least open my eyes to issues unvisited. *Wow! Why didn't I think of that before?* is a daily reminder of how technically incredible the writing world has become, rendering new possibilities to unfold on the page and in life itself. Thank you for all that and please stay in touch with me on my website at: www.JohnJGobbell.com. Or email me at John@johnjgobbell.com.

JJG

February 2019
Newport Beach, California

ABOUT THE AUTHOR

JOHN J. GOBBELL is a former Navy Lieutenant who saw duty as a destroyer weapons officer. His ship served in the South China Sea, granting him membership in the exclusive *Tonkin Gulf Yacht Club*. As an executive recruiter, his clients included military/commercial aerospace companies giving him insight into character development under a historical thriller format. An award-winning author, John has published eight novels. The books in his popular Todd Ingram series are based on the U.S Navy in the Pacific theater of World War II. John and his wife Janine live in Newport Beach, California.

john@johnjgobbell.com

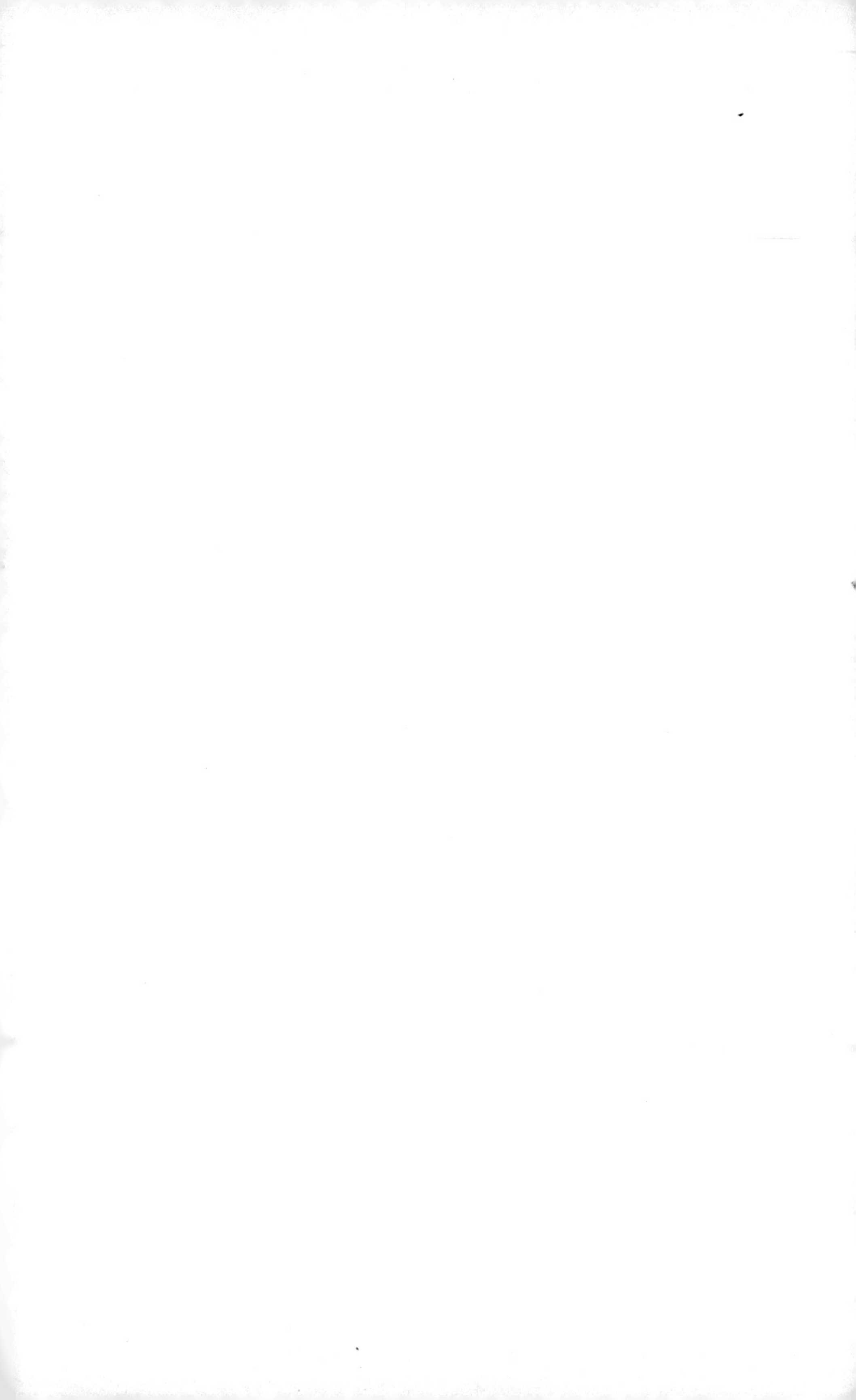

Made in the USA
Las Vegas, NV
08 January 2021

15498907R00256